Hoover's Nightmare

A SPECIAL AGENT GONE "NATIVE"

AN FBI NOVEL

Wade Shirley

Fulton Books, Inc.
Meadville, PA

Published by Fulton Books 2020

ISBN 978-1-64654-090-7 (paperback)
ISBN 978-1-64654-091-4 (digital)

Printed in the United States of America

The FBI Seal and Badge are proud and honored symbols
of America's finest law enforcement agency

The events which unfold in the plot line of this novel are heavily influenced by the FBI experiences of the author. Most of the names of the actual actors, as well as the name of some of the locales, have been changed in a sincere effort to protect the character and reputation of those real life individuals, who may actually be innocent, but for various reasons, were caught up in the storyline as it rolled forth.

Contents

Introduction

E nough books have been written, Hollywood movies scripted, stories told, and yarns spun about cases involving the Federal Bureau of Investigation to fill libraries. The common denominator in virtually all these story lines seems be the very high-profile cases that snap up national headlines and top spots on the networks evening news. These are the scenarios that grab public attention and usually concern famous politicians, drug lords, multimillionaires, celebrated actors or actresses, mass shooters, kidnappers, sex scandals, foreign counterintelligence, espionage, or any combination of the above. The majority of these narratives originate in one of the large FBI field offices headquartered in the nation's large population centers or in Washington, DC.

But somewhere out there in the vast rural areas of America was another breed of the FBI that is so different from that depicted in the popular television broadcasts as to be almost totally unrecognizable. I am referring to the few one-man resident agencies (RA) that were once scattered across this great nation, which J. Edgar Hoover reluctantly recognized to be essential to the operation of his Bureau. These offices were often hundreds of miles from the headquarters of their respective field offices and were as unique as they were valuable to the work of the Bureau.

Hoover was often quoted as having a general bias against Resident Agencies in general as he felt they were too far removed from the micromanaging eyes of his handpicked Special Agents in Charge (SACs). Therefore, they obviously must be, and were assumed to be, by those in Washington, *screwing off* a good deal of the time. This obsession caused him to refer to his Resident Agencies as Necessary Evils and other less-than-flattering phrases.

If he voiced that opinion about Resident Agencies with multiple agents assigned, one can only guess how he must have concerned himself with those far-removed offices scattered across the heartland of America like the old Pony Express relay stations. The one-man RA in Scottsbluff, Nebraska, was actually located near the old Oregon and Mormon Trails, near an old Pony Express station, only a few short miles from the picturesque and famous Chimney Rock in the heart of the historic West.

The writer was assigned to this outpost for a period of 20 years from 1971 to 1991 and came to know life in a remote setting like most other Special Agents never can imagine in their wildest dreams. The RA was located 452 miles due west of his headquarters in Omaha and 176 miles from the next assigned agent in North Platte, Nebraska. The Bureau car (Bucar) became his home as he worked the 14 very large but sparsely populated counties assigned to the RA territory. Road trips were the norm as he wore out an automobile approximately every two years, making his rounds covering routine leads.

Inasmuch as any FBI assistance was so far removed and distant, he developed extremely close working relationships and friendships with the many officers from the Nebraska State Patrol, the various police departments, sheriff's offices, and other federal agencies within the boundaries of his assigned dominion. He even worked closely with the Nebraska State Criminal Brand Inspector on matters pertaining to cattle rustling. Literally, his life depended upon their help and cooperation on almost a daily basis and the bonds of camaraderie ran very deep.

The picture painted in the movies of the FBI being at odds with the locals over jurisdiction and turf was not the case in the world of the Scottsbluff RA. Instead, there was an arena of friendship, helpfulness, and cooperation that was exemplary. The writer lived daily with the motto of "Don't embarrass the Bureau" and did everything in his power to foster an atmosphere of friendship, respect, and goodwill with these agencies.

The same working relationships were developed with most of the locals when the writer was transferred to another very small RA in the Salt Lake City Division located at Idaho Falls, Idaho, where he again worked, a good share of the time alone. There were two notable exceptions to this friendly working atmosphere which are detailed in the book, telling of the two Idaho counties where the FBI was not welcome per the instruction of the respective sheriffs of those counties. Interesting and troublesome situations developed in both cases.

With these working conditions in mind, it was only natural that his lifestyle, dress, and working relationships with the locals would be a fulfillment of one of the phobias of Director Hoover. From the earliest days in his FBI training, it was repeatedly emphasized that the reason the Director liked to transfer his agents frequently was because of his fear that if they stayed too long in any given assignment, they would become too friendly with the locals and be influenced too much by them.

Hoover referred to this condition as "Going Native", which he frowned upon.

The writer managed to live all but one year of his thirty-year career in a small RA meeting the description of necessary evil.

The entire perspective of this agent's view of the Bureau was totally unique as it was almost entirely from a great distance away. Sometimes, the further from an object or situation, the more clearly it's viewed. This writer's linear perspective of the FBI did not include any jockeying for leadership positions, rubbing shoulders daily with supervisors, or any need to brownnose or develop into a sycophant. But from a distance, he saw the workings of the Bureau and some of the politics involved and was able to be removed from it to a greater degree than almost anyone else. There was one period when he did not see any supervisor or another live agent for a period of over five months.

Scottsbluff was even in a different time zone than the rest of the Omaha division, and the high desert, mostly arid climate, was a pleasure to live in versus the humidity and congestion of the rest of the Omaha division.

When the writer left Scottsbluff in 1991, the decision was made to close that one-man outstation. There were protests from virtually every law enforcement and government agency in Nebraska's panhandle, but to no avail. After all, Bureau management is all knowing and beyond scrutiny of mere taxpaying citizens. This was the end of an era and a very unique one at that. The entire area would henceforth be covered by a road trip agent from North Platte.

As that RA faded into oblivion, so did the cases worked. It was partially for that reason this project was undertaken. The writer felt there were just too many untold stories from the American Indian problems (think Wounded Knee) to the small, sometimes humorous, cases that were 100 percent small-time rural Nebraska and rural Idaho.

Some years after the writer's retirement, the RA in Idaho Falls fell prey to the same Bureau logic and was retired to the dusty history books of so-called progress.

Now all living evidence of those two once-proud offices no longer are in the city directories or phone books serving those two great small cities. The thoughts of losing the experiences of those assignments forever were a part of the logic of pursuing this work.

The title of the book represents exactly what happened to the writer as he became the agent theoretically feared by J. Edgar Hoover himself.

Hoover's Nightmare: A Special Agent Gone Native is a fascinating and entertaining insight, like no other, into the everyday life of an isolated lone agent in this premier law enforcement agency. A view from the inside and yet from a great distance.

Although this book is written as a novel and the names of most of the characters changed, the events are based on real cases and incidents. You are invited to join with the book's main fictitious character, Agent McWade, as he takes the reader on an exciting and fascinating journey through this unique period of old west Indian wars, kidnappings, and often-humorous routine events, all specific to assignments unlike most others. All this in the remote rural reaches of the American West.

A special thanks is given to my good wife, Beth, and my children, who, so many times over the past several years, gave me the encouragement and support I needed to stay focused on seeing this work to a conclusion. Without their faith in me and their continued helping words of endorsement, it would have been all too easy to have put this all aside to gather dust in the recesses of a retired agent's mind. Thanks to them, the fictitious, but all too real, Agent McWade would never have come to life in this fun and informative novel.

Chapter 1

Yellow Thunder

It was a beautiful sunny day to be living in the panhandle of Nebraska.

The bright noonday Cornhusker sun was doing what it did best, which was trying to warm the gentle spring breeze that drifted nonchalantly in from the lush and sprawling sand hills ranch country to the south of the tiny town located on US Highway 20.

To the occasional passerby, who happened to stop in the sleepy town of Gordon, it would appear just like any other day. A closer look, however, near the municipal building and police department, may have revealed a hodgepodge assortment of news vans and strange TV antennas reaching toward the blue sky.

But something potentially explosive and maybe even sinister was brewing behind this peaceful-appearing setting. Inside the municipal building gymnasium was a large gathering of several hundred Native Americans who were not in Gordon to enjoy the scenery or to spread goodwill. They were angry, noisy, and passionate about their mission and were concentrating on the business at hand.

McWade was growing increasingly nervous by the minute as he sat perched high up on the top row of the bleachers overlooking the floor below. What he was witnessing was a spectacle like he had never before seen. Being played before his eyes was an entire landscape of activity resembling a frenzied powwow from an old Western movie. The kind of chanting and dancing done the night before a war party was sent off to battle.

The fact that the hardwood bench seats were pure torture on his backside had very little to do with the uncomfortable cold sweat that was beginning to form on his all-too-pale white forehead.

"Why am I here and whose brilliant idea was this anyway?" he muttered to himself.

Some three days earlier, he had innocently answered the telephone at his FBI office in Scottsbluff, Nebraska. Up to that point, his life as an agent had been relatively quiet as he had been working his routine average, run-of-the-mill cases, that drifted to the one-man resident agency (RA) from his headquarters in Omaha some 452 miles to the east. Sure, there were times when he felt overwhelmed as there were no backup agents to help, except in North Platte some 175 miles down the Platte River to the east. But for the most part, McWade felt like he was working in a hamster wheel of routine and sometimes nonessential busy work.

He loved the remote assignment and, for the most part, just wanted to be left alone, out of the limelight, in his isolated world where he could be his own boss and do things without supervisors looking over his shoulder and micromanaging every move.

His Special Agent in Charge (SAC) had once stepped out of his Bureau car (referred to as a Bucar) after driving over nine hours on one of his mandated tours of the RA and, after looking around, sighed deeply and exclaimed, "I hope you never screw up, McWade, because I could never find anyone crazy enough to live in this god-forsaken place."

Actually, McWade loved the place and played along with the bosses' ill-conceived notion of Scottsbluff being a hardship duty station to get possibly advantageous treatment in the future should it ever come up.

The ringing of the phone pierced the silence of the RA.

"McWade, old buddy," came the jovial voice on the line. "Armstrong here! What do you know about AIM?"

"A great toothpaste. Use it all the time," quipped McWade.

He, of course, was fully aware of the fact that AIM stood for the one and only American Indian Movement. Furthermore, it was common knowledge that AIM had gained national notoriety and worldwide media attention after the forceful takeover and eighteen-month occupation of the infamous Alcatraz Island and old penitentiary in California.

The major news networks and outlets had fed on this incident like it was their favorite dessert at a potluck church social until, virtually, every man, woman, or child capable of watching TV or listening to their car radio knew at least something about AIM.

Armstrong, a criminal investigator with the Nebraska State Patrol (NSP), was a cheerful, fun-loving, yet very capable and competent police officer. He and McWade had developed mutual respect and trust for each other on a variety of cases on which they had worked in the past.

"I have a snitch telling me that AIM is stirring up shit on the Pine Ridge. They are talking about getting as many Indian recruits as possible together, forming a caravan, then traveling to Gordon where they can spread a little hate and discontent."

When Armstrong referred to the Pine Ridge, he was talking about the massive Pine Ridge Indian Reservation located just across the border into the state of South Dakota, where there was beginning to be a considerable amount of tension and political unrest.

"My guy in the know tells me that none other than the infamous AIM activist, Chin Black Heart, is personally on the Pine Ridge rallying recruits as we speak and that the demonstration is to take place three days hence. Chin hoped to gather several hundred Indian supporters capable of mounting their cars and pickups for the thirty-five-plus-mile trek into Nebraska and on to Gordon. No other details were known at the time," said Armstrong.

The catalyst for the convoy and pending demonstration was the recent death, in February, 1972, of an Indian man by the name of Raymond Yellow Thunder.

McWade had followed and monitored the Yellow Thunder's death through close liaison and contact with the Gordon Police Department, the Sheridan County Sheriff, and the NSP.

The death of Yellow Thunder was truly tragic and bizarre. Little did McWade, or anyone else for that matter, envision, at the time of his unfortunate death, that this would escalate into a major national incident. But things like this seem to sometimes take on a life of their own, and wherever they stop is anyone's guess.

Raymond Yellow Thunder had worked for several years as a ranch hand in and around Sheridan County, Nebraska, and was known as a good, reliable, hardworking man who liked to pretty much stay to himself. He was a private, good-natured fellow who did his work unsupervised and then spent his free time on weekends, often by himself, with a bottle of his favorite spirits.

The particular weekend, and one to always be remembered, was in the month of February 1972, in the midst of a blast of frigid Canadian cold air, which had wrapped its arms around the Great Plains in a virtual bear hug.

Yellow Thunder had made his way to Gordon, had obtained a bottle of his favorite brew, and was walking down the main street in town, feeling the buzz. He was, as usual, minding his own business and looking for solitude as he made his way down the dimly lit street past the Borman Chevrolet used-car lot.

As fate would have it, four local cowboys and one female associate, also feeling the effects of their night of partying and drinking, pulled alongside the silhouette of the poor man wandering down the sidewalk. Some people are just naturally mean after a few drinks and our local cowboys fit this bill and even excelled in the stupidity department.

"Hey, Injun Joe," came the call from one of the rednecks.

The humble figure ignored the degrading slurs and kept on walking with his head down, trying to avoid trouble.

"What's the matter, chief? Cat got your tongue? Can't you hear that I'm talking to you?" another of the hillbillies cried out.

It seems minutes turn into hours when you are vulnerable and a pack of wolves surround you like a helpless lamb. So it was as the overgrown, immature bullies continued to taunt and harass the poor helpless Native American whose only thought at this time was to somehow elude them and be allowed to disappear into the solitude of the empty street stretching ahead under his worn work boots.

Then came the most brilliant idea yet out of the warped minds of the drunken partygoers. "Let's teach this Injun some manners and give him a little road trip in our trunk!"

With that, three of the tormentors leaped from the car, grabbed the slightly built man, and commenced to abduct him and physically toss him into the trunk of the vehicle. All this was not done gently, and Yellow Thunder sustained a substantial amount of bruises and marks from the incident.

Gordon was a small town of only around one thousand two hundred people, with only a limited number of streets for the hoodlums to rattle around on, so it did not take them long to get bored with the cries and pleadings of the man in the trunk begging for his freedom.

As the crew of ruffians drove past the American Legion Hall, one of them had another brain fart of a thought. "Remember how we used to pull down other kids pants in high school and throw them in the girls' restroom? Let's depants the dude in the trunk and shove him into the dance they are having at the Legion Club."

The good citizens in the dance hall were mortified when the poor man was shoved into the hall, partially clothed and totally embarrassed and petrified. He was offered help by some well-meaning people but refused their suggestions for assistance and left the hall on his own, stumbling aimlessly back into the dark cold shadows of the village.

Drunken bullies sometimes must have a grain of compassion, even though minuscule, as our carload of hellions, a short time later, saw him shivering in the cold along the abandoned streets. They stopped, threw him his own rumpled clothes they had earlier confiscated from him, and then laughingly left him to fare for himself.

Totally shaken, Yellow Thunder made his way to the Gordon Police Department, where he entered and asked the jailer for a night's shelter in one of their jail cells.

The next morning, he was given a routine jailhouse breakfast consisting of powdered scrambled eggs, bologna, and a piece of toast with peanut butter. Little did he, or anyone else, know that it would be the last meal he would ever eat.

He left the jail on his own and wandered back onto the city sidewalks.

His lifeless body was discovered a few days later curled up in an unlocked vehicle at Borman Chevrolet's used-car lot, not far from where he had been abducted and imprisoned in the trunk of the strange car only a few short days before.

Initial reports were that he was a victim of the weather and had frozen to death in the car where he had sought refuge and protection from the elements. But there were also noticeable indications of trauma on his body, which were obviously the result of the injuries received the night of his horrific nightmare encounter with Gordon's worst and least desirable product.

This whole fiasco was the typical stereotype of four fun-loving white cowboys roughing up an intoxicated Indian for the mere entertainment of just doing so, and AIM was having a field day with the incident as a rallying cry.

The truthful facts of the whole thing were completely off the radar and beyond belief, but AIM insisted on even embellishing that reality with added fiction, and it was getting ugly. Rumors were flying on the rez, fueled by Chin and his followers, that Yellow Thunder had been tortured, beaten to death, and even castrated by his white assailants while in their custody.

"Let's go to Gordon and see what the hell this AIM bunch is up to on this one," Armstrong had said. "It could be exciting, and besides what could possibly go wrong?"

Armstrong's brilliant idea for covering the upcoming protest and demonstration was simple. He and McWade would pose as newsmen, and using a dummy, nonworking camera, they would pose as cameramen, positioning themselves high up in the gymnasium, hopefully unnoticed, where they could take copious notes on what was going to report it all back to their respective superiors in a matter-of-fact manner. "After all, with Channel 4 News printed professionally on the camera, what could anyone suspect?"

Armstrong was persuasive, so McWade agreed to meet him in Gordon on the fateful day. The idea seemed, on the surface, to be totally bulletproof, but then so had McWade's friend's prenuptial agreement that had left the poor man almost penniless.

So good was the plan that McWade never even gave a second thought to call any of his three supervisors in Omaha to clue them in on that fact that he was going undercover for a day to film what could turn out to be a bloodbath by a frenzied war party. He hated paperwork, and to get Bureau approval on something so seemingly innocent could take weeks and amount to endless volumes of paperwork. After all, his buddy, Armstrong, seemed so confident and even had the dummy camera.

McWade had a favorite plaque on the wall of his RA, which was in the shape of a very serious-looking American bald eagle wearing earphones, such as would be worn on a wire intercept. Below the earphone-wielding bald eagle was the prophetic statement In God we trust, all others we monitor!

"So why not be like that truth-seeking eagle?" McWade rationalized.

Now, however, perched high on the top row of those bleachers, he actually wished he was an eagle and could spread his massive wings and fly the hell out of that hornet's nest below and back outside into the refreshing breeze that represented safety and freedom.

With the seemingly hundreds of very vocal and angry Native Americans milling all around, he was beginning to question, for the first time, the actual wisdom of Armstrong's planned undercover gig.

Glancing over at Armstrong, he, all of a sudden, took close note of his rather long and flowing blondish red hair which adorned his head. McWade mused that this was about as crazy as Custer and his sidekick trying to sneak into the camp of Crazy Horse at the Little Big Horn disguised as undercover medicine men to see what they were up to the night before the big battle.

Now, for the first time since meeting Armstrong, he also began to wonder about his ancestry and where his last name and long reddish-blond hair had originated.

McWade could not ignore the very suspicious and frequent glances coming their direction from the Indians filling the floor and the bleachers. It dawned on him that he and Yellow Hair were the only two white men in the entire building, and all eyes seemed to be glued on them.

The powwow on the gym floor below was complete with some guy in Native American dress wildly beating on a large war drum every time someone would speak. And speak they did!

Chin had set up a table in the center of the hardwood floor with a loudspeaker system, making it easy for everyone in the hall to hear all that was going on before them.

One by one, some Indian would rise to his feet and walk up to the microphone to relate some horror story, either real or fictional, about some mistreatment to him or his family by some evil white man.

After each emotional testimony, the costumed guy with the huge drumsticks would pound the drums loudly. The hall would literally echo from the outburst of drumbeats, accompanied by some loud chanting in the native tongue of the Ogalala Sioux.

These near-riotous proceedings were proclaimed by Chin to be designated as an official AIM grand jury, for the express purpose of highlighting to the whole world the mistreatment not only of Yellow Thunder but also of the entire Indian race.

The testimonies being born were recited with tearful conviction, passion, and overflowing emotion.

It reminded Agent McWade of a few religious testimony-type meetings he had attended where churchgoers would stand and bear the same kind of sobbing and emotional story of experiences or convictions based more on inner psychological feelings rather than history, real evidence, or actual fact. The only difference here was that after each sincere-sounding testimony, there was another outburst of chanting and wild beating on the drum.

As a case in point, one female protester, wearing a combination of traditional Western wear mixed with some tribal dress, stood before the table. The middle-aged woman took the microphone in her trembling hand and presented the following completely false and unsubstantiated fabrication with unshakable belief: "I have personally seen the mutilated and battered body of my old cousin, Raymond Yellow Thunder, before he was hastily buried by the white man to cover up the evidence that he had been barbarically castrated like an animal. I know this took place beyond a shadow of doubt. So help me God, what I am telling you is true, and I know it with every fiber of my being."

Following that impassioned invention or hallucination of facts, the drums beat wildly and the crowd reacted likewise with loud yells and cries for justice mixed with more chanting accentuated by some tribal language.

All this was having a real effect on the assembled gathering. They were all appearing to outwardly begin to show more and more hostility and anger as they were being manipulated by Chin and his cohorts. The atmosphere inside was beginning to change rapidly from just gray, overcast skies to stormy with a 90 percent chance of serious of hell-raising trouble. Was another destructive killer Nebraska tornado going to touch down directly inside the town building?

As McWade sat there in wonderment, he realized there were three common denominators in each of the testimonies being sworn to at the grand jury:

1. Indians were the innocent victims of blind justice over the past one hundred-plus years.
2. Evil white men were totally and 100 percent to blame for every injustice that had taken place.
3. Those evil white men, individually and collectively, as a society, must finally be held accountable and pay through the nose for every dastardly deed they had inflicted upon the indigenous peoples of the Americas.

Items two and three from the list gave McWade very little comfort, given the growing venomous mood from the mob and the continued unrelenting, rubbernecked peering in their direction.

Outside, he supposed the light fresh breeze was still blowing the refreshing smells of flowers and grass in from the south grasslands. But it was definitely stuffy on that top roost and getting more so by the moment. The tense feelings were mounting.

Naturally, both he and Yellow Hair were armed with their standard-issued law enforcement weapons, concealed neatly from the view of the searching eyes of the crowd. This fact, given the situation, now seemed more like a problem than any kind of solution as word now had been circulated that AIM had positioned its own security guards at each of the visible exits and were frisking persons entering or leaving the hall.

One closer look at the burly, tattooed hulks they had recruited as bouncers caused virtual chills to run the full length of McWade's spine. They looked more like thugs than security guards and appeared to be taking their assigned jobs all too seriously. Suddenly, survival pushed aside intelligence gathering as the number one instinct in both of the young crusaders minds.

The often-told story that went "When you are ass deep in alligators, it is hard to remember that your original goal was to drain the pond" now took on special personal meaning.

McWade wondered briefly about the tall special agent, who had recruited him from his peaceful life in the Butte Division a few short years ago. "Dangerous? Not really, and if so, only minimal!"

"Bullshit! You can add that one to the list of propaganda told," he now acknowledged.

So far, old Yellow Hair Armstrong had not said much, but now he leaned over to McWade and said, "See that woman over there?" as he nodded toward a well-endowed fine specimen sitting several rows to the right and four rows down.

How a well-trained Bureau sleuth had missed noticing this young, twentysomething-year-old beauty, sitting there in plain view, like a storybook princess from a Hollywood movie, was actually the biggest mystery of the day. Her dark gleaming hair was hanging about four inches below her shoulders. It was immaculately groomed and gracefully covered her long neck and picture-perfect light-brownish complexion. Her frame was suitable enough to be used on the cover of any woman's fitness magazine. The kind to make other women envious and most any man drool. She would easily have had McWade's vote for Miss Native America 1972 in any beauty contest.

Sexy, yet out-of-this-world classy, he thought.

She is my snitch. Her real name is Mandy Silk Hair," whispered Armstrong.

McWade assumed that when the earlier reference was made about his informant being a guy that Armstrong meant a man-type guy, not a gorgeous woman such as the one gracing the bench below like an angel without wings.

McWade had taken an oath and was "charged with the duty of investigating violations of the laws of the United States, collecting evidence in cases in which the United States may be a party of interest, and performing other duties imposed by law." At least that is what it said on his credentials in his vest pocket.

He took that oath seriously and was proud of the calling; however, that did not make the present situation any less fearful or disturbing.

He had been in the real world of law enforcement long enough to learn that the old adage "Follow the money" had real meaning and should never be overlooked.

Guys like Chin and his close associates were masters at the game of gaining public support and sympathy for their causes. If their game plan went as planned, in their eyes, the money would soon start flowing into their coffers from sympathetic sources worldwide. The glory about this plan was that the donated funds were usually quite generous and almost totally untraceable, allowing the leaders ample funding to live a lifestyle well beyond their normal means.

McWade realized that most in the building were being used as pawns on Chin's giant chessboard of drama and that the poor, unfortunate Yellow Thunder was their current Remember the Alamo slogan to propel them forward.

"So much for deep thinking and philosophy." He gradually drifted back to the reality of the moment.

"So what brilliant, clever exit strategy have you cooked up?" queried McWade.

"You are a doubting Thomas, oh ye of little faith," chuckled the round, red-faced Yellow Hair as he caught the eye of his snitch.

With a preplanned wink and a nod, the woman stood up and made her way to the far end of the gym floor to be lost in the crowd of disorganized bodies milling below.

Just as rehearsed, the pretty woman started screaming in a shrill voice, "Help, get your mangy hands off me, you filthy bastard, and let go of my purse."

All attention in the hall went in that direction.

Immediately upon hearing the noise, the gangster-looking security thugs abandoned their posts by the doors and rushed to the far end of the court to rescue our damsel in distress, who, by now, had recomposed herself and was standing there looking as helpless, although somewhat shaken, and innocently beautiful as ever.

"That woman is amazing!" mused McWade as he and Armstrong, seemingly on cue, grabbed their dummy camera, made their way off the bleachers to the nearest unsecured exit and sucked in a large breath of freedom as they inhaled fresh outside air.

Of course, the decision was made by McWade not to ever mention this ill-conceived undercover fiasco to the Bureau. Instead, he generated a short teletype to Director Hoover, reporting only a short summary of the facts of the protest.

The Director allegedly had a number of phobias that set him into orbit. High on the list would be reading about something in the newspaper that should have been reported to him in advance by his agents on the ground. The teletype had covered everything, giving the who, what, where, and why of the incident at Gordon. All the supervisor types in Omaha and DC would be happy as they headed for their favorite happy hour stop-offs on their way to their respective homes. Each would tell their wide-eyed listening buddies of how *they* had handled, and personally defused, the situation on the frontier of western Nebraska in the small town of Gordon and on the Pine Ridge.

But number one on the list of Hoover's biggest phobias, or nightmares, was the fear that one of his agents would "go native."

Going native, to the Director, was defined as one of his agents, like McWade, for example, getting so far removed from the normal mainstream cluster of other FBI agents that he would start to work with and, for heaven's sake, actually hang out with, in his free time, locals like Armstrong. The real clincher would be that one of his blue ribbon team would even start dressing like a local and even hang with them in the coffee shop to swap stories and information.

So for the sake of pure common sense, the undercover gig would remain undercover.

McWade enjoyed Letters of Commendation much more than Letters of Censure from his beloved Bureau in his personnel file, so this was a no-brainer. They had pounded into his head relentlessly, in new agents training, that one "ah shit" letter could cover a hundred "attaboy" letters. So it was important to have a good one always on the top of the stack.

But as pointed out, the Scottsbluff RA in western Nebraska was a remote, and mostly out of sight and out of mind, outpost. Sometimes months would pass without ever seeing another Bureau agent or employee, so naturally, the much-needed help on various cases came from the local departments all over the state's panhandle. These folks also became McWade's off-duty friends and were the ones he spent free time with frequently. So in many ways, he was already well on his way to becoming "Hoover's Nightmare."

As he headed his Bucar to the southwest, on the long drive back to Scottsbluff, he feared now, and rightfully so, that the Yellow Thunder incident may well change his life forever.

Could this AIM protest at Gordon be only the beginning of something much, much larger?

Could his "Beautiful Nebraska, Peaceful Prairie Land," as the state song described the beloved Cornhusker territory, be in for some radical changes on its northwestern borders in the near future?

The loud drums pounding relentlessly from the grand jury in Gordon were still reverberating and echoing in McWade's ears when other noises sounding something more like actual war drums began to be heard in the small towns and villages on the massive Pine Ridge.

Had it begun?

He checked his seat belt to make sure he was buckled up for the ride that was surely to follow!

Chapter 2

The Posse Arrives

S omewhat emboldened by the massive media coverage of their protest and subsequent grand jury indictments of the four rogue cowboys responsible for the death of Yellow Thunder, AIM seemed to be on the roll.

The completely false narrative of the torture, beating, and castration of Yellow Thunder had spread like the gospel of truth across the rez and through the Indian households surrounding the Pine Ridge and neighboring Rosebud. In fact, virtually every reservation in the United States, as well as the reserves in Canada, had been indoctrinated via the AIM social network.

Rather in politics, religion, investment schemes, or in the networking of racial propaganda, if a lie is repeated often enough, it soon becomes pure doctrine to the uninformed, who are so easily led. These folks, in each of those categories, always assume the position of being in the know and the only ones possessing the real truth. A person in such a state is not usually willing to set aside their know-it-all bias and even consider that facts may differ from their idea of truth by emotion.

Even after Nebraska authorities bowed to the wild and outrageous AIM accusations, a second autopsy was performed, which completely verified and validated the findings of the first. There was absolutely no truth whatsoever of the alleged torture and castration.

No one in local law enforcement, or in the Sheridan County Attorney's Office, was denying that Yellow Thunder was roughed up during the process of false imprisonment. But the cause of death was shown to be exposure to the elements. In other words, the poor man froze to death.

Those responsible were to be charged according to the Nebraska law, addressing the crimes committed. But to AIM, that was not enough. Chin, and his buddies, wanted nothing short of first-degree murder charges and the death penalty for all involved, and there was no reasoning with them about what the law would, or would not, allow.

McWade was working in close liaison with Armstrong and the other local authorities when the news came in from Armstrong's source, as well as numerous others, that yet another protest was being organized to target Gordon. This was to be a much bigger and better version of the original earlier protest as the word had now spread worldwide, with reports of Indian sympathizers, pledging support from almost everywhere.

As the day of the big event approached, the plans to cover it became more detailed and specific with each bit of new information received.

It was whispered that not hundreds, but thousands, of militants would flow into the now-wary town from the north and proceed down Nebraska State Highway 27.

Only those living in Gordon, and the surrounding countryside, could feel just how disconcerting this pending situation actually was to the good law-abiding citizens who lived, worked, and enjoyed life there. This was truly a sparsely inhabited county, where the population of cattle dwarfed the number of actual human beings by thousands to one. The idea of several thousand unruly militants invading their county, both outnumbering and overpowering them, did not set well with any of the locals, and it was not going to be tolerated. Ranchers and city dwellers both vowed to take up arms to protect their families, homes, livestock, and property.

The arming of Sheridan County was easy for most as it only meant checking the gun cabinets to make sure there was enough ammo for each of the several guns everyone seemed to own. Most had never envisioned any threat like this as the Indian wars were supposed to have been something of the past that their great grand-parents had to deal with in the last century.

Urgent pleas were being made to the Office of the Governor in Lincoln to send help to deal with the potential civil disorder and chaos.

McWade attended numerous planning sessions involving state and local authorities where the possibilities were planned and debated from every scenario and angle imaginable. The Sheridan County Attorney feared the civil unrest may tear his county completely apart, and everyone else had similar concerns as it pertained to their departments.

Always, in the back of everyone's mind, was the knowledge that this was Wild West ranch country and just how heavily armed and passionate the local population actually was about this matter. The thoughts of any cowboy versus Indian war of any type terrified everyone in the planning circles. Now it appeared, however, that the proverbial scab covering the still-festering tragedy of the original 1890 Battle of Wounded Knee was being scratched off and that blood may flow again.

It was unclear what AIM had up their sleeves when they once arrived in town, but from the looks of the steady arrivals of news agencies, it appeared the group planned to put on a good show for the reporters. When a news crew arrived from London, England, McWade just knew they must be looking for something really news-worthy. Equipment was arriving by trucks, trailers, and vans, and the antennas being assembled were reaching skyward in a fashion that made the earlier protest coverage look feeble by comparison. Something definitely big was expected by those arriving advance teams, and it was felt in the air.

So countless were the aerial fingers pointing upward in the area around the Gordon Police Department that it was beginning to look like the back of a porcupine with its quills standing erect and in attention mode.

The patch of the Gordon Police Department with
the patch of the Nebraska State Patrol

After all the planning by the authorities had been finalized, it was decided it would be best to only show a minimal presence of patrolmen in and around town. The group think on that decision was that they were afraid to show too much presence as it just might irritate the invaders and motivate them to create a conflict in front of the media to show how overpowering the white man's oppression had become. McWade was the lone dissenter on that decision and had advised them fruitlessly that the schoolyard bully only understood one language. That language was the show of strength and the fear that someone bigger or stronger could knock him on his ass. That was the pure language spoken in the tongue of our first known ancestors since this world began.

The proposed plan called for each and every NSP unit, which could be spared, from the entire great state of Nebraska, to be in town and ready to respond in case the matter escalated and got out of hand.

Since the AIM caravan would be entering town from the north, the patrol cars would be bivouacked, out of sight, on the south end of Gordon, across the Chicago and North Western Railway tracks, and across US Highway 20, in and around the county maintenance buildings and Quonsets. The whole idea was that they could be well hidden there, and yet very close, should their assistance be required.

The NSP in Lincoln, with the approval and full support of Governor J. J. Exon, was overly generous on the number of patrol cars volunteered to this potential insurrection.

McWade loved the look-alike patrol cars the NSP had purchased for their service at that time. They were full-sized Plymouth Fury cruisers with the special police package and big block V8 engines by Chrysler. Each unit was painted white, with the blue-colored state of Nebraska NSP emblem adorning the front doors, and each side of the cruiser had the large blue lettering identifying the car as NSP. Each unit was awesome to look at individually, and it could only be fantasized as to how it would look to see a huge assembly of these vehicles in one gathering.

Such a display of law enforcement might had not been planned in the panhandle of Nebraska since the glory days of the old Fort Robinson, which had been the Outpost on the Plains during the Indian wars of the late 1800s. The US Government had turned over the entire fort to the State of Nebraska after it had served as a remount training and K9 training unit during World War II.

When he and Armstrong had gone undercover as fake newsmen to cover the grand jury, they had been polite and stayed in the background. However, this group of out-of-town journalists were quite the opposite. For the most part, they were arrogant, abrupt, and generally lacking small-town social skills in the area of manners and etiquette. In other words, McWade thought they were "a collection of rude jackasses," who were in the same category as Chin and his sidekicks.

In the detailed planning for this event, there was a contingency plan, to be implemented only if everything went to hell in a handbasket and the NSP cruisers were needed for assistance. In the case of such a call for help, the NSP sergeant in command would give a special 10 signal for help on the radio. If that happened, the assembled NSP units would respond in haste, lights and sirens activated, across US 20, across the CNW tracks, and up the main street of Gordon to defuse whatever problem was occurring.

The plan seemed as rock solid and bulletproof as McWade's aforementioned friend's prenuptial, which actually, despite his planning, had left the poor bastard bleeding out like a stuck pig after his divorce.

Of course, it was hoped by all that this show of muscle would never be required. But the plan was put together by humans and would be carried out by humans, so McWade only hoped for the best.

There was really no surefire way to factor in Murphy's Law into the planning equation, so fingers were crossed and silent prayers mumbled by those in charge.

On the day in question, calls came in from sources stationed along State 27 that the convoy was moving and that it was massive. Exact numbers were hard to come by, but it was clear that several hundred vehicles were descending, like an invasion of locusts, upon the wheat field called Gordon.

Tension was mounting in the minds of each and every person in town sworn to serve and protect. Those on the battle lines in town were most apprehensive, and those in the temporary secluded encampment to the south of town were dry mouthed also.

New territory was being explored as McWade was absolutely sure he had not been offered any classes by the FBI at Quantico in Indian warfare. He was equally positive the NSP had not been offered any courses in that area either.

He, like everyone else, waited with varying degrees of apprehension as the caravan of militants snaked its way, mile after endless mile, through the grasslands toward the waiting sworn, and heavily armed, officers. Since the FBI had no law enforcement jurisdiction in this matter, McWade was monitoring the entire situation in his Bucar, which gave him mobility as well as the ability to assess and respond. He did carry the official card issued by the governor of Nebraska assigning him the unique title of Special Nebraska State Deputy Sheriff. This was primarily just for emergency situations, much like this, enabling him to respond with legal State of Nebraska authority. He hoped this would not be necessary, but he had the proper Bureau issued firepower at hand, if the need should arise.

Soon the large convoy entered the city limits and progressed toward the small Gordon Police Department, which was the immediate focus of AIM's apparent game plan.

Chin, and his militants, saw the small contingent of officers at the PD and sensed a brazen feeling of superior force on their side of the equation. This was evidenced in their behavior, which soon got entirely out of hand.

As the convoy continued to stream into town, Chin stormed into the office of Bob Boxer, the chief of police (COP). He had demands! They (AIM) wanted justice. This meant they wanted to arrest and take possession of the four cowboys that had been indicted earlier by their kangaroo court called a grand jury.

Chin pushed his frame up against the body of Chief Boxer and was yelling at him nose to nose. Like the schoolyard bully McWade had warned about, he ripped the police hat from the Chief's head and placed it upon his own to symbolize victory, similar to the taking of the scalp of the enemy's leader in bygone times.

Chief Boxer, a mild-mannered professional, did not take the bait being thrown out by Chin, who very much wanted to start a fight and incite some kind of riot right there on the spot in front of the story-hungry press. The taunting, belligerent, and demeaning comments were mostly ignored even though the Chief, as he later . admitted to McWade, would like to have crushed Chin like the sour and rotten grape that he resembled.

As AIM sympathizers continued to pour in and mass around the PD, the TV cameras were humming and busybody reporters were taking snap shots from every angle of everything that moved or breathed as they scrambled excitedly through the robot-like gathering. Like a flock of buzzards circling above their anticipated prey, the army of outside press were frothing at the mouth to outdo one another even if it meant creating some fake news to show their followers. They had already shown themselves to excel in the false narrative area based on their reporting of inflated of numbers and embellished proceedings following the earlier grand jury fiasco. So the bar had already been set at about knee level on the high jump pit of honesty.

Before Chin and his group of ruffians could get their troublemaking landing gears fully extended and before their planned chaos could be fully implemented, there was a total breakdown of communications over at the NSP command post. The sergeant in charge, by the name of Corns, inadvertently sent an SOS mayday call over the radio to the anxiously waiting posse on the south edge of town.

Suddenly, and within seconds of the inadvertent call for help, over sixty of the gleaming white NSP cruisers fired up their oversize engines and roared into action.

The posse quickly formed, and as if on command, they raced across US 20, the CNW tracks, and north up the main street of Gordon with lights flashing and sirens screaming.

McWade witnessed the spectacle in awe as the procession roared toward the PD, as if in full attack mode, with riot gear in ready position. The incident could easily have been the inspiration for the police cruiser scene in the later Hollywood movie *Smoky and the Bandit*, where the imaginary rogue sheriff, Buford T. Justice, gathered scores of police cars in effort to finally catch his prey.

Not only did the approaching posse riding their ponies of iron and steel get the full attention of the townsfolk but also of the wide-eyed AIM invaders from the north. The chilling effect on the protest organizers was profound and immediate. The message was loud and clear and in a language even the overbearing bully thugs completely understood.

Never had McWade seen anything so impressive. This fleet of cruisers in action was even more inspiring than the military jets flying over Memorial Stadium in Lincoln before a Husker home game. These were the things that made loyal Americans have chills run up and down their spines and make hair on the neck stand at attention.

Some kind of attention was also noted on the part of Chin, and his gang, as they seemed to immediately size up their opposition and instantly lost their enthusiasm for troublemaking. A new game plan by AIM was implemented, and the retreat began.

With their collective and figurative tails between their legs, the marauders scrambled into their vehicles and hastened back toward the rez, which they felt was their own sovereign nation and where they would be safe from arrest by the oversize posse that had surrounded them.

A mistaken command signal had completely defused a very dangerous and potentially costly civil disruption in the little village and had sent a clear message to AIM about what to expect if they caused trouble in Nebraska.

Law enforcement nationwide should have taken note and paid attention to what had taken place that day in the middle of a vast grassland empire. The lesson should have been incorporated into every police training program and pounded into the heads of every politically correct attorney or Bureau supervisor.

The lesson was ever so simple. When confronted with a much superior and more powerful force, AIM and most other demonstrators will usually melt into the background as it has a tendency to suppress their cowardly behavior. Much trouble could have been avoided in future confrontations, and perhaps lives saved, in the upcoming dealings with AIM if the lessons learned in Gordon that day would have been taken to heart. But who listens to a lone agent in the middle of nowhere?

The real geniuses all seem to live behind desks at FBI Headquarters (FBIHQ) and in the fancy field offices throughout the land. These leaders seem to have to consult with armies of attorneys and PC specialists before making critical decisions.

So why would anyone give any credence to an agent on the verge of going native?

The summary teletype to FBIHQ gave some of the facts about the day's activities.

McWade would imagine the Director reading it and knowing that the evening news was fake when it reported thousands of protesters rather the actual number of eight hundred. The word *thousands* sells more newspapers than the lower truthful number, and McWade was beginning to feel more educated about the media.

It was beginning to become more clear about the fourth branch of government, the media, and how they could be just as deceitful and unscrupulous as the other three. The word *self-serving* seemed to come to mind.

Feedback from FBIHQ soon became less frequent and, after a week or two, ceased altogether as far as the AIM matter in Gordon was concerned. It all seemed to fade into yesterday's news cycle.

But something inside whispered to McWade in a convincing tone, "AIM is far from dead, and the worst is yet to come."

Then came the communication dated May 2, 1972, that sent shock waves and would certainly create adjustments throughout the entire Bureau. J Edgar Hoover was dead! The man who seemly could live and rule his Bureau empire forever had died of an unexpected heart attack. The head of arguably one of the most powerful government agencies since its founding in 1935 and the only FBI Director since its inception was now gone.

The Bureau was in collective shock, and all waited in eager anticipation to see what would now happen to the agency he had been so instrumental in creating.

McWade somehow sensed the days ahead would be uncertain and unsettling, even for agents like him, residing in remote assignments, hanging out with local cops in small-town coffee shops, working mostly the bread-and-butter cases of the Bureau, who were, most of all, living examples of Hoover's nightmare.

Chapter 3

Hoover

There were some who claimed, jokingly of course, that he never really existed. That he was just the figment of someone's imagination. That the powers to be had needed to create a superhero of sorts to convince the masses that everything possible was being done to combat the crime wave sweeping the nation in the form of gangsters like Bonnie and Clyde, Pretty Boy Floyd, John Dillinger, and others who had dominated the news on their interstate crime sprees.

Hence, the fictional creation of a man who could represent a strong bulldog-looking appearance, coupled with a name, like a vacuum cleaner, representing a cleanup of crime.

The name Hoover was chosen and attached to the stern, boxer-like face of the image to be known as J. Edgar Hoover.

The supersleuth character to be portrayed to the public, as the fiction writers claimed, would be created through all sorts of smoke and mirror PR, complete with look-alike stand-ins and mannequins for interviews and photo ops.

Although McWade knew this to be BS, he could not testify otherwise as he had never seen, shook hands with, or spoken to anyone claiming to be Hoover.

Sure he had some "attaboy" letters signed by the man's pen with his unique blue ink signature. There was also the Western Union telegram on the official yellow-and-black format with the offer to work for the Bureau. The message was on ticker tape strips glued to the telegram showing it was from John Edgar Hoover. But then couldn't anyone generate paper communications?

In October 1969, when McWade attended his three months of new agents training in DC and Quantico, Virginia, he was never allowed to see the legendary man as there was always a story or situation to prevent such a one-on-one meeting.

An example of that was as follows: Each new agents class, consisting of fifty new recruits at the inception, was assigned two class advisers. McWade's class was designated as NAC #8 (New Agent Class 8), and the two assigned class counselors were old-timers from out in the field named Joel and Clyde. Both were well seasoned and full of all sorts of war stories to feed the eager young men. It was definitely a class of all men as the Director was adamant about not hiring any female agents for various reasons. Counselor Joel, with a convincing gleam in his eye, related to the class how the Director no longer met and shook hands with the new agents.

Apparently, in a class, a month or so before, the new agents were to meet the man and were in a line standing outside his office in the Department of Justice (DOJ) Building. Their suits were all pressed, their teeth all brushed, and, above all, their hands were all dry, and each held a new clean handkerchief. They had been warned that Hoover was emphatic about shaking hands with someone with a limp handshake and, above all, someone with sweaty, moist palms.

Hoover had no real love for newsmen unless, of course, they were writing something very glowing about him or his beloved FBI. Interviews with reporters were scheduled in advance so he could be prepared and on his best game plan. On this particular day, as Joel relayed the experience, this uninvited reporter, who had been denied access to Hoover, saw the line of new agents outside his office and merely did what reporters do. He silently stepped in the line behind the last agent and waited.

According to Joel, "Holy hell reigned down upon those two poor counseling class schmucks. No one has seen those two since, and who the hell knows to which galaxy in outer space they were sent?"

Hence, the new edict from the head office according to Clyde: "This will never happen again. No more new agents classes will meet with the Director again—ever!"

The two NAC "mother hens" were overjoyed to be able to stay away from big corner office as they both claimed that no good could ever come from most meetings with the Director.

They began telling, in machine-gun fashion, horror stories about new agents' classes' meeting with the man in the big office. One such class had just marched through, shaking the Director's hand. When the line of agents had all exited, he made a note with his bold handwriting, saying that one of the agents was a pinhead. The class nannies were in a state of panic, trying to determine to which of the fifty new agents he was referring. Joel related that those poor class counselors even were seen "out in the hall looking at all their hats to see who had the smallest head."

Clyde then just had to tell about another similar case where Hoover allegedly made a note that "one of these guys walks like a duck." The next few weeks put everyone in that particular class under a microscope of surveillance to determine who the duck walker could be. They even wondered if it could have been the guy in the class who was from Oregon and had played football for the Oregon Ducks. Such infectious paranoia seemed to surround those who had those positions.

Joel then told McWade and his anxious classmates of another poor agent who had just been transferred to his office of preference (OP) in the Northwestern part of the country. He and his wife were so happy to finally be back closer to family and to his home. The agent was hardly finished unpacking his boxes when he had to go back to FBIHQ for some kind of routine in service training. While there, the guy foolishly decided to make an appointment with Hoover just to meet him.

The Director was impressed with the guy and made a note in the margin of the page in his file, in the bold blue ink, that said, "Great agent, we need guys like this at WFO" (Washington Field Office).

When the guy returned back home to his wife and kids, there was a transfer letter waiting for him, changing his assignment to WFO. "You just can't make this shit up," warned Joel with enthusiasm. "I am telling you to just stay clear of that office because good things usually just do not happen."

Then not to be outdone, Clyde jumped in to tell of another well-seasoned agent from the New Orleans office back in DC for training. The man had allowed himself to become somewhat portly and was visually overweight, not conforming to the Bureau weight chart for his height. He foolishly did not avoid the Director, who immediately pulled out his blue pen after seeing him and gave him six months to transform from fat to fit, according to Clyde.

The story continued that the chunky agent went back to the field and became the talk of the New Orleans office as he did nothing to lose any excess body mass and, in fact, was seen by most as actually increasing in size. When the time for the meeting with Hoover arrived, he flew to DC, but not before buying an oversize suit for himself at the local Salvation Army outlet.

Clyde laughed about how he met with the Director in his oversize baggy surplus suit and how he was congratulated on his weight loss and sent back to New Orleans to, once again, fight crime.

McWade had a classmate, John Riley, who was an Irishman from the great state of Indiana. He had traded his badge as a highway patrolman there to proudly carry the badge and credentials of a Special Agent of the FBI.

From day one, both Clyde and Joel harped to the attentive new agents about the three Bs and how they could give you nothing but trouble and even get you fired. They were Booze, Broads, and Bucars, not necessarily in that order.

"This is the gospel according to Hoover!" Joel emphasized. "Violations of these laws constitute a sin in the eyes of the Director and will be dealt with harshly."

A few days later, Agent Riley chose to go out on the town, drinking to excess. While allegedly in a drunken state, he call the FBI switchboard and tried to hustle the female operator who answered his call. He reportedly made a real ass of himself in trying to solicit sex from the innocent young girl. In his brain fog, he let her know he was a new agent and identified himself.

In the holy trinity of Bureau commandments, he had just violated two.

Joel had explained that the one sure way to get fired was to dip your pen in government ink! "Does anyone need me to explain what I mean?" he asked.

Only silence followed as there was no doubt.

McWade would forever wonder if the whole Riley thing was for real or just a staged setup to show and illustrate what would happen to sinners.

Every single person in NAC #8 was aware of the incident as agents are great at gossip and excel in obtaining information. So everyone stared in stone silence the next day when an official-looking man came into the classroom asking for Agent Riley, stating the Director's Office wanted him. The man then escorted the white-faced guy out the door.

His official notebook, pen, and other classroom paraphernalia were left abandoned on his desk, standing as ghosts of his disappearance.

Whether for real or a setup, the man known as Agent John Riley was never seen or heard from again by anyone in NAC #8, and just like poor Charlie riding the MTA, his fate is still unknown.

McWade was beginning to get the big picture as his NAC days began to pass.

"The best way to handle this Hoover issue is to stay as far away from him and his corps of yes-man as humanly possible and completely below his radar screen," he reasoned.

He knew by now that if anyone screwed up and, in the eyes of J. Edgar, needed to be disciplined and taught a lesson, one of the worst possible things, short of firing, was to banish the poor soul to the Butte Division. However, the front office was so far out of touch with reality they hadn't caught on that living in Idaho or Montana was one of the best things that could happen to most agents. In fact, McWade had mustered in through the Butte Division and would love to be assigned there someday. But to list Butte as an OP would be a sure guarantee that he would be sent in the other direction, or so he had been told. This was the unwritten policy under Hoover unless, of course, you had a rabbi in management to pull strings for you in the transfer unit.

Joel stood before the class early on and in subdued tones, as if he was being monitored, told of how both he and Clyde were sort of in a limbo state as far as their careers were concerned. He told in detail of how they had both been a part of a big city office team, monitoring the activities of a violent group now named the Weathermen. This was a domestic terrorist group with both bombings and blood on their hands, which posed a threat to the United States.

Now his voiced became even more secretive as he almost whispered how they had been ordered, by Bureau management, to break into the living quarters of these terrorists in order to plant listening devices so they could be monitored. Thus, hopefully to save lives and property, this was done, according to Joel, "with the full knowledge and blessing of Hoover."

However, the cover for the black bag operation had somehow been blown, and now those involved were being literally thrown to the wolves as the Bureau seemed to be backpedaling and disavowing knowledge of the operation. "Clyde and I are here as nannies because the Bureau wanted us out of sight while this matter was being resolved," he added.

McWade could observe that even though Joel acted macho about the matter, he was actually concerned and frightened over the possible fallout and how it would affect both he and Clyde, as well as others. He had expressed concern that he could be financially bankrupt if he had to pay for his own legal defense attorneys.

Clyde then stepped in to try to lighten the atmosphere with another story about the Director and the curtain of nervous fear that hung over all who had to deal with the man.

"There was a case involving a fugitive, who was being considered to be placed on the FBI Ten Most Wanted Fugitives. The case agent drafted the required memo and sent it up the chain.

When Hoover saw the memo, he was agitated and irritated as the agent had only left very narrow margins on each side of the page.

This obviously left no room for the signature blue pen to make the all-knowing remarks. So to correct the writer's error, in his bold fashion, he wrote, "Watch the borders!"

Clyde laughed and embellished in detail how the order then went out Bureau-wide to put up checkpoints and get more agents on both the Mexican and Canadian borders.

"I couldn't make this stuff up," he smiled.

The stories continued throughout the three-month training. Stories like how the Director required all new agents to purchase, with their own money, the book *Masters of Deceit* by J. Edgar Hoover. The problem was that Hoover did not write the book and, instead, had ordered his own agents to do it on Bureau time using Bureau resources. He then allegedly kept the money from the proceeds.

"Now try to beat that for being a master of deceit," said Joel.

"Okay, try this one," Clyde stated as he stepped in front of the classroom. "How about after his FBI limo was hit by another car while making a left turn? The poor chauffeur was ordered, in the future, to avoid making any more left turns. The problem was therefore solved as there were no more accidents involving making those pesky left turns in front of oncoming cars! Brilliant solution." Clyde laughed.

Not to be outdone just yet, Joel stood and moved his muscular body forward to the ears of the waiting and eager trainees. He cleared his voice, then lowered it to a secretive whisper. "I have a friend in the lab who claims the old boy ordered him to design and make blinds and shutters that would open with the first rays of the morning sun and close at sundown for his bedroom windows at his home. Yet another agent from the lab had been ordered to design and build a step around his toilet because Hoover's legs were too short for him to reach the floor."

"The Bureau has a minimum height requirement of five feet, seven for anyone they hire as an agent. Would any of you budding Einsteins dare guess how tall Hoover was?" Joel asked.

He smiled as the answer five feet, seven inches came from the rear of the classroom, which, by the way, was located on one of the upper floors of the historic old Post Office Building in DC. The answer was obvious to McWade as the Director, the fearless leader, would certainly not want to be the shortest guy in the entire Bureau.

He already was rumored to have a step built behind his desk so he could stand on it as he did not want to appear to be short in photo ops and while meeting taller people.

"No personality complexes below the surface there," theorized McWade.

When McWade drifted into Scottsbluff, Nebraska, in March of 1971, he was pleased with the small town and excited about hopefully spending the rest of his Bureau career there out of the limelight and far from the micromanaging eyes of supervisors in Omaha and FBIHQ.

He had not yet unpacked his bags when the word came down that some radical anti-Vietnam War protesters had broken into the unsecured RA at Media, Pennsylvania, and stolen some Selective Service case files.

These files, pertaining mostly to routine cases being worked there, had been leaked to the news outlets, which caused the Director to be embarrassed and, thus, outraged. Another of the things pounded into the skulls of the new budding scholars in NAC was the cardinal rule that was, by far, the most important: "Do not embarrass the Bureau!"

To do so was a sin above all others as the "Bureau was all about image and worldview," according to both Clyde and Joel. "There is no way to separate Hoover from the Bureau, so to embarrass one is to embarrass the other, and beware if you do," added Counselor Clyde.

The break-in and information leaks to the newspapers at Media, Pennsylvania, had embarrassed the Director. His shoot from the hip, shotgun reaction was to "close each and every RA in the entire United States of America!"

"That should solve the problem," laughed McWade when he was told about the proposed closures. No RAs, no break-ins, end of story!

Eventually, cooler-headed would prevail, and it was decided to install alarm systems in each of the hundreds of RA that dotted the country. Until that could happen, the Director ordered that every RA should be guarded by an agent each and every night.

Since there were then two agents in Scottsbluff, guess what that meant?

"Do you have any idea what it's like to sleep on the floor in a small RA?"

"This too shall pass!" McWade had seen on a plaque once. And soon an alarm was installed and his bags were finally unpacked.

The larger question in young McWade's mind was, why wasn't there an alarm system in every office years earlier? Wasn't Hoover's FBI the blue ribbon team at the forefront of innovation in law enforcement?

The bags were just unpacked in Scottsbluff when another edict came down from the Director stating that "every agent in the Bureau would develop a ghetto informant." This was because, McWade supposed, of the riots in the ghettos of DC and other larger cities over the recent past. If there were more informants, the Bureau would know what was going on in advance and stop any riots before they started. The plan from the ivory towers at FBIHQ was simple and made complete sense as they looked out their windows at the city below.

McWade soon found he had a problem. Scottsbluff, Nebraska, was a ranch-farming area with nothing that even resembled a ghetto. A quick surveillance of the town revealed a colored population of less than twenty, which included six basketball players on the local Nebraska Western Junior College team.

McWade drafted a brilliant memo and sent it back to his office in Omaha, stating in a matter-of-fact manner: "You send me a ghetto and I will send you a ghetto informant!"

That message put Hoover's order to rest in the Scottsbluff RA and made for a good story for other agents to tell, pointing out how out of touch some in management were.

Maybe there was something to what nanny Joel had told him in NAC. "Screw up, move up!"

Books have been written on J. Edgar Hoover, both pro and con. His critics have painted him to be a power hungry, dictatorial, and ruthless man who was controversial in every way. Those singing his praises are not only more understanding of his shortcomings but also point out the positive things that took place during his long tenure as FBI Director.

McWade tried to judge him using a liberal measuring stick, showing facts, efforts, performance, and accomplishments and asking if the country was better off because of his leadership in the Bureau. Unfounded rumors, political hatred, and bias was given very little credence in this formula.

Was he dictatorial? "Yes!"

Was he totally honest in his actions? "It sometimes appeared not to be the case."

Was he somewhat paranoid? *Seemed to be!* thought McWade.

Was he a cross-dresser as his critics allege? "Who really cares? I certainly never saw any such behavior," McWade answered.

Was he too powerful and did he abuse that power? "A lot of the agents who worked for him seemed to think that was the case."

Was he a true patriot who loved the United States? "Yes!" McWade replied emphatically.

Did he play the numbers game for Congress, emphasizing quantity over quality on the cases he encouraged his agents to work? McWade seemed to think that was true on many of the cases assigned to him. Minor car thieves, army deserters, and draft dodgers seemed to come to mind. After all, an interstate car thief arrested by a local police officer but prosecuted by McWade seemed to count the same as an organized crime conviction in New York City.

Did he live up to his last name (Hoover) by vacuuming up minor criminals instead of focusing on harder and more important issues of national concern? Again, McWade would have to answer, "Yes, it seemed so."

Did he maintain files on political figures for his later use? "Reportedly at times."

Was he a short man with an oversize ego? "Probably," McWade stated, adding, "But I am not a psychologist, so how should I know?"

So with all the negatives thrown out there about the man in the corner office, what was the average agent to think?

McWade sensed that most agents, like himself, who served under him felt a great deal of pride in being part of his Bureau. He was not perfect; in fact, he was far from it. But McWade respected him and realized that he was a pure genius in the area of image building and had projected the Bureau to the public as the number one crime-fighting investigative agency in the entire world. Since image is so important, McWade was grateful for his dedication in that particular area.

A white-collar criminal in a fraud scheme once told McWade the secret of his success: "Once you learn how to fake sincerity, the rest is easy!" he had bragged.

McWade was not comparing sincerity with image but knew that image, whether completely warranted or perceived, went a long way in the art of gaining the trust and confidence of an otherwise wary victim, witness, or subject of any investigation. He acknowledged that Hoover had paved the public perception road very well and made things easier.

He had received a letter from Hoover, signed in his bold blue handwriting, in April 1972, congratulating him on the birth of a son. But now there would be no more letters, no more of his spur-of-the-moment epistles telling agents to find a ghetto informant in the North Platte Valley of Nebraska. He was gone from his beloved Bureau. That same Bureau to which he had given his life.

Will he be remembered as a hero, a legend, a celebrity? *Whatever anyone thought of him, he was a phenomenon, a giant in the field of empire building*, thought McWade.

With all this said, McWade always smiled to himself when he thought of the fear Hoover had that one of his agents could "go native."

This occasional thought would pass as soon as he entered the coffee shop to BS with his friends, the men and women of the local, county and state law enforcement agencies in his RA towns.

In fact, on occasion, his thoughts would drift back to the months of his training and his short years in the Bureau under Hoover. He had never met the man, he had never seen the man. Could he, therefore, personally testify that he really was a real person?

He laughed at his own ridiculous thought as he took another bite of a glazed doughnut and began swapping stories with Armstrong and the rest of the guys.

*****

Nearly all men can stand adversity, but if you want to test a man's character, give him power.

—Abraham Lincoln

Hoover had more power than most!
You be the judge of his character.

J. Edgar Hoover, the man and his legacy

Chapter 4

Hoover High

When the man in the suit, calling himself Joel, one of the class counselors, began calling the roll, organized alphabetically, of new agents at NAC 8, no one answered to the name Smith. Calling the name yet again in a louder voice, an answer came meekly from the back of the room.

"He isn't here, sir!"

"And just who are you?"

"I rode here with him from New Orleans yesterday, sir. He looked around the city, saw two homeless people energetically making love under an old blanket right next the old run-down Hotel Harringbone, where the FBI had made us reservations. While he was staring at them, a rat the size of an alley cat ran across his shoe."

The reporting agent said Smith then got back in his car and said, "Screw this! I'm outa here. Tell them to keep the damn job. I'm going home!"

"Shortest FBI career yet," chimed in Clyde, the co-class counselor. "Apparently he must not have been too impressed with the nation's capital."

McWade recalled his own experience the night before when the limo driver had told him he was insane to carry his suitcases two blocks from the drop-off point to the Harringbone. "You won't make it!" he had warned.

McWade, proving the driver wrong, had made the journey safely anyway without being robbed, mugged, or shot and chuckled to himself that they would not be reading about him just yet in *Washington Post* obituaries section after all.

The Harringbone reminded him of a twelve-story candidate for the mayor's next urban renewal project. But it was still standing, and it was no big deal because he was only propositioned once on the elevator while taking his bags to his room.

She had seemed friendly enough and had half whispered, "I only wanted to make your stay here a great one, if you know what I mean?"

McWade knew exactly what she meant and wondered silently if she was actually a real hooker or a Bureau snitch lurking in the lobby to test the integrity of the new hires being housed there. His mind-set was already entering the Twilight Zone as far as trusting people. This characteristic (of people trust) would continue to develop to a PhD level in the years to come.

After a night of distant sirens and creaking pipes popping from the room's antique radiator heater, combined with squeaky bed-springs and the moaning and gasping from the next room through the old plaster wall, he was beginning to see why Smith had decided to be a no-show.

The thought did enter his mind, *What have I got myself into?*

The first couple weeks seemed to be a continual parade of specialists parading before the class, explaining this program or that program, with most always telling the new group that if they violated their particular policy that it would be "the quickest way to get your ass fired!" This list was growing longer each day with no apparent end in sight.

Every speaker felt like he or she had to relate a horror story that was bigger and better than the last lecturer. It was always about someone who had not taken their advice seriously, therefore had gotten into trouble and ended up either fired or in Butte. The Butte idea sounded good to McWade, and he considered maybe breaking that rule.

During one of the breaks, a new agent nicknamed T Shirls, from one of the Rocky Mountain states, suggested that this whole indoctrination thing going on seemed to him much like a Nazi training camp. Everyone in the small group laughed but, deep down, wondered themselves if this was the case.

Five of the weeks of training would be at the United States Marine Base at Quantico, Virginia, with the rest being in DC.

Just like in the movies, Quantico was a full-time frenzy of firearms, self-defense, and crime scene scenarios. At night, the new inductees crowded into the old brick Marine barracks built during WW I, on Army cots that appeared to have come with the building, lined up similar to those in homeless shelters.

NAC 8 had to decide if the time there was more like a school or a prison, and after much lively, off-the-record debate, it was aptly named Hoover High. The short self-important man in charge, Ty, was christened Headmaster Ty. Every class needed a name. NAC #8 was no different, so the unanimous choice was "Hoover's Groovers."

After being assigned to the field, McWade returned to Quantico a few years later for a two-week-long white-collar crime in-service training session. This was after the great and spacious buildings at Quantico were all finished and the new FBI Academy was operational. It was soon discovered that the same little self-important guy with the huge ego was now in complete control of the brand-new "Hoover High."

ID cards with flimsy alligator clamps to attach to the collar were issued to allow entry to the academy and to the chow hall. They were laminated and looked about the size of a driver's license.

On the second day at the academy, McWade's ID cardholder had a clip malfunction and the card was lost. Too nervous to report it to Headmaster Ty, McWade just flashed his Texas driver's license at each meal and when entering the academy grounds. In other words, he could come and go at will and eat good meals in the cafeteria like everybody else using his Texas driver's license.

On the last day of training, McWade was summoned to the headmaster's office and told that his ID badge had been turned in by someone who had found it under the walkway between two buildings. Not since being called into the principal's office in fifth grade for throwing snowballs at the Union Pacific train that passed by the schoolyard had he seen a more stern-faced look from a bald-headed Kojak-looking man.

Ty is really taking this serious, and this isn't good! thought McWade.

Out came the badge from the lost and found, and Ty Kojak began his lecture as to what would happen if enemy spies got this and gained access to the FBI Academy to wander at will. He then asked McWade, "How have you been eating these past two weeks?"

"Quite well actually, thanks to my Texas driver's license."

The beady-eyed, round-faced, bald-headed man was livid when he found out that a mere street agent from a remote Nebraska outpost had been able to outsmart and go around his brainchild of a security system that he himself had designed to thwart the enemies of the world.

McWade wondered about this seemingly delusional man who was caught up in his James Bond spy mentality and why he was actually running the place. Then he remembered another old saying tossed around the Bureau that said that in the dairy barn, just like the Bureau, "Shit always floated to the top of the bucket." That seemed to explain everything.

"Be more careful!" he mumbled dejectedly as McWade left his office.

Later, it was rumored that there was a complete and total overhaul of the ID card system at Hoover High. McWade was sure Kojak probably received a cash award for pointing out the weaknesses of the old system. That was the way things worked.

Ty was only one of the unique persons running the show at the time of NAC 8.

There was Charlie O'Donnell, the agent lawyer who taught constitutional law. Being Irish from Boston, full of drama and enthusiasm, he made the otherwise boring constitutional law lectures come alive. He was one of a kind with his role-playing using his fictional characters woven into his presentations.

There was the criminal in all his lectures named "Balls O'Leary."

There was the sleazy defense attorney, the eminent "Springer McCarty."

The list of characters, all with catchy Irish names, seemed end-less, and the class gave him a standing ovation after each days lecture.

There was Agent Peach from the Baltimore Field Office, where he had worked WSTA (White Slave Traffic Act) cases most of his career before coming on staff at Hoover High. He must have cheated on the height requirement as he looked smaller than five foot seven. His lack of height was more than made up for with his deep fog horn voice.

He liked to relive his years in Baltimore, telling his juicy stories of busting prostitution rings and of the girls involved. He loved to warn the new agents by telling them that these girls would offer any favors to keep from going to jail. He would get his own very serious demeanor, lower his gravel voice even lower, look the eager faces in the eye, and say, "Now, boys, these women will be desperate. They will offer you sexual favors in exchange for looking the other way. But don't you do it! It will seem exciting at the time, but remember my words. Under the covers, it is all pink and wet, and it is not worth risking your career."

The whole class wondered about his "pussy posse" assignments and joked about his experience and just why he always, when he went to the restroom, washed his hand before urinating instead of after like the rest of the guys.

Outside the classroom, far below on the Washington Mall, people had been arriving from all over the United States. The word around the halls of Hoover High was that it was to be the largest anti-war demonstration in the history of Washington.

McWade had never seen so many hippies in his life, and the sight of it all was crazy. Peter, Paul, and Mary could be heard in the distance cranking up their anti-war and peace music as it was blasted to the masses, who crowded the mall below the Washington Monument.

It all turned out mostly peaceful although class was canceled one day because of a tear gas grenade someone lobbed into the building.

Each morning, either Joel or Clyde, would try to shock the new student-agents with some new gossip or story being circulated around FBIHQ.

"Last night, the Metro Police arrested some schmuck in the act of have sex with a camel at the DC Zoo," Clyde reported. With that news story being of the nature it was and the fact that camels have humps, the story took on a life of its own as "Hoover's Groovers" added their own wit and manufactured spin-off jokes from the incident.

Soon the training days began to wind down and everyone was now looking forward to and focusing on graduation. This also meant receiving their assignment to one of the fifty-nine field offices which would determine where they would relocate to begin their actual careers. Good assignments were hoped for by everyone, and all had fears of undesirable destinations.

When the big day came, the tension mounted. One by one, the class calling themselves "Hoover's Groovers" would hear their name called. They would then walk nervously to the front and open the envelope that determined their future and fate. Alphabetical again, McWade waited patiently. "Agent McWade," came the voice of Joel. The long walk to the front, the anticipation, and then the relief.

The transfer gods had smiled on him. "San Antonio!" he exclaimed with almost tearful relief.

"Goodbye, DC, and hello, Texas!"

"Honey, pack the car, get the kids ready, we are heading for the Lone Star State!" he told his wife excitedly on the phone that night.

In looking back on his months of training, brainwashing, and intense indoctrination spent in the halls and classrooms at DC and on the base at Quantico, he tried to comprehend it all in his mind. He thought a sign he once saw summed up his questions quite well: "Is it my imagination, or are all these rules designed for the sole purpose of being huge inconveniences?"

He would find out soon enough!

Chapter 5

The Real Fun Begins

San Antonio is truly one of the few unique cities in America with its own character and charm.

The FBI office was surprisingly situated directly across the street from the historic Alamo. The walk from the contract parking garage for the Bucars took McWade through the beautiful gardens around the old mission. *What a peaceful setting!* he thought.

Mail was already piling up in his inbox by the time he found his way to the office. To his surprise, the first piece of mail he looked at was an Identification Order (IO) or a Wanted flier with a picture of an old buddy from fifth grade back in Idaho. Good old Melvin had apparently finally found his niche in life as a bank robber out of the Salt Lake City Division.

"It's all about choices!" he mumbled as he found his way back to his assigned squad and desk.

Then McWade remembered buying stolen candy bars from Melvin at scout camp when he was thirteen years old. Melvin had already chosen the life of crime and was at the same camp as part of the Idaho State Reform School troop. They had good food, including candy bars, and McWade's troop had pretty dull and bland food only. Good old Melvin would steal candy and other goodies from his troop's commissary, offering them for sale to McWade's troop, who naturally bought them up with reckless abandon. The first Boy Scout law (to be trustworthy) didn't seem to register to anyone concerned.

And buying stolen candy bars didn't compute as wrong anyway at that young age.

The fugitive squad assignment meant McWade could have as much action as he wanted as there was always an early-morning raid on the house of some unsuspecting escapee or deserter. Whether knocking on the front door or stationed at the back, it was always a way to get your early-morning adrenaline fix. There was always the chance of a good footrace if the guy came bolting out the back door hurdling hedges and fences as he beelined down the back alley. For the first few months, it was hard to believe that doing something so fun could be called a job and could pay so much.

The Vietnam War was still ongoing and as unpopular as ever for those who were drafted and did not want to be shipped to the Asian front. For those already serving, there were always tons of deserters from the ranks. Adding those numbers to the draft dodgers and with San Antonio being the home to so many military bases, this was a hotbed of fugitive activity.

And lest anyone think that deserters and draft dodgers were simple cases, McWade always reminded folks that these guys (and women) were passionate about not wanting to be shipped away. They were young, usually inexperienced at the cops and robbers game, and, therefore, totally unpredictable and likely dangerous when being arrested.

Hoover was known by some as the "Czar of National Law Enforcement," and rounding up draft dodgers and deserters for the war effort was something his men just did to show his patriotism. McWade also suspected the Director liked the large numbers of arrests of deserters and Selective Service violators because, on paper, a Top Ten or IO fugitive made the same size mark on the report to Congress. A great report could justify an increased budget for the next fiscal year.

The war stories surrounding deserter arrests could keep McWade's listeners entertained for hours. One such story was when neighbors had told McWade and his partner that good old Francisco had been living at his grandmother's apartment for weeks and had just been seen going into the apartment minutes ago.

Lying grandmothers were now to be added to the ever-growing list of people you can't trust as she looked McWade in the eye, and with elderly conviction, sincerely stated, "Isn't he in the Army? Why, I haven't seen Francisco since he was drafted over six months ago and have no idea where he might be!"

"You don't mind if we take a look around your apartment then?" McWade asked as he and his partner brushed past the elderly woman.

"Go right ahead, sonny," she half-heartedly agreed.

When the clothes in granny's bedroom closet began to move on their own, the guns came out and, at the same time, "FBI, come out with your hands up!" The beady eyes of the frightened young desperado appeared between the elderly woman's bathrobe and slip.

"You have a search warrant?" came his panic-stricken question.

"No, Francisco! But we have you." McWade smiled.

He was then turned over to the Military Police (MPs), who took possession of him. The uniformed MPs were not smiling at their deserting comrade as they carted him away in cuffs and leg irons. The last words heard from Francisco were "This sucks!" The last words from the MPs were "Shut your damn mouth or I'll show you what sucks!"

Meanwhile, back at the office, McWade was being introduced into the real FBI, not the one talked about at Hoover High. In his infinite and boundless wisdom, the Director had determined that his agents in the field could not solve crime while "sitting on their asses in the office!"

His solution was to mandate that agents could spend no more than two hours per day at their respective desks. This was called Time in the Office (TIO) and was to be monitored by supervisors. It didn't seem to occur to the FBIHQ policy makers that the time spent in the office doing paperwork sometimes could require all day or at least most of the day, depending on what kind of cases were being worked.

Each agent would handle this ridiculous requirement in his own way.

During the first week, a fellow Special Agent by the name of Bruce was observed by McWade to grab his portable radio and enter a small closet not far from his desk.

"SA 19" (code for San Antonio car 19).

"Go ahead, 19," came the reply from the dispatch just around the corner and down the hall.

"SA 19 is 10-8" (code for in service).

SA Bruce then came back to his desk and continued his paperwork. Twenty minutes later, he was back in the closet with his radio.

"SA 19 is 10-7" (code for out of service).

And so the game continued as he created a record on the radio log down the hall to cover his tail, as if he was out in the car covering leads while he was actually busy doing his required paperwork at his own desk.

A few weeks later, McWade came up with his own foolproof plan to get his hours of paperwork done while still complying with the TIO mandate.

He bundled up all his paperwork and files, stuffed them in his bulging Bureau briefcase, found a Bucar, and headed out. Of course, going home was forbidden, so he had found a very secluded and quiet library on the campus of Trinity University. Since there were very few occupants in the lonely place, he was able to spend the required time there getting his work done.

The elderly hawk-eyed woman librarian wondered for months about the young man with a suit and tie, carrying an official-looking government-issued leather briefcase. *Was he a spy, or was he a businessman too tight to rent his own office?* she mused without ever asking. Little did she know he was a new FBI agent trying to learn how to navigate and survive in a world of crazy and impossible rules and regulations handed down through the official channels of a bloated government bureaucracy.

Speaking of rules, McWade, on his first day, had been introduced to the Bureau's concept of AUO (administratively uncontrolled overtime). Each agent who qualified would receive a 25 percent bump on his salary based on the starting salary of a new agent, which, at the time, was just over $10,000 per year.

This AUO was to compensate for all the time an agent spent while on call and signed in at the office. The genius behind this plan was that, to qualify, McWade had to exceed the San Antonio office average overtime hours claimed every other month. To manage the office average and to keep it at just over two hours overtime per day, McWade was assigned a partner with the agreement that they would coordinate their claimed AUO and one would go high one month and low the next.

McWade thought to himself, *This is so unbelievable that I can't even tell my wife or she will think I am dishonest and crazy.* And so he suffered the AUO secret in sacred loneliness. But to not play the game meant to lose 25 percent of his take-home pay, so this was a no-brainer.

And so it went. Between TIO, AUO, large binders containing the Rules and Regulations as well as the Manual of Instructions, it was virtually impossible to not violate some rule or policy several times before lunchtime each day. He was reminded again about his earlier thought about draining the pond when you are ass deep in alligators. That challenge was becoming more difficult daily.

An old-timer in the office, Tom Crabford, who had been around the block in Hoover's Bureau several times over the past thirty years, encouraged young McWade to keep focused on the finish line. If you ever happen to be lucky enough to be transferred to a lonely RA somewhere in the middle of nowhere, just put down your roots, do your job, and stay completely out of sight. In other words, Go Native Young Man!

Getting to know the other agents in the office was one of the highlights. Most were hardworking, sincere, and honest and possessed a variety of skills. One agent stood out from all the rest as he was captivating, talented, friendly, very fun to be around and seemed to have a magnetic personality. In other words, thought McWade, he was just plain over endowed in the social skills department. His name was Freddie McNickle, and here is his truly unbelievable tale:

McNickle was undoubtedly the most charismatic agent McWade had met during his short time in the Bureau. Was it the fact that both were of Scottish descent, or was he just one fun guy to be around?

Freddie was generous with his home and had parties there frequently where he served burgers and good times for all who were invited. His dad, he claimed, had been an FBI agent, which seemed to give McNickle expertise and an inside track on just about every question that came up. Whenever he told a story, there were always several huddled around, seemingly captivated by every word from his mouth.

He was always happy to show off his Corvettes that he had in the garage to fix up and sell. He had developed several informants, he claimed, who operated salvage yards where he could get parts for this endless stream of cars he appeared to run through his small garage. He really appeared to have all the answers about anything to do with automobiles.

McWade was in the market for a new family POA (personally owned automobile) and hoped to find a nice low mileage station wagon. "No problem!" exclaimed Freddie. "Do I have a beauty for you?" He went on to explain that he had been at the races last weekend up in Austin, and one of the guys from the famous Smothers Brothers had a tow car they wanted to sell. It was a fully loaded 1969 ruby red Chevrolet Kingswood wagon that was a beauty to behold.

That wagon's 396 V8 guzzled more gas than McWade could ever imagine possible, but Freddie again came to the rescue. He soon had it over to his garage, reworking the carburetor, installing smaller jets, and making all the necessary adjustments on McWade's new purchase. This automobile was the pride of the neighborhood, and all eyes followed it whenever it passed.

He was at the height of his talking game when telling about his contacts and the latest good deal on a Corvette.

One day at the office, old Crabford pulled young McWade aside and told him in a fatherly voice, "I know he is a guy easy to like, but you just can't afford liking people like him."

Time would prove Tom to be a man with prophetic insight.

One day, Fast Freddie, as those on the squad had nicknamed him, left the office at exactly 8:15 AM in his Bucar, a plain-Jane-looking 1966 four-door Chevrolet. He was supposedly on his way to fight crime as his Number 3 locator card had been properly filled out and left at the switchboard, showing where he was planning to be the rest of the day. Only two blocks from the office, Fast Freddie, blew a red light and T-boned another poor soul who was going through on the green.

The Director had a policy in effect for everything, and this was no exception. If an agent is at fault in an accident, he will be charged for the cost of a new Bucar or for the cost of repairing the one he damaged. Running a red light was a no-brainer, and young McNickle was ordered to replace the Bucar, which was declared a total loss.

Now Fast Freddie was not a highly paid employee as his starting salary, like other new agents, was only $10,252 per year plus the AUO amounting to and additional $2,558. "How could he possibly pay for a new Bucar?" asked McWade and others on the squad as they visited around the watercooler.

Freddie was glum, but not for long. Remember, he was a man with junkyard informants and contacts all over town.

Within a week, he presented the Bureau another vehicle just like the one he destroyed.

Freddie and his team of scavengers burned the midnight oil and resurrected from the graveyard of old automobiles a new Bucar, just like the one he had totaled. He bragged that he had found another '66 Chevy that had been rear-ended, which he bought for mere peanuts.

McNickle had led his team of auto surgeons as they performed a truly masterful lifesaving operation. Using a cutting torch, the rear end of the wrecked Bucar was severed from the demolished engine and front seat by cutting it just behind the front doors. The front part of the donor car, including the engine and transmission, was implanted by welding the two halves together, painting it, and placing the proper VIN (vehicle identification number) on the finished product in all the proper and secret locations.

The car Freddie presented to Mr. Hoover's finest was arguably the best-looking Bucar in the San Antonio fleet. The details of the resurrection of old SA 69 were laughed about by each and every agent as Freddie was looked at as a small-time hero for getting the best of management. "Score one for the little guys" was the general agent consensus.

The secret of the rising from the dead of the car was never mentioned to management and, certainly therefore, never up channeled to Director's Row.

Freddie's stature as a courageous young rebel made him even more admired by his comrades. Even the old-timers, the office heavies, who smoked cigars while leaning back in their chairs, with their feet planted on top their desks, in the secluded back offices of the bank robbery squad, chuckled and were amused by the caper.

McNickle had a real talent for doing gutsy things and living on the edge. "This guy is a rising star in the Bureau. We will hear more about him," McWade overhead someone say.

One of the main functions of the FBI is the gathering of information to be used for prosecuting criminals concerning national security. It was also learned that any spicy story or out-of-the-ordinary conduct by any agent soon became widespread knowledge (or gossip) throughout the organization.

So it was with McWade's good friend, Fast Freddie McNickle, who, like one of Mr. Hoover's finest groomed sheep, went totally astray from the flock and embarrassed the Bureau. He definitely would, someday, stand out as the black sheep in the Director's herd.

After leaving San Antonio, good old McNickle was transferred to a field office down south close to the home of his father, now a retired Bureau agent. *Now that was a lucky impartial stroke of good fortune*, thought McWade. *Maybe, just maybe, it does pay to have connections in this outfit!*

Rumor was that young Freddie, shortly after arriving in his new field office, was called out with almost the entire office to look for an armed and dangerous madman who had just done his latest robbery. Black Bart, the notorious thug, was last seen entering into a very secluded field of tall grass, which was waving gently in the southern breeze.

This case was so big that even the SAC was out there with his boys on the hunt, hoping to be there in case they captured Bart. A Bureau-friendly newsman had been advised by that same SAC to be in the wings for a good story. A little positive press always seemed to go a long way for any supervisor's career when reported to the

Director as long, that is, as the SAC also threw in the name of the Director in the news release.

Without warning, Black Bart leaped from his hiding spot in the tall grass and pulled a gun on the SAC's back. Our man Freddie was several steps behind and covering the back of the SAC when this unfolded before his wide eyes. Remembering all the intensive training from his days in Quantico, McNickle instinctively raised his Bureau-issued 870 Remington 12-gauge shotgun to a ready gun position and warned the culprit, who ignored the command. When the gun smoke finally cleared, Black Bart's body was lying in a bloodstained heap in the waist-high grassland. He should have known better than to have taken on Fast Freddie McNickle with his 12-gauge pump-action weapon. At close range, our bank-robbing gangster should have given more respect to a magnum load of 00 buck. He would never be given that chance again.

When a Special Agent saves the life of an SAC, one of Hoover's personally anointed, he attains instant superhero status, and McNickle was no exception to this rule. He could have been granted most any wish the Bureau genie offered. He could have been given his OP or any number of other offers. But our youngest celebrity instead just wanted to be part of a Bureau unit that only existed in secret. A unit so confidential that even one of McWade's closest friends in the FBI laboratory was unaware of its existence for several of the years he was thusly assigned to the lab.

Fast Freddie was the ideal candidate to be trained as a Bureau locksmith and break-in artist for the planting of listening devises and monitoring equipment. He learned quickly and soon was in demand throughout the country. His reputation continued to grow as his talent was used in more and more field offices on supersensitive cases.

He had proudly gone from welding two cars together to inventing and obtaining a patent on a revolutionary new lock which he was selling on the open market. He reportedly was able to open safes quickly and was a natural in coming up with innovative ways to plant court order devices undetected.

Once, McWade had heard that Freddie was summoned to plant a monitoring device in the business of a Mafia-owned storefront used to launder money. The problem with getting into the building was that the only entrance was on a very busy sidewalk on a large city street. "No fear!" said our man as he devised a great plan to make an impression of the lock.

No one noticed as a delivery truck bearing the name Freddie's Appliances pulled up next to the entrance in the middle of the day. A large refrigerator-sized box labeled "Westinghouse" was unloaded and placed directly next to the door. Inside the box was our trusty sleuth secretly equipped with the necessary tools of the trade. Through the small holes in the box, precut at exactly the right height to match the door's lock, Fast Freddie lived up to his name as he made impressions of the locks with lightning speed. The box was then taken away by the same delivery men who had placed the box there only fifteen minutes prior. It was then loaded into the van where Freddie, with a broad smile on his face, exited the cargo container on his way back to the secret chambers of his lab, where he went about making duplicate keys from his impressions on the gangster's lock. He loved the challenge and loved the risk. "Happy is the man who loves his work!" he chuckled to himself as he admired himself in the mirror.

Thanks to our man's innovative mind, the agents working the case, accompanied by McNickle, were able to enter the building, bypass the alarms, install the bugs, and leave undetected. He was good, and he now knew it! *Nothing can stop me now!* he thought clandestinely.

Freddie's reputation as a genius in the black bag arena was growing like a raging wildfire driven by strong Santa Anna winds, swallowing up everything in its wake. He was whispered about privately as being the best there ever was in his field.

Soon he was making trips on the Bureau's dime all over the country. No one seemed to question why he would fly to his destinations on commercial flights and return home to his place in rural Virginia driving a Porsche automobile. Also, no one seemed to question how he could afford an expensive estate in the Virginia countryside complete with an acreage, nice Thoroughbred horses, a swimming pool, lush trees, and beautiful landscaping.

Add to the estate a large shop to house his ever-growing collection of Porsche sports cars, and one could only wonder how he could afford all this on the salary of an FBI employee. But those who may have wondered would rationalize in their minds that he was now a Bureau Supervisor, and after all, didn't he invent a new type of lock for which he was receiving royalties? Maybe he had inherited money? Maybe he had invested well in the markets?

With all the good life seemingly going his way, Fast Freddie was still ultra generous with his good fortune. Parties were always being held at his estate and were very well attended by those he invited, both street agents and Bureau supervisors. Everyone loved to be part of his circle of trust. His charisma was intoxicating, and all seemed to be drawn to him like a moth to the flame.

McWade's close friend in the Laboratory reported also that Freddie was getting a little too friendly with his wife and actually tried to plant a French kiss on her at a Christmas party and had to be put in his place with harsh words of warning. The warning was something to the effect, "Do that again and I will kick your ass up between your shoulder blades!" But this cavalier behavior toward women only seemed to signal a side of his life that was being, at that time, kept very close to McNickle's vest and escalating.

Only a few knew that he also had a secret love nest suite in the suburbs of Alexandria, Virginia, where he schmoozed women of all walks of life that had joined him for one of his love rendezvous. His schedule was such that he could come from an assignment a day earlier, and no one was the wiser. This extra day of fun and frolic would be spent with his latest conquest, whether it be an airline stewardess or a beauty he had picked up at a bar. His wife either looked the other way or never questioned his innocent-looking face when he finally arrived home, seemingly totally worn-out from his activities.

Fast Freddie's skills and his bravado enabled him to abscond with a Porsche parked on a side street, in a driveway, or some parking lot without any difficulty, and the thrill of the theft seemed to give him a definite buzz. He prided himself in just how quickly he could steal the car and be down the road undetected.

Upon bringing his latest treasure back to his well-equipped shop, he was able to do the magic of changing the VIN on the stolen car to correspond with the VIN of some salvage title he had acquired through his junkyard sources. It really came in handy to have all the information through his FBI channels as to where all the CVINs (confidential vehicle identification numbers) were stamped on the particular models he happened to be pilfering. If there was a CVIN on a tag attached to a particular seat cushion, he knew how to find and either remove it or change it. A CVIN stamped on the underside of the frame, no problem; he knew exactly where to look and how to handle that issue. Freddie was on the roll.

You might be wondering just who purchased these stolen Porsche cars.

"Anyone who McNickle knew was a potential buyer, including Bureau Supervisors looking for a good deal," reported McWade's plant in the Lab.

In 1980, all hell seemed to rain down on poor Freddie. Needing some extra cash, he was caught inside the FBI Federal Credit Union located right inside the J. Edgar Hoover Building.

A night janitor was making the rounds and noticed the door to the credit union was not locked. When the man opened the door to investigate, there was our friend Freddie crouched like a cheetah beside the open safe with over $250,000 in bills stacked around him. With the speed of light, Freddie leaped to his feet, drew his sidearm, and yelled, "FBI! Freeze!"

The poor janitor was to be blamed by McNickle for his own break in and safecracking.

What balls! thought McWade. *The FBI's own credit union?*

Freddie's life started a downward spiral at that point as he soon became the target of an investigation by the OPR (Office of Professional Responsibility).

The poor janitor was cleared of the accusation against him as Freddie became the focus of a series of thefts and crimes all up and down the eastern seaboard. Soon he was tied to thefts of loose diamonds, rings, jewelry, and even Mercury outboard motors for boats. When word was sent out around FBIHQ about his car thefts, it was advised that all unsuspecting supervisors who had purchased any stolen Porsche from McNickle had until sundown the next day to surrender that car or risk prosecution. Word was whispered around the hallowed halls that around thirty stolen vehicles magically showed up and that about that many Bureau supervisors had vacancies in their garages that night.

When McWade heard the story, he could not help but wonder if the same leniency would have been shown if those purchasing the stolen cars would have been mere agents rather than supervisors. "Just a passing thought," he said to himself.

McWade's snitch in the Lab was aware that several stolen diamonds had also been sold to unsuspecting friends of McNickle both inside and outside the FBI. Since these diamonds all had certified papers describing them, they were all traceable. Soon the word went out and to HQ, and loose diamonds also came flooding into the evidence room. One young man from a police department in the suburbs of DC used one of Fast Freddie's diamond rings to become engaged to his fiancée. The same guy was to take the oath as a new special agent in two weeks. He failed to self-disclose his purchase and was fired the same day he showed up to be sworn as a new recruit.

McWade laughed that this guy, and Smith, the no-show to NAC 8, the kid from New Orleans, probably were tied for having the shortest Bureau careers in history.

OPR thought they would be coy and monitor who would come and go from McNickle's estate in the suburbs by covertly installing a concealed camera in a tree near the entrance to his driveway. The plan was to capture the license plate numbers of every car and subsequently interview them as to the purpose of their visit, hoping to get some poor agent lying in some way.

McWade was amused when he heard that Freddie was again ahead of the competition and knew all about the secret monitoring device. So whenever a friend would visit, McNickle would warn him that OPR would probably be calling them in within a few days. The geniuses at OPR were livid when they, again, found out they were behind in the spy game with their subject.

Freddie's ship was sinking fast as it was even found out that he had stolen FBI portable radios and sold them to a big-name NASCAR race team in North Carolina.

As physical evidence piled up against our famous celebrity agent, there were still many agents who knew him that refused to believe he was guilty of anything. The right side of their brains said, "Look at the evidence!" while the emotional left side of their brains said, "No way, I refuse to believe he would do this!" Such were their beliefs and testimonies borne to his innocence. But soon, even those doubters were convinced.

He was acquitted on charges of breaking and entering the FBI Credit Union but was convicted of jewel theft, Interstate Transporting of Stolen Property, tax evasion, giving false statements, and obstruction of justice. He was sentenced to eight years in prison on those charges. In another trial, he was convicted of receiving over $100,000 for stolen cars and other items.

The thing that most disgusted McWade was when Fast Freddie was convicted of having sex with the twenty-year-old handicapped daughter of one of his defense attorneys. For this, he was given twenty years on a sex offense which he was to serve concurrent with his other charges.

After all this had gone down, McWade now wondered about the real origin of the 1969 Kingswood wagon Freddie sold him. Was it really the tow car for the Smothers Brothers' race team? He guessed he would never know.

Through the magic of the internet, McWade found McNickle's obituary in a faraway western part of the US. It read as follows: "Fast Freddie McNickle (1940–2012) passed away surrounded by his family. He followed his father's footsteps into the FBI, becoming a Special Agent Supervisor. He held lock patents and was involved in boat and NASCAR racing. Freddie never met a stranger and was often heard to say, 'If I don't have it, you don't need it' and 'I can fix anything but a broken heart.' Visitation will be held March 1, 2012."

The lengthy obituary outlined his many talents and accomplishments. Absent was the dark truth of a potentially great agent gone astray who just could not seem to help himself when it came to his appetites and his greed.

While serving his time in an undisclosed federal medium-security prison facility, McWade was told—surprise, surprise!—that Fast Freddie soon won over the warden with his charm and smooth talk. When he wasn't busy preparing income tax returns for the administration, he was busy in the prison shop, working on sports cars. He reportedly made several guards happy when he showed them how they could write off the sports cars they bought from one of Freddie's friends on the outside. With his new position as "trustee" and given that he had full access to the prison van to make deliveries and run errands, McWade could only shake his head and say, "Wow, nobody will ever believe this stuff!"

These are just some of the numerous things not covered in the obituary.

Freddie had once told McWade, "When you set your one goals, the sky is the limit." So it was with Fast Freddie McNickle, truly charming, but a dark legend in McWade's ongoing FBI experience.

After his death, McWade tried to imagine Freddie approaching at the Golden Gate. "In your wildest dream, do you really think old St. Peter could keep him out? After all, he was the very best locksmith in the entire world, and by the way, who ordered a new refrigerator up here anyway?" RIP.

Meanwhile, back in San Antonio, time was flying by as young McWade, like a dry sponge, was daily soaking up little things to help him navigate the rough Bureau waters ahead.

Old-timers were full of advice when he gave them his youthful ear.

Old Charlie, an accountant agent, told him his motto was, "If you can't convince them, confuse them!" This came from the same guy who had an old chest full of US savings bonds collected over the past twenty-five years. Every time he got a raise, he increased the number of bonds until this stash resembled that of Captain Kidd. McWade smiled when the old-timer mentioned that his wife still thought they were making the same salary as twenty years ago.

"Never go into management. They perform a lobotomy on your brain once you join their ranks. Your ability to think decreases in proportion to the increase in your ego until you are disliked by almost all the working agents," advised old Crabford. "I have seen many good agents turned into unlikable morons and jackasses!" he concluded.

Another old-timer, Richard Meyers, gave McWade more advice that had worked well for him: "Always carry a folder, look concerned and walk as if you were a man on a mission and never set where the SAC can see you or you will get more of his stupid busy work." Again, out of sight, out of mind.

All this advice was still being processed when the year to be spent in his first office as an FOA came to an end. With barely enough life lessons learned for survival in the real world, his much-awaited letter of transfer finally arrived.

Omaha Division! Now I can live with that, he thought. *Sure beats the crap out of Detroit, New York, or Chicago.*

Before he ever left San Antonio, he had already submitted the form changing Omaha to his OP.

Chapter 6

Nebraska: The Good Life and the Notorious Third Street Gang

As the city limit sign reading "Leaving San Antonio" disappeared into the rearview mirror, McWade could only have good memories of his FOA experience in that quaint city with its beautiful river walk and Spanish missions. He knew he would probably never see again so many good agents who had tutored him on his way.

As he passed the sign to Breckenridge Zoo, he recalled how he had been only minutes away from a Wild West shoot-out on the small train that circled through the forest around the zoo that previous summer. He and his small family had boarded the train for the fun-filled ride of two miles through secluded trees and tall bushes. It was a fun ride, but the next group of fun seekers who boarded the same train were ambushed by armed masked men who relieved all passengers of wallets, jewelry, and valuables.

The great train robbery made national news, and every time McWade thought about it, he fantasized in his mind what would have been the outcome had the robbery involved his train with him being armed. Any scenario he pictured ended up with one of two endings or outcomes: "Hero or Otherwise." Either way, it would have come to the attention of Hoover, and whether a good or bad outcome, it would mold his future into something he was trying hard to avoid. He wanted to just fly low and remain totally undetected by that front office on Pennsylvania Avenue.

He felt he would have been able to handle that, or any situation, as he was still pumped from his he-man training at Quantico and could still hear the gravel-voiced defensive tactics instructor telling in a manly voice, "Things out there are going to be a tough sport, so wear a cup!" That advice would help McWade and would stick like glue throughout the rest of his life. However, the he-man feeling would soon mellow in favor of using more common sense until the odds on the balance beam tipped more in his favor.

The stay in Omaha was but a flash as the SAC there asked if he would consider the assignment in the most remote part of the two state division (Iowa/Nebraska) at the Scottsbluff, Nebraska, RA. The place had never been heard of by the young refugee from Texas, but he accepted it on the spot as it fit his master plan. What better place to get lost from sight than an RA situated 452 miles to the west on the Nebraska-Wyoming border? It was even in a different time zone. Was this lucky or what?

He had always remembered the quote from the *New York Tribune* by Horace Greeley in the mid-1800s: "Go west, young man, and grow up with the country." Now he hoped to do just that.

Chimney Rock, located along the visible remnants of the old Oregon and Mormon trails, meant McWade's new home was coming into view. When massive rock formations rising over eight hundred feet over the lush farmlands of the North Platte River Valley appeared in the distance, he knew he was nearing the Scotts Bluff National Monument.

The cities of Gering and Scottsbluff were snuggled in the shadows of the impressive bluffs separated only by the North Platte River. That river was said by the early pioneers passing by—en route to Oregon, California, and Utah—to be a foot deep and a mile wide.

One glance at the small remote oasis, one drive around the twin cities, a jaunt down Broadway passing by the Panhandle Co-op Oil Refinery and it was love at first sight. With a total county population of only around forty thousand and the mighty Scotts Bluff Monument standing like a giant sentinel guarding the whole complex from a position to the southwest, McWade said to his good wife with enthusiasm, "Screw Salt Lake City. This is the place! We can and will make it work for us!"

McWade had coined a phrase to guide his idea of where he wanted to live out his Bureau life while in San Antonio, it was simple and matter of fact. "Anything east of here is worse than here." This place was ideal for now.

The next morning, he found his way to the RA and met his partner, the SRA (Senior Resident Agent), an old salty agent nearing mandatory retirement age of fifty-five. His name was Bob Frinsey, and he had been in Scottsbluff as a one-man show since the late 1940s when the RA was established. One look at him and McWade guessed it wouldn't be long before it was again a one-man show.

"How isolated can you get? This could be a dream come true."

"They sent me out here because I was socially clumsy, and they thought I might embarrass the Bureau," Frinsey joked. "So why are you here?" he asked with a twinkle in his eye.

McWade could see the old boy would be a good sport.

"I'll tell you up front that we are going to split the workload right down the middle at 80 percent and 20 percent. Is there any question in your mind who gets the 80%?" he quipped.

"I am going to take the south counties of the panhandle along Highway 30 and the new I-80 that is still under construction. You will take the northern counties along the South Dakota border as nothing much ever happens up there anyway."

Frinsey went on to explain that the Indian reservation in South Dakota was handled by the RA in Rapid City, South Dakota, and that it was a peaceful place up there. McWade was given the impression that he would have to scratch for work up there to justify his existence.

"Those Indians up there are no trouble at all. The last Indian problem in Nebraska was in the late 1800s when some soldier shot Crazy Horse at Fort Robinson as he was allegedly trying to escape the stockade."

He went on to tell McWade that "my retirement could be tomorrow, next week, or next year, depending on how I feel and how much this job interferes with my golf game. After all, I am a proud member of the KMA (kiss my ass) club."

Of course, the KMA club thing McWade fully understood as the very comfortable age at which an agent is at least fifty years old, with at least twenty years' experience as a Special Agent. The age he could retire with full benefits. The age when he could quit before they could fire him if he screwed up. The age when the fears of being disciplined and transferred to a big city office ceased to be an underlying anxiety-producing concern. It was the magic age that every one of the ten thousand agents under Hoover's tight reign looked forward to and dreamed about both night and day.

McWade was just getting used to his territory when Ed Coal, Special Agent for the Burlington Northern Railroad (BNRR), appeared at the RA with a problem. Virtually every railcar carrying new automobiles arriving at their West Coast destinations was arriving without the spare wheels in the trunks of the new vehicles.

Coal had deducted that the thefts were probably taking place in the small town of Crawford, Nebraska, where the BNRR would receive these train cars from the CNWRR.

This TFIS (Theft From Interstate Shipment) case sounded like it could be a fun whodunit matter to get baptized into the fiery waters of rural Nebraska FBI work.

The small picturesque town of Crawford was snuggled peacefully under the silhouettes of the surrounding buttes and cliffs. Here, the population was less than the 3,600-feet elevation posted on the Entering Crawford sign on the edge of the aging village.

Fort Robinson was located a few miles to the west of the old declining township and was now only a memory of the Indian wars of the past. Its remaining buildings were now turned over to the state of Nebraska as a tourist attraction and a haven for history buffs. During its prime days of glory as a fort, nearby Crawford was the place of action for off base nightlife. A place where soldiers could have a drink, find a woman of the evening, and generally let loose and party.

Now Crawford, like the old fort, was struggling to stay alive, and many there longed for the bygone days of action and a thriving economy.

McWade found the Crawford PD easily enough as it was in the old red brick city building. There he was met by a true American patriot, the COP, a man by the name of James Primer. The old man had the wrinkled face of a cowboy who had worked all his life in the hot sun, with the horses at Fort Robinson, when it was a remount station in WWII. He had helped train the horses and riders for the US Army. Those same horses were purchased from all over this great land. They were then trained for battle and sent to the various theaters of war in Europe and the islands of the Pacific. He told stories that kept McWade at attention for the better part of an hour before they finally got to the matter at hand.

The old man held a cigarette clinched in his weathered lips, and as the smoke curled up around his eyes, he asked, "Did you see that butte on the way into town?" Not waiting for an answer, he continued, "That is Crow Butte, where, in 1849, a Crow raiding party stole a band of horses from the Sioux and headed west through this area." He went on to tell how the Sioux pursued the Crow marauders, who took refuge on the top of the butte that now bears their name.

With the Sioux circling the butte, the trapped Crow warriors eventually devised a plan to build many bonfires which they kept burning brightly at night while they escaped by sneaking past the sleeping Sioux.

From the excited tones in his voice, McWade could have been fooled into thinking Primer could have been there himself had he been fifty years older. This place definitely had a proud heritage and was easy to fall in love with almost instantly.

The old man took McWade on a tour of his city, down past the rail yards where the two railroads came together to exchange cars, allowing the CNWRR cars to be connected to the BNRR engines, for their trip through Montana, Idaho, and into Washington and Oregon. The layouts of the railroad sidings were studied and visually mapped out in McWade's mind. It was determined that these railcars loaded with new automobiles often sat on the sidings in town for one to two days, waiting for the right BNRR train to attach to them for the westward trip.

A perfect opportunity, he thought, *for thieves to break into the vehicles and remove the spare wheels and jack.*

These thefts had to be taking place at night, under the cover of darkness so plans were devised to catch the brazen thieves in action.

The following night, the CNWRR was scheduled to place four open railcars on the siding. Each of the cars would carry six new automobiles of various makes and models, and the cars would be on the siding for two nights. They were to be the bait, and hopefully this could turn into something fun.

Primer located an old, almost abandoned, house only a few hundred yards from the rail siding, and McWade and Primer positioned themselves inside with their automobiles hidden close by and out of sight. After nesting down, the long wait began. A detailed written log was kept during the daylight hours of any cars or pickup trucks that happened to drive by. Nothing seemed unusual when a pickup truck carrying four high school boys drove slowly by at about 3:30 PM, apparently after the Crawford High School had sounded its last bell, ending the school day.

"Just a bunch of kids looking for a secluded place to drink a beer and score with their girlfriends," drawled the old chief. "Not much else to do for fun around this damn place these days."

Night soon closed in as the bright full moon started to peek above Crow Butte to the east. *This moon is great. We can actually see if anything goes down*, McWade thought to himself as the minutes turned to hours. The sandwiches and pop were not that exciting, but James still continued, nonstop, with his stories of the good old days when this was a happening place, full of soldiers, whores, saloons, and dance girls.

Suddenly, a pair of headlights appeared from the south and then another. Almost as if on cue, both pickup trucks turned off their headlights and slowly crept along, stopping next to the first railcar, using only the moonlight to inch along.

At least five to six dark silhouettes emerged out of the trucks, and as if carrying out a well-rehearsed game plan, they split up, spread out, and began their work.

One thief would pop open the wing window on the passenger side of the car, swing it open, grab the extra set of keys that were hidden in the glove compartment, go immediately to the trunk, open it with the keys, remove the spare wheel, and throw it to the waiting arms of the accomplice below. The operation went like clockwork with wheel after wheel loaded into the back of the waiting trucks. The keys would then be placed back in the glove compartment and the wing window closed to look normal.

"That little bastard is Arlen Hedge!" said Primer almost in a shout. "And that fat guy is Casey Breen. Well, I'll be damned, they are just snot-nosed high school kids."

Just then, a set of headlights appeared about three hundred yards from the other end of the yard, apparently scaring the boys, as within seconds the thieves leaped into their trucks and sped off into the darkness. The car coming from the other directions turned out to be a couple kids looking for a secluded place to get down to their lovemaking business at hand.

Since the ringleaders had been identified, McWade and Primer let them escape until the next day. Then one by one, they were pulled from class, taken to the PD and questioned about their thievery. They began rolling over on each other like a bunch of trained circus dogs until the mystery of the vanishing wheels was not only solved but many of the wheels were also recovered from their storage barn, where they were cooling off. The ink was hardly dry on the statements when their story unfolded into a prosecutive report that read like a Huck Finn novel.

Arlen Hedge was sitting in English class a few weeks earlier bored out of his gourd while the class was studying Shakespeare. As he was gazing out the window of good old Crawford High, he saw a freight train loaded with new automobiles creaking and grinding slowly to the siding. He noticed two things: (1) the cars were completely open and unprotected, (2) they usually stayed on the siding overnight, again unprotected, until taken away by the BNRR.

"Just how hard would it be to get the wheels out of those cars and send them on the way without anyone knowing?" he smiled to himself.

Since five of his classmates lived close to him on Third Street, he organized the infamous "Third Street Gang" and appointed himself as the leader. One of his gangsters had a dad who owned a tire store to the south of town, which made it a great place to remove the stolen tires from the wheels. The poached tires then made it onto the wheels of most of the high school kids automobiles as well as countrymen looking for a good deal. It was indeed a lucrative and thriving business in the small town.

A good night's work could net twenty-five to thirty wheels of various sizes. McWade noted that, unlike most kids tires on their cars, those parked at Crawford High School all seemed to be new. No bald tires were to be found on the cars of teenagers in Crawford.

McWade suggested to the AUSA (Assistant United States Attorney) handling the matter that leniency be given as these were basically good kids who had been sucked into Hedge's plan.

They were all indicted by a FGJ (federal grand jury), arrested, and placed in the pretrial diversion program for youthful first-time offenders. They all promised, some tearfully, to leave their lives of crime behind. If they did stay crime free their records would be wiped clean as if the whole ordeal had never happened.

McWade also learned something that was very important to understand in the FBI. The indictments, arrests, and convictions of six young high school boys counted just as much on the stat sheets in Omaha and at FBIHQ as did the indictments, arrests, and conviction of six armed and dangerous bank robbers.

The new boss in Omaha was impressed and very happy.

When the boss was happy, McWade was happy. He was even happier when an "attaboy" letter was placed on top of his personnel file signed by J. Edgar Hoover. A nice cash award accompanying the letter was also appreciated.

He laughed to himself when he thought of the old ex-cowboy-turned-chief, saying as he pinched his cigarette butt in his finger to get the last puff, "We sure got them sumbitches, didn't we?"

True, this case did not crack a Jesse James-type operation. But it did involve thefts from the railroad, and the Third Street Gang was now part of history. Besides that, the 1971 graduating class of Crawford High School could boast a record never achieved before or since by any other class. The most federal indictments, arrests, and pretrial diversions!

"Who knows? That might be a class record for the entire state of Nebraska or the whole country," smiled McWade.

Also, not long after the notorious high school gang was busted, it was noticed that, gradually, both railroads started to enclose and secure the railcars to protect the new automobiles being shipped. Had McWade's famous Third Street Gang caper changed the way these railcars would look forevermore?

He was going local and loved every minute of the journey. The locals were really nice people and they spoke the same language. The words *those little sumbitches* still echoed in his ears as he relaxed, leaned back, and propped his feet comfortably on the desk of his RA. *This could be a fun ride*, he thought to himself as headed for the doughnut shop to hang out with the guys.

Scotts Bluff and Chimney Rock towering above the North Platte River

Chapter 7

Strange Ransom

The road seemed to stretch into itself as the hot Nebraska sun was beating down without mercy on the young man trudging westward on US 26 with his backpack, containing his earthly belongings, flung over his back. You don't seem to accumulate that much while serving time in jail for sex crimes. His thumb was being ignored by hundreds of cars as they hurriedly passed him on their way to Scottsbluff and beyond. In fact, his arm was getting cramped from the hours of holding his thumb at attention. The only thing he was getting was a middle finger wave from some redneck speeding past in a pickup truck.

"Need a lift?" came the voice out the front window of an older model sedan that had stopped beside him.

Jumping in the back seat, he noticed a fairly attractive sixteen-year-old girl named Linda and her eight-year-old sister, Susan. He settled himself next to Linda, and the car was off into the sunset.

"Your name?" asked the driver. "Kelvin, Larry Kelvin, sir!" came the reply.

"We live just outside Scottsbluff and you're welcome to go that far with us," said the driver, identifying himself as Earl Jones.

Over the next seventy-five miles or so, the hitchhiker had managed to convince the family that he was between jobs and was heading to Wyoming in search of work as a ranch hand. He portrayed himself as a hardworking, honest man who had been taking care of his sick mother until she had died two weeks ago. Even though he was easily ten years older than Linda, he was instantly attracted to her youthful body as something deep inside his pedophile brain started churning out those same hormonal cravings and desires that he had been busted for five years ago.

By the time they had arrived at the Jones home in rural Scotts Bluff County, located a few miles off the old Oregon Trail and just west of the Scotts Bluff National Monument, his attraction had now drawn the young inexperienced maiden into his snare.

In fact, when the little sister had fallen asleep, Larry had cautiously let his hand touch the hand of Linda, who did not resist in any way, thus giving him a green light to go even further down the forbidden road of lust and horniness.

"Since you don't have any place else to bed down, we have a room in the back you are welcome to use."

"Much obliged, sir," Larry politely responded as he was shown to the bunk in the spare room to the rear of the rural and isolated home.

Since he was handy and volunteered to help around the yard, he had stayed on for at least three weeks before old man Earl started to suspect some extracurricular activity going on between young Linda and the strange bedfellow. It seemed that Linda had been introduced to something her young, blossoming, budding female body found to be quite to her liking.

After the lights were doused around the Joneses each evening, young Linda would sneak from her room and share the rest of the night cuddled in blissful intimacy with the man who was acting as her sex education lab instructor. She would then sneak back to her bedroom before the rest awakened and seemed always to come to breakfast with a newfound smile on her glowing young face.

Father Earl may not have been the sharpest kid in his high school class when he graduated at age twenty-two, but he suspected something was going on when he found the two sleeping soundly in Kelvin's bed at 4:00 AM one night when he got up to answer a call of nature. His daughter's sleepwalking excuse just didn't add up, so he ordered Larry to hit the road, which he did, but not for long.

He soon was caught back in the daughter's arms, which, he surmised, left him no alternative but to secretly ship young Linda out of town to stay with her aunt in Hot Springs, South Dakota.

Meanwhile, back at the RA, McWade had just managed to get rid of an old man wearing bib coveralls from Oshkosh whom he had foolishly opened the door and allowed into the office. The old geezer wanted to be an FBI informant and would not take no for an answer. During the brief conversation, he suddenly volunteered that he had a scar, and before McWade could tell him to hit the road, he had dropped the front of his bib overalls and revealed a scar at least eighteen inches in length.

That was enough. "Please leave before you get thrown out on your butt, buddy!" McWade commanded. The old man left still muttering about how he could help solve crimes on the farm if only given the chance.

Now curious, McWade called the Garden County Sheriff in Oshkosh about the old guy who was well-known to the whole sheriff's office. The sheriff laughed and then told about how the old boy got his scar.

He had been reading in a health magazine about the benefits of taking enemas for health reasons. He figured, according to the sheriff, that if a little water was that good, then why not go for the grand prize of total health and happiness. In his farm shop, he devised a small tube, which he connected to his garden hose. After inserting the small tube securely in his rectum, he turned on the faucet.

The good sheriff accompanied the ambulance to his farm and could not believe his eyes. "Do you have any idea what fifty pounds of water pressure up your butt will do to the colon? It looked like someone had inserted a small explosive and then ran for cover. What a shitty deal!" he said.

The Garden County Sheriff had just hung up the phone when another call came in from the Scotts Bluff County Sheriff that there was a kidnapping in progress. The victim, McWade was informed, was an eight-year-old girl by the name of Susan Jones.

Rushing to the sheriff's office (SO) across the river in Gering, Nebraska, McWade helped them set up a command post in the conference room. A small-town version of a big-city task force was quickly set up consisting of McWade, the entire Scotts Bluff County SO, and the NSP. The difference between this task force and the big-city type was that everyone involved in this operation happened to be good friends and got along great in every way. "Sort of like family, except there were no sibling rivalries," McWade observed.

In constructing a time line, it was soon established that the subject was none other than Larry Kelvin, who had crept back to the Jones home under cover of darkness, snatched young eight-year-old Susan Jones from her bed, forced her into a pickup in the Jones's yard, and drove away in the stolen truck with his frightened hostage in tow.

Not wanting the stolen truck to be seen, he had ditched it in the small town of Mitchell, Nebraska, and proceeded to steal a 1955 Ford Fairlane from the detached garage of an elderly woman who had trustingly left the keys in the ignition. Now this car, even though sixteen years old, only had only eight thousand miles on the odometer. It was a cherry, and half the town of Mitchell was secretly waiting for the little old lady to die so they could jockey themselves into a position to buy the car.

Kelvin, with the abducted eight-year-old, then drove to Torrington, Wyoming, where he made his first ransom call to the Jones. The home phone, of course, was being monitored and recorded the ransom demand.

"Listen, and listen carefully. This is Larry Kelvin and I have your daughter Susan with me. She will not be harmed if you do exactly as I tell you. I will give you Susan in exchange for Linda. I will call you back in two hours to arrange the exchange."

The call was quickly traced to the phone booth across the state line into Wyoming. NSP cruisers were speeding in that direction as was the full contingent of available FBI agents (that would be only McWade as Agent Frinsey was in Lincoln practicing his golf game). With the interstate aspect of the case, it now fell within the full jurisdiction of the FBI.

As McWade's Bucar was rushing toward the city of Torrington, a radio transmission was received from the Wyoming Highway Patrol that the stolen Fairlane was in view and was being pursued at a high rate of speed just north of town by one of their units. Another report shortly came in that Kelvin was turning back toward the state of Nebraska on country roads. The chase then was to be handled by the NSP.

When the stolen car was observed reentering Nebraska, it suddenly turned off the dirt road and into the sagebrush ranch lands. The previously flawless classic vehicle was about to obtain a few flaws as it bounced through the brush, above ditches, over grassy knolls, and around small sand dunes, trying to elude one of the NSP's finest troopers, the infamous "Action Jackson."

Just outside the small village of Morrill, Nebraska, McWade veered north in hopes of intercepting the fleeing felon and the eight-year-old victim. *She must be totally petrified*, thought McWade, who was fearing for her safety being held hostage in the car with this madman.

Almost like a mirage, the dust trail of the escaping automobile was spotted streaking across the barren landscape with Action Jackson in hot pursuit, his own vapor trail closing in fast. The whole scene, amazing as it was, looked much like the Road Runner cartoon as he streaked across the badlands trying to elude Wile E. Coyote. As the gap closed between the two vehicles, Kelvin suddenly turned the Ford sharply to avoid a bump from the cruiser. In doing so, he tried unsuccessfully to make it to the top of a small dune. With the car high centered and mired axle deep in the white sand, Kelvin upped the stakes by drawing his gun and aimed it at the NSP unit which had stopped some fifty feet away.

Apparently, Larry had not paid attention to his fellow inmates when swapping stories with them about shooting guns from a vehicle. Instead of leaning out the window and aiming, he, with all windows closed, pointed the gun through the back window and pulled the trigger. The projectile shattered the back window just like the blast from the muzzle did Kelvin's eardrums. Luckily, the hostage, being so frightened, had hidden her head in a blanket, which helped prevent any such injury to her.

As Kelvin staggered out of the getaway car, his ears still ringing, both McWade and Action Jackson chased him down like two cheetahs would a wild boar. He was hurriedly disarmed, handcuffed, searched, placed under arrest, and ushered into the wire cage in the back of the NSP Plymouth Fury for a long and lonely ride back to the county jail.

"Whoever heard of demanding that a parent trade their sixteen-year-old daughter to a known sex predator in exchange for their eight-year-old daughter that he already had in his possession?" McWade asked the AUSA (Assistant United States Attorney) handling the prosecution of this case from Omaha. "Fascinating!" was his reply.

With the action part of the kidnapping now resolved and with Kelvin back where he belonged, now came the endless time-consuming task of interviewing the entire Jones family, to include Susan, Linda, the subject, the law officers involved in the chase, and any other person who could possibly be called as a witness. Each of these interviews would be placed in an FD-302 (Bureau report of an interview), which would, in turn, be placed into a prosecutive summary report for the AUSA.

Being a man of action at that time of his young career, McWade dove right into things by going again to the isolated country home of the Jones family. The place could have been used for the filming of an episode of the *Hatfields and McCoys* as it was sort of hillbilly on steroids. There were more old cars and trucks in various stages of disrepair than at most junk yard. They were parked on blocks, under trees, in old tumbledown sheds, and in small fields behind the barn.

Isolating and interviewing the family members was an experience, but they were good folks who had experienced a traumatic ordeal. A room in the house was set up as, one by one, they paraded through to tell what they knew about Kelvin and the kidnapping.

It was getting dusk by the time McWade wrapped things up. He grabbed his folder containing the statements and headed down the sidewalk toward his Bucar while talking with Earl, the father of the Jones clan.

Suddenly, from out of nowhere, a large animal jumped undetected from under the culvert and attacked McWade's right leg by wrapping its strong front paws around the calf area in a death grip. Not knowing what was happening, he looked down only to see a masked face glaring at him. The first impulse was to try to draw and shoot the attacking animal. But the damned thing was too close to his own leg, so he thought better. Just then, Earl laughed and shouted, "Down Bandit!" to his leg-grabbing pet raccoon.

It was funny afterward, but while it was happening, not so much!

Thinking that was enough of crazy for one day, as they approached the Bucar, Earl suddenly, like a drama queen, fell to the ground groaning in pain, explaining that he had a gunshot wound in his gut area. As they waited for the ambulance to arrive, Earl apologized, saying that he did not want to tell anyone until now as he wanted his girl safe and didn't want his problem regarding the shooting to interfere with Kelvin's capture.

He explained that the previous night, he feared that Kelvin, after snatching his daughter Susan and his pickup truck, may return to the house. With that in mind, he armed himself with his .22 caliber rifle and sat around the compound on guard duty.

At about 3:30 AM, a loud horn from one of the many cars in the yard pierced through the cool night air, sending chills up his spine. Thinking it was Kelvin, he grabbed his gun and ran at breakneck speed in the direction of the honking only to trip and fall. His rifle discharged shooting himself in the gut area.

He lifted up his shirt at that time to show a small entry wound which luckily had missed his vital organs. He continued his quest only to find that it was not Kelvin, but rather Bandit, the playful pet raccoon, who had crawled into a car and honked the horn.

Larry, the amorous lover of younger girls, received a twenty-five-year sentence to a federal prison after pleading guilty to kidnapping in US Federal Court, District of Nebraska. McWade thought to himself that "twenty-five years should give him some time to cool off his lustful desires and maybe to rehearse his kidnapping skills."

How he ever planned to pull off the mechanics of the "girl for girl" ransom exchange without getting caught or shot would forever be a mystery.

Again, McWade received kudos from his SAC in the form of a letter to place in his small, but growing, personnel folder. The Director himself followed with a small $150 cash award, saying "Attaboy" in official Bureau jargon.

He smiled and wondered silently to himself (that's what you usually do in a one-man office) as he thought about how the sweet young eight-year-old Susan would raise her hand in her third-grade class the next day at show-and-tell and explain to the class her ordeal to the other wide-eyed kids.

But the most satisfaction of all was a note McWade received in the handwriting of the tenderhearted Susan thanking him for saving her from her night and day of terror.

This metamorphosis was beginning to seem more real each day as he was even starting to feel a bit more *native*.

What a fun case!

Soon he would realize that if the same case would have happened in or around Omaha, the entire office would have been called out to work the case and every agent on the case would have received an "Attaboy." The case agent would have been given a much larger cash award and the SAC, ASAC, and any other supervisor who happened to be in town would have written themselves up to get a yet larger cash award. He was learning the facts of Bureau life quickly. But it was still much nicer to be as far from the office politics as possible.

His love affair with the territory and the people of western Nebraska was becoming a very real thing. And he had only been there long enough to barely get his feet wet in North Platte as it meandered its way toward the east.

Chapter 8

We Just Wanted a Woman

Our man of the hour, Sam McCarty, and his dim-witted buddy, Matt Gregory, were kicking around in the countryside near Placerville, California. Since his childhood, Sam had heard stories told of gold nuggets gleaming in the clear mountain streams just waiting to be plucked up, and he wanted a piece of the action. The fact that he may have been 130 years too late to file a claim at the same place James Marshal discovered gold in the area had not occurred to him. He just wanted to be rich and thought panning for gold would be his answer.

What did finally occur to Sam and Matt was that sleeping on the ground in sleeping bags, crammed in a tent, and eating beans from a tin can was getting old. The stinking clothes also created a laundry problem the two Boy Scout dropouts did not want to deal with either. Sitting there shivering around their small campfire, they put their collective heads together and came up with a brilliant solution.

"Sam, old buddy, what we need for ourselves is a good woman!" Matt drawled. "Why, she could keep this place tidied up a bit and do our cooking for us."

The two sat in silence for a long time until finally Sam spoke up, "You know, my ex-wife, Sarah, may have had other problems, but she was one hell of a cook and always kept the house spotless. She was also great to snuggle to on cold nights."

"Where is she now?" asked Matt.

"Last I heard she was still back in our old hometown of Logansport, Indiana, working at some care center of some kind," answered the other gold seeker. "But she hates my guts after the separation."

Before they retired back to the small tent reeking with the smell of dirty socks and week-old underwear, they had agreed on a plan to get Sarah back to the gold country with them one way or another.

The next day, their beat-up old Chevy sedan was heading back to Indiana.

There is absolutely nothing about the sound of the telephone ringing at midnight that is pleasant. Could it be the SAC calling to tell what a great job you just did on that last meaningless survey that had taken hours to complete? "Yeah, sure!" jested McWade to himself.

"McWade, we have a situation here you might want to take a look at," came the voice of the COP at Kimball, Nebraska.

Yes, it was yet another kidnapping, and the Chief and his officers had two men in custody at the Kimball County Jail. It was agreed that since the victim was safe and the car was secured as a crime scene, McWade would travel the forty miles to Kimball and help them sort things out in the morning.

The old Chevy looked like it had been lived in for weeks. It would have qualified for federal disaster funds if there had been a hurricane around to blame. Inside the trunk was a mountain of evidence to collect and process as confirmation of an abduction. There was gray duct tape appearing to have been used to tape arms, legs, and mouth as human hair was clinging to the sticky side. There was rope, an old pair of handcuffs, blankets, old pillows, and other items to lead one to conclude that someone had been tied, gagged, and held against their will in the trunk for a long period of time.

The arrest had taken place after the manager of the Shady Rest Motel in Kimball had checked a man and a woman into room number 13, which ultimately proved not to be a lucky number for good old Sam and Matt. During the check-in process, the woman appeared upset and acting as if she was not all that happy about being with the guy posing as her husband. Sam had used the names Mr. and Mrs. Joe Smith on the sign-in sheet and had paid in cash.

After getting the room key, "Mrs. Smith" managed to slip the manager a handwritten note, saying, "Please help me. I have been kidnapped. Call the police!"

After they checked into their room, the alert manager noted they were driving an older model white Chevrolet bearing a license plate from the great state of Indiana. He also noted there was another man, also a white male in his thirties, who was sleeping in the passenger seat of the car. This also seemed a bit strange as usually people at his motel rented a room and then slept in it rather than in a car parked outside in the parking lot. Besides all that, it was a cold night and this just seemed weird. So the call was made to the Kimball PD.

Now Move the Clock Back Three Days

Even for Sam, it wasn't all that difficult to ask around Logansport and find that his ex-wife, Sarah, was employed in the health-care business. Locating the facility where she worked was even less of a challenge. Her car was familiar to him, which parked in a secluded area of the parking lot, so he waited for her swing shift to end at about midnight. He and his sidekick, Matt, joked about their well-thought-out plan of getting a woman to satisfy all their manly needs as well as taking care of their tent and cooking.

They smoked the better part of a pack of Marlboro cigarettes before they saw the small-framed blond walking alone through the parking lot toward her parked car. Sam still had the hots for this lady and thought her to be a fine specimen of womanly perfection. Sarah, on the other hand, did not share that view of her ex but now fully agreed with all her friends that had tried to warn her about marrying such a brain-dead creep. When she saw him standing there close to her car, her first reaction was not that of fear but rather of total anger as she had hoped never to see him again.

"How you doing, Sarah?" came the feeble attempt at conversation.

"What the hell are you doing here?" she demanded. "The restraining order is still in effect, and I suggest you get your ass away from my car."

"No need to get your undies in a wad. I just wanted to say hi and to see how you are doing."

Sarah didn't notice the shadow of another tall bearded man lurking close by and to her rear.

At just the right moment, after getting close enough, Sam grabbed her arm firmly. Matt then jumped out of the shadows to assist as the two men quickly subdued the petite blond, who proved to be no contest for their determined conquest. Before the surprised woman could even scream for help, she was bound with cords and duct tape placed over her mouth. Sam then pulled out a rusty pair of handcuffs and placed them firmly on her wrists with the cold metal gripping her bone and flesh like the jaws of a steel trap.

She winced with pain as they manhandled her small body and flung it into the trunk of their old car. Her muffled attempts at screaming went unheard as the parking lot was empty, with the exception of her small Toyota Corolla and the white sedan with the cramped trunk where she now found herself imprisoned.

Matt had grabbed the keys to her Corolla, which he unlocked and drove with haste to a preplanned wooded area by a park where it was abandoned.

Matt jumped in the passenger seat, and the dynamic duo were California bound with their captured female prize locked in the trunk.

"This could be the perfect crime," Sam bragged. "No one saw us, and they won't have a clue as to where the hell she disappeared to."

They were cautious to keep the speed limit as they left Indiana and followed I-80 through Illinois and Iowa, stopping only to grab junk food and gasoline. They would stop in isolated off-road areas when they thought Sarah needed to relieve herself but always made sure no one saw them letting her out or placing her back in the trunk.

Sarah realized her only hope for escape was to try to be nice to her half-witted captors and to somehow convince them that she was not going to try to escape. When she overheard them talking about using her as a sex slave and housemaid, she decided to convince them that she would do all they asked willingly.

Sarah had heard about the Stockholm Syndrome, where the victim starts to bond with the kidnapper, and decided to fake that same effect in order to gain the trust of her former mate. She rationalized that she had learned to fake it with him nightly when they were married and therefore felt she was an expert in that area.

The process was gradual, but soon Sam was developing a trust in her. He soon even removed the handcuffs that bit her wrists. By the time they had crossed most of the state of Nebraska, everyone was getting exhausted from the nonstop driving and the anxiety of the ordeal. When she heard Sam talking about stopping at a motel, she started planting the seeds in his mind that she might be able to help him relive the wild sex they had enjoyed on their honeymoon to Niagara Falls.

When they pulled into the Shady Rest at Kimball, Sam was eager to leave Matt in the car alone as he fantasized about rekindling his love life with his seemingly eager hostage and, of course, wanted privacy.

While in a rest area near Sidney, Nebraska, Sarah had managed to get some paper on which to write a note. This was the same note she managed to leave with the manager of the motel.

When the police arrived at the Shady Rest, they rousted the sleeping Matt from the front seat of the car. Within minutes, he was singing like a canary and jumping through loops like a trained monkey in a circus act. He was soon doing everything within his power to save his own skin at the expense of roasting Sam, who was, at that very moment, shacked up in room number 13 with his unwilling captive. After getting his statement, the police officers planned the rescue and arrest.

Like stealth warriors and with the aid of a master key, the police swooped down upon Sam's room where he sat on the edge of the bed with nothing on but a surprised look of panic. The object of his crime was rescued without so much as shot being fired or any major injuries. She was able to smile genuinely for the first time in three days.

When McWade arrived in town to conduct the interviews and process the evidence, the whole matter was mostly wrapped up within three days, which was record time by any Bureau standard.

The FBI in Indiana had already been made aware of Sarah's disappearance and was quick to get a kidnapping warrant. After transporting the two budding gold miners to the nearest US Magistrate in the North Platte, Nebraska, they were given a free ride, compliments of the US Marshal's Office, back to the Hoosier State to face charges.

Sarah was happy to give a detailed statement as to her abduction and the subsequent ordeal of her terror in the trunk. Her legs, arms, neck, and stomach areas all bore witness to the forcefulness of the kidnapping as she displayed bruises and abrasions consistent with her nightmare.

Her black-and-blue, bruised limbs and torso were photographed, and she was then examined by a doctor who gave his okay for her to return back to her home.

Her folks were happy to wire her money, and she was last seen boarding the eastbound Greyhound bus to Logansport. She smiled and waved as the black diesel exhaust smoke curled up around the rear of the large silver coach disappearing around the corner.

During the interviews with Sam and Matt, it seemed to McWade they were in a contest trying to outdo each other in placing blame and supplying details of their misguided escapade. It was amazing to see such a lack of common sense and denseness all wrapped into two rather small heads.

McWade could only wonder about the fairness of her having to buy her own bus ticket back home while the abductors both rode free, compliments of the US government. They also ate well while Sarah, on the other hand, had to buy her own hamburgers and greasy fries at the bus terminals along the way. *Some things just seem upside down*, he thought.

On the drive back to the RA, a warm feeling again came over McWade as he reflected upon a pretty damsel in real distress being saved from a life of further humiliation and debauchery in the gold fields of California. Even though his part was small, he had helped give Sam and Matt secure lodging for the next twenty years.

Mr. Hoover again smiled on the success of the case with a small cash award and a nice letter to grace McWade's personnel file. Meanwhile, with a satisfied smile on his face, again he joined his law enforcement buddies at the local doughnut shop to rehash and laugh about the two not-so-bright criminals. It all made McWade reflect upon a saying he had heard that seemed to apply directly to this matter: "Think how stupid the average person is—and then realize that half of them are even stupider."

Chapter 9

The Dangers of Genealogy

Sheridan County was now back to normal again and, at least for a short time, seemed like the little piece of ranch country paradise the locals all loved.

Chin, and his band of wannabes, had somehow seemed to fade into the recent past in the wake of the Raymond Yellow Thunder seemingly botched protest in Gordon a few months earlier.

The cattle were back safe on their massive ranches, and the ranchers, no longer fearing an Indian uprising, had put away most of their weapons and were back to just carrying a rifle and a hand-gun in their pickup trucks. Peace was reigning supreme again in the Nebraska Sand Hills.

Geoffrey Poacher, the Sheriff County Sheriff, had requested FBI help in locating a local ranch hand, who had fled Nebraska to parts unknown, after stealing a pickup truck from his former boss, the owner of the sprawling Hidden Lakes Land and Cattle Company (HLL&CC). To add insult to injury, the man had taken several other items of value, along with a stack of company checks. Using the stolen Hidden Lakes checks, he managed to cash one at every store or busi-ness in the towns of Rushville and Gordon. There were people in the home-decorating business that did not hang as much paper around the county that weekend as our departing ranch hand, Chuck Beans.

True, the FBI normally would not get involved in such a seem-ingly small local crime, but this was Rushville, Nebraska, where this stuff was not taken lightly. The owner of the HLL&CC also just happened to be a close friend of the sheriff and was a big supporter of the local high school athletics booster club. The Hidden Lakes owner, Michael Rich, did not appreciate Beans tarnishing the good name of his ranch, and he wanted this guy back to pay for his sins.

McWade explained to Sheriff Poacher that a letter from the sheriff would have to be sent to the AUSA in Omaha, requesting that the FBI help locate Beans as there was reason that he had fled Nebraska. The AUSA would then authorize the FBI to file a federal warrant charging Beans with Unlawful Flight to Avoid Prosecution (UFAP), and a fugitive case would then be initiated. Normally, after the subject of the fugitive matter was arrested, the UFAP warrant would be dismissed and the subject would be extradited back to the local jurisdiction where the state charges were filed. Hence, the UFAP warrant was only a tool used by McWade to locate Chucky Beans for the sheriff.

With the warrant now filed, McWade first headed for the HLL&CC ranch headquarters located in the heart of the Sand Hills about thirty miles south of the Sheridan County seat.

The trip to the ranch was like a trip into another world as he aimed his Bucar south on a road that soon turned into a single-lane paved black top. The road was just wide enough for the car but would not be wide enough for two cars to pass each other. He hoped that if another vehicle did appear, it would be a four-wheel drive as it was sand on both shoulders that would spell trouble for his Bucar.

The unique beauty of this isolated area was unmatched by anything McWade had ever witnessed, and it went on mile after endless mile. The rolling hills were lush and filled with green grass and colorful flowers like nothing you see on interstate highways.

"Was there no end to this landscape?"

Added to the flowers and grass there were literally dozens of small lakes, fed by the massive Ogallala Aquifer, that appeared over almost every other rolling sand hill.

Just when McWade thought he had gone almost to the end of the earth, he crested a hill to see a magnificent ranch in the oasis below. The white-framed ranch house was snuggled in the midst of giant cottonwood trees surrounded by bunkhouses, sheds, haystacks, corrals, barns, shops, and windmills. The lawn in front of the ranch house was manicured and the whitewashed wooden picket fence looked like it had been placed there as part of a Hollywood movie set for a modern-day Western.

He had wondered just how one would deal with living in such a remote area away from the rest of the world. That question was answered when he noticed a large airplane hangar with two small aircraft, one a two-engine plane and the other a small Piper Cub, seemingly ready to depart at any time.

Thankfully, Sheriff Poacher had educated McWade about proper ranch etiquette, which was that any stranger appearing at the ranch within an hour of the noon dinner was expected to stay and dine with the owner and his wife.

"Just call me Clara," the rancher's wife said as she greeted McWade. "You are just in time for dinner, and Michael will be here in a few minutes."

The meal was excellent and reminded him of his own mother's cooking back on the farm in Idaho. With the meal finished, the trio sat down together to allow McWade to glean any information about Chuck Beans that would lead to his location and arrest.

Chuck, also known as Chucky by his fellow ranch hands, had drifted into Rushvillle six months ago, looking for work. He had furnished a social security number and other information, but Clara admitted that it could all have been fabricated.

Michael Rich added that he had been a hard worker and had caused no problems at all while living at the ranch. He never was seen to be intoxicated, and in fact, Rich didn't think he even consumed any alcohol. He just minded his business and kind of kept to himself.

At this point, McWade was thinking to himself, *If I ever got in trouble and needed to disappear from the world, this place would be better than the witness protection program. This would be like going native on steroids.*

Michael then asked McWade if he wanted to go up in the Piper to shoot a few coyotes. It was tempting, but the visual of the headlines "PETA Outraged at FBI Agent's Coyote Massacre," and the Director's reaction to those headlines made the invitation easy to reject.

"Anything else about Chucky before I leave?" McWade asked as he headed for the Bucar. "Did he leave anything behind?"

That seemed to jog Clara's mind as she ran her fingers through her auburn hair and added, "You know, come to think of it, I think Chucky was one of those peculiar Mormons. I found sort of a Mormon Bible in his room after he stole the truck and left. It had a lot of family names and history written in it. Here, let me get it for you."

Looking at Beans's Mormon Bible, McWade found it actually was titled the Book of Mormon with his entire genealogy written on special sheets attached to the book. Beans, being staunch in his beliefs, had the names, addresses, birth dates, and other identifying data for not only his parents but also generations of family history.

The trip back to the hustle and bustle of the real world was uneventful.

The material on his genealogy sheets proved to be valuable as leads were sent out nationwide, eventually resulting in Beans being apprehended at some faraway isolated ranch near Ely, Nevada, owned by some relative, who was harboring him.

"Genealogy can be catching!" chuckled McWade as he had the UFAP warrant dismissed.

Thinking about the Hidden Lake Land and Cattle Company, McWade wondered if this would have been a great place for Fast Freddie McNickle to have hidden out if he had escaped from prison. He could have hidden there forever. But then McWade guessed that before long, he would have seduced Clara and conned Michael Rich out of the deed to the ranch.

Perhaps some big-city agents, sitting in their smoke-filled squad rooms, would look down their self-important noses and snicker at cases like this one. But the good sheriff appreciated the work, and it was an experience like none other to live like a local on the big ranch even though for a short time.

Two lessons were learned, McWade thought:

1. Genealogy can be dangerous, and some people can get caught up in it.
2. Life in Nebraska was really good. This case was an example.

Chapter 10

The Chin Man Returns

It has been said that sometimes just getting out of bed ruins the whole day.

Well, during the year 1972, if you were to hang around the city of Scottsbluff long enough, you were sure to see the Chin show up sooner or later.

The Gathering

Since Chin and his band of jolly followers had been scared out of Gordon, Nebraska, during the spring of 1972 by the sight of all those NSP police cruisers descending upon them like seagulls after Mormon crickets, they had been mostly unseen and were keeping a low profile. But protesters do get impatient and eventually have to show their hand again. After all, they are what they are.

"Could I rent a room for the night?" came the request from the Native American man to the manager of the old Sands Motel. "My friend Red Wolf also needs a room next to mine."

The man seemed clean-cut and pleasant enough and paid with cash, which always was a plus to the middle-aged manager.

As the evening progressed, it was noted that first one, then two, and then more men and women began to appear, as if by magic, all gravitating toward rooms 13 and 14, where Chin and Red Wolf had set up quarters. Before 10:00 p.m., the folks in the rooms adjacent to those began to lodge noise complaints to the front office.

When the overwhelmed innkeeper looked out his window, he was alarmed to see at least twenty-five to thirty individuals congregated in his rooms. His call to Chin in room 13 fell upon deaf ears, and he was told in so many words to chill out and leave things be if he knew what was good for him.

Repeated calls from adjoining tenants reported rampant liquor consumption along with loud and lewd behavior by those who continued to congregate.

At this point, the frightened landlord paid a personal visit to the scene of the affair and pleaded with Chin to quiet down and have all the nonpaying visitors leave the premises. It was evident at this time that damage was being done to the rooms as they were in the process of being trashed.

The Police Appear

Within minutes of the 911 call from the near-frantic manager, four units from the Scottsbluff PD appeared in the parking lot, blocking off all avenues of escape, lest anyone were to try to make a run.

By this time, intoxication was the order of the day for almost everyone present, and the accompanying barrage of vulgarity and insults filled the evening air like the putrid stench from the nearby cattle feed yard. The restraint used by the police officers was commendable under the circumstances, and within minutes, twelve of the militants, including our friends Chin and Red Wolf, were arrested, handcuffed, placed in the cages of the patrol units, and transported to the nearby city jail.

The Booking

The small holding cells at the Scottsbluff City PD and Jail were not designed for the long-term holding of prisoners as they were normally transported across the North Platte River to the Scotts Bluff County Jail in Gering. But since those being arrested were for drunk and disorderly, the decision was made to house them at the PD until morning.

There was only a dispatcher/jailer/clerk on duty at this late hour, and he was overpowered by the booking of this many at one time into the small facility. This was definitely not a normal occurrence at the sleepy facility.

Needless to say, those arrested were quickly booked into their cells and were soon on their bunks, sleeping off their night of planning, partying, and overindulgence.

At midnight, there was a change of the guard, and all seemed quiet in the old cellblock number one and two. There was nothing out of the ordinary as all seemed relaxed, comfortable, and peaceful.

At around 2:30 AM, the jailer walked by the cells and, upon looking in on the inmates, happened to note a distinct bulge in the right front pocket of Chin's pants. Alarmed at what appeared to be a failure on the part of the original booking officer to properly search the prisoner, the jailer called for assistance to investigate.

Chin was abruptly roused from his drunken slumber where he was lying peacefully on his jail bunk. A quick frisk and search of his person revealed a fully loaded snub-nosed .38-caliber Smith and Wesson Chief Special revolver concealed in his right front pocket of his Levi's pants.

His immediate reaction was that of an apparent well-rehearsed denial as to the knowledge of any gun.

"I have never seen that damned thing!" he convincingly and emphatically stated.

"You bastards planted that on me while I was sleeping!"

"You searched me before you jailed me, so how else could it have been in my pocket?" he yelled. "This is a damned setup to get me! You are going to pay for this one big-time."

Chin was still playing the part of the victim when the day crew arrived, and he demanded his call to is attorney.

National News

The first call did not go to his attorney but rather to the local Scottsbluff *Star Herald* newspaper. Even before the reporters' morning coffee was finished, they were at Chin's side with pen in hand, listening intently to his orchestrated and well-arranged claim of police corruption, collusion, and their deceitful scheme to set him up.

The charge was carrying a concealed weapon, and he was not going to let this one die. He seemed to know in smirking way that this one was going to give him more mileage than he had planned in his wildest dreams. He was overheard by a small-time jailhouse snitch talking to Red Wolf concerning the police, "I've got these pigs by the short hairs on this one. They'll be sorry they messed with me this time. Before this is over, I'll own the goddamned town of Scottsbluff."

The Civil Rights Complaint

The news of Chin's arrest and weapon violation charge was national news within twenty-four hours. He was his normal masterful self in spoon-feeding the hungry reporters with his version of how he was completely innocent and was the obvious victim of a much-larger plan to put him away for something he did not do. Whether or not the media bought his story was not relevant as they printed it the way he laid it out to them, and the bleeding hearts from all over the world were on this one, like flies on stink.

The very next day, an official civil rights violation case was filed by Chin, charging the Scottsbluff, Nebraska Police Department and the city of Scottsbluff with a violation of his civil rights. It was alleged, of course, that the gun found on his person was planted by the police in a well-planned-out scheme to harass him and get him incarcerated for a crime he did not commit.

No matter how this played out, the Scottsbluff PD was going to have egg all over their face. Either they screwed up royally on the search during the booking or, as Chin alleged, they planted the weapon on him as he slept innocently in his jail cell. For the PD, this was a PR nightmare.

McWade met and shook hands with a very well-groomed and cordial Indian man identifying himself as Chin. He had entered the small, stark two-story FBI office located on the second floor of the First State Bank Building alone. Since this was a high-profile case,

McWade was accompanied by his soon-to-be-retired partner, Bob Frinsey, who could act as a witness to whatever transpired.

The FBI policy clearly pointed out that any civil rights violation cases against an agency, such as the Scottsbluff PD, where McWade frequented almost daily and, furthermore, was personal friends with several of the officers and detectives, should be assigned to an out-of-town agent not familiar with the agency. That was the policy, but in the real world, the powers to be in Omaha felt they could not spare anyone to come 452 miles west to work a case of national importance. So McWade was their native on the scene as usual.

Chin was pleasant, fluent in his conversation, and very interesting to converse with about the arrest and the gun *planted* on his person. He maintained that he had never seen the weapon, did not own a gun, had never possessed a firearm, and was incensed that he was being accused like a common criminal. He assured McWade and Frinsey that he was just a peace-loving individual who was a complete victim of blind justice and was sickened by this false accusation and what it could do to is fine reputation as an ambassador and broker to the Native American movement for equality and fairness.

He maintained that his very position in AIM could be adversely affected by this false accusation as AIM never would condone anyone in their movement to possess any kind of a firearm. He held back a wink as he made that knowingly false statement.

McWade realized that he was a young agent and probably did not look old and salty but was amused that Chin assumed he was naive enough to swallow the bit about no one in AIM having weapons. McWade had seen armed individuals in the mock grand jury fiasco earlier in Gordon when posing as a newsman. At this time, he was glad that Chin did not recall him from that fateful day or this thing could really boomerang.

The official interview finally ended and Chin was shown the door. McWade could understand why he was able to get a following as he was a man of rather muscular stature who was charismatic, fascinating, and appeared to be a natural-born leader.

"You will be notified of the results of the investigation when the DOJ (Department of Justice) Civil Rights Division determines the merit and outcome of the entire investigation," McWade told the departing Chin as he descended the staircase to the street below.

The Verdict

After collecting all police reports and interviewing all officers involved and any and all potential witnesses having knowledge, the report was submitted.

Within a record time of three weeks the answer came from DOJ that this case lacked prosecutive merit and was to be closed. McWade promptly informed Chin of the opinion, but he had already been informed by DOJ directly through his own attorney he claimed. Case closed? Not so fast, partner!

Chin's Gun

Being the PR genius that he was, Chin had milked this case to the max in the media arena. Worldwide news agencies covered his plight and drew real tears from bleeding hearts who know no better. It was an amazing phenomenon to behold that so much could be made out of so little. But McWade mused, *This is the world of the 1970s where fake news seems to reign supreme.*

Just when the smile over the seemingly outrageous audacity of Chin was beginning to disappear, the phone call from the Scottsbluff PD made the smile return broader than ever.

"Guess who just left my office?" Detective Livingbone laughingly stated.

"Your friend Chin Black Heart just had the gonads to come here and ask me if he could get his gun back since the case had been dismissed! Imagine that! The gun he had never seen and claimed we planted in his pocket, he now claims is his and wants it back."

McWade was betting correctly that the rest of the story would never make the six o'clock news anywhere.

Chin was last seen by McWade's snitch heading back north to the rez. Somehow, though, McWade had an idea he and his AIM comrades would be heard from again in the near future.

Chapter 11

Sex in the Heartland: The X-Rated Room and More

The question seemed to always be asked, "So just what do you do in a place like Scottsbluff?"

McWade would thoughtfully gaze into the questioner's eyes and reply, "I do whatever comes my way, and unlike most other agents in other places, I do it without much Bureau help."

The smile about Chin asking for *his* gun back, the same one which he had never owned, had not had time to fade when Action Jackson and Detective Livingbone cornered McWade at the coffee shop and presented another small-town dilemma which they thought needed federal assistance.

Apparently, a young voluptuous woman known only as "Denise" had hit the sleepy little Nebraska town of Scottsbluff like a white tornado. The fact that she was the ultimate in the looks department was not the problem. It was the way she was brazenly going about the advertising for her particular employment.

Now Scottsbluff was no stranger to an occasional prostitute peddling her flesh for a modest price on the circuit from Kansas City to Denver to Rapid City. But this young lady and her pimps were taking things a bit far in the advertising department, making it hard to ignore as a police problem.

Not only was she available for appointments 24-7 but had also printed up business cards, drawing attention to her talents. The cards simply read, "For the Time of Your Life in the X-Rated Room, call Denise, telephone 308-632-xxxx."

The business cards seemed to be no big deal, but even Action Jackson thought that placing them under the wiper blades of every car in the downtown area was a bit over the top. When he had found one of these cards on his own windshield and had tossed it on the front seat of his car, there was still no concern. But when his spirited and suspicious wife, Suzie, happened to see it, there was some explaining to do as, apparently, the trust level had dwindled in their marriage.

The church ladies of the small town were horrified. Soon they had pressured their husbands to at least also act concerned, and soon the complaints started to arrive at the Scottsbluff PD.

The suggestion by the NSP and PD was that they work the case with the FBI to allow it to be prosecuted federally under the ITAR-Prostitution (Interstate Transportation in Aid to Racketeering-Prostitution) statute. It sounded like a logical plan, and so another small-town task force was born.

Our girl of the hour was soon properly identified as a professional from Minnesota, and her two handlers were also soon known by their real names.

McWade noted that Denise was the kind of woman most others dream of looking like in the beauty department. She was 28 years of age, 5'4", and weighed in at 120 shapely and well-toned pounds. Denise had a perfectly shaped nose placed on a face that other women would envy. Her emerald green eyes were mesmerizing, and her naturally colored dark eyebrows and rose-tinted lips blended together in perfect harmony. Her perfectly formed sparkling white teeth would flash when she smiled her rehearsed infectious smile. The gods of beauty had blessed her with glowing dark brown hair with a hint of auburn that would look as appealing sloppy wet from her morning shower as when blow-dried by the summer breeze.

"She would look as good getting up in the morning as when she was dressed up for a night on the town," exclaimed Action Jackson as he looked on from the window of the surveillance van. McWade chose not to ask how he seemed so certain about that factual observation about her morning looks.

The place of business was an old hotel room just a block away from the FBI office dubbed, of course, the X-Rated Room. It was on the second story and in a room at the top of an old dusty hardwood staircase that creaked a warning with every step.

Finding the Undercover John

The assignment seemed easy enough. All the clandestine stealth had to do was make an appointment, get properly wired for recording the transaction, wander up the stairs, and get Denise on tape offering her services for money and then making some kind of overt action to show she was going to follow through on her specific promised services. The "closet John" could not do or say anything whatsoever that could be construed or used as even a remote defense-claiming entrapment.

Now who do we choose for the assignment was the next task force decision?

Action Jackson was ruled out as he seemed way too anxious to volunteer and some still had lingering suspicions that he already had a prior "friendship" with the young woman.

McWade could possibly have received Bureau permission for the sensuous chore, but he knew better than to suggest that possibility to his own beautiful trusting wife. She believed in the statement that "if good men do nothing, evil will prevail." But she also was a firm believer in the statement that "if a man hangs out long enough in the barber shop, he will end up with a haircut." The latter statement, of course, trumped the first in her mind. So McWade was counted out quickly.

Livingbone was too well-known and could jeopardize the whole operation.

Agent Frinsey would not have been up for the task due to his advanced age and feeble demeanor. He would have had to settle for a cuddly kiss on the cheek and possible a lap dance from the energetic dark-haired bombshell. So there was another no go.

The lot finally fell upon young Baron Radar, a muscular young detective from the Scottsbluff PD. He was not only a physical specimen, but he was articulate, very attractive to the opposite sex, and one who could bullshit his way in or out of any possible situation. He seemed like the perfect match.

The Plan

"Hello, this is Denise!" came the sexy voice on the other end of the line.

"Yes, I have an opening at four o'clock this afternoon. Can you be there?"

"Sure. I have your address on the card you left on my car. Sounds great, and I'm excited to meet you and to see what you have to offer." Radar almost drooled.

He finished with, "Four o'clock it is, and I will be using the name Mr. Smith, of course."

As the time for the liaison neared, "Mr. Smith" was wired with all the latest electronic technology, and McWade and three other task force members sat just outside the old hotel in the back of the van looking like aliens with their large earphones for monitoring the encounter.

Every step on the old staircase squeaked a warning that someone was approaching the den of iniquity. Radar was met at the top of the stairs by a thirty-five-year-old burly white male who looked him over suspiciously before allowing him to enter the mysterious room.

Radar was taken aback by just how strikingly stunning the young temptress was as he entered the dimly lit room and looked at her face-to-face.

"What can I do for you?" she said seductively.

"I was intrigued by your card and wondered just what you were offering."

The small talk proceeded for at least three minutes before, finally, Denise volunteered that she would do an around the world for $100 unless it lasted for more than thirty minutes. It would then be $50 more for each additional fifteen minutes.

She explained in detail exactly what she would do, and the deal was made.

Radar pulled out his wad of marked twenty-dollar bills and counted out loud until the $100 total was received.

At that point, the young damsel seemed all too eager to get on with her services and told him to just lay his clothes on the chair. Before he could pull out his badge and say that she was under arrest for soliciting, she had already dropped her blouse and exposed her braless breasts to the now-wide-eyed supersleuth.

At this point, McWade and two of the other officers hurriedly exited the van and took the stairs two at a time to finish the arrest of Denise and her two handlers.

After conducting a thorough search and seizing various strange items used in the trade, McWade only had one thing to say about the X-rated room. "It was educational and certainly lived up to its name."

After pleading guilty to the ITAR-Prostitution statute, our two pimps and their "sex slave" received a couple years in a minimum security federal facility to reflect on the flaws of their game plan and how to improve it in the future.

However, Denise was never seen again in Scottsbluff and the X-rated room became another small-town legend.

So the church ladies, Beverly Better-Than-You, and all the others on the self-righteous and sanctimonious pew could relish in the fact that this evil temptation was removed from their midst.

However, the jokes and jesting about this case lived on sporadically around the morning table at the local doughnut shop.

Interstate 80 Lowlife

It was a cold and rainy miserable night along I-80 when John Brown pulled his Peterbilt 18 wheeler off the four lane and into a rest area near Elm Creek, Nebraska. As he sat there waiting for the rain to let up he heard a light knock on the driver's door of his rig.

What he saw sickened him as nothing he had seen before in his rough and wild life. There, standing shivering in the rain, were two small barefoot girls, looking to be ages ten to twelve. They were soaked and appeared to be frightened as they kept glancing over toward an older-model car with North Carolina license plates occupied by two adults, a male and a female.

The older of the two girls started to weep as she commenced to offer herself and the younger girl to the truck driver in a sex-for-money proposition. All the time the girl was talking, she was nervously looking toward the parked car in an apprehensive manner.

Brown, an honest and upright man, sent the girls back to the car and, as soon as possible, called law enforcement. Within minutes, the two little girls were in the protective custody of the NSP who ushered them to a safe haven in Kearney, Nebraska, and gave the two adults a room at the Buffalo County Jail.

It was a long three-hundred-mile drive to Kearney, but when McWade pulled into town the next morning, the puzzle unfolded quickly at the county sheriff's office.

The woman, Lizzie McCoy, was the aunt of twelve-year-old Patty and ten-year-old Sarah. The man, Earl Hatfield, was the deadbeat boyfriend of Lizzie and the owner of the car in which they were living out of at the time of the incident.

The entire crew were from North Carolina and were en route to the state of California, looking for a change of scenery. Aunt Lizzie, due to other problems in the extended family, had temporary custody of Patty and Sarah.

Since they were short on cash, Earl, the deep thinker of the party, decided to prostitute the two young girls at truck stops and rest areas across the country.

Statements from all concerned revealed the girls had been violated for money at least four times at different truck stops and locations prior to being picked up in Nebraska.

It literally sickened McWade as he interviewed the cute little innocent girls and determined how they had been forced to act as sex slaves to unidentified dirtbag cab lizards in Illinois, Iowa, and Nebraska. They had been coached by the two brain-dead, low-life adults and had collected gas money for their travels, turning it over to Earl.

The report containing the vivid statements was forwarded to the AUSA in Lincoln, who decided to throw the book at both Earl and Lizzie. They were charged under the WSTA (White Slave Traffic Act), and after having the facts of life discussed with them, they wisely decided to avoid a trial and enter a guilty plea. Both were given twenty-five-year sentences to think about just how despicable they actually were.

A part of McWade's inner mind hoped that other prisoners would deal out the appropriate justice usually reserved for child sex offenders in federal prisons. He knew, without a shadow of a doubt, that it would be known in advance that they were the loathsome pimps of Lizzie's nieces. He knew how the system worked and almost smiled that some justice may actually take place behind prison walls for these two monsters.

The two little girls were returned to, hopefully, more responsible relatives and offered some counseling to help repair their damaged fragile lives.

McWade was certainly not a scriptorian but recalled the good book, saying, "And whosoever shall offend one of these little ones, it is better for him that a millstone were hanged about his neck, and he were cast into the sea." He thought maybe Lizzie and Earl might start practicing holding their breath just in case this were to be applied to them.

He recalled old deep-voiced agent Peach, assigned to the Pussy Posse where they worked the WSTA cases in Baltimore, saying to his NAC 8, "It can be a sick, sick world out there. Cling to what you have at home, boys, and remember that if you don't like what you see, true beauty is only a light switch away!"

This seemed to be the new norm! Going native in the heartland seemed to have its own variety of kinky spice.

Chapter 12

Nixon's BIA Blunder

Richard M. Nixon was running for reelection, and the countdown was on toward the November 7 casting of the ballots. It was shaping up, according to the national news outlets, to be a close race between Nixon and the anti-Vietnam War liberal Democrat George McGovern.

In the days leading up to this all-important election, there was another rather interesting movement taking place across America.

AIM, along with other Indian groups, had organized a rather large caravan of concerned Native Americans and were calling this the Trail of Broken Treaties Caravan.

The convoy was headed for the nation's capital after starting out on the West Coast. It was adding participants as it was winding its way eastward from state to state toward Washington, DC.

The party snaking its way across this great land consisted of cars, pickups, vans, Volkswagen microbuses, scooters, motorcycles, and any other mode of transportation they could find.

Given the previous trouble with AIM in the Scottsbluff territory, McWade was paying special interest to the phenomenon as it was being reported by news reports as well as in Bureau communications, asking for any informant information concerning this matter.

As the group convoyed into DC, it turned out to be the largest group of Native Americans ever seeking an audience with federal politicians since the Little Big Horn.

Nixon was uneasy as he felt his reelection could be sabotaged by what he thought to be an uncalled-for freakish sideshow and unanticipated protest.

McWade surmised that because of Nixon's insecurity about the situation, the Indians sensed weakness on his part. Obviously, the incident at Gordon, Nebraska, had not been properly channeled or heeded. The big boys in Washington had not learned anything from McWade's reports, so there was almost no show of force whatsoever to the invading Indians as they headed toward the BIA (Bureau of Indian Affairs) Headquarters Building.

News reporters salivated and drooled uncontrollably over themselves as over five hundred Native Americans literally poured into town and stormed the BIA building. This was the kind of news they thrived on as this was the day of their glory.

As McWade watched helplessly from his own living room, his RCA black-and-white television set showed some of the same familiar players he had dealt with in Scottsbluff and Gordon, Nebraska, smiling widely for the cameras as they trashed, looted, and pillaged this beautiful government building. It was indeed hard to watch, knowing that his earlier reports on how to prevent this kind of behavior had gone completely unnoticed and had fallen on deaf ears and eyes blinded by those in positions of sanctimonious authority and overrated self-worth.

He swore he even saw his old friend, Chin Black Heart, smirking at the camera and grinning like a Cheshire cat that had just stolen the cream. He appeared to be in his full glory, doing what he seemed to do best.

Instead of the raiding party being met with available overwhelming force, law enforcement was ordered to stand down and sit on their proverbial hands showing no force or opposition. There was no parade of police cruisers, no SWAT teams, no cavalry of any kind to slow the attack and takeover of the building.

Unknown to most of the uninformed public was the fact that the BIA building contained a virtual collection of early Indian artifacts, valuable paintings, and antiquities that were not replaceable.

Government leaders, too weak and insecure to open their politically correct mouths, watched and wrung their uncalloused hands as this theft and destruction took place only blocks from their ivory towers.

Windows were broken, fires were started inside the various rooms, holes were bashed in walls, and graffiti was the order of the day as McWade and other taxpayers looked on in frustration at the inaction by their duly elected and appointed government officials.

But their main objective was achieved as Nixon won in a landslide. McGovern finished almost 20 percentage points behind in a humiliating loss. But the damage to the BIA building was massive and disgusting and stood as a virtual monument to failed policy and inaction.

Now adding insult to destruction and after sitting by with ample resources at their disposal within a few blocks away, McWade received a teletype instructing him and any other agents working Indian matters to do the impossible. The insanity of the order boggled his mind under the circumstances. It was to identify and attempt to recover any stolen BIA property, artifacts, or paintings in their respective territories throughout Indian Country.

Again, try to grasp just what happened, HQ agents and supervisors watched the looting, allowed the thugs to leave the BIA building and, subsequently, leave town with their contraband, and now wanted the likes of McWade and others to do what they should have done. "Why didn't they just arrest them as they left with their stolen treasures?" seemed like the logical question.

As the Native Americans filtered back to their reservations and homes, the stories of their conquest were heard by sources. Stories such as a teacher in Alliance, Nebraska, who reported to McWade that one of her students in third grade bragged to the class in show-and-tell that her dad had brought back some "really cool stuff from Washington, DC, last week."

Of course, nothing came of the recovery efforts but denials and accusations of harassment. The Trail of Broken Treaties had become a trail too old and faint to follow and the artifacts gravitated to someone's front room, basement, or to a pawnshop for some quick cash.

This whole escapade obviously tended to embolden AIM and other militant Indians in general toward future similar activity.

McWade predicted to his fellow local law enforcement buddies that a heavy price would be paid in the near future for the mishandling of the BIA fiasco.

The bungling leaders in faraway DC had proven again to McWade that the "Peter Principle" was still alive, well, and working within the FBI and in government as well. This principle was based on the theory that individuals in leadership positions all seem to rise eventually to their level of complete incompetence.

Thanksgiving was just a few days away, but how was McWade to know that his prophecy about resulting Indian trouble would be fulfilled so quickly and that he would spend the upcoming holiday with the Indians as they carried out the next phase of their battle against white rule at the historic old Fort Robinson, the legendary Outpost on the Plains.

Just like when donating money or untold hours doing volunteer work for churches or clubs or Bureau supervisors, to McWade, it seemed the same theory applied to AIM protesters and looters: "Enough was never enough!"

Chapter 13

Thanksgiving at the Fort

Fool me once, strike one! Fool me twice, strike three!

A sign hung proudly over the entrance to the main headquarters building at Fort Robinson announcing in a-matter-of-fact way, *Through These Portals Passed the World's Finest Horsemen.*

"Armstrong here!" came the voice on the phone. "Looks like we have more Indian action at Fort Rob."

The Fort was a place to visit, love, and stay now that the State of Nebraska had taken ownership and made it into a state park. A great place to take the family, rent one of the old officers' quarters buildings, and relive history in the picturesque butte country. A place where the stories could be told of the incarcerated Cheyenne Indians that were trying to keep from being forced back to the reservations actually escaping and being hunted down and killed by soldiers known as the Fort Robinson massacre.

The NSP was requesting assistance as apparently some thirty to fifty of the same troublemakers from the BIA takeover had now forced their way into the museum, and the fort was under siege. They were making demands, threatening damage and refused to leave.

The self-proclaimed leader of this takeover was a local Indian and AIM member by the name of Bob Yellow Canary, who apparently was not aware that the Army had deeded the old fort to Nebraska. He hadn't taken into consideration that this was not Washington and that, in cowboy country, this sort of crap was not to be tolerated.

When McWade arrived at Fort Rob, he was met by Armstrong and three other NSP troopers, as well as Fess Benson, the Dawes County sheriff. Fess was an old cowboy turned sheriff, who looked like an aging Wyatt Earp, and was already pissed that he was going to miss his supper. He used the same adjectives for the interlopers as James Primer had used to describe the Third Street Gang of railroad tire thieves.

The first thing he was heard to say was, "Them mangy sumbitches better get their sorry asses out of there before I have to go in there and kick their butts up between their shoulder blades." McWade got the idea from that comment that the good sheriff had lost patience with the hostiles who were now threatening to burn the place down if any efforts were made to remove them with force.

Fess and his good wife, Helen, were considered genuine friends and, on more than one occasion, had McWade eating with them at the old Dawes County Jail located on the third floor of the courthouse in Chadron. After supper, the stories would go on about the good old days, and then when he was ready to retire, out would come his false teeth and off would come his six-shooter. He would place them both inside his refrigerator for safekeeping and be ready to watch TV and retire.

McWade never quite guessed the reasons for the refrigerator as a hiding place but had learned there are some things you just don't ask.

The demands by the Indian raiders were simple although totally unrealistic.

"Give Fort Robinson back to the Indians to control and do as they pleased," commanded Yellow Canary.

As the first two days passed by in a standoff, the enthusiasm inside the museum was beginning to wane at the sight of more and more Plymouth cruisers pulling up on the parade grounds and forming a large circle around the building that had been compromised. Inside, the beautiful Mandy, now one of McWade's sources, overheard Yellow Canary talking on the phone with Chin Black Heart, saying something to the effect, "I think we might have bitten off too much to chew this time. Can you send help?"

After day two passed, Fess commented, "Helen is doing Thanksgiving dinner, and this is bullshit!" McWade got the impression he was not happy with the lack of progress in removing the thugs from state of Nebraska property.

By 6:00 PM, a deputy arrived with a large box of Helen's sandwiches, which calmed him a bit.

As the occupation dragged on, it seemed as if the attorneys in Lincoln were being paid by the hour.

A meeting was demanded with Nebraska Governor J. J. Exon, who replied back that he did not look at Yellow Canary and his flock of followers as representatives of the Indian people of Nebraska and, therefore, refused to meet with them. Essentially, he had just told them to pound sand, which was a new experience for them to ponder.

At that time, McWade and Armstrong arranged a meeting with Yellow Canary and his two sidekicks, Elroy Pasados and Tom White Eyes, in a small room just down the hall from the museum. This gave McWade the chance to explain to them what it means to be outnumbered, outmaneuvered, and left holding a losing hand.

"You absolutely cannot go back and make a new start here, but you can start now and change the ending to this whole matter," McWade explained. It seemed much easier to negotiate from a position of power with at least fifty NSP units visible from the window.

The militants did not want to leave in total defeat, so they decided to spend Thanksgiving at the fort also. They would give up their takeover of the museum, assuming they could leave without being arrested or charged with anything.

The brokered agreement was that they were to leave Fort Robinson ASAP. However, they had been blabbing to the news media that they were going to spend Thanksgiving at the Fort to show a symbolic victory. To save face, the State of Nebraska allowed them to eat their dinner and have a small victory celebration along the sides of US Highway 20, which passes directly through Fort Robinson. Since technically, the highway was not part of the Fort Robinson State Park, both sides could claim victory, and no damage was done to the museum or to the fort. And Crazy Horses artifacts stayed put in their glass cases where they belonged.

The fifteen to twenty cars carrying sixty to seventy Native Americans parked along the highway, peacefully feasting on their sack lunches while McWade and the cavalry of troopers looked on from a short distance away, having their own lunch that Helen had prepared and sent over with another deputy. They were all keeping a close eye out for a pair of Fess's false teeth that might have accidentally made their way into the potato salad from the fridge.

As Thanksgiving with the Indians ended in the early afternoon, McWade pointed his Bucar south toward Scottsbluff with the words of his old friend Fess, the Dawes County sheriff, still ringing in his ear, "This is a bunch of bullshit!"

Perhaps the good sheriff was absolutely right and McWade tended to agree with him 100 percent, but peace had prevailed; no looting or damage had taken place, and the high plains would be at peace for at least another month or so as AIM moved on to softer targets they thought to be more like the BIA building.

McWade was but one agent, and with the coordinated help of the NSP and the SO, they had done what the federal government and the FBI in DC had been unable to do with unlimited resources. If this was what going native was all about, he was loving it more with each passing month.

Turning the other cheek makes for a great Sunday school lesson topic, but in the real world dealing with the likes of AIM, it could spell disaster. If the truth were known, McWade didn't mind missing the turkey with the kids that day, but if that thing would have dragged on, he would have missed the Nebraska-Oklahoma football game the day after. But then the Huskers blew the game 17–14, so there was statewide mourning anyway.

On second thought, the more he considered what Sheriff Benson had said, he was probably right on target and saw all this for what it really was—a bunch of bullshit!

As he pulled into his driveway, he recalled the last few weeks and wondered almost aloud concerning the AIM problem, "Where is all this going to end?"

That question would be answered sooner rather than later. But for AIM in the state of Nebraska, at this point at least, it was strike two and you are out!

Chapter 14

Elroy's Invasion

The Christmas holiday season came and passed quickly. Peace had been the order of the day since AIM had lost the game at Fort Robinson after the checkmate move by law enforcement and the NSP.

After a New Year's vacation, Chin and over one hundred other AIM followers resurfaced at the Southeast Recreation Center (SRC) in Gering, Nebraska. This was to protest some supposed or real injustice they thought was taking place there against the Native Americans that used SRC.

Lincoln Whitaker, a good personal friend of McWade's, was the volunteer chairman of CRC, and when the protest turned to a pushing and shoving incident, Whitaker called the Scotts Bluff County Sheriff's Office. Deputies and officers from the NSP quickly responded to the scene to restore order.

It seemed that Chin actually enjoyed the attention of getting arrested as he refused to comply with police orders and ended up in handcuffs and then off to the county jail.

Not much came of this as the national media did not seem to care that much about pushing and shoving by AIM, and Chin getting arrested was beginning to look like part for the course. Disappointed in the whole thing, he made bail and disappeared again to the Pine Ridge.

McWade yawned, sent in a short teletype to the Bureau outlining the incident, and went back to updating his thirty-plus routine cases assigned to him. He had learned by now that to justify your existence in the RA, there was a magic number of cases he should have pending at any given time. That number was between twenty-five and thirty. The older cases would be closed as new ones arrived, but at any given time, a caseload was absolutely required or the boss would start mumbling or threatening to close the RA. Every ninety days, there was a required file review, requiring a trip to Omaha, for a sit-down face-to-face with the supervisors there. They would look to see and make sure each case file was current with some type of investigation posted in the last ninety days.

Most of the supervisors reviewing the cases had never actually worked that kind of case in their whole career, but somehow they knew just how to work them anyway by virtue of their mantle, so McWade would smile, thank them for their help, and head back to the RA to do things the best way he saw fit.

The general term thrown around the Bureau to reflect this outdated system was known later as posting and coasting.

So McWade was getting ready to retire to his sweet wife after a long day of posting and coasting when he received a call telling him they had another incident.

Fresh off his looting trip from the BIA building and the later takeover at Fort Robinson, it seemed good old Elroy Pasados was at it again. An informant in Alliance, Nebraska, fifty miles to the northeast, had reported that Elroy and three of his AIM buddies had just been seen filling half-gallon glass bottles with gasoline at a local service station.

The bottles full of gas, plus firearms under a blanket and torn rags, looked a bit suspicious, especially since someone had thrown a Molotov cocktail onto the steps of the Scottsbluff Junior High School only a week before. That bottle did not break and, therefore, no explosion or fire happened as planned. A Molotov cocktail was known universally as a poor man's grenade. A rag would be stuffed into the neck of the bottle, lit, and then thrown. When the bottle broke, it would explode into flames.

By now, Elroy was well-known to every cop in western Nebraska, and his old VW bus was easy to recognize as it seemed to show up at every AIM incident.

McWade and Action Jackson raced eastward out of Scottsbluff on US Highway 26, past the small town of Minatare, only to find that NSP units, already advised of the situation by McWade, had intercepted the VW about five miles east of the massive Minatare Feed Yard.

As McWade arrived on the scene, he saw a beautiful sight. Elroy was already facedown on the cold snowy pavement, screaming about his civil rights, police brutality, and being set up again. The open side door of the old bus revealed at least twenty Molotov cocktails with the rags already inserted into the open bottles, four military-type assault weapons, and a host of smaller handguns and weapons. In the rear of the van were flak jackets, black stocking-cap-type masks, and various other devices of the terrorist trade, to include a small propane torch and even a good supply of flares.

The NSP and the Scotts Bluff County SO were busy taking inventory of the weapons of war while Pasados, now sporting a new pair of handcuffs and leg irons, continued to scream about his rights, claiming that all this evidence was being planted in his van by "white pigs."

Back at the county jail in Gering, our local wannabe terrorist, Elroy, was completely frustrated that his plan had been thwarted once again. "By now, he must be starting to feel like a failure at his trade," Action Jackson laughed.

McWade found that the foiled plot, which was soon uncovered, was to have taken place as follows:

1. The van was to stop at the Minatare Feed Yard and commence firing into the cattle with semiautomatic weapons, killing as many cattle as possible. This was to create a diversion to bring as many county and state cops as possible to that crime scene.

2. They would then proceed to the Panhandle Co-op Oil Refinery, located on the south end of Scottsbluff, where

they would torch the facility and cause a huge fire as another diversion. This would hopefully ensure that most of the Scottsbluff PD, the Scotts Bluff County SO, and the NSP would be at the scene of those two incidents.

3. They would then proceed to the NSP Troop E Headquarters, located in the Nebraska National Guard Armory on the north end of Scottsbluff. By now, all the NSP units should be sucked away by the chaos at the refinery and feed yard, leaving the NSP dispatcher, the Troop E NSP offices, and the armory all unprotected and ripe for the takeover by Elroy and his men. After securing the NSP HQ and the armory, a call was then to be made to his old friend Chin, hoping that AIM would rally behind him. Another call was then to be made to Porky Gonzales, the infamous leader of the dreaded Brown Berets, a Chicano activist group in Denver, Colorado. Elroy had visions that, by combining the Indian power of AIM and the Chicano forces loyal to Porky, he could take over the entire city of Scottsbluff and hold the city hostage, thereby getting his way with the evil oppressive US government. But alas, while the city slept, unaware of the sinister plan to hold them hostage, those charged with the duty to serve and protect did both. Everyone in the twin cities of Scottsbluff-Gering went to work or about their lives as usual the next morning, and only a few read in the local *Star-Herald* or the *Gering Courier* about the arrest of Elroy Pasados and others on charges of illegal firearms and explosives possession.

Perhaps this whole thing was not a big deal by big-city FBI standards, but then again, maybe it was even more important. Whatever, it still gave McWade a warm and fuzzy feeling as he and his old friends Action and Armstrong related the night's episode to the wide-eyed morning coffee shop crew.

As he met with Mandy Silk Hair that day in Alliance to compensate her for the information that saved Scottsbluff, he thanked her again. She smiled, tossed her long black hair into the wind, and headed back toward the Pine Ridge, ready for the next action that she assured would happen all too soon.

Hoover would have loved this stuff! he silently thought to himself as he headed back to the Bluffs. He automatically reached down to turn up the music on his country radio station, which, by now, was becoming his constant companion.

A Bucar, a good country station, a great family, and great friends. No wonder the official big green sign at the state line read, Nebraska, the Good Life.

Chapter 15

Wounded Knee

"Successful People primarily Focus Only on One Thing."

Assuming there is some truth to that statement, McWade observed that the one thing Chin Black Heart focused on more than anything else was the image he saw looking back at him in the mirror. How did he look to the media? How did he appear to his fellow AIM groupies who seemed to follow him as if he were an all-knowing prophet sent from above? What's in this for me?

In addition to his fascination with how he looked to his peers and the larger world audience, he was continually looking for a softer target that would have widespread, even worldwide, impact. Being the genius that he was in the area of protests, he found what he was looking for right under his nose on the Pine Ridge Reservation.

The name Wounded Knee was well-known to anyone who had even the slightest knowledge of the old west and the history of forcing the indigenous people of the area onto reservations. Diaries and records told and retold of the events on that cold winter day in 1890 on the snowy banks of Wounded Knee Creek when something went terribly wrong, resulting in the US Army soldiers opening fire on a group of Sioux men, women, and children, killing at least 150. Forgotten is the fact that 25 soldiers also were killed in that horrific bloody battle to become known forever as the Wounded Knee Massacre.

Most action taken in life is a result of rising tensions until it becomes a crisis. The PRIR was no exception.

The situation on the Pine Ridge was now at a fever pitch, and the political kettle that had been boiling for the past several months was ready to explode. Needless to say, Chin and his band of jolly followers were throwing as much fuel on the fire heating that pot as possible and were gleefully awaiting the eruption.

The once and somewhat peaceful reservation had become very divided. On one side of this political equation was the duly elected tribal president, Will Dickson, and those who followed him. His supporters were referred to by others as Dickson's Goon Squad or, simply, the Goon Squad (GOON stood for Guardians of the Oglala Nation).

On the opposing side was AIM and those who supported Chin Brave Heart and his henchmen. AIM accused the Goon Squad of dishonesty, corruption, and other crimes associated with political corruption and cronyism. The Goon Squad replied back with force, brutality, and even deadly violence as more than fifty of Dickson's opponents were allegedly killed over the next three to four years in the early to mid-1970s.

Chin, although born on the Pine Ridge, had moved from the rez early in his life. The Goon Squad looked at him as an outside agitator being financed by well-meaning do-gooders, church groups, and others liberals whom they thought should just mind their own business.

Dickson, his Goon Squad, and the PRIR tribal council definitely considered themselves a sovereign nation and thought they should answer to no one, including the US Federal Government or the state of South Dakota. Many defiantly displayed their own special license plates on their cars, trucks, and pickups, showing themselves as part of the Oglala Sioux Nation rather than the state of South Dakota.

Finally, lightning struck in the form of an armed takeover by AIM of the small village and trading post at Wounded Knee, South Dakota, located on the PRIR on February 27, 1973. Chin had found the ideal target. It was unprotected, isolated, and the name unique and synonymous with Indian mistreatment and injustice.

Books were later to be written on this seventy-one-day siege, but McWade only witnessed the action from his own territory in Nebraska through overheard radio transmissions and stories told around the coffee shops by fellow agents who were staying on TDY (temporary duty) in any and all available motels in Chadron, Rushville, Gordon, Crawford, and Hay Springs. These agents had been sucked in on the Wounded Knee Special from each and every one of the fifty-nine FBI field offices around the country.

As hundreds of FBI Agents, Deputy US Marshals, and others arrived on the scene, they quickly set up a perimeter around the besieged village complete with roadblocks and checkpoints to control movement in and out.

"You have got to be kidding. The Bureau has five SACs on the scene each thinking they have equal authority? What a way to make sure no meaningful decisions can be made without a committee meeting," commented McWade to a fellow agent who had just arrived in Chadron from checkpoint one. The agent laughed and related that one of the more liberal SACs had decided to send out orders on how to respond to being fired at by AIM. The order on the Bureau radio was that, if fired upon, the agents were only to return fire, trying to wound the assailants. Obviously the SAC did not even know Bureau policy and was contradicting it with his stupid instruction.

After hearing the rather bizarre order, a reply came back over the airwaves, "Right, I copy that, boss. Just try to nick the bastards in the head."

"Who said that?" screeched the infuriated fearless leader.

"I'm the Green Hornet," came the reply over the Buradio.

"ID yourself this instant, Green Hornet!"

"It's 10-0 on that, leader one. I may be Green, but I'm not that green!" came the reply as the radio went dead.

As the stalemate continued day after endless day, the agents at one of the roadblocks overlooking the village, became bored and were looking for a little excitement. They decided to cause a little tension among the folks holding hostages in the small cluster of buildings.

The Bureau had furnished an APC (armored personnel carrier) for protection since there was an occasional incoming round from AIM.

They found an old, rather long, stovepipe and attached it to the APC, which looked, from a distance, to be a barrel resembling one on a military tank. Then as evening approached, a few flares were sent out the stovepipe to look as if the fake tank was shooting at them. The panic-like scrambling for cover by the occupants below was humorous to witness and worth yet another laugh.

One lazy Saturday, a hotshot firearm instructor from Quantico appeared at the same roadblock overlooking the scene below. Brandishing his 30.06 hunting rifle, he told McWade's friend Ron that he would bet him $20 that he could shoot and hit the bell in the steeple tower on the little church below. After the bet was made, out came a much larger sniper rifle from the gunman's trunk, and the hot dog instructor commenced to ring the bell three times in a row from over a half-mile distance.

Ron paid him the $20, which was laughingly returned as a bigger gun had been used rather than the 30.06. Ron chuckled uncontrollably because after the third shot hit and loudly rang the bell, a man, who had been placed in the tower, jumped up from nowhere and scrambled below for safety. So much for the watchman in the tower.

On yet another day, McWade's snitch from the village reported to him that AIM had given an official Indian name to the now-famous female FBI agent working the roadblock at a visible checkpoint. Noting that this woman could apparently go her entire twelve-hour shift without a bathroom break, she became known affectionately as Princess Iron Bladder.

Initially, the cluster **** of leadership for the Special, being big-city types, had required the agents to stand out at the checkpoints in the middle of nowhere in their business suits and ties. The February and March cold was unbearable until they managed to get some army surplus winter jackets and defied the orders from above. All the SAC types, by the way, found warm places to hang out to contemplate their next brilliant move.

From his own Buradio, McWade heard an agent at a roadblock report that he was being fired upon by AIM and requesting instructions. With his own ears, McWade heard the order to "stand down until we contact DOJ to see if it was okay to return fire."

Somehow, after hearing that order, he knew this was going to be long and drawn out. He kept thinking that the NSP would have surrounded the militants with one hundred cruisers and ended this thing in a few days if it had happened in Nebraska.

When it was reported to him that a car full of DOJ employees pulled up to the roadblock requested permission to enter the village only later to return without the gas cans and ammunition seen in the vehicle earlier, he knew the situation was out of control. Later, orders were given to not even detain DOJ cars coming and going to Wounded Knee. *Could our own beloved DOJ actually be aiding and abetting the militants?* he wondered. Deep down he knew the answer, but it appeared to be much, much bigger than him, and he decided the approach to the whole thing was to take the stand that "it was not my circus and not my monkey."

Again, his old NAC instructors, Joel and Clyde, had not covered the topic of Indian wars and village takeovers by militants, so this was a learn-as-you-go experience.

On occasion, when McWade slipped over the border to see his old friend Ron and to bring him a real McDonald's burger, he found him eating freshly barbecued venison. It seems they had become tired of eating those boring K rations and had poached a deer that had wandered too close to the action. A good gutting and a hot fire later, they were all enjoying a real cooked meal, compliments of the hunting skills of one of the agents from the Salt Lake City Division. Even a game warden from the South Dakota Game, Fish, and Parks Department dropped in for a sampling of the wild game dinner and gave his approval as "dire times call for dire actions," he mused.

A command post for the operation had been set up in Rapid City, South Dakota, at the National Guard Armory and for a period at an elementary school. A six foot six agent friend told McWade that the biggest challenge he had personally encountered in the whole

Wounded Knee matter was using the restroom at the elementary school and trying to hit the urinal designed for use by a second grader.

"That took more skill than hitting a silhouette target with a Bureau-issued four-inch Smith and Wesson .38 revolver from the fifty yard line," he quipped.

Finally, after seventy-one long and anxious days, a second cease-fire was initiated and the takeover ended. The incident was not without casualties as two AIM sympathizers were killed and a US Marshal wounded at one of the checkpoints when he reportedly did not take cover, thinking he was too far away from the village to be hit by incoming fire.

Chin was among those arrested for inciting the incident, but the federal grand jury indictment against him was dismissed due to alleged misconduct by the US Attorney's Office handling the matter. The bottom line was that good old Chin Black Heart and others at the top of the AIM hierarchy were free again. In the case of Chin, now having gained national fame, he could pursue his career as an actor or maybe even resurface somewhere to stir up some more trouble in between Hollywood movie shoots.

During the aftermath of Wounded Knee, McWade was subpoenaed to federal district court in Pierre, South Dakota, as a witness on some very minor case he had limited knowledge about. The only thing leaving a lasting impression about that case was the fact that Pierre seemed to have the notable distinction, at the time, of being the only state capital in the lower forty-eight states without a McDonald's.

Often forgotten by those telling about the long seventy-one-day takeover is the financial and emotional damage done to the owners of the Wounded Knee Trading Post. Their lives were literally turned bottom side up, and their means of livelihood were forever altered.

Long after the cease-fire, there were hundreds of cases to be worked and hopefully prosecuted. This work was to be continual, tedious, ongoing, and difficult as prosecutable pieces of complex puzzles were increasingly hard to find with every month that passed.

McWade's peaceful territory, which included all the small towns and villages in the northern panhandle of Nebraska, would never quite be the same in the wake of the invasion of federal law enforcement. Stories would be told by locals of how the local bars thrived and prospered from the free-spending agents, marshals, and others there with expense accounts and pockets full of money to be spent. It was rumored that more than one rancher's daughter lost their virtue by falling victim to the smooth-talking big-city visitors hanging out in Chadron.

Virtue and morals are one thing, but how would you explain an arrow sticking in the hood of your Bucar parked outside the Roundup Motel? Boredom and horseplay were twin sisters to such events that took place. All this thanks to Chin and his band of jolly AIMsters!

"Don't embarrass the Bureau" had been the motto of McWade since arriving at his assignment in the Scottsbluff outpost on the high plains. The foremost goal in all his liaison with local law enforcement and other folks in his RA towns had always been to enhance the reputation of the FBI. Now he conceded that his objective just might have been derailed and sent down a sidetrack for the time being. Thanks again, Chin!

As life began to settle back into the normal RA routine, he would go home, pop some popcorn, and put in the movie *Last of the Mohicans*.

He thought out loud, "If they ever update this movie, I think Chin Black Heart should have a starring role. He would be a natural for the main part."

"If integrity is the shield between greed and vanity, he (Chin) should be a shoo-in as he had none" was McWade's final thought as he dosed through the last part of the movie.

While resting, he recalled the story of a day when agents at checkpoint one again became bored with the lack of progress taking place in the standstill negotiations. One particular overly frustrated agent jumped into the trusty APC, fired up the engine, and raced at breakneck speed toward the blockaded village. The startled AIM militants looked on in horror at the oncoming machine of war, wondering just what was happening. The armored vehicle roared up to a trench, which had been dug by the oppressors to be used as a protective bunker. Directly over the top of the trench, the APC stopped, did a full 360-degree spin, and fled back up the hill to the roadblock, leaving the bunker half full of loose dirt. The onlooking agents wildly cheered the action but pledged to deny that it happened should some liberal DOJ attorney or stuffed shirt Bureau supervisor inquire.

Later, reports from the beautiful Mandy, McWade's source on the ground, was that it scared the occupants of the bunker so badly that the trench was used as a latrine from that day forward.

Nevertheless, the thoughts of Wounded Knee, the loss of life, property damage loss, money spent, and lives altered weighed upon McWade during his lonely hours spent in his Bucar. Why didn't the sanctimonious hotshots running the show just read reports and learn how things like this were handled in Nebraska? Sometimes it may not hurt to at least pay a little attention to some agent going native and perhaps prevent a shit storm like Wounded Knee.

Chapter 16

RESMURS: Horror on the Pine Ridge

When an organization has lost its shadow, they say it has no conscience and its soul lacks redeeming value. Such was the case with AIM. The shadow of this organization was being eaten away piece by piece as their leaders and criminal types were being hunted methodically, one by one, by dedicated agents on TDY and those assigned to the Rapid City RA. It was a daunting task to identify lawbreakers from the brutal takeover of Wounded Knee. Gathering information from reliable witnesses was difficult, but the work went on from the time of the cease-fire in the spring of 1973, through all of 1974, and into the first half of 1975.

During this time period, McWade had frequent contact with the agents working hundreds of cases as they continued to stay in the border towns of Nebraska surrounding the Pine Ridge. Many hours were spent in motel rooms and eating joints discussing the names, crimes committed, and necessary strategy to build prosecutable felony cases against the AIM insurgents guilty of federal crimes.

Juggling the CIR (Crime on an Indian Reservation) leads from the Wounded Knee fallout, plus the unending flow of regular cases routinely flooding the lonely RA, kept McWade on the go constantly. His old sheriff friend, Fess Benson, told him one day that he needed to slow down and breathe the fresh air. The actual words, as McWade recalled them were, "You run around any more like a fart on a skillet!"

A case came by phone late on a Friday afternoon during the fall of 1974 when the big-city-type agents were mostly all on their commute home. The Denver FBI had reason to believe that a UFAC-Murder (Unlawful Flight to Avoid Confinement) subject by the name of Freddie Conway had moved to Scottsbluff and was working at a service station on East Overland Street using an alias. Conway had escaped prison in Ohio while serving time there on a murder conviction.

FBI Denver had a photograph but no way to get it to Scottsbluff until at least Monday or Tuesday of the following week. The clerk in Denver did mention that their office had just installed some brand-new device called a fax machine, but that would require a similar FAX on the Scottsbluff end of the phone line to receive and print off the photo.

McWade's eyes lit up as he recalled that the local *Star-Herald* newspaper, where one of his kids worked as a paper carrier, had one of those newfangled machines to get news stories and photos.

A call later and a trip to the newsroom resulted in a very fuzzy shadow of a photo appearing before his very eyes of Conway. The quality of the fax was so poor there was no way to tell if the subject was black or white or from another planet. There were stringy lines running vertically through the sheet.

Now there was a choice to be made. "Should I wait for a good photo to arrive and risk Conway being tipped off and leaving town? Or should I grab some help from Action Jackson and bag this sucker now?" McWade asked himself.

An Armed and Dangerous warning in bold type at both the top and bottom of the incoming teletype describing the escapee and outlining his crime was impossible to miss.

McWade had worked on the fugitive squad in San Antonio and had been in the Omaha field office when similar arrest matters had arrived. These were the cases that were assigned to the office heavies—the guys with the deep voices, dark glasses, and reputations for kicking ass and taking names. Usually, every available agent in HQ would be summoned to the planning room where the SAC or a squad supervisor would be there to offer his *expert* advice even though they had skipped firearms and fit tests for years and were mostly clueless about these things. One SAC that McWade recalled could not even find his gun as he hadn't carried it for weeks.

But the HQ operations were executed similarly to a Barnum and Bailey circus performance complete with press releases, letters of commendation to all the assisting agents, and sizable cash awards to the case agents and especially to the SAC for his invaluable help. McWade had just returned from Omaha two weeks prior where this exact scenario happened for the arrest of some poor truck driver who had stolen a load of lettuce and abandoned his rig.

But this was an RA and McWade was trying to go native. The plan was simple and totally uncomplicated.

McWade's unmarked Ford Bucar pulled into the station as if for gas. Noting that only one person was inside and, furthermore, that he resembled the subject's description in every way, they exited the car and wandered nonchalantly into the station.

"Do you have change for the pop machine?" asked McWade.

He gave change for a five-dollar bill and stepped back away from the counter.

At that moment McWade, drew his gun and issued the order, "Freddie Conway, this is the FBI. Freeze! You are under arrest!"

It all happened so quickly that he was on the floor and in cuffs before he even thought to deny he was Conway.

The short trip to the county jail with Conway was made, and soon he on his way back to prison in Ohio that next week.

The next week brought nice telephone calls and a memo from the fugitive squad leader in Cleveland and from Denver. Nothing was ever heard from the SAC Omaha as he was too busy cashing his reward check for his great and valuable work on the arrest of the lettuce king. By now, McWade fully realized that was standard operating procedure in the Bureau, but out of sight, out of mind was still working well for him.

In the spring of 1975, McWade received a telephone call from an agent by the name of Ron Williams from the Rapid City RA, requesting help on a case from the Pine Ridge reservation.

"An eight-year-old girl was abducted in Pine Ridge over the weekend and taken to the old Travelers Hotel in Rushville, where she was brutally and repeatedly raped."

He wanted a hand with the crime scene and interviews in McWade's territory.

Within minutes, the Bucar was northbound to Rushville where McWade met with Ron, a very nice-looking, clean-cut agent.

It was determined that an Indian male, in his thirties, had abducted the little girl, brought her to the old hotel, rented a room on the third floor, and had repeatedly raped her over the weekend. The poor little girl's screams had gone unnoticed or unheeded while the pervert pedophile had his way over and over again.

The interviews were completed, and a seemingly solid case for prosecution was built. The abuse was so horrific that the poor little girl was literally ripped apart, leaving large stains of her blood, which had soaked deep into the old mattress.

The semen and bloodstained areas of the mattress were cut out and bagged as evidence to be sent to the FBI Laboratory by Ron as soon as he arrived in Rapid City.

Over the next few weeks, the case brought McWade and Ron together by phone and in person several times until a friendship had been forged. He was the kind of good-looking guy that would attract the attention of the opposite sex and was pleasant and fun to be around.

McWade never followed the outcome of the CIR-child sex abuse case as something totally unexpected and tragic happened on the ridge.

"Two FBI agents killed on the Pine Ridge Reservation in South Dakota" came the news alert on the country station. "Details to follow!"

McWade sat in stunned silence as the news began to sink into his brain. He knew a good number of the agents working the reservation and waited breathlessly for the release of their identities. From unofficial information, he quickly gleaned from other agents he learned that it was Ron Williams and another agent he had only once met by the name of Jack Coler.

Details were still limited, but reports were that they had been lured into a rather large AIM encampment, later known as the Jumping Bear Compound, in an isolated part of the Pine Ridge. This compound had been apparently unknown to them, and it turned into a massacre and execution-style murder scene by the scores of AIM militants who surrounded the helpless and outnumbered agents.

The date of June 26, 1975, would never be forgotten by McWade. As the facts rolled in daily, it was very difficult not be become very emotional, knowing that such fine and upstanding men had senselessly lost their lives. This loss had hit very close to home and was sobering beyond anything he had before anticipated.

Everyone knows that life is fleeting, but no one expects this kind of tragedy to happen to end good young lives so prematurely.

The Bureau opened a huge special task force case to resolve this and other pending AIM matters and code and named it RESMURS for "REServation MURderS."

"If ever there is anyone who deserves the death penalty, it is the heartless slime that shot and killed these two good men" became McWade's standard comment.

Within days, the hotels, motels, state park cabins, and any other place for rent were being swallowed up as agents again from all of the fifty-nine FBI field offices began arriving in western Nebraska. This time, the RESMURS Command Post was moved to the Nebraska National Guard Armory on the hill in Chadron near the Chadron State College campus.

McWade again wondered if all this would be happening if the spineless politicians and attorneys in DC would have taken a firm stand at the BIA building and incarcerated those same AIM leaders who had been allowed to leave and further their rampage.

"A higher judge will have to sort this out and answer that question," he guessed.

But for now, he was preparing for the second and even larger onslaught of the hundreds of big-city agents into his formerly peaceful prairie land empire.

Meanwhile, the names of the two brave young agents were placed on the FBI Hall of Honor at FBI Headquarters. This honor is reserved for those agents who lost their lives as a result of adversarial force.

Elsewhere, somewhere inside a cell in a US Federal Penitentiary, an AIM coward by the name of Leonard Peltier is currently serving two consecutive life sentences for first-degree murder.

McWade knew there would be calls by liberals and other bleeding heart Hollywood types for his release, but he only wished they could meet with the families and friends of the murdered victims, look into their eyes, and see the heartbreak that has been theirs to live with since that terrible day on the Pine Ridge in South Dakota.

As McWade closed his mind to the sad events of the RESMURS ordeal, he did smile at one or two sideline events not talked about by history buffs who chronicled this case.

When the word of the shooting deaths of the two agents hit the news, it seems two Bureau agents had gone AWOL for a couple days to go home to see their families. They were reportedly somewhere in the state of Wyoming when they heard. They panicked, knowing they should be there to assist. The news, through the agent underground gossip channels, was that they drove so fast for so long they burned up the engine in their Bucar trying to get back to their post. The cover-up of this was sure to have taken some ingenuity, but it never seemed to surface higher than street-agent level.

Another crazy incident that brought a wide smile to McWade's face involved a suave East Coast agent by the name of Jim (last name withheld for obvious reasons) that McWade met at the National Guard Armory in Chadron. He mentioned in casual conversation that he was paying most of his paycheck to two ex-wives back in his home state for alimony. His SAC had sent him on TDY so he could hopefully earn a little extra money on overtime and per diem to get ahead of the curve.

He was a handsome, good-looking man with an overabundance of charm, which attracted the local ladies. He apparently met a local rancher's daughter and, after two or three drinks at the bar, decided he had met soul mate number three and asked for her hand in marriage

A quick trip to the local minister and he was again happily married and enjoying all the honeymoon benefits of a newlywed lover.

When he next visited the command post, he was proudly flashing his new wedding band, much to the amazement of the other agents. The news quickly was passed on to the ASAC over the RESMURS special who called him in to the front office for a visit. His boss did not see that congratulations were in order as he had not followed any of the Bureau guidelines about name checks and backgrounds on prospective brides. In fact, the head man was pissed that he was so stupid and told him he better figure out a way to undo the mess he had gotten himself into. He was summarily dismissed and sent on his way.

Word filtered back to McWade that a call had been received by Jim from the local minister the following Monday, reporting that there was a problem. It seemed that someone, over the weekend, had gained entry into the rectory and that each and every paper, form, and document pertaining to Jim's marriage was missing and, therefore, could not be forwarded to the state of Nebraska to be officially recorded.

"You and your bride will need to come back into my office and refile all the papers," the good pastor instructed. "If you don't, it will be as if you were never married."

Jim faked a smile of concern to hide his real feeling of relief and headed for Pine Ridge to fight more crime and corruption.

Detective Vasman, the stalwart of the Chadron PD, also a graduate of the FBI National Academy (FBI-NA) was never able to solve the case of the missing marital papers, and poor Jim was once again a lonely single man. But he smiled broadly when he realized he was not paying any additional support money to a third wife in Nebraska.

Again, McWade pondered if the reputation of FBI in his RA territory would ever survive this massive agent invasion. "Don't Embarrass the Bureau" didn't seem as important to this breed of macho G-men from the big-city asphalt jungles of society as it did to the likes of McWade. They were definitely cut from a different cloth, and this was not their territory, so many seemed not that concerned about Hoover's views. After all, to many of these musketeers, J. Edgar was a fading legend and his words were, to them, no longer gospel doctrine.

Chapter 17

AIMless

As the leadership of AIM increasingly became embroiled in their own legal matters, they had to worry more about their own earthly salvation, meaning keeping out of jail and saving the money they had collected from charities. This meant they obviously had less time to devote to their specialty, which was causing chaos.

Finally, life began to return slowly to the pre-AIM norm in western Nebraska. That is not to say that things would ever be the same when handling routine leads, which involved interviewing Native Americans. Attitudes had seemingly changed in a very noticeable fashion with a definite tone of defiance.

An example of this was when McWade received a routine lead to interview the elderly distant relative of an Indian fugitive on a simple horse theft case from Pine Ridge. When McWade went to the rural address, it seemed almost abandoned other than for several old cars in various states of disrepair setting around the yard. There was no signs of life anywhere even though it was in the early afternoon.

The elderly woman answered the door and was in the process of denying any knowledge about her fugitive relatives whereabouts. Then from the living room couch came one man, and from the small kids' room came two more. Two more men, who had been sleeping in the old cars, came from behind McWade. Suddenly, it was no longer the grandmotherly lady involved, but McWade found himself completely circled by five Indian males who were demanding in an aggressive tone to know what the hell was going on and why they were being harassed.

Four of the men were bare chested, proudly displaying their jailhouse tattoos, and the circle they had formed was closing in on McWade.

"You are in Indian country now, white man!" came the familiar AIM jargon. "Nebraska was our country before you stole it, white man!" snarled another.

For the first time in his life, McWade wished he had not used so much sunscreen and maybe he could have blended in a bit better.

At this point, realizing the odds, McWade did what Custer was not smart enough to figure out and do. He planned and executed a full retreat.

As he backed out the front door, he tried to look as if he was leaving anyway and mentioned that if their horse thief cousin came around have him call the FBI.

Even the three lazy mongrel dogs in the yard seemed to snarl at him as he drove away and back to Alliance.

It was unmistakable. Even a simple nonthreatening lead involving Native Americans in Box Butte County or anywhere else in his RA territory would now be handled with an NSP, city, or county lawman backing him up.

Shortly after the horse theft matter, Ted Vasman, a good friend and now the head detective for the Chadron PD, was challenged in the street by William Walking Buffalo, wielding a bow and arrow and threatening to shoot Vasman. Ted, a handsome ex-Marine and former California Highway Patrol (ChiPs) motorcycle trooper, stood face-to-face with the militant former AIM renegade. It was a standoff much like in the movie *High Noon* with both facing each other at a distance of less than fifteen feet, looking each other squarely in the eye. With his unflinching, ever cool voice, he stated in a matter-of-fact drawl, "If you think you can get an arrow on that string and pull it back before I can draw and shoot your sorry ass, then why don't you just go for it?"

Thinking it over, Walking Buffalo slurred, "I'm letting you off the hook this time, you paleface pig, but you better watch your back!"

The once-calm atmosphere between the Native American community and law enforcement seemed now to be full of tension and added suspicion, thanks to the work of AIM. Many Indians acted more emboldened and less respectful toward the law than a few short years earlier.

In the cold of winter February 1976, the body of a young, attractive Indian female, Panda Marie Squash, was found by a local rancher along his fence line just off the road shoulder of Highway 73 on the Pine Ridge.

It seemed very routine and appeared to be just another body found decomposing on the reservation. Panda had been known to be associated closely with Chin and others in the upper echelon of AIM and was frequently seen at AIM demonstrations and protests.

Dr. P. D. Quick, a pathologist from Scottsbluff, Nebraska, had a contract at the time to conduct autopsies for the BIA on the Pine Ridge reservation. He was very efficient and was as quick as a fiddler's elbow in rendering a cause of Panda's death. "She died of exposure," stated his typed report. It was plain and simple!

With this report in hand, the verdict on this matter was case closed.

However, in the meantime, Mandy Silk Hair and the other sources were advising McWade that Panda had been ordered shot by the top hierarchy of AIM as they had falsely accused her of being an FBI snitch.

Enough testimony finally was furnished to the FBI in South Dakota to convince them that Panda Marie Squash had been executed and died by being shot in the head.

A court order was obtained and her body exhumed for a second autopsy. This time, a different pathologist was employed who, this time, did a thorough examination of the body and determined something entirely different. There was an entry wound in the back of her head, a hole as big as a chubby finger through her brain, and a projectile from a handgun lodged on the inside of her skull in the forward portion of the brain. Dr. Quick had obviously missed something rather significant in his haste.

Since Quick lived in Scottsbluff, a lead to interview him about his apparent botched exam was naturally assigned to McWade. After all, he was now the only agent assigned to the RA.

Dr. Quick appeared to be a bit defensive as McWade entered his office in the West Nebraska Regional Hospital. It was obvious he knew what the interview was about and he wanted it over.

"Your report, which I have here in my hand mentions nothing about any bullet in the brain, and furthermore you concluded that Panda Marie Squash died of exposure to the elements. In other words, in layman's language, you say she froze to death. In view of the second autopsy finding a bullet lodged in her brain and semen in her vaginal area, neither of which you mentioned, how do you explain this?" McWade asked.

Trying to save face, the good doctor explained that "the bullet weakened her body, but she did absolutely die of exposure."

He had no explanation for missing the bullet and the semen and seemed in a hurry to end the interview. He was just living up to his God-given name.

Based on his shoddy work, he was never again given an opportunity to bill the government for another $600 autopsy on the Pine Ridge. His work there was over!

Over the next thirty years, the blame game continued as to who killed Panda Marie.

AIM obviously blamed the government. Other rank and file AIM members blamed AIM leadership. Other rumors circulated that she was killed by other AIM women who thought she was being treated like a princess by leadership and were jealous.

As McWade did not work the Pine Ridge, he soon was back with his more routine cases. But that did not mean the anxiety level was any less.

The entire Omaha Division was now on red alert as the entire office was in shutdown mode, preparing for the most feared and nerve-racking, recurring ordeal in the Bureau. The Omaha Division had just been informed that their annual office inspection by the Inspection Division was quickly approaching. Preparation for the invasion of these dreaded inspectors was being anticipated, and self-preservation plans were being implemented.

McWade was again happy to be snuggled safely in the arms of his little lonely remote RA 452 miles west of the tension, anxiety, politics, and paranoia associated with this phenomenon in Omaha. He was beginning to realize, more now than ever, that he was not a people person when it came to the office politics, drama, and uneasiness surrounding the office shell games.

Chapter 18

Trauma: The Office Inspection

"**O**m-1 to Lincoln!" (Om-1 was the SAC, Omaha Division.)
"Go ahead Om-1."

"Uh, uh, Lincoln, what is my 10-20?"

Long pause on the Bucar radio as Parry, the clerk in the Lincoln RA, tries to contain his laughter and come up with some kind of response to this uninformed and juvenile clueless request.

"Boss, could you look out the window and describe what you see to help me get a fix on your 20?"

This was a true-to-life, actual radio broadcast over the Omaha FBI frequency.

Unusual?

Now here is the setting.

The Omaha Field Office is under their routine inspection by the FBI's feared Inspection Division. A team of inspector's aides, headed by an Inspector, has been in Omaha for about a week, combing through agents' case files, office statistics, communications, claimed accomplishments, and anything else that goes on in a field office. It was now time to have an Inspector's Aide visit each of the RAs in Nebraska and Iowa for one-on-one interviews with each agent.

The SAC OM-1 is driving his Bucar to Lincoln on I-80 with an aide in the passenger seat. He has made the fifty-mile trip to Lincoln hundreds of times but, trying to impress the inspector, asks the impossible question.

Poor Parry told him just to follow the highway signs to Lincoln and tried to contain his amusement. The guy in the passenger seat just rolled his eyes. Again the Peter Principle was alive and working in Omaha. This man had clearly been promoted to his own level of complete incompetence.

McWade's first experience with an office inspection was when he had only been in Scottsbluff a few weeks. Actually, he was completely bulletproof and safe as he had not been there long enough to screw up and, therefore, had nothing to fear.

But the senior RA (SRA), Bob Frinsey, was a bundle of nerves. McWade and old Frinsey were to meet the inspector's aide at the Scottsbluff airport at 6:00 PM, or so they thought. Frinsey had forgotten to factor in the one-hour time change, and they met one very unhappy, disgruntled inspector pacing the floor of the small airport when they pulled up. Not a good way to start, and poor Frinsey was now shaking as if he was clinging to a ninety-pound jackhammer breaking up concrete.

The fact that agents tended to have high blood pressure was now starting to be understood by young McWade. There was apparently a good reason for required annual physical exams. Stress kills, and these inspections seemed to up the stress to the fight or flight level. Now this was a dangerous situation as once a person gets to that stage, their measured IQ drops as much as twenty points, increasing the chance of screwing up even more causing even more stress.

The unwritten rule, learned from day one in the field, was that an agent never tells an inspector there is a problem. If you say there is, then you actually will have a much more serious problem and will always regret not just answering with yes or no and volunteering absolutely nothing.

"These guys are not your friends and do not trust them!" This was pounded into the head of almost every agent.

McWade's favorite description of the inspection staff is comparing them to the scene in the movie *Planet of the Apes* where the apes are riding horses and chasing the humans through fields, lopping off the heads of those helpless beings they can catch.

Inspection staff horror stories had been told since the first week in NAC 8 and were added to annually.

One favorite story concerned an SAC in one of the FBI field offices in the Rocky Mountain region who had a girlfriend. The SAC would allegedly leave at a given time every day and meet the fair maiden in an apartment a few blocks from the office where he would do whatever SAC's do when they meet lovers for a midmorning rendezvous.

Several agents were aware of this hanky-panky and started following him and noting times, dates, places, photos, etc.

Finally, one brave agent could tolerate this fraud no more and sent an anonymous letter to the Inspection Staff in Washington.

The inspectors descended like locusts on the field office. But amazingly enough, the main thrust of the investigation was who sent the unsigned letter rather than if the allegation was true. From sources at the Bureau, McWade even heard the letter had been processed for fingerprints to try to identify the author. But most agents are not stupid, and wearing rubber gloves when handling anonymous letters would be a given.

Eventually, the letter writer was identified and punished for not minding his own business and opening an unauthorized case on one of the FBI's royally knighted SACs.

The SAC was also punished as he was caught in the act (actually he was caught in the sack) of falsifying his Number #3 locator card and putting down a falsified address as to where he was headed when he left the office. It was his claim that he was attempting to develop the woman he was caught with as an informant and was conducting some deeply penetrating interviews.

Lying to an inspector was reason for termination unless you were in the management program, and then apparently it was more or less expected and sometimes rewarded.

This protective attitude of management originated from Director Hoover. Since he, Hoover, personally chose each and every SAC and since he, Hoover, considered himself infallible, much like the Pope, any screwup by an SAC would be looked at as if Hoover had made a mistake choosing him in the first place. This just could not happen, and therefore, SACs did not make mistakes, they did not cheat on their wives, they did not have alcohol problems, they did not misuse Bucars, and they were pretty much perfect in every way. Thus, the narrative lived on, and the inspection staff, all in line someday to hopefully become SACs themselves, played the game to perfection.

So again, the answers to the questions asked by the inspectors aides during the one-on-one interviews were "Yes, sir!" "No, sir!" "Everything is great, sir!" "No suggestions whatsoever, sir!" "I love it here!" "My management is great, sir!" "I'm not aware of any problems or improprieties whatsoever, sir!"

And so went the interviews with the inspectors. And guess what? No letters of censure, no derogatory findings, and no ugly cases opened against the boss you would have to live with daily after the inspectors turned tail and left.

As old Tom Crabford had told him so many years ago, "the secret to a happy life in the Bureau is to ride the waves, don't rock the boat, stay off the radar screen, and put in your twenty." It seemed to be working well so far.

The Bureau had devised an incentive plan for its managers much like other government agencies. This plan did more to broaden the divide between agents and managers than anything else they could possibly have drawn up if that was, in fact, their purpose.

The government placed money in a large pool to be divided among the Bureau's elite management staff according to the accomplishments. The more accomplishments reported, the larger the piece of the money pie that SAC or other supervisor was awarded. But guess who generates the stats? If you guessed the agents working under these leaders, you were on target.

How does a supervisor get a larger piece of the pie? Right again. "More stats!" How does he get more stats? Simple. "Make his agents work harder, longer and be more productive."

One of McWade's SAC's received a nice $20,000 yearly bonus as his piece of the management money pie after a rather productive year by the Omaha Division. He was so appreciative of his agents' work that he even allowed McWade to buy his own diet Pepsi when they went to the coffee shop while on tour to Scottsbluff the week after getting the bonus.

Hence, McWade had another sign made up and mounted on the wall of his rural one-man office that stated, "The floggings will continue until the morale around here improves!" Working cases in a small town can touch lives and create situations different than in the bigger offices where the agents are not public figures known by so many.

This was the case when McWade's junior high son came home from school one day and said, "Dad, my friend JJ says you are trying to put his dad in jail for gambling. Is that right?"

As a matter of fact, JJ's dad was the subject of an ITAR-Gambling (Interstate Transportation in Aid to Racketeering-Gambling) case, but this could not be discussed with family. So JJ, who happened to be a great kid, continued to hang around as the friend of Shirls right up until his dad was indicted and convicted. These are strange situations spawned by the small-town assignment.

McWade knew there were *givers* and *takers* in the FBI just like in society in general. But somehow, this saying seemed to be twisted as one of his supervisors told McWade that "it was much easier for him to cause stress than to learn to deal with it." McWade turned to him and told him to his face, "You seem to be good at achieving your goal."

Most street agents were observed to be givers (producers) and were good quality men and women.

As the office inspections would come and go, annually and then later they occurred every other year, life continued and lessons were learned. These visits were necessary blips on the radar screen of life in the RA and soon to be taken in stride. The lesson learned from his old mentor in San Antonio so many years ago about carrying a clipboard or a folder and walking as if in deep thought or in a hurry seemed to work well in headquarters and during those dreaded visits. It also helped to have sufficient stats and assigned cases in relatively good order.

Doing those things seemed to keep the apes on the horses from getting close enough to lop off your head.

Chapter 19

The Head Hunter: A Journey to the Dark Side

The office inspections became routine and no longer feared by the lone agent in Scottsbluff. More than one SAC had told him, after driving the 452 miles from Omaha, that it was a god-forsaken assignment and insinuated that it would be hard to get a replacement. So why would he fear an inspection? The only thing they could threaten him with was a transfer, and they, in their lack of understanding, had taken that bargaining chip off the table.

Management in the Bureau looked at RAs in general, and small ones in particular, as *necessary evils*. They were necessary because that was where so many statistics came from to make them look good. The evil part was mostly the perception that the resident agents were out of their daily visual contact. "If we can't see them out the corner of our eye, then how can we micromanage them?" was the question that was talked about in their conferences. "And they must be screwing off most of the time" was the other comment tossed around their conference tables.

In reality, as pointed out earlier, McWade loved the one-man assignment in the panhandle. The people were great and his law enforcement friends were totally helpful and fun to work with. The resident agents in North Platte and Grand Island, even though 175 and 300 miles away respectively, were there to lean on and were helpful when necessary. They all became great friends, and their comradery was enviable.

There were times after the decline of AIM, the worry was that there might not be enough work to justify an office. Then within the blink of an eye, this would change and the cases would flow in so fast that it was as if McWade was trying to drink water from a fire hydrant.

Let's just say he loved the Bureau from afar and enjoyed life to the fullest. Negative thoughts about management were quite normal, and as he went on, he realized these were the same concerns most people have. Whether it be work, church, clubs, or any other group involving people, the same concerns about out-of-touch managers seem to persist. Soon, it was smile, say "Yes, boss," and then disappear and do the work the way it should be done. He learned to expect nothing and was usually right on target.

The ship was stable and life was good. Then the blasted phone rang.

"McWade," came the voice of his Omaha ASAC, "how would you like to go to the Behavioral Science Unit (BSU) at Quantico to become a Criminal Profile Coordinator (CPC) for the state of Nebraska?" Things were a bit slow that week so the answer was, "Sure, why not?"

He had always had a fascination with profiling, and now the opportunity to study under the world's finest in this new burgeoning field was exciting. Three in-service classes lasting two weeks each, seemed manageable, so soon he was on the plane heading east for the first scheduled session at the Xerox Center in Leesburg, Virginia.

A virtual smorgasbord of the world's most celebrated experts in the art of behavioral science were paraded before the small class of agents selected from their respective field offices to be trained. McWade sat at attention and absorbed the new information like a dry sponge in a bathtub.

Authors, university professors, and, of course, the BSU experts in the various fields of their own expertise came in a seemingly endless stream. *Where else could a person learn so much from the masters in their fields?* he thought. Processing simulated crime scenarios, reviewing photos, and studying police reports and a myriad of other evidence in attempts to reconstruct the crime was a daily activity.

Then using known behavioral patterns associated with various types of people, attempts were made to draw up profiles of the person who committed the crime. Hopefully, the field could be reduced significantly to show that the likely offender fit a certain race, sex, or economic subgroup. The overall study of the victim, crime scene, and evidence could possibly determine if the person was an organized or an unorganized type, which also helped tell a lot about the subject, his personality, and his social type.

All this reinforced something McWade already firmly believed: "There sometimes is nothing creepier than the truth!"

Roy Cottonwood quickly became McWade's favorite instructor and could hold the class spellbound with his lectures on sex crimes. It was from his lectures and photos the class learned of the term autoerotic deaths and how they could be differentiated from suicides. He explained that many insurance companies had been calling autoerotic deaths suicides and thus avoiding having to pay the beneficiaries. In fact, an autoerotic death is an accident and could even kick in a double indemnity payment, depending on the policy.

Cottonwood was the world's best in this field and had even written books on the subject. A typical autoerotic death could be as simple as someone arranging to hang themselves with a rope or ligature. He would allow the rope to tighten around his neck until the last instant before losing consciousness. At that last second, he would cut the rope and allow the blood to rush back into his brain, causing a euphoric thrill, resulting in an orgasm and ejaculation. However, if his plan went awry and he didn't cut himself down in time, these became accidental deaths and not suicides as frequently reported by authorities.

When dealing with crime scenes, part of the technique taught was that of being able to isolate your feelings and normal thought process about the crime, the victim, and the criminal. All this must be done to allow yourself to be able to think like the criminal thinks.

This was all beginning to feel like a very real journey into a dark world of criminal and sexual deviance. Trying to wrap your own mind around the fact that so many folks with such deviant thought processes walked among the general population was difficult but quite necessary to accomplish the desired goal.

New words were added to McWade's vocabulary at a lightning pace—words like *paraphilia, preferential rape, pederast, necrophilia,* to name but a very few.

Each new word came with a story, it seemed. An example was *necrophilia,* which meant "having sex with a dead corpse." One agent in the class relayed that he had worked as an assistant mortician during his college years and that he had caught the mortician doing just that.

It was explained that such behavior would fit the norm. A pedophile normally seeks employment or volunteers in work that would put him in contact with his targeted field of victim, such as scoutmaster, schoolteacher, bishop or clergy, etc. A necrophiliac would normally seek the field of a mortician and so forth.

The old saying "Fiction is truth until real truth (or more fiction) comes along" was taking on more meaning.

You name the abnormal conduct and another member of the BSU staff would step to the front of the classroom and bring expertise to the subject.

Multiple personalities? Who better to address that topic than the author of *Three Faces of Eve* who enlightened the wide-eyed agents.

The anatomy of the sex act was explored in detail (touch, sight, taste, smell, and hearing) was thoroughly explored in light of the understanding that the actual sex act was, in fact, a sensory act and part of a sensory experience rather than purely physical.

The possible early indicators or predictors of future criminal behavior in later life were also explored as follows:

1. Bed-wetting after the age of six years
2. Cruelty to animals
3. Fascination, well beyond normal, with fire and the setting of fires

McWade wondered what chance of staying out of prison some poor kid would have who was into the torture of cats in front of a fire he had just started right after wetting the bed. That would be known as the perfect classic triad of predicting criminal behavior.

Before leaving the third two week in-service session, Roy Cottonwood pulled McWade aside and wanted him to submit a full report on a very unusual case he told Cottonwood about from the Scottsbluff RA. Roy said, "I thought I had seen every type of auto-erotic death case there was to see, but yours is unusual enough I want to add it to my next book on that subject." The case went as follows:

A young man from western Nebraska had just finished serving in the US military at a radar tracking station in the South Pacific. He claimed he had some expertise on the tracking of enemy ships and aircraft in the area and, when mustering out, had smuggled some documents he thought to be of importance to some foreign government.

On his way to his home in Nebraska, he contacted the embassy of a foreign country and tried to make an appointment to sell them the stolen documents. So our want-to-be-spy tried to contact a certain cold war enemy by phone, which was an amateur move on his part. Before long, he and his briefcase full of documents were in a West Coast FBI office where he was being debriefed on his attempted potentially treasonous act. How was he to know that he had called the FBI into the matter?

It was determined that his stolen papers were not that great and that a good check of documents in a public library could have given the same results.

When our James Bond arrived back in Nebraska, McWade was called into the matter to talk to both he and his father to explain the facts of life to him about how he was being let off the hook this time but to cease and desist his life of wanting to be a double agent. He promised to live a normal life and stated he would rededicate himself to a life of patriotism.

Our budding Bond soon grew tired of Nebraska and moved on to the state of Georgia, in the land of Dixie, where he settled down to a not-so-routine life. There he soon found a good-looking Southern belle, as do all spies, and quickly fell madly in love with the lass. He apparently wanted desperately to impress this young sweet thing and told her that he was being followed by Russian KGB agents. When she scoffed at the idea, he decided to make his story more believable by shooting himself in the buttocks and claiming the Russians had done it. So far, his warped plan was working, or so he thought.

When he shot himself, however, instead of it being a minor wound in the fleshy part of the butt, as he had planned, he ended up hitting a major nerve and became paralyzed from the waist down. The cops soon proved his wound was not by the KGB but rather was self-inflicted. Soon he was back in Nebraska, dejected, depressed, and without his impressionable southern girlfriend. Besides all that, he was confined to a wheelchair and bed for the rest of his life.

His family could not handle him and soon he was moved to a single room of an old hotel right next to the FBI RA.

One day, the landlord came to his room, found him unresponsive, and called the PD. The responding officers found him to be quite dead surrounded by a set of very unusual circumstances.

As McWade assisted the PD on the matter, it was soon determined to be an autoerotic death of a most unusual nature.

Bond, being mechanically inclined, had built a triangular metal derrick-like structure, allowing him to lie in bed with the device over his pelvic area. He had a pendulum attached to the tripod which would swing back and forth, making contact with an electrode. A direct current transformer was his power source, and each time the swinging pendulum made contact with the electrode, it sent a surge of electric current through a set of wires. These wires were attached to a probe, which was inserted into his penis and to two clips that were attached to his breast nipples. The recurring surges of current would apparently give him a sexual charge, resulting in an anticipated arousal and orgasm.

He had not made contingency plans for the tripod tipping over, which caused a continual current to pass through his three contact points, slowly electrocuting him.

His body was found in that condition surrounded by a goodly supply of porn magazines. His days as a double agent had ended without glamour in a small, dusty two-story low-rent hotel room. An autoerotic death! An obvious accident!

The whole experience at the BSU was unlike any other. McWade felt he had been exposed to behaviors, lifestyles, fetishes, fixations, obsessions, manias, fascinations, fantasies, fads, hang-ups, compulsions, and disorders of which most of society was unaware. But when this evil rears its ugly head and is acted upon, innocent people are harmed, raped, tortured, or put to death. When this happens, the knowledge of the dark side may well be the best tool law enforcement has to identify and prosecute these demons masquerading as people.

Returning to Nebraska, McWade was now fully qualified as the "Criminal Profile Coordinator" for that state. As such, he helped and assisted local law enforcement agencies throughout the entire state properly prepare, package, and submit evidence, including police investigative reports, crime scene photos, and other necessary items to the BSU for analysis to enable a profile report to be made. In other words, he was the qualified liaison between local departments and the BSU.

Realizing that most of the time spent at the BSU was dealing with mind games and the study of the criminal mind, it was understandable that, gradually, McWade would find himself silently doing his own profile of people he met and with whom he visited. Sometimes this quiet game was quite enjoyable.

The words of advice by Cottonwood would echo in his mind at times: "You have to be able to turn your emotions on and off at will in order to cope with this kind of job. Because of the sensitivity of the job, we have to learn how to fake our emotions. Never go home at night and make your family any less happy than they were. Try to make them even happier."

Trying to show how everyone looks at things differently and that everything is a matter of individual perception, Cottonwood added the following, "Remember, guys, crowded elevators smell different to very short people!"

The time at BSU had been life changing. How would he ever have known that a man (or woman) rubbing against a woman (or man) in a crowded elevator, bus, or subway to get his sexual gratification was a fetish known as practicing frottage?

So many things learned! Things such as to ignore facts does not change them.

He had accepted so many facts as truth beyond a shadow of a doubt. *But then do doubts actually have shadows?* he wondered. How would he actually know for sure in this life?

However, "The Evil men do" was starting to sink in more now than ever before.

Also in passing, as he reflected back to the auto erotic death with the transformer gone bad, he wondered if that was like his own mom had said, being tickled to death.

Chapter 20

Fraud in the Heartland

"Look at this! I can get 20 percent interest on my savings, plus a free toaster, for opening a new account at the Platte Valley Federal Savings and Loan (S and L)." This was a typical conversation around the dinner table of many city dwellers across the Nebraska panhandle, including at McWade's.

"How the hell do they expect us to make it? The bank has upped interest rates to 24 percent on our farm-operating loan for next year. With the price of cattle, beans, sugar beets, and corn in the tank, we are one step away from bankruptcy." This was a common discussion around the dinner table of farmers and ranchers in the same area.

"Sorry, sir, the math just isn't there." This was the all-too-frequent response to the farmer's loan request by the bank loan officer after reviewing his loan application, financial statements, and projections. The farmer and his wife would leave the office depressed and with the wife usually in tears. Suicides were becoming more common.

The family farm was under attack. Desperate times call for desperate actions, and soon the phone at the Scottsbluff RA was ringing off the hook.

In a last-ditch effort to get the cash needed to survive, many had fallen victim to the ruthless and heartless schemes of those promising abundant money at a much lower rate than the local lenders, who had turned a blind eye to their loan requests. Each fraudulent scenario seemed to have the same familiar theme: (1) We have money to lend you from some Mideastern oil prince or some other made-up source to fit the current news cycle; (2) You need to fill out the forms and submit them, along with an advance or processing fee. This was usually a percentage of the actual loan being requested. Rarely was it under $10,000; (3) The money was never delivered; (4) Promises and excuses of all types were made for the never-ending delays. These stall tactics gave the criminal time to hook other victims until, finally, one day, he closed up shop and the phone line went dead.

It was at this point they would make the frantic call to the FBI.

Another frequent storyline was when McWade already was working a case under the Fraud By Wire (FBW) statute, and the name of the farmer/rancher came up as a victim. Perhaps his name surfaced as a result of documents obtained in a search warrant in another state or division.

When this happened, the desperate victim would refuse to believe he had been duped and McWade would have to set him down and plainly explain the facts of life. There were times the victim would have already received a telephone call from the fraudster, telling them that the FBI had been seizing their records and not to cooperate as this would make it so they could not get the promised money.

In these cases, often the biggest part of the interview was to convince the farmer that he had been screwed out of his $10,000 and that the FBI was not the villain.

If the farmer had a loan on the land itself, this could compound his dilemma and bring the financial grim reaper literally to his back door in the form of a foreclosure.

Fighting cowboy and Indian wars with the likes of AIM was one thing, but setting in the humble living room of a third-generation sixty-year-old farmer was quite another.

"My wife sold her wedding ring and heirloom silverware to get money to process our loan. That, along with the cash value of our surrendered life insurance policy, made the $20,000 we sent the guy," the farmer said, trying to choke back tears.

"We have absolutely nothing left now. How do you start over at our age?" his wife wept, wiping her eyes with a tissue.

"Damn those bloodsucking bastards!" was the only thought in McWade's head as he watched helplessly. He knew that even if there was prosecution and restitution ordered by the court the chance that any of the $20,000 would be seen by the farmer was nonexistent.

Three weeks later, the name of the farmer showed up in the obituary section of the local *Star-Herald*. "He died at home" was the only listed explanation.

He was obviously just another victim of the farm recession sweeping rural America at that time. But to McWade, this poor man was more than a statistical victim of failed policies. The image of his sad and desperate eyes and his sun-wrinkled, dejected face would be a lifelong haunting memory. Yet McWade knew this was not an isolated situation, and his feelings waffled between anger and sadness.

The words of Roy Cottonwood at the BSU now had a little more meaning: "You have to learn how to turn your emotions on and off in order to cope with this kind of job."

During a severe financial recession, the one institution many people look to is the local bank. After all, in most cases, they are the ones with the thing everyone needs more of—money.

Robbers try to rob the bank in a variety of ways. Burglars attack the bank in off-hours, employees get good at coming up with embezzlement schemes, bank officers go to jail when caught in various fraud schemes, and, of course, customers seeking loans falsify financial statements to make them look more like wish lists instead of their verifiable collateral. All these assaults on the federally insured funds usually resulted in another case being added to the already overly generous caseload assigned to the lone agent manning the RA.

It was a crazy world out there as farmers would claim equipment belonging to neighbors on their financial statements. When the bank officers would come to the farm to verify the items, the farmer would "borrow" them from the neighbor, enabling the inventory to match the statement. Oftentimes, cattle not belonging to the rancher was shown as his own. There were also times when the bank officer sent to verify the inventory conveniently miscounted or looked the other way for some kind of favor.

"You can buy anything in this world with money." The love of it seemed to be the catalyst that created the bulk of the work that kept McWade crisscrossing the lonely roads of panhandle wearing out a new Bucar every two years.

Spawned by the same need for farm capital came the theft of very expensive farm equipment. Everyone seemed to love the color of John Deere green, and the company had produced a model that made farmers fall in love with it at first sight. In the early 1980s, the big 8850 diesel four-wheel drive tractor was a monster boasting a 955-cubic-inch V8 which cranked out 370 horsepower. This pride of Illinois also had a healthy price tag of over $120,000, reflecting just how proud the company was of this powerhouse.

One brisk morning in Oshkosh, Nebraska, it was noted that one of these big boys had disappeared during the night as if by magic. Over the next few months, the same dealership reported the theft of a large John Deere grain combine valued in excess of $100,000. By now the Garden County Sheriff was asking for help as it was strongly suspected they had crossed state lines and were being housed in another state.

Within the next month, if that wasn't enough, the very same dealership took delivery of a new Lockwood center pivot sprinkler system worth in excess of $100,000 only to find it missing from the backyard before it was even assembled.

With no leads to follow up on at this time, McWade sent out a communication to the surrounding FBI field offices to be on the lookout for the equipment and opened a routine ITSP case (Interstate Transportation of Stolen Property).

During the same time period, a couple of rednecks from Kinnear, Wyoming, located near the farming area known as Ocean Lake, were arrested in Bridgeport, Nebraska, with some small-time stolen farm implements in their possession. McWade had them prosecuted, but they were as dense as a sack of rocks and claimed to know nothing about the Oshkosh thefts.

They reminded McWade of a saying he had once heard from an old preacher, "And they dwindled in dumb belief!" These two seemed too mentally challenged to be involved in the big thefts anyway.

Just when the case was to be put out to pasture, a rancher called from east of Casper, Wyoming. "I hired a young kid on my ranch from Ocean Lake whose dad is a hired man on a big farm over there. This kid is bragging about a big 8850 Deere that will kick butt and take names. He says his dad operates the farm for the owners."

Bingo!

Many interviews later and a three-hundred-mile trip to Ocean Lake resulted in the recovery of all the Oshkosh items, plus a truck-load of other stolen items. The whole farm was being operated with stolen implements.

The owners of the new farm turned out to be a doctor and a dentist from Casper. The doctor purchased the land as his part of the agreement, and the dentist agreed to furnish the equipment for the operation. It was like trying to pull teeth to get any straight answers out of the dentist, who claimed he had paid for them with cash from an unknown stranger at a rest stop. No bills of sale or receipts were exchanged.

Eventually, the AUSA in Wyoming declined prosecution on the matter, saying it lacked prosecutive merit. It was hard to miss the brand-new dentures he was sporting.

Oh, did I also mention that our friendly dentist/farmer from Casper had previously lived and worked several years in Oshkosh, Nebraska, and knew the area well? While honest established farmers were struggling and many were losing their farms, this enterprising guy thought he had figured out a way to steal his way into farming.

Tough times call for innovative farming. Such was the case with one poor man from Sidney, Nebraska, who sent several thousand dollars of his hard-earned money to a flimflam shyster in Oregon for a franchise in a worm farm.

During World War II, the US Army built hundreds of rein-forced underground concrete storage bunkers and covered them with dirt. These were part of the Sioux Ordinance Depot on the northern edge of Sidney. The purpose for these bunkers, used to store ammunition and military hardware, being in western Nebraska, was to make them harder for Japanese planes to strike in case of an attack, plus they were extremely hard to spot from the air looking more like mounds.

These old bunkers were now being used by farmers and others for storage. Our potential worm farmer had rented one and spent thousands making worm beds, complete with warming devices, lamps, lights, and moisture control equipment. He opened his new business, Wonderful Worms Inc., and waited for the overly priced equipment to arrive. The starter worms came, and with proper feeding, they grew and grew until it was time to harvest them.

By now, the con artist was long gone and there was no market, as promised, for his tons of worms. It seemed the taste buds of the American people did not prefer worm protein over beef just yet as promised. And McDonald's and other national chains were not switching to earthworm burgers as he had been led to believe. His entire investment was lost. Now multiply this one farmer by several others sucked into the scam and it was no small matter.

"I feel so violated," the man said. "My wife and I are so destitute now we may have to develop a taste for worm burgers and worm soup as we have nothing else."

Meanwhile, just down I-80 from Sidney, Truman Pacman, the president of a small-town bank, reported he was getting letters demanding that he place $50,000 under a culvert on State Highway 71 in a remote area near the Colorado state line. The letters were threatening the banker and his family with great bodily harm if the demand money was not obtained and delivered.

McWade investigated and soon determined, in his own mind, that the letters were prepared by the banker himself. The letters were furnished for examination at the lab and also to a non-Bureau linguistics expert McWade had met while at the BSU.

The report from the Identification Division was negative for prints, but the report from the linguistics expert was a gem dandy. It described the bank president in very minute detail—his age, his race, which section of the country in which he was raised, his education level, his marital and family status, and more.

Truman was curious about the linguistics report and requested permission to see what it said. Since the case was going nowhere anyway and since McWade wanted to get on to more productive work, permission was granted for him to hear the report as it was read aloud.

The scene in Pacman's office was truly priceless. As the letter was slowly read, the color drained from his face. As the report continued to describe him in detail, his lips and throat got so dry he had difficulty speaking. Then little beads of perspiration appeared on his forehead. Now he was in his classic flight mode as his IQ appeared to drop at least twenty points, and he mumbled incoherently about the fact that he really didn't think there would be any more letters anyway. He still maintained that he did not write them but just had a gut feeling the matter was over.

The case was closed administratively, and McWade was, along with Truman, quite sure the mysterious letter writer would never strike again demanding money from the bank. This proved to be true, and once again the tools of linguistic profiling seemed helpful.

As for Truman, the words of Ben Franklin seemed to fit him like a too small Speedo at the beach: "We are all born ignorant, but one must work hard to remain stupid."

About this time period, the craze of the ugly little creatures called Cabbage Patch Dolls swept the nation. "So ugly they were kind of cute" was the way some described them. They were made of fabric and came with the doll's official name on a birth certificate, plus a healthy price tag.

Soon counterfeit dolls were being offered, and the newspapers were going a bit crazy over this story. "Good grief, Charlie Brown!" mumbled McWade when his first Cabbage Patch case was assigned. "Hoover, even though an avid gambler at the track, would never have bet on any horse named Cabbage Patch." And now the FBI is working cases on dolls.

Before the doll counterfeit cases were history, McWade was also being assigned cases involving Girl Scout Cookies. These were driven by the national news media and involved complaints of someone putting needles in the cookies or otherwise tampering with them. After scores of copycat leads were chased down and proven to be a hoax, such as some twelve-year-old kid in the family screwing around with the cookies his mother had bought from the Girls Scout next door, these cases also became part of yesterday's news cycle.

But then how could any local, small-town agent solve cookie and doll cases when they couldn't even solve the mystery of thirteen scrawny buffaloes slaughtered at a meatpacking plant in Gordon, Nebraska. These small critters suddenly, as if by magic, turned into forty-nine thousand pounds of high-priced buffalo meat to be sold to tourists traveling to Yellowstone National Park in Wyoming. Unconfirmed sources claimed that after the government inspectors would leave at night, some almost-worthless, tough, old bull meat was labeled Buffalo and sold at a premium price.

The buffalo meat case was never solved, but the owner of the plant did serve jail time on another unrelated matter for allegedly selling contaminated adulterated meat from already dead and diseased cattle to the government for use in school hot-lunch programs. The processing plant involved in this was also located in western Nebraska and the criminal investigators from the US Department of Agriculture seemed to frown on that sort of thing.

By the end of the 1980s, Scottsbluff was one of the very few one-man offices still being operated in the FBI, and soon the Bureau map of field offices and resident agencies would fail to reflect that it ever existed. It was a sign of the times as working alone in a changing world of crime was proving to be too dangerous.

Soon gone would be the times when the agent of a foreign government would be followed by a lone FBI agent.

McWade's predecessor told of following a spy across the heartland for several days to make sure he was going where his filed papers with the State Department said he intended to go. After a couple days of following the foreigner, Frinsey knocked on his door and asked him if he would just pound on the wall of their adjoining rooms in the morning a half hour before he planned to leave so Frinsey didn't have to lie awake listening. He also gave the foreign spy some suggestions as to where to eat in the small towns, noting that he was eating in dives that were not that good.

The knock on the wall came at 7:30 AM, and the surveillance over the next two days went without a hitch.

Part of McWade died when the doors of Scottsbluff RA were closed. For over twenty years, he had been the eyes, ears, hands, and feet of the FBI in that panhandle territory, and now all that he was taking with him was the sign from the door which stated Federal Bureau of Investigation, Scottsbluff Resident Agency. In addition to the sign, he would also leave with a lifetime of memories too numerous to mention.

Going native had its downside. How do you ever leave the best friends a man could possibly ever have behind? Where could you ever work for the FBI where the guys you work with are your best friends? Where do you ever get assigned where your best running buddy is also one of your snitches? Where do you live where your money could go further and your kids could play safely in the canyons and ravines without fear?

While in Nebraska, he had been converted and was baptized into a new religion. No, this was not just joining a new tribe such as "the International House of Handshakes." He was now a bona fide Cornhusker. He would bear testimony to this new religion every Saturday during the fall football season and was proud to be part of the Husker Nation.

He would soon start his very own Idahoans for Nebraska as he was headed off to his new assignment in Idaho Falls with Go Big Red decals in his car window.

This sign was once proudly displayed on the door of the
Scottsbluff, Ne RA. The wall hanging came to symbolize
McWade's experience in dealing with most people

Chapter 21

Some Cases Just Stink

I daho Falls is a beautiful city in the Upper Snake River Valley less than a two hour drive from West Yellowstone, Montana, and Jackson, Wyoming. The FBI operated a small two-man RA there to cover the cases drifting in from the rural counties surrounding the city previously known as Taylor's Crossing and then Eagle Rock.

Since he was not yet even unpacked when the phone rang with the first problem to solve, McWade visually thought of a sign that he had displayed in his Scottsbluff office just out of public view. It was a picture of the cartoon character Sylvester Pussycat with a very stupid irritated look on his face and an outstretched hand with a pointing finger. The caption above the figure showed Sylvester saying. "Would you be very upset if I asked you to take your silly ass problem down the hall?"

But he answered the ringing device despite his temptation to ignore its irritating sound.

"Is this the FBI?" came the matter-of-fact voice. "This is Detective Scott Free of the Idaho Falls PD, and we need a little help on a break-in and attempted burglary at the credit union on South Boulevard."

Soon McWade was playing crime scene investigator with Free as they gazed at a rather large toolbox left behind by the burglars when they were obviously frightened off by officers who responded to the activated alarm.

With a thoughtful Sherlock Holmes look on his face, he uttered a prophetic statement that ended up solving not only the credit union matter but also several other burglaries around Eastern Idaho over the past six months.

"This toolbox smells like cow shit!"

It wasn't BSU or any FBI training here, and this was not rocket science. You see, McWade had been raised on a small farm with dairy cows and had been on the Future Farmers of America (FFA) dairy judging team in his high school days. He had actually competed in district finals against Napoleon Dynamite and his buddy Pedro. That smell was both unmistakable and unforgettable!

"We need to be looking for a couple locals who work at a dairy!" he proclaimed.

Some great police surveillance work at 3:00 AM had noted and made record of a rather old Chevy pickup truck from a dairy in neighboring Bingham County near Blackfoot. The faded decal on the side door of the old truck read Reeking River Farms Inc.

"Now this looks like a great lead!" McWade stated as he and Free hit the road south looking for Reeking River Farms.

The owner of the dairy farm identified the employee who milked the cows and drove the old truck. The cow hand was not at home, but his attractive thirty-year-old wife dropped the dime on him in a heartbeat, stating that he had not arrived home the night before until 6:00 AM and that she suspected that he had been up to no good. She seemed to act relieved when she found out about the credit union as she admitted her thinking was more along the lines of an extracurricular action in another woman's bedroom.

Earl, the young cow-milking farmhand, was easy to find and, within minutes, was not only confessing but also giving up the name of his buddy in crime, Troy. His confession rolled off his lips as if he was confessing to his local Mormon bishop and that if he left out any details it would just not be right with God.

He told how they had gained entry into the credit union with a pry bar but soon realized they had set off an alarm. The police arrived while they both hid in a basement storage room after pulling some boxes over the opening, leading to their secret hiding spot.

For the next two hours, they hid and listened as the police searched above them. They could hear the cops talking and when the police dog paused, sniffed, and then pawed at the carpet on the floor directly above them. "I thought sure we were toast when the dog hit on us. But the handler thought he was smarter than his dog and pulled the animal back," Earl gushed.

After an hour or so, they felt the coast was clear but set off the alarm again as they exited the door. "We just got the hell out of there as fast as we could, jumped in our truck, and got out of Dodge, leaving our toolbox behind."

Even though they got no money, it was still a break-in and attempted burglary. Before the young men were through confessing and asking for forgiveness, they had admitted to fifteen additional unsolved burglaries in warehouses, grain elevators, and other businesses in a four county area.

After charting their activities on a spreadsheet, it appeared these two amateurs were putting in more hours at night than on their day jobs milking cows. "No wonder Earl's wife suspected him of an affair," McWade chuckled.

Their wish for a little time to relax was granted by the federal judge in Pocatello, who made the following statement to their parents after sentencing them each to a year in jail and restitution: "By Idaho standards, I guess you have done reasonably well raising your kids. But this behavior must stop!"

By Idaho standards! Just what was meant by that made McWade smile. It reminded him of his own mother's favorite saying every time he did sometime wrong.

"What will people think?" He never did find out who the *people* were that she was so concerned about, and as he got older, he tried to care less what they thought as he noticed most were too worried about what people seemed to think about them to really care.

His new supervisor in Boise, M. T. McMillon, was impressed about the new guy in Idaho solving a case the first week and, as a reward, issued him a newfangled thing called a cell phone. The new device was called a brick phone as it was the size of and looked like a brick with a stubby antenna sticking out one end. This new phone meant the end of an era for McWade. From this point on, the Bureau leash hooked to the collar around his neck just got much shorter. He was starting to wonder about some of the new technology and the impact it would have on the freedom he had learned to relish in Nebraska.

He was still wondering what the good judge meant by Idaho standards when his new brick phone rang.

"Pack your bags, buddy! You will be calling Deer Lodge, Montana, your home for the next few weeks," explained McMillon.

There had been a massive takeover and riot by inmates at the Montana State Prison. Deaths had occurred, and property damage in the millions had taken place.

"You will be part of a team of about twenty seasoned agents who will be addressing numerous allegations of civil rights violations at the prison. Meet your team leader in butte the day after tomorrow and have fun,"

This meant lots of FD302 reports as all the inmates, guards, and any other witnesses were slated to be interviewed, and these interviews were to be written up on reports bearing that name.

This could be fun! he thought. "Some of the most interesting people I have met have been prisoners. They all have their own stories, and maybe I can learn something about another side of life," he said as he pointed his Bucar north on I-15 toward the Monida Pass with his suitcase in the trunk.

The proud souvenir logos of the Montana State Prison

Chapter 22

Don't Pee in the Milk

The Montana State Prison (MSP) was located a few short miles in a westerly direction from the shopping area and main street of the small town of Deer Lodge. It was an impressive facility with its formative outer fences, guardhouses, and walls surrounding the cellblocks and other sturdy buildings. The whole image of the prison in an isolated area and remote setting seemed to be daring anyone locked inside to try the impossible. At first glance, escape just did not look like a good thing to try.

In the late summer of 1991, all the news outlets were flooding the airwaves with details of the deadly riot and takeover by inmates of the prison. McWade had listened passively to these newscasts telling how inmates had killed other inmates and destroyed prison property, but this was in another state, and besides, *How could this affect me?* he thought. That was all before his call from his fearless boss McMillon.

The FBI was at the prison at the direct request of the Governor of Montana to look into the numerous civil rights complaints lodged by inmates claiming to have been mistreated both before and during the riot.

Two teams were organized to carry out the daunting task of interviewing all the inmates and guards at the prison. McWade was assigned to team up with another agent and would be taking statements from the long list of guards furnished. "It looks like we may be here awhile," he muttered in a matter-of-fact tone to his partner.

A briefing was held, giving all concerned agents a background of the case and the specifics of the complaints:

The Incident

Five guards were escorting three prisoners from the exercise area in the inner courtyard back to the maximum security unit. Nine prisoners left in the exercise area broke through the chain-link fence, rushed toward the cell block, and made it in before the sally port doors could be closed.

With the outnumbered guards trapped inside and the riot now in full gear, they were fearful of their lives and locked themselves in the shower area of the maximum security unit. Furniture was destroyed and mattresses piled against the doors to prevent guards from seeing the mayhem going on inside. Fires were started activating the sprinklers.

The trapped guards in the shower area were being threatened, cursed at, and felt their lives were in jeopardy.

Three hours after the takeover, the Disturbance Control Team (DCT) began a direct assault on the building in effort to regain control and save the trapped guards. The effort to save the guards was carried out successfully by entering through a roof hatch built for that purpose.

Upon regaining control of the cell block, the DCT discovered the bodies of five dead inmates and several others with varying degrees of injuries. The prison population, at the time of the incident, was 1,160 inmates, 68 of whom were assigned to the maximum security cell block unit.

There were over 200 guards assigned to the MSP with well over 200 other civilian employees.

The Complaints

1. A month or so before the riot, an inmate in maximum security had tried to hang himself. MSP regulations, for

safety reasons, prohibited a lone guard from entering the cell to save him. By the time help could be summoned, the inmate was able to successfully hang himself and was dead.

2. The inmates who had killed the five other inmates, trashed the place, and set fires claimed they were kicked by guards after being handcuffed.

3. The maximum security inmates complained that after being removed from the facility that they had themselves trashed and burned, they were then housed in a make-shift facility that was unsuitable. They claimed they were stripped naked, handcuffed, and made to sit on a concrete floor for several hours.

4. Inmates claimed that guards and other officers verbally harassed and called them names. They accused those supplying their food of placing hair in the food. Supposedly everyone from the warden to the last officer was aware of this unchristian behavior yet did nothing about it.

One by one, interview after long interview, each of the guards gave detailed accounts of that tragic day, what they saw, what they heard, and what they experienced. All four of the alleged civil rights issues were addressed, written up on FD-302s, and set aside to be placed in the final report.

To the casual person reading the reports of the two sides of the equation, it would have seemed they were reporting two separate and totally different events. On the one side, all the guards were professional, followed the MSP rules and regulations to the letter, and saw nothing at all out of the ordinary.

On the side of the hardened criminals, their interviews were obviously seen through a different windshield. They claimed to be innocent victims of blind justice who all had to endure abuse, unprofessionalism, insults, and taunting.

It was a classic case of inmate said versus guard said and would be written up the way each told their story. So who are you going to believe?

The average person would undoubtedly answer, "Oh please, give me a break!"

On about the third day, McWade was getting tired of trying to find decent food downtown when one of the guards suggested, "Why don't you just have lunch with us at the mess hall?"

"Who prepares the food?" was the return question.

"Oh, the prisoners do, and they do a great job."

McWade had heard stories of what some people do to food when they know law enforcement is on the consuming end of it, and it was not pleasant to think about.

Things like hair, foreign objects, fecal material, and body fluids, just to name a few, had been reportedly documented at restaurants and other facilities over the years. If an officer was in uniform, there were just some places, usually with criminal types in the kitchen and serving area, that were just not recommended.

"Oh, no worry here! We eat the exact same food as the inmates, and they just don't mess with the food. The Montana Department of Health told me that we have the cleanest eating place in the entire state of Montana," the guard proudly stated.

He went on to tell how a few years before some inmate, who worked in the prison dairy, had been ticked off over something and decided to piss in the prison milk supply. When word of his misdeed was spread among the prison population, he was dealt with appropriately by the other prisoners.

"After the misguided idiot got out of the infirmary and his bruises and abrasions were healed, he had less status in the prison population than a child molester," he continued.

There is an unwritten rule here that you don't mess in any way with the food supply. You certainly don't pee in the milk.

After hearing this invitation from the guard, McWade enjoyed a great meal at the mess hall in the cleanest facility in Montana. Or, at least, so he was told!

Looking around the prison, he noted inmates of all ages. He visited with three prisoners who represented a close-knit family. There was the grandfather, his son, and his grandson, all serving time together. McWade thought, *How nice it is that the state of Montana places so much value on family-oriented activity and helps them stay together this way.*

Looking out the window, the guard pointed out a very large man who was one of their most famous inmates known as Pork Chop.

"He is unique in that he weighs over five hundred pounds despite his five foot three height. His number one goal in life is to see how big he can get. He is so fat he can smuggle huge amounts of food into his cell by hiding it in his fat folds." He went on to laughingly say, "I have found this guy with tuna sandwiches hidden inside those fat folds. At least I think it was tuna as that's what it smelled like. In fact, his whole body smells sort of like the toilet seat on a tuna boat."

McWade had seen more and now heard more than he needed, and at the end of two weeks, his work there was completed.

The sound of those large sally port doors clunking shut could mean either hell or freedom, depending on which side of the closed door you were standing. The two- to three-mile trip down the hill to Deer Lodge would be hopefully his last.

Since he was thirsty, he stopped at the local quick stop for a diet Pepsi for the road and noticed a down-and-out-looking man sitting on a bench.

McWade was curious and asked the man if things were okay.

The man related the following, "Up until about a month ago, I had it all. Plenty to eat, clothes all laundered daily, a solid and secure roof over my head, online college classes, television to watch, great gym in which to work out, access to a library, no debt, and complete medical coverage."

Thinking the worse, McWade asked him what had happened. "Divorce, drugs, alcohol, loss of job? Why the lifestyle change?"

"Oh, nothing like that at all. I just got released from the prison up the hill there where I worked in the dairy," he almost tearfully said as he pointed toward the MSP. "By the way, man, could you spare a buck for a glass of milk?"

Before leaving, McWade grabbed a copy of the *Montana Standard* newspaper and glanced at the headline of the opinion section: "Prison Staff Behaved Well." The writer went on to explain that 90 percent of the inmates would claim they were innocent and shouldn't be there in the first place.

"Would you believe the inmate over the professional guards and staff who daily put their lives on the line? After all, these are the same convicts who murdered five of their own fellow inmates and now we are supposed to be alarmed about their civil rights being violated?"

McWade felt pretty much the same as the citizen in the paper. Eventually, the folks at the DOJ also felt that way as nothing earth-shaking came of the investigation.

A letter of commendation and a warm fireplace was his reward that first Christmas in the Salt Lake City Division. "Life in a small RA was great!" he reminded himself each day after the five o'clock rush minute.

Saturday was a big game on television between Nebraska and Oklahoma, the first since organizing his own Idahoans for Nebraska Chapter. The FBI small-town good life was continuing in the great state of Idaho.

After the time in the MSP, it was really comforting to know that any one person does not own all the problems in the world and that real peace comes from within.

McWade also gained another twist or outlook on the old saying, "When one door closes another opens." Recalling the sally port doors in the prison, he mused that when this happened you might actually be in jail. Or, as one inmate had told him, "Surprise sex is great to wake up to unless you happen to be in the old cell block." It's all a matter of perspective.

Chapter 23

Willful Ignorance

M ajestic Mount Moran could not have looked more impressive. The view of that beautiful mountain from the window of the Jackson Lake Lodge was a bit breathtaking.

The crisp fall days were signaling the end of summer and the beginning of the fall leaf spectacular in the Grand Teton National Park area.

This was the setting for the Salt Lake City FBI management conference, a two-day series of meetings headed up by the management of that field office. McWade was requested to be there by virtue of being the SRA of the small two-man Idaho Falls office. From the get-go, it seemed like an FBI-sponsored boondoggle to spend money before the end of the fiscal year, September 30. This was the kind of meeting in a resort setting that seemed to infuriate taxpayers. The SAC and other management seemed content to justify the expenditure using the "Use It or Lose It" slogan aimed at budget money that would be lost if not used.

The attendees consisted of management types from headquarters and the SRAs from Utah, Idaho, and Montana, which made up the SLC Division. The conference went without anything noteworthy taking place until the boss, Glen Geno, opened things up for discussion. Since almost every SRA at his little meeting was older and part of the enviable KMA Club, it was soon apparent that most were going to speak their minds a little more than the average younger agent who was not eligible for retirement.

The boss, in his all-knowing wisdom, was telling the agents in the room that he wanted them to alter their Number 3 cards to make them reflect that the agents were working cases that would have a higher priority classification rather than a routine type.

Over the years since Hoover's death, HQ had developed a brainchild system called Time Utilization Record Keeping or TURK. This morphed into an outlandish system whereby the cases any agent worked had a priority classification number attached to it and the agent would list this on his number 3 card.

HQ used this system to determine which offices needed more manpower using the thinking that any office working a higher priority of cases needed more agents than those working lower priority cases.

So back to SAC Geno and his instructions to only use high-priority classifications regardless of which type of case you actually were working. "Suppose you are going to firearms for the day. Put a high priority number on your Number 3 card anyway."

After listening to this reasoning, McWade raised his hand to get his attention and asked a simple question. "Boss, wouldn't altering the TURK classification be dishonest?"

The room became ghostly quiet as every old salt in the room waited for the next gem of wisdom to roll forth out of the mouth of their fearless leader. Everyone expected his full wrath to be channeled toward McWade, a common agent no less, who dared to even ask a question challenging his moral discernment.

He stopped, as if thinking for a very long and uncomfortable time. His face then became stern and a thoughtful expression overtook his countenance. Ever so slowly, he began to pace back and forth like a cat stalking its prey. Everyone in the room waited with great anticipation, expecting some great Socrates-type eternal wisdom to be revealed and roll forth from his lips, which, by the way, he was slowly licking with his tongue. It was as though whatever he said would actually burn his lips rue or otherwise.

Then after what seemed like an uncomfortable, everlasting eternity of expectation, he stopped his pacing and gestured with his right hand by placing his right finger on his temple. He cleared his throat and began speaking.

His uncanny statement would stick with McWade and some of the others in the room like flies on stink. This profound, deep doctrine coming from his mouth verified everything McWade had previously theorized about FBI management both past and future and captured in one sentence what they were all about and what motivated most.

Each word came very deliberately and ever so slowly. "When you can't run as fast as the other guys, *you cheat to win!*"

What a deep-seated tell-all statement from one of management's ordained and ever-so-wise chosen leaders, McWade thoughtfully smiled as his notepad captured this gem of Bureau Management wisdom.

Going back to his days in San Antonio, McWade recalled working with Glen Geno where they were both FOAs on the fugitive squad. After an early-morning raid, the entire group of agents came back for lunch at a small, quaint Chinese restaurant along San Antonio's famous scenic River Walk. Geno was a young agent, seemingly overly endowed with confidence, so it was of no surprise to everyone when he actually was given two fortune cookies.

The first stated, "Confidence is the hinge on the door to success."

But the second fortune read with a warning, "Be honest in your dealings and beware of false pride, lest you misinterpret the meaning of success."

Fast-forwarding Geno's FBI career from the point of his famous "cheat to win" pronouncement was somewhat tragic. Apparently, years later, he was accused of mishandling sensitive information pertaining to the Ruby Ridge matter in Northern Idaho, and for whatever reasons, he was stripped of his SAC position and banished to the basement of the J. Edgar Hoover Building, where he served out the remaining years of his now not-so-glamorous career.

His time there was reportedly lonely as he was considered toxic. Other agents really did not want to even be seen talking to him for fear of it negatively impacting their budding climb up their own Bureau management ladders.

His wife later divorced him, and several years later, he passed away quietly as a forgotten man, a partial product of his own pronounced and flawed philosophy.

How sad. He had so much more potential! It was an unhappy final chapter to a Bureau star who flamed out, a product of apparent willful ignorance to the principle of honesty. McWade, though saddened by the outcome of Geno's life, was always appreciative of those many fellow agents who were brave enough to stand up in the Bureau canoe and risk tipping it over by speaking up against wrong. These were the agents to whom the words *Fidelity, Bravery,* and *Integrity* were their guides along their Bureau paths.

These are part of the 99 percent of agents who chose to believe and act in a way that is honest and sensible, not merely as they had been programmed, not like a force of mindless robots wearing suits and ties, but real men and women with values, morals, and a strong work ethic. Agents who believed sincerely they could help make America a better place to live, love, and enjoy.

Chapter 24

The Amazing Popcorn Caper

Headlines

National Inquirer: "Cops Arrest Two Grannies in Movie—for Buying Popcorn."

Post Register, Idaho Falls, Idaho: "FBI Checks Out Popcorn Arrests."

Standard-Journal, Madison County, Idaho: "Women to Spend Day in Jail as Punishment in Popcorn Battery Case."

The state of Utah seems to look at Idaho as their very own state park and recreation area. At least it would seem that way to native Idahoans each holiday weekend as an endless stream of automobiles from the Beehive State migrate north to spend a few days away from their crowded, self-created asphalt nightmare.

Most of the time, the migrants are welcomed by the natives as they bring wallets full of cash, which is eagerly placed in the pockets of the business owners. However, other natives are not so happy to see their peaceful Gem State suddenly overwhelmed by the hoards. Like locusts devouring up available camping spots and sand dunes, these tourists come. Some natives are heard calling them derogatory nicknames, such as Utards, while others just pray for locust-gulping seagulls to come to the rescue.

Needless to say, on Memorial Day weekend, a spunky grandmother from Utah named Maxine journeyed to Madison County to visit Mable, her grandmotherly sister. Since Madison County was not exactly the hub of excitement, the two grannies soon got bored watching the potatoes grow in the nearby fields.

"What is there to do around this place?" asked the weary Utahan.

Since it came down to either watching a violin concert at the local Ricks Junior College (now BYU-Idaho) or a Disney movie, they chose the latter.

Mable, with her teen daughter and three teen friends, headed to the twin theaters to feast on the excitement of a Disney rerun. Maxine arrived a few minutes later but was unable to find her sister in the lobby. Thinking Mable had gone into the wrong movie house, she ventured next door for a peek into the other venue. Not seeing her, she innocently purchased a bag of popcorn and went back to the lobby of the movie house showing their Disney film.

Meeting up with Mable, they purchased tickets and proceeded to enter the theater.

"Sorry, ma'am, you did not buy your popcorn here and cannot take it into the theater. Company policy!" stated the stern manager taking tickets.

"So what do you want me to do with it?" snarled the perturbed Maxine in a huffy tone.

"I don't really care, but you're not taking it in our theater!" the manager retorted.

"I have a notion to dump it right on the floor," Maxine growled as she physically pushed past the now-motivated and red-faced young man in charge.

"You're trespassing now, and I'm calling the cops to get you out of here!" he yelled.

Maxine and Mable settled in to watch their favorite character, Cinderella's wicked stepmother, when they were interrupted by four armed police officers, who entered the showhouse at the request of the manager, and politely asked them to leave.

Instead of complying, our ladies of the corn doubled down and told the cops to buzz off, resulting in their eviction physically from their seats. With the eviction came actual arrests as the middle-aged grandma-type church ladies did not behave the way they had been taught in Sunday school.

Johnny Carson on his *Tonight Show* highlighted the incident with several jokes about popcorn, movies, Idaho, and police action. McWade actually saw humor in the whole matter until a call came from his office assigning him to investigate the matter.

Jokingly he asked his boss, McMillon, "So what's the violation? Illegal Transporting of Contraband Popcorn (ITCP)?"

Actually, the grannies had filed a civil rights violation complaint against the officers who had arrested them, claiming they had been brutally manhandled, resulting in several bruises and other injuries both physical and mental.

McWade's classmates from NAC #8 who were working organized crime cases in New York and Los Angeles would snicker at this case. "But my pay is the same as theirs, and I wouldn't trade my commute for the big-city rat race." He smiled as he headed north to Madison County, the home of the Rick College Vikings.

Interviewing the two parties, the ladies and the police, made McWade wonder if they had been there on the same day and at the same movie. The grannies were now well-behaved and displayed the manners of someone singing in the Mormon Tabernacle Choir. They used phrases like "I have never been so humiliated in all my life. These four huge police officers came down the aisle, grabbed us for no reason, and pulled us out of our seats. They marched us out like common criminals, twisting our arms behind our backs."

Maxine did admit to the *National Inquirer* that "I think I may have unintentionally actually have hit one of the officers."

Witnesses in the theater told a better story of what happened, saying that the two women used language that would have made a sailor blush. "Here I took my kids to see a G-rated movie, and these two women taught them four-letter cuss words that were beyond R-rated," said one man.

The two were seen by other witnesses as out of control. They were screaming, swearing, scratching, and kicking the officers as well as yelling slurs at them at the top of their lungs.

"Five days in jail, $50 fine for resisting arrest and obstructing a police officer, and five more dollars for trespassing!" pronounced the judge as he brought down his gavel on the courtroom desk.

"The commotion in the movie house was the closest thing to a riot Madison County had ever experienced and the most excitement since the 1976 flood after the Teton Dam broke," exclaimed one movie house witness.

Who wants to watch a movie without popcorn? Never before had so much fuss been made of a $2.50 bag of popcorn.

On the other hand, one witness wondered what would have happened if the two culprits would have attempted to smuggle in M&M's and a cola drink. "Would they have called in the SWAT team and cleared the whole building?"

McWade envisioned the DOJ attorneys laughing uncontrollably as they read his civil rights report before declining any prosecution for police brutality.

Could this possibly have happened anywhere else in the entire world?

"Only in Idaho! Only in Madison County!" he chuckled. "Only in my RA territory!"

Then he saw something that seemed to explain it all. A college-age shapely young woman walked by wearing a T-shirt with a message boldly displayed on her back: Madison County, We Are All Here Because We Are Not All There!

Is this what the good judge meant when he told the parents of the cow-milking burglars? "By Idaho standards, I guess you have done reasonably well raising your kids."

By Idaho standards! This phrase would always linger in McWade's brain as he puzzled over the full depth of its meaning. And to this day, he never watches a movie without a good bag of popcorn.

Chapter 25

Spicing Up Our Sex Lives

McWade once read a survey stating that only 4 percent of the participating population actually considered themselves to have a below-average IQ. Reading this, he therefore concluded that at least 46 percent of the folks out there are not only below average but a bit delusional. The reader can determine where the following couple, again from Madison County, Idaho, involved in the next caper, should fit.

McWade once again reflected back to his own sheltered childhood and teen years where his very religious mother always prefaced things he did with the phrase, "What will people think?" He was gradually able to work toward the mind-set that what other people thought of him was none of his concern and really none of his business.

Most people he knew were too busy looking, figuratively speaking, into their own mirrors to really care that much about what other people were doing anyway.

When the telephone call came into his office from a young woman, with young children, wanting to file a complaint with the FBI against her soon-to-be ex-husband, charging him with tapping her telephone, it sounded interesting. As her story unfolded, he glanced at the telephone's digital display to make sure the call was not coming in from Peyton Place instead of Eastern Idaho.

The young mother, a stalwart in her church and a pillar in the community, had obtained a restraining order on her husband prohibiting him from coming into or near the house. In total disregard for this, her husband had repeatedly walked right through that court order and had placed a recording device on her telephone junction box just outside her home.

Realizing domestic matters can be very ugly, he ran the scenario past the AUSA before jumping in with both feet. He was told the law was very specific and prohibited this kind of behavior, so he pointed the Bucar again toward the home of the famous 1M Idaho license plate—Madison County.

The unusual story unfolded as follows:

McWade found a middle-class churchgoing couple, married almost ten years, who felt their sex life was getting stagnant and downright boring at times. To their credit, theirs was a marriage where they had open communication skills and could talk about these matters, hoping to make their relationship better.

Longing for the same thrills and excitement experienced as newlyweds, they put the kids to bed and had a regular family counsel, the same way they had been instructed to do by their religious leaders when they wanted to plan or resolve problems within the family unit.

Between them, they soon came up with what seemed like a foolproof way to bring back some zing and zest into their lackluster relationship.

She was to dress up in her skintight blue jeans, with a low-cut blouse, and venture out to possibly the only bar in the entire county, where she would try to hook up with some cowboy for a one-night stand complete with frolic and adventure.

She would then return and report.

The plan was executed. She quickly found that her shapely body and cute face was not hard to sell, especially for free, and takers were more than willing to give her the tutoring she desired.

She soon settled on a suave middle-aged cowboy with the macho looks and apparent pickup lines to win the job.

The plan was to learn new techniques, skills, expertise, and talents suitable to take back home to her eagerly waiting husband. They would then try to duplicate the things the frisky wife had learned in her very own lab experiments from the hookup artist.

Now the first few times seemed to work very well as our girl, Ruby, turned out to be a very willing, capable student and an extremely fast learner. The smiling instructor, John, also was apparently able to tap into everything he had learned as well as things he had dreamed about and been wanting to try his entire life. "Life is really good!" he told the bartender as he would leave with Ruby for their weekly sessions.

To Ruby, our love-starved lady, her weekly lessons were like shots of heroin to a drug-starved addict. She was beginning to love her newfound exercise program way too much as her face was now radiant and glowing like never before.

The first month or so, Fred, the stay-at-home husband, really enjoyed his wife's newly discovered skills, and it just seemed to be the thing they needed to spice up their bedroom antics. The thing neither Ruby nor Fred had built into their equation was that soon Ruby realized that, in the lovemaking arena, John was like an NBA star and poor Fred was more like the slide rule-carrying geek struggling to make the seventh-grade ball team.

Soon Fred was benched and John was center court in Ruby's life. After all, it seemed Fred was much better at baby-sitting than doing slam dunks or three-pointers from half-court, like his competition. The once-burning flame of lust between Fred and Ruby had now turned to cold embers that no longer even glowed or smoldered during the long cold Idaho nights.

Back at the BSU, Roy Cottonwood, the sex crimes expert, had told McWade specifically that "sexual conduct always begins as a fantasy. According to mental health professionals, everyone harbors forbidden desires and fantasies, if only fleetingly."

He added, "For most, the simple contemplating of the forbidden act seems to suffice, and most never seriously consider bringing those fantasies to reality."

But for now, our young and very unhappy married couple had crossed that line into the uncharted territory of the forbidden and could see no way to make a U-turn.

Fred now tearfully told McWade that he had totally misunderstood his Sunday school teacher when he said, "In the end, you will only regret the chances you did not take." He guessed now that he must have been talking about something else.

Poor Fred was playing the country song "Ruby, Don't Take Your Love to Town" night and day and was pleading with her using lines from that song that said, "Ruby, for God's sake, turn around." But she was not interested in the benchwarmer anymore as she found him to be unexciting, dull, and, quite frankly, very poor at dribbling the ball up and down the court. He was now yesterday's news!

Fred was mortified when Ruby filed for a divorce and continued her rendezvous with cowboy John. So he hired a local attorney and presented this lawyer with the idea of tapping his wife's phone to get evidence that could be used in court to show she was an unfit mother. Fred claimed the attorney agreed this would be a great idea.

So a trip to Radio Shack for equipment and a visit at 5:00 AM each morning to the junction box outside his old bedroom window to change cassette tapes led to Fred's present state. He would listen to the steamy intercepted conversations between Ruby and John and cry himself to sleep each night, longing to be back in the saddle himself.

Fred had filled three shoeboxes full of cassettes before young Ruby caught him in the act of changing tapes and soon figured out he had been tapping her phone. He had given them to his attorney for safekeeping and to be used as future evidence.

Of course, when McWade interviewed Fred's attorney, the potato farmer turned lawyer, quickly realized he could be prosecuted as an accessory and began categorically denying ever ordering the tap or even knowing the history of the tapes. Even in Idaho, you can't intercept and record a conversation without the consent of at least one party.

"What a waste of skin this guy would be as an attorney," McWade quickly concluded. "Doesn't he understand anything at all about the law and the expectation of privacy?"

Fred was indicted and plead guilty. He was sentenced to two years' probation.

Fred's less-than-competent attorney, not surprisingly, was determined innocent of knowingly committing any federal crimes by the AUSA, his old law school friend. The unwritten rule of the attorney brotherhood remained intact, which was that attorneys do not go after other attorneys unless it is totally unavoidable.

Fred's attorney, shortly thereafter, retired from his law practice and is now raising Idaho spuds. Rumor is that he is now something that he never was as a barrister. He now is a man truly "outstanding in his field!"

When hearing of Fred's probation sentence, McWade was reminded of the words once again of his old friend, the Sheridan County, Nebraska, Sheriff: "Hell, McWade, that ain't no punishment. You and I are on probation every day."

"Who said small towns are boring?"

People in small towns are just as capable of royally screwing up their lives as anyone else anywhere," he thought as Tammy Wynette's country song "D-I-V-O-R-C-E" began to play on his Bucar radio. He tearfully told McWade that he should never have fallen for the old saying, "If you don't sin, then Jesus died for nothing."

You just can't fix stupid! thought McWade as he headed back home.

Chapter 26

Into Thin Air

"Challis Girl Missing" (*The Challis Messenger*, Challis, Idaho 10/14/93)

"Searchers Desperate for Clues" (*Post Register*, Idaho Falls, Id 10/15/93)

"Hoping for a Miracle" (*Post Register*, 10/17/93)

"Challis Residents Still Searching for Answers" (*Post Register*, 10/18/93)

"Sheriff Says no Firm Leads in Challis Abduction" (*Post Register*, 10/20/93)

"Psychics Aid Search for Girl" (*Post Register*, 10/25/93)

"Law Enforcement Has New Lead in Challis Abduction" (*Post Register*, 10/27/93)

"Officials Have Positive Leads in abduction (*Post Register*, 10/28/93)

"FOX Network to air Special on Stephanie" (*The Challis Messenger*, 12/9/93)

"Two Months Later, Still No Leads in Disappearance" (*Post Register*, 12/10/93)

"Slaying Suspect Cleared in Challis Case" (*Post Register*, 12/14/93)

"Sandi Crane, Stephanie's Mother, Age Thirty-Two, Deceased" (*Post Register* Obituaries, 8/13/97)

Ben Crane, Stephanie's father, age forty-eight (Evans Funeral Home Obituary, 10/12/2012 Eastsound, Washington)

S nuggled in a picturesque storybook setting along the Yankee Fork of Idaho's famous Salmon River, dubbed the River of No Return, was the small town of Challis, population one thousand.

US Highway 93 runs through the eastern part of town, winding its way along the river toward Salmon, some fifty miles to the north.

Entering Challis, the welcoming sign states Explore Historical Challis, Founded 1878, the Wilderness Gateway. There was truly wilderness and isolation in virtually every direction with a quaint old west and mining town flair bestowing upon it a personality like no other. This was a town where old and new four-wheel-drive pickups and Jeeps outnumber conventional cars and could be seen, on any given day, parked around the old brick Custer County Courthouse in the center of town.

It was a friendly town where most folks seemed to know one another, bothering no one, and relished the idea of minding their own business. Many came here for the isolation, some to leave a past behind, some for recreation, and others to work the nearby mines.

This was the peaceful scene painted on the day of October 11,1993, which was forever to change this peaceful village on the frontier.

Stephanie Crane, a beautiful, fun-loving nine-year-old third grader, had been to the bowling alley located on the east side of US 93, asking her mother, Sandi Crane, for money to pay for bowling. Some thought maybe the little girl's mother may have acted upset about something while she was exchanging words with the little girl.

The mother left the bowling alley with the apparent understanding that Stephanie was to walk to her home, located about one half mile farther to the east toward the river near her grandfather's sawmill.

She never made it home that night or ever!

Reconstructing her travels from the bowling alley showed her crossing Highway 93 and heading west, in the opposite direction from her home. She was seen at approximately 6:00 PM at the Challis High School football field near the long jump pit, playing in the sand. She then left that area, headed south from the sports complex, again turned west and into the unknown.

Witnesses, tracking dogs, and interviews with hundreds were to give no further clues as to the mystery of Stephanie's disappearance. The entire town of Challis turned out en masse over the next few days to comb the town and surrounding outskirts. The river was searched, and abandoned buildings, old vehicles, wooded areas, parks, and every conceivable nook and cranny were methodically examined.

The little girl had literally vanished into thin air.

With no solid clues coming forth, the family members obviously became increasingly frustrated and naturally channeled those feelings toward law enforcement. At this point, the Custer County Sheriff and his understaffed department seemed to be the target.

Three days into the ordeal, the good Sheriff contacted McWade, requesting FBI assistance. By now, including the FBI, there were eleven law enforcement agencies participating in this investigation, including Bureau of Land Management, Forest Service, Idaho Fish and Game, Challis PD, and others eager to help in any way possible.

At the request of the Sheriff, the FBI (which equaled McWade at this point) was to lead the loosely assembled task force assisted by an investigator from the Idaho State Police (ISP). By the next day, the Salt Lake City FBI had dispatched fifteen agents to assist in the monumental task of interviewing virtually every man, woman, and responsible child in Challis and the surrounding countryside, hoping to find any leads whatsoever that could help solve the Stephanie puzzle.

It was quickly determined by the door-to-door contacts and interviews that the isolation of Challis seemed to be a magnet for unregistered sex offenders trying to lose themselves in the general population. By the end of the second day, six of these red-faced offenders had been identified, thoroughly interviewed, and cleared through alibi verification. Their names were also shared with appropriate Idaho authorities anxious to place the missing predators into their database to enable their neighbors and townspeople to know who they were and to warn the towns children of the dangers of being surrounded by folks with that propensity.

A command post was established in the commissioner's room in the basement of the old courthouse. There was almost zero air circulation in the large room, which soon became a very real problem, given the fact that several of the local lawmen were chain-smokers.

Since McWade and his FBI family were invited guests of the sheriff, who himself was a heavy smoker, this seemed to be a delicate situation as no one wanted to offend the good Sheriff and his deputies. After a quick consultation with other agents, McWade posted a sign in the smoke-filled room that stated simply, Computers In Use, No Smoking! That seemed to solve the first logistics problem as it was now actually possible to see across the room, which previously had worse visibility than downtown Salt Lake City during an inversion.

The very next problem to surface created a very delicate dilemma for McWade.

While conducting citizen interviews, at least five townspeople came forth in private and expressed grave concerns about one of the local lawmen on the task force.

Since he had an alibi for the day Stephanie disappeared, this matter was soon put to rest also. "Sometimes it's hard to tell the cops from the robbers in these small towns," McWade observed.

The same lawman also had a habit of hanging out in the local bars almost nightly, talking boastfully to his buddies. It was soon reported that he was telegraphing everything the task force was coming up to everyone within earshot to look like a big shot to his wide-eyed crowd.

Again, he was summoned in and given the lecture about "loose lips sink ships." He was told, in no uncertain terms, that he would be prosecuted federally for divulging any more information from the morning and evening briefings. The problem was solved when his boss decided to ban him from attending meetings or hanging around the task force command post altogether.

So far, McWade felt great progress had been made on administrative task force issues, but there was nothing positive coming forth about our missing girl.

By now, this was national news, and soon the calls were coming in from all over the world, offering their services. There were psychics, clairvoyants, divining rod dowsers, fortune-tellers, wiccans, and any other believer in the occult or black magic. One self-pro-claimed practitioner of the occult appeared on the scene claiming to have the ability to look into his hat at a seer stone and get lead information regarding the disappearance. When it was all said and done, he was as dense as the rock he had buried in his stovepipe hat.

Another guy from Twin Falls, Idaho, claiming to be an expert dowser insisted that when he held his divining rod over a map of the city of Challis, it pointed to a specific address where the little girl was being held. The address happened to be that of the elderly retired chief of police who smilingly welcomed a thorough search of his house and basement. Of course, the search proved fruitless as this old gentleman was a pillar of moral character and as clean the spar-kling water of the Salmon River on the east edge of town. These were interesting distractions as far as law enforcement was concerned, but unfortunately, several of these psychics made direct contact with members of the Crane family, giving them very cruel false hope and expectations with their convincing charades.

Once one of these mystics got into the mind of a desperate family member, someone wanting to believe, someone willing to try anything, it was problematic. The information fed into their minds by the very convincing seers was quite real to them. Now with this confirmation bias firmly planted in their brain, the person would reject solid evidence or logic. They only wanted to hear things that would confirm the beliefs they already were now clinging to firmly and persistently. With logic out the window, their emotional brains could sometimes run wild, which was very sad to see and difficult to deal with rationally.

Within two weeks, the task force had chased down everything that remotely even resembled a viable lead. Every living breathing human in the area that could be located was interviewed. One by one, the FBI agents and others comprising the task force packed their bags and returned to their normal lives. Soon it was a mere skeleton crew assisting McWade, consisting of the SO and an ISP investigator.

Before long, it required banker boxes to hold the pages upon pages documenting the dead-end leads and other information col-lected. Each lead had been pursued, hoping to cast something positive into the mix. But soon, after months of endless days and sometimes nights of investigation, the stark truth and disappointing reality had set in firmly. "We may never know what happened to Stephanie!" was now the topic of the remaining investigators.

Theories about the disappearance were as numerous as any single person could fantasize. Was she abducted by a pervert who used her and disposed of the body in one of the hundreds of abandoned mine shafts in the area? Did she wander off and fall into one of these open holes in the ground to be lost forever? Would her remains be stumbled upon in the wilderness by some hunter during hunting season, thus giving clues and some closure? Was she taken by someone passing through town to be sold into the thriving white slave trade as a child prostitute? Since her parents were poor, could she have been sold for much-needed cash? Did she run away and become lost and then killed and devoured by wild animals?

The truth of the matter and the hard and cold reality of the situation was that, as the days, weeks, months, and then years rolled by, no more was known about her disappearance than was known shortly after 6:00 PM as she left the Challis practice field and wandered into the eerie shadows of the unknown. The case was quickly becoming a frustratingly difficult journey toward the unsolvable.

The ghost of Stephanie, the smiling dark-headed nine-year-old girl, still haunts McWade at night as it does countless others whose lives she touched so many years ago on that sunny October day in the small town that she forever changed.

Perhaps kids in the small town now don't enjoy the freedom to play outside unescorted as before. Maybe previously unlocked doors are now secured. Strangers passing through are now often looked at with more suspicion than in the past. Neighbors look and take note of the person next door with more caution and pay more attention to what is happening in the shadows.

The little girl who vanished into thin air, like it or not, impacted the entire town and even the entire state of Idaho.

McWade has, at times, in the still of the night, asked himself soul-searching questions—questions such as, could the SLC FBI have given more manpower and offered technical support similar to what was given in high-profile cases of wealthier victims in larger cities on the West Coast and around the country?

Sometimes being isolated from the main stream FBI is a plus, but he wondered if in this case the phrase *out of sight, out of mind* could have meant less resources being offered to help with the investigation before it became a cold case.

The little girl's parents divorced and died prematurely. Undoubtedly, the stress and the hell they experienced during this nightmarish ordeal factored into this.

The picture of the cute, bubbly girl dressed in purple, her favorite color, is painted indelibly in the minds of those left behind.

Purple was, and forever will be, Stephanie's very favorite color.

Chapter 27

The Baker to Vegas Extravaganza

"Boss, should we really be spending this much time and money on a relay race?"

The agent was cut short by the same SAC who earlier was credited with the now-famous "If you can't run as fast as the other guy, you cheat to win" quote. "We are taking a team to Las Vegas, and by damn, we are going to win this year!" snarled the SAC.

"But what if…what if there are differing opinions on this?" the questioning agent began, only to be abruptly cut short by the man in charge.

"Bullshit!" came the irritated voice of power, "There is only one opinion around this place that agents are allowed to have and it is *my* opinion!"

And so it came to pass that much preparation began for the annual 120-mile relay Baker to Vegas Challenge Cup.

The edict went out from SLC to all the RAs in the three state division that, come hell or high water, 1995 was going to be the year the SLC Division of the FBI would win their respective classification and bring home the first place trophy.

This event was touted as the largest law enforcement event in the entire world and would take place in the upcoming April. The "all agents" memo stated there would be 160 law enforcement teams with each team using 20 runners and being allowed five alternate runners to be used in case of illness or injury. Each of the 160 teams would be required to have a support vehicle with flashing red-and-blue strobe lights in front of their particular runner at all times. The 20 runners on each individual team would pass the baton to their next awaiting team member in the designated exchange stations spaced approximately 5 miles apart.

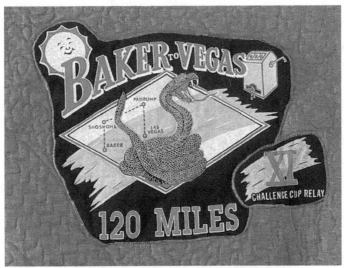

The shirt emblem showing the official route of the "Race" and the coveted first place chalice highly prized by SAC Geno

The rules showed the staggered starting time as being 4:00 PM in Death Valley at Baker, California. Because of the heat, any team whose runner wore a hat would be disqualified.

The word on the street was that if you wanted to score points with the man in charge, you should try out for the team and try to be one of his elites.

Why not? thought McWade.

Amazingly, his time during the tryouts qualified him for the team, with his assignment being leg 12, a 3.8-mile uphill grade on the eastern outskirts of Pahrump, Nevada. The SLC baton was anticipated to be at the exchange area at approximately 2:00 AM, some 8 hours after the race started in Baker.

The boss was so excited that it became his absolute number one priority. It was rumored that he ordered the FBI pilot to fly from SLC to Billings, Montana, to haul one speedster agent to the tryouts who had been unable to make the regular test runs.

Some teams from California were so competitive they were rumored to hire new officers based more on how fast they could run a five-mile course than on their qualifications as police officers. Unverified sources claimed some law enforcement units in Southern California would actively try to recruit officers from competing departments, depending on their running skills.

McWade knew, from his own sources, that SACs from several western divisions would visit Quantico and put dibs on the new agents who were the best in their classes. These claims placed on targeted new agents were not based on shooting skills, defensive tactics, knowledge of the law, academics, or any other normal qualification but primarily on running times down Quantico's famous Yellow Brick Road.

McWade was at the exchange station a good hour before the 2:00 AM anticipated arrival of the SLC team. The excitement in the cool night air was intoxicating as the adrenaline fix was starting to take hold.

In the distance, several miles away and up the mountain grade toward Baker, the red-and-blue flashing lights started to appear. First one, then another, and soon a long unbroken line as far as the eye could see into the still darkness of the Nevada night. The image creating itself before McWade's eyes was beyond anything imaginable. Never before had he seen such an unusual and breathtaking spectacle. Soon the sounds of the music and voices urging on their runners to run faster could be heard over the speakers of the pilot cars.

Where were the Hollywood camera crews? he wondered. *This is an amazing sight found nowhere else!*

As the snake of flashing lights crawled ever closer to exchange station 12, the tension and anxiety mounted. Famous faces in the world of law enforcement, from the Los Angeles area, pertaining to the OJ Simpson incident and ongoing trial, even arrived at the gate to urge their teams on.

McWade smiled when he thought how frustrated his own SAC, the infamous Glen Geno, was right now knowing there was no way he could actually cheat to win.

The baton came, and McWade was now center stage in his own drama as the hill seemed to get steeper and the baton heavier. *This is crazy!* he thought. *I must be the human centipede of stupid to do this.*

But as he finally staggered to exchange gate number thirteen to pass off the baton, he sucked in fresh air and thought of a saying he recalled from *Runner's World* magazine, which read, "It's not that you had the courage to finish the race, but that you had the courage to start!"

And so is each day of our life, he mused.

Back in Las Vegas the next morning, at the MGM Convention Center, SAC Geno was smiling ear to ear as he accepted the winning trophy. Each runner received a large glass mug with a coiled rattlesnake and the inscription 1995 Challenge Cup 120-mile relay, Baker to Vegas. To Geno, this was sweet revenge as he himself had bombed out in the previous year's relay.

Agents involved in the 1994 relay whispered that Geno had taken one of the first legs of the relay in Death Valley himself and apparently failed to take in sufficient liquids. He became severely dehydrated and wandered off the main road into the vast desert, mumbling strange things as if speaking in tongues.

Some agents riding in the support van questioned if it was dehydration or if he was just living up to his stated advise about cheating and was actually looking for a shortcut to Las Vegas. Whatever his situation, he had to be carried back out of the desert and into the van while his alternate finished his leg.

McWade's good time on leg 12 translated into a happy Geno, which, in turn, meant a new Bucar that year.

This made him think of a saying he had heard once in a movie that basically said, "Action is the only truth." And the truth of the matter was that a new car was coming.

The week after getting back to Idaho Falls, the word was that SAC Geno was back at Quantico on a scouting trip, looking for a new athlete for the 1996 relay.

The recruiting trip must have gone well at the academy as McWade found himself replaced on the 1996 team by a much younger and faster new agent who could run like a gazelle and had miraculously just happened to be assigned to SLC shortly after Geno had paid his visit to Quantico.

To expect a bad SAC not to do predictably questionable and wrong things is pure madness, McWade thought as he placed his first-place rattlesnake relay stein on his memorabilia shelf. But to try to change a person like Geno would be like trying to change the wheel on a speeding and out-of-control locomotive.

"Director Hoover probably just did another quarter turn in his grave over this one!" McWade laughingly smiled as he headed to the doughnut shop to report on his weekend in Vegas and begin preparing for his new Bucar.

After all, it's more fun to go native in a new Bucar rather than a beater.

Chapter 28

Welcome to Thompson County

There was once a sign on US Highway 20 in Eastern Idaho that stated in a matter-of-fact way: Entering Thompson County, Set Your Clock Back Fifty Years.

When seventeen-year-old McWade and his buddy Mort ventured into this "land of deliverance" one Sunday afternoon in 1959, they dragged Main Street once and made a U-turn on Bridge Street near the bridge over Henry's Fork of the Snake River. Within seconds, there came the piercing sound of a screeching siren and the unmistakable red flashing lights atop the older-model police sedan that pulled up behind. A burly-looking unkempt man, wearing old denim work pants, an oversize revolver and a badge pinned to a faded and wrinkled police shirt, slowly swaggered up to the 53 Chevy Bel Air.

"What did I do wrong?" the petrified young McWade humbly stammered.

"You really have to ask? You are even dumber than you look! You made an illegal U-turn you stupid little ass!" growled the hulking figure with the badge.

"But they are legal in—" began the wide-eyed teen, only to be cut off in midsentence.

"Hey, you little bastard, call this your lucky day. I'm going to give you a break. You and your fat-ass buddy can just turn this car around and get your lily-white sorry asses out of my county. If I ever see you again in Thompson County, hell will rain down on you like a shit storm and you will regret the day you were ever born!" he snapped as he spun around and climbed back in his patrol car, leaving the ghost-faced, terrified teens shaking in their boots.

That was McWade's very first contact with law enforcement, and he was not impressed. This ordeal was too traumatic to ever be forgotten, and he vowed then and there that if he ever went into law enforcement himself, he would never be the rude and vulgar disgrace of a man he had just seen. Was this the 1959 version of Thompson County's idea of how to serve and protect?

Someone later had told him the officer's name was Red, a man who had stayed on in town after being incarcerated at the Idaho State Juvenile Reform School as a delinquent. He had worked his way into law enforcement after his release at age eighteen but had managed to maintain his bullying attitude as he climbed through the ranks.

"What a county!"

Keep this story in mind and fast-forward your time machine thirty-five years to the year 1994.

It was a rather cold February day and McWade was trying to get things together to make the three-hour road trip to Challis on a couple of new leads on the Stephanie Crane matter. A phone call seemed to throw a wrench into the spokes of that plan as the Chief of Police in Woods Cross, Utah, said he had a problem with the Thompson County SO refusing to help him out on a matter involving a stolen Kenworth truck.

The Kenworth and the trailer it was pulling had been stolen in his city two months ago. The trailer had been recovered from a truck stop in Thompson's county seat, St. Anna, by the truck's owner about two weeks earlier. The operator of the same truck stop had just called the Utah chief telling him that a Kenworth, thought to be the stolen truck, was scheduled to be serviced that very afternoon.

The stolen unit was being operated by a local trucking company, Rich Transport (RT), from the little town of Parker, just west of St. Anna. The owner of the company, ironically, was named Rich.

Since the SO had been unresponsive, McWade agreed to follow up and see if the RT Kenworth was the same rig stolen from Utah.

A quick call was made to Butch, the Chief Deputy at the Thompson County SO, who willingly agreed to check out the truck that afternoon to see if it was the stolen rig. He said he would seize it, if necessary, when it came in for servicing. How was McWade to know that Butch and Rich were best drinking buddies and that Butch would knowingly cover for him on the stolen RT Kenworth?

Just before heading for Challis, a call was made to Butch as no promised return call had been received. The following is a brief time line, which is mind-boggling:

3:00 PM: Call to Butch who said this was a civil matter and that per the Thompson County Attorney, he was not doing one more thing on the case. He was reluctant to give details, and it was apparent he was covering for Rich Transport.

3:15 PM: A call to the truck stop owner was made who gave unique and detailed information about the truck positively identifying it as the stolen Kenworth although the VIN numbers had been ground off. McWade advised him to secure the truck until the FBI could seize it as required by law.

3:30 PM: Obtained verbal authorization from the AUSA, District of Idaho, Boise, Idaho, to seize the truck and was informed that a seizure warrant would follow.

6:00 PM: McWade, accompanied by his young ex-Marine partner, Bill, arrived at the truck stop to seize the truck but found the truck was now gone. It seemed Rich's son, Danny, had been alerted and had hastily taken the stolen truck to hide it away from the FBI, inasmuch as Rich was out of town on a long-distance run.

6:20 PM: So hastily had been the truck's removal by Danny that he had not allowed the air brakes on the trailer to build up pressure, and his skid marks were followed for over a half mile until he had unhooked the trailer by the old abandoned stud mill.

6:55 PM: McWade returned to the truck stop and telephoned Butch at his residence. The Chief Deputy was updated about the seizure warrant and that the truck had been apparently hidden. His help was requested to assist in its location and seizure. "Come into *my* county and accuse one of *my* people of having a stolen truck?"

he screamed over the landline. He was clearly out of control, and his buttons had obviously been pushed.

"Now you and your half-assed partner can just get in your car and get the hell out of our town!"

This outburst was beginning to sound exactly like that Sunday afternoon in 1959, some thirty-five years earlier, when Chief of Police Red had thrown McWade out of St. Anna. The tone, the cursing, and the similar verbiage seemed to be coming from the same DNA.

Amazingly, McWade later learned that Butch was the beloved son and offspring of the late Red, who had served the city of St. Anna so professionally all those many years ago. It was very apparent that the father had taught the son well.

This whole corruption and bullying thing seemed to be the truth hidden within the lie of the small town on the Snake River. How bizarre that both the 1959 teenager and the FBI version of the same person could be thrown out of the same town by a father-son law enforcement duo spanning over three decades. "How many more victims of their official terrorizing and police abuse and corruption were out there unreported?"

The out-of-control officer, Chief Deputy Butch, was reminded by McWade that the last time he checked, Thompson County just happened to still be in the United States of America and that the FBI therefore did not need his permission to cross the border into Thompson County and that it was not *his* area to order anyone from. He was further reminded that if he would have carried out his sworn duty and upheld the laws of the state of Idaho by seizing a stolen truck with an altered VIN, this whole thing would not be happening.

St. Anna was not a large city and therefore the search to locate the notorious Danny was not that hard. The fact that he drove a white Chevy pickup bearing the personalized Idaho license plate DANNY made it easy enough that McWade could locate it, unassisted, in a town of two thousand people without much difficulty.

The pickup was soon located a block east of the only stoplight in town parked on the south side of the road across the street from an older two-story white apartment building.

It was now very dark and approaching 8:00 PM. McWade had already missed the road trip to Challis, and neither he nor agent Bill were all that happy about this whole ordeal at this point. The wait was less than a half hour when, at least, fifteen redneck-looking men came pouring out of the apartment staircase and out into the street below. By then, it had been learned that the gathering was actually to plan the annual Island Park snow machine race in the mountain country west of Yellowstone National Park. The meeting involved the Thompson County Search and Rescue team. Young Danny, being the upstanding citizen that he was, reportedly was a member of that fine group.

As the gang of rough-looking men approached the parked vehicles, they were met face-to-face by the two waiting FBI agents in the middle of the dimly lit street.

"Which one of you would be Danny?" asked McWade.

"Who the hell wants to know?" came the reply from the bully-looking man fitting the description of Danny. McWade guessed he had found his man.

"We're with the FBI and want to talk to you about the stolen Kenworth you drove out of the truck stop a few hours ago. We have a federal seizure warrant for that truck and want to know where you are hiding the damn thing," McWade advised as he displayed his FBI credentials to the now-belligerent man standing by the white pickup.

Danny was known to have a short fuse, and at this point, it was apparent he was in fight mode as he moved in nose to nose with the young, muscular ex-Marine-turned-agent Bill. They were both in flight, fight, or freeze mode and the fight part looked real.

"I'm Danny, and I am pissed! Who the hell do you bastards think you are that you can come into our town and take my dad's truck? I should just kick your ass right here and now!" he yelled into the crisp night air loud enough to be heard a block away.

By now, all of Danny's fellow search and rescue crew were assembling in a semicircle around young Bill and Danny as if they were coming to his actual rescue. At this point, McWade turned and directly confronted the group of curious, eager onlookers. "This is FBI business and does not concern any of you. My advice is to stand down and do not interfere in any way if you know what is best for you!"

The recovered stolen Kenworth which was the
catalyst for the Thompson County fiasco

The group reluctantly withdrew a few steps back, much to McWade's relief.

As this scene unfolded under the streetlight, Danny was yelling that he was going to punch out young Bill's lights while the agent was boldly standing his ground, telling him to give it your best shot!

Danny's biceps were twice the size of his brain as he stupidly growled, "I know exactly where the damn truck is, but I'm not telling you and you can go straight to hell."

"I thought we arrived in hell already about three hours ago! But thanks for just giving me all the probable cause I need to roast your sorry ass on this!" smiled McWade in an almost gleeful tone to the dim-witted Danny.

As Bill and Danny backed slowly away like two dogs who had been itching for a fight, McWade breathed easier and was able to move his hand away from his holstered revolver.

At this time, he thought of an old saying he had once heard. "You know, Danny, life is like a jar of hot jalapeno peppers. What you do today just may be a burning issue tomorrow," he told the fuming you redneck.

The gathering broke up, and as everyone disappeared into their own shadows, McWade turned to Danny. "Get a good night's sleep, Danny. You haven't heard the last from us. We shall return."

It was a sleepless night for McWade as he relived each and every possible scenario and possible outcome of that previous evening and how close it had almost come to going to hell in a hand basket.

Jim, the AUSA in Boise, listened carefully as the story of the Thompson County incident was relayed to him. Unlike most in the US Attorney's Office, Jim was an aggressive, prosecutive-minded attorney. He was a pleasure to work with despite his unusual hobby of photographing roadkill animals along the highway and putting them in his famous Road Kill Album.

"You are in luck. There is federal grand jury in session here in Boise as we speak, and I will have them issue a subpoena for the stolen Kenworth truck to be delivered before them by 5:00 PM tomorrow."

In his entire career, this was a first! Usually subpoenas were for documents, but a truck? "This whole Thompson County gig is good enough for a movie script," he said to himself as he hung up the phone.

McWade now knew Danny and his uncooperative style and therefore showed up with the subpoena the next day at his place of employment, where he worked as a Chevrolet-GMC car salesman, accompanied by a uniformed ISP trooper.

"You can give me the truck or be arrested for contempt and do jail time right now Danny," smiled McWade as he served the document on him.

In predictable Danny fashion, he snarled, "I'll be damned if you will get the truck! I'll call my attorney, Springer Hoster!"

"Please do," came the forced excuse of a courteous answer.

Soon his attorney had been fully briefed by Danny, who then smugly handed the phone to McWade. Hoster demanded to know the name of the AUSA so he could educate him on these matters.

Hoster, who had once served as the Thompson County attorney, apparently thought he was one up on everyone else in all things pertaining to the law. He promptly called Jim and apparently received an education himself. AUSA, Jim explained to him that the truck better be turned over to McWade by 5:00 PM or that both he and his client (Danny) would be arrested for contempt and placed in jail for the remaining duration of the impaneled federal grand jury, which would be up to eighteen months.

Springer Hoster must have dosed off in law school and missed the part about the fact that when he admitted to the AUSA that his client had told him where the stolen truck was located that he now also knew and was now was part of the cover-up.

The expression on Hoster's face was pale and ghostlike as he appeared and asked McWade just where they should deliver the stolen truck. He looked like he was run over enough to have been photographed and placed in AUSA Jim's road kill album.

McWade was amazed to discover that the stolen Kenworth was tied into a group of thieves centered in Three Forks, Montana, headed by the notorious Ben Ward, who had been stealing trucks and farm tractors all over the western part of the US. The stolen units were taken to an isolated Quonset building, used as a chop shop where VIN numbers were altered and often the stolen trucks repainted. The group loved the farm tractors, loaders, and heavy equipment as they were valued well over $100,000 each and required no titles, making them easy to sell for cash to anyone shady.

Rich passionately denied knowing anything about the truck being stolen. All the evidence showing otherwise, even though very strong, was circumstantial. His attorney, Springer, helped him avoid prosecution, and he was only out the money he fronted for the purchase. He continued in the trucking business as owner of Rich Transport. He reportedly turned to religion in his old age, repented of his truck thefts and other sins, and died a peaceful death in his beloved town of Parker.

Danny, his loyal son, was humbled a bit by the whole incident but stayed a cocky bully until he died a premature death a few years later. He was still the South Thompson High School football legend, in his own mind, to his last breath. His mind-set was similar to and captured in the fictitious Uncle Rico character in a later low-budget Idaho based movie called *Napoleon Dynamite* referred to earlier.

Butch was arrested, in his own county no less, by an ISP trooper for driving while intoxicated. He told the arresting officer, "I guess I drunk too much!" He then refused to take a breath or blood alcohol test and was therefore stripped of his driver's license. He hired St. Anna's famous attorney, the eminent Springer Hoster, who failed to live up to his nickname Springer. Butch's phony claim of being a diabetic with an insulin problem did not fly in court as he was convicted of DUI.

He was promptly given a special award by Thompson County for being a stellar officer. It was headlined in the local newspaper as "Chief Deputy Wins Award for Good Work." He soon retired from the SO, reportedly continued drinking with his questionable buddies every afternoon until his obituary.

Springer Hoster continued to be one of the most respected citizens in St. Anna. He was last reported trying to help a fellow patient escape the St. Anna Nursing Home by helping to crack the code on the inside of the front door of that facility. The escape was short-lived. He subsequently passed on to a reportedly more peaceful place. Folks attending his funeral observed that his obituary was very kind to him.

Ben Ward was convicted in federal court of ITSP and given ten years in the federal penitentiary.

A few years later the US Probation and Parole Office, serving the District of Idaho, called McWade to inform him that Ward had found a sponsor and was being granted an early release and parole because of his fine behavior in prison.

You guessed it!

He was being sponsored by a very questionable farm equipment dealership right there in St. Anna.

"You can't make this stuff up! Ben Ward is now going to be a new future citizen of Thompson County, Idaho," McWade told his buddies at the doughnut shop that day. "This is the same Ben Ward that shot over the heads of law enforcement officers in the state of

Montana when they tried to arrest him at his Three Forks Quonset shop."

"He will either be the mayor of St. Anna or the Thompson County sheriff within the next ten years to keep the legend alive," McWade quipped. "I'm sure the implement business will know exactly how to make use of his expertise in concealing serial numbers and repainting stolen tractors. Wow!" he exclaimed.

McWade was a firm believer in only punishing those who had committed the crime. But there really didn't seem to be much justice here.

"Sometimes going native in the Land of Deliverance is not what it is cut out to be," he mumbled to himself as he realized just how close he and his partner, Bill, had come to being in the middle of an old west showdown and possible shoot-out with seemingly corrupt county law enforcement, thieves, and redneck bullies.

The whole thing that night in the shadows of the dim streetlights could have turned into a gunfight mirroring the one in *Tombstone* at the *O.K. Corral.*

"What a country! But the commute to work was sure great!"

Could it be that Thompson County was one of Idaho's attempts at being a sanctuary county where outside law was not welcomed? But then being ordered out of the county is even a step above the mere sanctuary status claim.

As McWade reflected back on the infamous Thompson County incident, he thought of all the players involved in the game. They were a colorful bunch. There was Red, Butch, Rich, Danny, and, of course, Springer. At one time in his life, his ego may have felt somewhat injured by the derogatory and inflammatory comments made by the players there.

But then the famous line from a favorite Western movie *Tombstone* always came to mind and made him feel almost gleeful. This was when Doc Holliday coined the statement, "If I am to be insulted, I must first value your opinion!"

And so it was!

Chapter 29

The Minister's Daughter

F ishing in the beautiful vacation area of Thompson County had
been great for Bonnie Bosserton and her husband, Sam. The
seemingly unending carpet of Lodgepole Pine trees of the Targhee
National Forest stretched as far as the eye could see across the volcanic caldera known as Island Park. The seclusion of this area on
the western border of Yellowstone National Park had prompted the
young couple to comment on how great it would be to live there.
Sam had commented to his young wife, "Wouldn't it be great to be
able to get a log cabin and just settle here?"

This modern-day version of Bonnie and Clyde were traveling
through the area in the 1994 Jeep Cherokee they had stolen in the
state of Florida from a retired New Jersey police officer, who hadn't
learned yet to remove the keys from his parked car.

With the stolen Jeep in their possession, they liked to stop at the
state line each time they were about to enter into that particular state.
Out would come the camera, and photographs would be taken of
themselves, the stolen car, and the Welcome signs in the background.

Welcome to Tennessee. Click, click went the 35 mm camera.

Welcome to Colorado. Click, click!

Welcome to Nebraska. Click, click!

The thought didn't seem to enter into their heads that these photographs just might be important in proving Interstate Transporting
of a Stolen Motor Vehicle (ITSMV) if they were ever to be caught in
the pilfered Cherokee.

Thompson County was a place now known to McWade as a place of showdowns, and this was to be no exception.

Our cross-country thieves were heading south between the small town of Ashton, Idaho, toward St. Anna on US Highway 20. They had just crossed over the Fall River bridge when their small dog, Puddles, lived up to his name and peed in the car. In complete frustration, Sam made an abrupt and sudden U-turn across the two-lane highway and pointed the car back in a northeasterly direction.

As fate would have it, a dedicated ISP trooper just happened to see the car whip around in somewhat of a reckless fashion and decided to pursue the situation. The siren and red lights came on as the ISP unit closed the gap behind the stolen car.

Inside the car, a preconceived plan was immediately put into action. Bonnie reached into the glove compartment and handed Sam their concealed Bersa .380 semiautomatic pistol, which she herself had loaded earlier the previous evening.

Sam pulled the vehicle over to the shoulder of the highway about three-fourth mile from the Fall River bridge which they had just crossed a minute before while heading the opposite direction.

The young good-looking trooper, James Gomez, exited his patrol unit, thinking this was just a routine traffic violation. He approached the stopped car from the rear driver's side in a cautious fashion, and with his right hand, he routinely unfastened the holster on his service weapon. Little did he know what was in the mind of the two occupants of the car and what was in store for him.

The Bossertons had both talked about this moment in great detail should it arise and were in complete harmony as to what their contingency plan was and how it was to be executed. It was simple, specific and to the point. "Kill the officer!"

Sam was no stranger to prison and had no intention of ever going back. His new, somewhat naive bride had been talked into and was in harmony with his plan.

Sam's hatred of police was later to be well-documented throughout his life of crime. At the young age of twenty-five, Sam had already managed to build a rap sheet résumé that included burglary, theft, and possession of cocaine and, at the time, was an escapee from the great state of Florida. Unknown to trooper Gomez, Bonnie had aided and abetted in his escape from the Franklin County, Florida, jail, where he been incarcerated on a variety of other charges.

"Hello, sir, how are you doing today?" trooper Gomez asked politely.

The trooper did not see the concealed Bersa being held, out of sight, beside the driver's right leg, in his right hand. The plan concocted by the two occupants of the car was in full operation at this point. Sam was very cool and seemed clean-cut and friendly.

Bonnie, on the other hand, knowing what was about to happen, was very nervous and actually squirming in the passenger seat as if to prepare herself for what was to happen next.

"Good!" came the reply from Bosserton.

Then with a lightning move with his right hand, the concealed pistol came flashing from his side and was aimed point-blank into the torso of the young officer.

Three shots were cranked off in rapid succession by the young thug directly into the troopers chest area.

Good police training now kicked in, as if the trooper was on autopilot. He quickly spun around in a counterclockwise direction, pulled out his own pistol, and fired at the Jeep as it was now speeding from the scene toward the town of Ashton.

The rear side window of the Cherokee was shattered, and another shot never found its intended mark. Due to the intense emotional state of the officer, after having just been shot, attempts to fire more rounds were unsuccessful as the trigger was not fully released enough to allow the weapon to fully function.

"It felt like I was hit with a sledgehammer when those .380 slugs hit me!" he later recalled to McWade. "I seriously did not know if I was going to live or die as I had no idea if my vest stopped the slugs or not."

Miraculously, Gomez was not injured, thanks to his protective equipment doing the intended job.

When the young trooper realized he was still alive, he jumped into his cruiser and began the pursuit of the vehicle, which had now disappeared around the bend and over the Fall River bridge.

As he raced to find the attempted murderer, he called for help but, at the same time, realized he had lost sight of the fleeing vehicle.

Sam and Bonnie had mistakenly thought they could elude the police by going off-road with the four-wheel-drive Cherokee. About a mile from the scene of the shooting, Sam had turned the Jeep to the east and crossed over the Union Pacific railroad tracks. His intention was to bounce through the sagebrush, sand, and pasture land toward the towering Teton Peaks that stood on the horizon about sixty miles to the east. He hoped to escape into that wilderness area undetected.

This plan did not work any better than his plan of killing the officer as about three hundred yards into the sagebrush the Jeep hit a large lava rock sticking up from the sandy grassland. The unit hit with such force that it was damaged, high centered, and immediately was out of commission. Apparently young Sam was unfamiliar with four-wheeling in the desert and avoiding large outcroppings of lava rocks.

Now in a very unfamiliar countryside, Sam and Bonnie grabbed a few of their belongings. Abandoning the disabled Jeep, they set out into the unknown as the cool evening air in the high country began to settle in around them with a distinct chilling effect.

As night began to approach, they saw a large barn in the distance and headed toward it with haste. Their shoes were designed more for the Florida beach than the cactus, sagebrush, and sharp lava rocks of the high desert along the north shore of the gushing Fall River as it carried its clear, precious water from Yellowstone to the Henry's Fork of the Snake River a few miles to the west.

Tired and cold, they took refuge in the old barn and snuggled in the hay, which was piled in the far end. Bonnie's feet were bleeding and both were cold, wet, and shivering after slipping into the cold icy waters of the river a half-mile downstream.

A virtual posse of law enforcement had gathered by now, and the stolen getaway Jeep had been located, impounded, and was being processed. Officers from the ISP, the Thompson County SO, and other local jurisdictions had assembled and were, with the aid of trained dogs, tracking the two subjects.

Leading the charge for the Thompson SO was none other than Chief Deputy Butch, who had sacrificed his nightly happy hour to be there with the troops. He was already at odds with the ISP as he was demanding that the SO have possession of the Jeep while the ISP, with much more expertise, wanted to process it for evidence. After all, the shooting was on a major highway and involved an ISP trooper, so the ISP was demanding jurisdiction to gather evidence into the shooting of one of their own.

After a very heated exchange, the ISP allowed possession of the car to go with the SO and requested assistance from McWade to help with interviews and processing of evidence. This turf war between agencies would continue as time passed.

Through the chilly night air, the couple in the barn, huddling together for warmth, heard the sound of dogs on their scent followed by voices as the posse circled the structure trapping them inside.

Butch repeatedly called for them to come out with their hands in the air, but it was in vain as young Sam had vowed he would not, under any circumstances, go back to jail.

About seven the next morning, the officers surrounding the barn heard Bonnie call out that she wanted to surrender. Soon the figure of a sobbing, tired, and cold female appeared in the open sliding doorway of the barn. She was quickly placed under arrest and whisked off in a patrol car to the Thompson County Jail. The stand-off continued at the barn as the hours dragged on endlessly. The pleas to surrender were ignored or verbally refused.

Back at the county jail, McWade had arrived and was interviewing Mrs. Bosserton in detail, trying to get all the elements of an ITSMV case covered as well as the shooting of the trooper.

Bonnie was in a very talkative mood and was confessing to McWade the same way she would to the pastor at her Evangelical church.

She was the daughter of a minister in the state of Tennessee when young Sam visited the congregation to hear her dad preach. She, being a bit naive, found love at first sight and was swept off her feet by the handsome young stranger. It was not long before she accepted his hand in marriage to become officially Bonnie Bosserton, teenage bride of Sam.

When they married, little did she know or suspect that the ring Sam gave her was one he stole in a burglary. The journey with Sam was to only go downhill from that point on. The new marriage was rocky, but love seems to be totally blind. The BS from Sam made her think she was on cloud nine, but then anything can look tasty when served on the right dishes.

She told McWade that she loved the guy. She said that she really had a strong feeling for him but asked the question aloud, "But what was I thinking?"

When he was sent to jail in Florida, she played the part of the loyal bride thinking that he, like so many others, was just the innocent victim of blind justice. He always said the police "just had it out for him and accused him of things he really did not do."

She talked freely about how she coordinated his escape and drove the getaway car after picking him up from a work camp project. Again, she claimed she believed that he was innocent. "I guess I'm just a poor judge of people, but I do truly love him," she freely confessed.

The minister's daughter denied any involvement in the shooting and claimed she knew nothing of the plan and did not even know he (Sam) had a gun. This story later fell apart when her fingerprints were found on the extracted .380 shell casings from the pistol, indicating that she had actually loaded the cartridges into the magazine herself.

McWade was noting that Bonnie, just like almost all other persons he had dealt with in the past, tended to use their religion as a protective shield to hide behind. All too frequently, they were very good at the game of deception and lying.

She claimed she did know the Jeep Cherokee was stolen but did not witness the theft as she was around the corner when Sam took possession of the vehicle. He was gone for a few minutes and came back driving it and smiled that some idiot had "left the keys in the ignition." She passionately and categorically denied driving the car herself. This was also later proven to be untrue when the 35 mm film from her camera was developed, which showed her smiling face behind the steering wheel of the stolen car as they entered the state of Idaho.

About an hour into the interview, the door to the SO interview room opened and someone informed her of some very bad news.

Back at the barn, it seemed that Sam was not planning to give up even though he was trapped like a caged animal in the old barn and had exhausted all avenues of escape. Soon Deputy Butch grew impatient and tossed in a couple tear gas canisters. Within a minute, two shots rang out from inside the barn and then total silence. Nothing was heard but the sound of crickets from the nearby pond. The silence was deafening, and it didn't take a brain surgeon to guess what had happened inside.

When no voice response came from inside the building, the surrounding posse carefully entered the barn only to find the lifeless body of the young fugitive with his weapon still in his hand. He had been very honest with himself, for the first time in a long time, when he had earlier told Bonnie that "I will not go back to jail."

Thanks to the person interrupting the interview to tell about the death of Sam, the questioning came to an abrupt end. Bonnie turned into an emotional basket case and was ushered out of the interview room and back to her cell.

The turf war between the ISP and the Thompson County SO seemed to make it into the local newspaper, the Idaho Falls-based *Post Register*.

The headline was "Thompson Sheriff Demands and Gets Respect." Excerpts from that article told the Thompson County story: "I just don't have that problem (respect)," the sheriff said. "They always go through me, whether it's the FBI, the ISP, the IRS, or whoever. That doesn't mean there aren't some grumbles," the sheriff continued.

The article continued, "One state (ISP) officer tried to take Bosserton's (stolen) car to Idaho Falls (to be processed). Thompson County Deputy Curt Hillman, with the sheriff's blessing, told him (the ISP officer) that he would take him to jail if he tried to move the car. The car stayed put and the dispute was quieted with little controversy."

Again, headlines from the *Post Register* gave a chronology of the events:

5/30/95: "Gunman Shoots Trooper, Self"

5/31/95: "Gunman's Crime Trail led to Standoff"

6/6/95: "Widow of Florida Fugitive Faces More Felony Charges"

6/8/95: "Trooper Shooting Hearing Delayed"

6/14/95: "Bosserton Indicted in Shooting" (Bonnie Bosserton)

6/15/95: "Trooper Testifies at Hearing"

6/20/95: "Florida Woman Is Bound Over, Federal Grand Jury Returns Indictment Based on FBI Investigation and Testimony"

9/19/95: "Judge Orders Widow Released from Thompson County Jail"

11/14/95: "Bosserton Pleads Guilty to Federal Stolen Motor Vehicle Charges Stemming from Trooper Shooting Incident"

3/19/96: "Woman Sentenced in Stolen Car/Trooper Shooting Incident"

For her part in the whole crime spree, Bonnie was sentenced in Federal Court to a mere six months in federal prison and ordered to pay $14,000 for the damage to the stolen Jeep Cherokee. In Idaho State court at St. Anna, she was given a withheld judgment plus 150 hours of community service. As usually is the case, McWade noted she showed great remorse for her crimes.

The Thompson County Attorney, Penny Stanford. doubted her sincerity calling her "someone who has been very sorry she was caught."

The Bonnie and Clyde-type crime spree across the US left a trail of burglaries, thefts, and who knows what else? There were numerous false ID cards found in the vehicle, and the young widow only told McWade what she thought he already knew about her involvement.

During the time between her court-ordered release from jail on September 19, 1995, and her sentencing on March 19, 1996, she was free as a bird to go wherever she wanted. But like others in the past, she found Thompson County to be a very criminally friendly community and decided to stay and blend in with the good folks of St. Anna.

"But then, if the truth was known, Bonnie might, despite her criminal background, be as trustworthy as a lot of the folks in law enforcement." McWade chuckled to himself. "After all, this was Thompson County."

Thinking back to the case of Sam and Bonnie Bosserton, McWade recalled a quote he had once heard that stated, "Sometimes, the first step toward forgiveness is realizing that the other person was born an idiot." He was not saying that Sam was, in fact, an idiot, but he was a young man that seemed to be always striving, but never arriving.

As for Bonnie, hopefully this whole experience would be her education into the real world. She, as the minister's naive daughter, was last seen on the front row of his little Tennessee chapel taking notes, having hopefully gained a new perspective in life.

Not a night goes by that now-retired trooper Gomez doesn't thank the manufacturer of his lifesaving bulletproof vest. He still undoubtedly has moments where he is also eternally thankful that young Sam was instinctively shooting for the torso and not the head area of his target.

Chapter 30

Are You Where You Want to Be?

Every agent that McWade ever knew, just like most people out-side the Bureau, went through different phases of their FBI lives. There was the anticipation of the hiring, the excitement of the academy experience, the big adjustment to life in the first field assignment as an FOA (first office agent). Then there was moving on to the challenge of being virtually on his own and the accompanying solitude as an RA (resident agent) in one of the most remote one-man offices in the entire FBI. Twenty years in Scottsbluff and then back home to his OP (office of preference), his early-life roots in Eastern Idaho. The place where he always thought he wanted to fin-ish his career and fade away into the next phase of his life, wherever that happened to take him.

At some point along the way, McWade took up the sport of running with one of his friends as a partner. Given his personality, it was not long before he thought, *Wouldn't it be macho to actually run a couple of marathons?*

A memorable quote from his *Runner's World* magazine soon became a phrase he would often use to motivate himself or to try to shame one of his kids to reach higher goals. It went something like: "Somewhere in the world, someone is training when you are not. When you race him he will win!"

When McWade transferred to Idaho Falls, he already knew that the Idaho National Engineering Laboratory (INEL) operated by the

Department of Energy (DOE) was part of his RA territory. This place was known to the locals as merely "the Site."

It appeared to McWade that one of the seemingly important things the DOE did at the Site was to change the official name frequently.

Established in 1949 as the National Reactor Testing Station, it was known as such until 1975 when it became the Energy Research and Development Administration. In 1977, it became the INEL, by which it was known until someone added the word *environmental* to the mix in 1997. At that time, it officially became the Idaho National Engineering and Environmental Laboratory (INEEL).

In 2005, the name was modified again and is, to this date, known simply as the Idaho National Lab (INL).

The site is a huge complex of over 890 square miles located in the high desert sagebrush area west of Idaho Falls in a remote area somewhat conducive to atomic energy experimentation. The site has a long history of impressive technological achievements in the field of next-generation energy study and other development.

In the late 1990s, Bill Garrett, Investigator for the OIG (Office of the Inspector General) DOE, contacted McWade for assistance.

Garrett was very well versed in all the rules and regulations pertaining to the handling of nuclear waste and hazardous materials and was troubled about certain information he had received from his sources.

It was alleged that two rogue INEL contract employees were randomly dumping and disposing of hazardous waste materials around the site, in total disregard for all existing rules and safety regulations.

The two villains were identified as Trey Yonson and Cleve Cigeria.

Garrett reported that "these two clowns are supposed to be disposing of waste samples from the lab in a legal and well-established manner. Instead, they are reportedly dumping this material anywhere and everywhere they could."

"Reports are that Yonson even takes these samples home in an INEL van and then, under cover of darkness, disposes of them in the

Shelley, Idaho, landfill or possibly even in the irrigation canal behind his home," the investigator added.

It seemed that these two cavalier mavericks had taken things entirely into their own hands when getting rid of hazardous waste. Over the fence into the desert! "Just dump it!" Yonson instructed Cigeria. If fifty or one hundred samples, or containers, were still in the van at the end of the day, it didn't really seem to matter.

After Yonson had driven the van home at night, these samples just seemed to magically disappear under the cover of darkness and were mysteriously gone by morning. *After all, who would ever know the difference?* thought Yonson.

Whatever happened to the waste was never to be fully known. One source heard that "Yonson had been dumping the samples into his garbage can to be taken to the Shelley landfill."

Another tipster had seen the bottles and boxes of unknown hazardous waste in the INEL van when Yonson left the Site the night before and noted that it was absolutely not in the van the next morning when he returned to work.

McWade and Garrett looked at each other and concluded almost simultaneously, in unison, "Could all this hazardous material still be at Yonson's house?"

"Let's pay Yonson's wife a visit and see what we come up with," suggested McWade.

The pretty young housewife answered the door of her home in the small farm town of Shelley.

"Why, yes, I'm Mrs. Yonson," she replied. "What can I do for you?"

She soon realized the two lawmen were not there at her front door to pay her a social visit and, upon that realization, became very guarded and defensive in her answers. Being a loyal wife, she was covering her husband's butt and seemed fully on board with whatever was going on at the Yonson household. She was an honest and somewhat religious woman, which made it difficult to lie without the signs of her deception covering her entire person. Within a couple of minutes, she was beginning to sweat like the proverbial whore in church. Her mouth became dry and her words deliberate and forced.

It was evident she wanted Garrett and McWade gone, but then she knew she wanted to appear cooperative due to her husband's job being at risk.

"No, I haven't seen Trey bring any bottles or containers home. Gee, I have no idea about any of this," she stated innocently.

Suddenly, from behind her skirt came the high-pitched voice of her little six-year-old son who had been listening attentively. "Mommy, those bottles are down at the bottom of the stairs. I saw Daddy carry them in last night!"

Mrs. Yonson's face lost all color. She suddenly had no interest at all in helping.

"No!" was her abrupt answer when McWade asked for a simple consent to search the basement for the contraband.

"We will be back with a search warrant, and those items your little boy saw better still be there or you too may be in very serious and deep trouble."

Being the "Lone Ranger" and going "native" may be great and have some advantages, but when trying to get a search warrant from the US Attorney's Office three hundred miles away, it can be an all-day thing.

With the aid of the fax machine and telephone at the Shelley PD, by nightfall a search warrant was finally in hand. The Chief of Police and one of his officers had volunteered to watch the Yonson residence to hopefully prevent Trey from sneaking in undetected and removing the evidence.

The house surveillance proved not to be all that great as Yonson himself answered the door when they knocked with the search warrant in hand.

Naturally, the evidence was gone and the search of the home proved fruitless.

Finally, McWade confronted Trey bluntly. "We know the waste containers are here in your home, and unless you want to sit here and watch as dismantle your house board by board, I would suggest you show them to us. Furthermore, you better have and explanation as to how you got into your house without entering through the garage or any door."

Soon Yonson was confessing to McWade as if he was confessing to his local Mormon bishop at the church just down the street. He was even pleading for forgiveness in the process.

"I parked the INEL van at the old sugar factory about a mile away and sneaked into the house through a back basement window that my wife opened for me," he stuttered. "I took all the samples I had stored in the basement and hid them outside by the canal bank under a utility pole."

Within minutes, boxes and bottles of unknown waste in every size and shape were seized, photographed, and placed into evidence. Most of the labels had been scratched off by Yonson to avoid undue attention.

Yonson assured the investigators there was nothing radioactive or dangerous as long as the material was kept in their containers.

Back at the Shelley PD, Yonson gave a full statement telling how he and his accomplice, Cigeria, had dumped the materials for several months at unauthorized locations around the Site. He very wisely denied dumping any materials in the city of Shelley landfill, thus shutting down any potential state of Idaho criminal violations.

The next day, his very anxious young accomplice, Cleve Cigeria, was located at his office at Central, the main office complex, at the Site.

His statement, though damning, was that everything he did, "I was just following instructions from my supervisor, Yonson. I knew it was wrong, but after all, he was my boss and I was following instructions."

Both of the black sheep of the desert claimed the motive for their actions was that their management had swamped them with work beyond what they could physically do, and the illegal dumping was the only way to get rid of the stuff and keep ahead of the game. They both used the word *overwhelmed* to describe their work situation.

Word of the illegal dumping soon got around the town of Idaho Falls, which, to a large degree, owed its existence to the Site and its thousands of high-paying jobs. The *Post Register* headlines were as follows:

1. "Investigation Has INEL Worker Nervous as Heck as Federal Grand Jury Meets, FBI Keeps Quiet on the Nature of Alleged Illegal Dumping"
2. "Illegal Dumping, Two INEL Workers Face Charges after Investigation"

After the federal grand jury indicted Yonson and Cigeria, it seemed allegations at the INEL came out of the woodwork. Sources proclaiming and asserting all kinds of practices that either had happened were ongoing or were out of compliance with rules of environmental law flooded the IG's office daily.

Time card fraud was alleged. Not reporting hazardous waste spills as required by the law was asserted. Cover-ups by supervisors of known illegal activity was insinuated. This case was starting to take on a life of its own, and the last thing McWade wanted was to get bogged down on a full-time matter with the OIG as it would prevent him from doing all the other work assigned to him.

At first, this looked like a routine matter. Yonson pleaded guilty and was to be sentenced. But then it was learned that Cigeria was claiming he was now innocent and was demanding a trial. It was soon learned that the INEL contractor for whom he worked was providing him with one of the sharpest defense attorneys in Idaho, all at the expense (indirectly) of the taxpayer, of course.

The contractor was taking much longer than seemingly reasonable to respond to simple requests.

McWade was quickly learning that large corporations—whether these corporations are disguised as churches, businesses, charities, political action groups, or otherwise—tend to circle the wagons and try in every way to protect the good name of their corporation when anyone asks questions or investigates them. This situation appeared to be no exception.

Since the DOE was paying the bill, it only made sense that they could ask the contractor to do whatever they requested. But this proved not entirely to be the case, and soon McWade realized that this was a classic situation where the tail was wagging the dog. And the tail in this case was that of a somewhat sassy Pitt Bull!

It was suggested to McWade that perhaps the reason for this lack of interest in helping with the investigation was the fact that many of the DOE attorneys and staff, those making oversight decisions over the contractor, would be in line for great retirement jobs when they retired. The contractor always seemed to find a way to hire these folks into great high-paying and lucrative positions. This was just pure speculation, but there seemed to be numerous examples of that very thing in every hall and office of the contractor's headquarters building. "What better way to get a cushy retirement job than to show favors to the contractor you are hoping will hire you," McWade concluded. The trial of Cigeria in Pocatello, Idaho, came all too soon and was to become a fiasco.

The AUSA handling the matter had, without McWade's permission or knowledge, allowed one of the defense witnesses, a supervisor with the contractor, to change her statement she had made to McWade during an interview. The AUSA permitted this witness to change her testimony on the official FD-302.

Then during the trial, the slick defense attorney used this to impugn McWade and cast doubt on his credibility. The question to the witness was "So was Agent McWade just mistaken, or was he lying?"

The lying phrase was repeated two or three times to get the point across to the jury.

Since the AUSA was the one who had allowed the change of the FD-302, he wanted to distance himself from his official blunder and refused to allow McWade to be called back to the stand to explain what had happened. To save his own face, this guy threw McWade under the bus, which adversely impacted the case outcome. What should have been a slam dunk was a dismal defeat and a failure on the part of the government.

Cigeria smiled as he left the courtroom.

Yonson, who had earlier plead guilty and then testified against Cigeria, could not believe his eyes and must have wondered about the wisdom of his own guilty plea.

Within a week of the conclusion of the ill-fated trial, McWade received a confidential visit from a person who had served on the federal grand jury (FGJ) in Boise during the entire process. Since FGJ proceedings are strictly confidential, this person did not reveal anything that would put the process in jeopardy. What this person was upset about was the behavior of the AUSA during the whole FGJ process.

The juror reported that the AUSA tried, on at least two occasions, to lead the FGJ into not focusing on the Site contractor as being culpable in what had happened regarding the environmental violations at the INEL. This was done by having the AUSA excuse the court reporter at a scheduled recess. Then without any reporter present, off the record, the AUSA would downplay the part of the contractor and try to imply that there were no prosecutable violations that could be proven against them. This was a very serious allegation, and McWade pondered what to do with the potentially dynamite information. The logical conclusion was to up-channel the whole thing to his immediate supervisor in Boise. So the phone call was made and a full verbal report given regarding the unprecedented changing of the testimony in the FD-302, which cost a conviction at a trial, plus the allegation of the FGJ manipulation.

There was a long period of complete silence on the other end of the line as the wheels inside the high-paid Bureau supervisor's brain were obviously churning like two hamsters on a wheel. By now in his Bureau career, McWade had learned that sometimes the absolute biggest and most important accomplishment was just being able to keep his mouth shut. So with that in mind, he waited for what seemed like an eternity.

Finally, his supervisor spoke deliberately and slowly to allow his words to sink in and to be understood. "There is no single case that we ever work or no single incident that happens that is worth jeopardizing the excellent relationship we have with the US Attorney's Office."

This comment came as no big surprise as he knew his supervisor was a personal friend of the supervisor of the AUSA in question. They were known to go to coffee together daily and had associations outside the office in a friendship capacity.

McWade put the information in a memorandum to the appropriate file to cover his own posterior, mumbled a bit to himself, and went about his other work.

Any thought of going any further with the information was put to rest two weeks later when McWade was visited by his ASAC from the Salt Lake City Office. The Idaho Falls RA was not due for a routine inspection or visit by anyone, so it was suspected there was some unannounced agenda and that it was not just a social call.

After a few minutes of routine small talk, the boss, who seemed well versed in the entire fiasco involving the AUSA, moved the conversation to that matter. He tactfully had McWade review the entire set of circumstances and listened patiently, only interrupting for clarification. When the case had been rehashed, he leaned back and cleared his throat. His question was a real clincher, and it was apparent he had given the matter considerable thought.

"Are you where you want to be?" he asked slowly and deliberately.

He knew full well that this was McWade's office of preference (OP). He also knew that it had taken over twenty-five years for McWade to get to this assignment and that it was the place he wanted to finish out the last few years of his career.

"Yes, it took a long time to get here!" came the obvious reply.

There was another long silent pause. McWade could hear the faint whistle of a freight train in the distance and the second hand on the office clock pounding like a jackhammer.

The visiting ASAC broke the silence and again asked, "Are you absolutely sure you are where you want to be?"

McWade was no dummy; after all, he had graduated from prestigious Utah State University with honors, and he knew exactly what was being implied.

He knew that if a formal complaint was filed against that lackluster AUSA, it would be forever impossible to ever work again with the US Attorney's Office in the District of Idaho. Since all cases worked by the FBI had to be presented to and prosecuted by the USA, this was a total no-brainer.

McWade also knew by now that nothing whatsoever would ever be done to the AUSA in question. These folks seemed to be above the law, and he knew it. It was also crystal clear at this point that there would be zero support from his own FBI.

This appeared to be a bit of a hostage situation. Report it further and be transferred, or just keep quiet and retire in Idaho Falls on schedule.

Nothing more had to be said. The entire incident was typed up and submitted to SLC, FBI. McWade highly doubted that memo made it into the official file.

However, McWade continued to smile each morning as he drove to his small RA in Idaho Falls, where he was out of sight and mostly now out of his supervisors' minds. He only had to recall how bad the traffic was in Los Angeles every time he wondered if he did the right thing. When that thought passed through his mind, he just smiled even wider.

McWade continued to work with the zeal of an FOA and learned how to pick and choose which AUSA he presented his cases to for a prosecutive opinions. He was even accused of attorney shopping but wore that title like a badge of honor. Office politics was something he detested when it came to getting things done, and his name was long remembered at the USA office in Boise. Attorney shopping had a good ring to it, and to be accused of it was a compliment as he wanted results and someone who would actively prosecute a worthy case.

The slogan about someone being out there training when you are not meant more to him now because he knew on race day he had actually won this one.

Someone had once said, "I would rather be dead than to quit living."

And almost daily he reminded himself, "Yes, I am where I want to be. This is living!"

Chapter 31

Cream Rises to the Top of the Can (Guess What Else Does)

Growing up on a small Idaho farm, McWade learned something about growing potatoes, alfalfa hay, and grain. But there was also the dreaded chore of milking that small herd of Holstein cows every night and every morning. Those creatures kept him fastened to the farm like Elmer's glue. They were there after football practice, they were there on Christmas morning. When it came to reliability and dependability, nothing could match that small herd of black-and-white animals—always waiting, always wanting, and always there.

In those days, the milk was poured through as funnel-like strainer into ten-gallon galvanized cans to be picked up each day by a milkman from the local creamery where the milk was hauled for processing into butter or cheese. It was a fact of life to the young budding agent that the cream would rise to the top of those cans and become very thick.

It was also very much a fact of life that any dirty, worthless foreign material such as crud (called cow shit on the farm) that happened to get in the milk cans also would rise to the top of the can.

This very simple observation was to carry over and have greater impact to helping him understand and evaluate the management program in the FBI.

Jokingly, regular street agents would repeat a saying something to the effect that "in the FBI, like nowhere else, does the cream struggle so hard to stay at the bottom of the can." Conversely, when referring to the FBI management program, these same regular, hardworking agents would also make reference to the fact that "shit always rises to the top of the bucket!"

In discussing the FBI management program, McWade always pointed out that he was not being overly critical of many of the individuals in the program but, rather, was attacking the system itself that attracted and then fostered so many truly incompetent and often narcissistic individuals into positions of leadership.

As a young agent in San Antonio, he only had to look at the requirements and expectations for those who signed away their lives to go management. After looking at the steps required, he soon concluded that it would take a certain personality type to voluntarily sign away so much of his normal life to this pursuit.

First, the agent would have to sign up for the program and then usually act as a "Relief Supervisor" in the field office for a period of time. He would, at some point, be sent to some type of management training at FBI HQ for an in-service.

Regular agents joked that normal fun-loving agents whom they knew as friends before the training would often come back transformed. The office talk was that these new soon-to-be management types were given lobotomies while there as they came back greatly changed and not for the better. They now distanced themselves from their former friends, acted more self-righteous, and were referred to by many around the office, behind their backs, as just plain pricks.

Assuming the agent newly entering the management program impressed the right people and was able to develop into a polished sycophant, he would be in line for assignments as a desk or squad supervisor and other lower supervisory assignments. Back in the 1970s through the 1990s, the recruit would often be transferred to larger cities with higher costs of living, longer commutes often with the corresponding strains on family life, if he or she was married.

Somewhere in the process, the budding supervisor would be assigned to the inspection staff for a period of one or more years and would travel with that staff to terrorize the various field offices they happened to be inspecting. This meant living in hotels and motels, away from home for weeks at a time, with the resulting strain on normal family life and marriages.

As was mentioned earlier, the program seemed to attract a special type of personality. McWade recalled a regular visit to his main office in Omaha for an all-agent conference on one occasion, where fifteen agents went out to eat at a local favorite restaurant. Every agent at the table ordered a hamburger-type sandwich from the menu, except an agent from Iowa named Jim. This guy ordered the most expensive steak on the menu, and when the bill came around, he was the one to suggest we just do the "New York split." He wanted the total of the bill divided by the number of agents (fifteen) and that every agent pay that amount. Essentially, he wanted his steak to be the same cost as a hamburger. The other agents told him to go to hell. But it was a good try.

McWade followed Jim's career path over the years, and you guessed it. He jumped into the management program and climbed through the ranks rapidly to become an SAC. Here was a man who had what it took to be an FBI leadership icon.

Over the years, the Bureau seemed to increase the leadership ranks at a pace much faster than the street agent growth. In looking back, McWade was very much convinced that a lot of the bad supervision was a direct result of too much supervision. There were soon offices with multiple ASACs, where in the past one had done the job. Squad and RA supervisors seemed to be tripping over themselves in some field offices. "All these chiefs and so few warriors," McWade would observe.

The beefing up of supervisors led to increased micromanaging. This really didn't bother McWade so much until it was observed that many agents were jumping into the program to become managers with very little time in the trenches. Soon the young micromanaging case supervisor, who had never worked that kind of case, was telling McWade how things should be done. The only salvation was that most of these eager beavers did not remember the great suggestions given during the ninety-day file reviews. Therefore, most of their less-than-brilliant recommendations and proposals could just go in one ear and out the other. When back in the RA territory McWade worked the cases in the established logical manner he had found to be effective.

McWade, in no way, wanted to insinuate that all Bureau supervisors and leaders fit the mold described above. Some were genuine, honest, and helpful. Those were, however, not the norm in his Bureau experience. It is not those that he talks about next but rather those who truly stood out as being genuine examples of poor leadership and the subjects of office jokes. Those who truly exemplified the Peter Principle in action.

Probably one of the most flagrant examples of managerial narcissistic behavior witnessed by McWade was outlined in chapter 23 ("Willful Ignorance"), where SAC Glen Geno stood before the group of seasoned agents at a management conference to proclaim his famous statement, "When you can't run as fast as the other guys, *you cheat to win!*"

Priorities

This guy just could not stand being anything but in first place in any kind of race or contest even if it was quite meaningless.

During the mid-1990s, the SLC Division would sponsor a SWAT Olympics event each year and invite SWAT (Special Weapons and Tactics) teams from various law enforcement agencies in the Utah, Idaho, and Montana area to compete.

Geno was still fuming and visibly upset at the fact that the SRT (Special Response Team) from the INEL in Idaho Falls had handily won the previous year's competition. They had actually beaten his beloved SWAT Team.

McWade had heard him muttering how this was not tolerable and that they were "just a bunch of ragtag security guards who were not even actually real law enforcement."

To make sure that his FBI SWAT team did not go down in defeat again, he had doubled down on the number of times they practiced. On this particular day, they were at Camp Williams, Utah, a Utah National Guard Base, south of Salt Lake City. This was to be a no-nonsense, balls-to-the-wall training exercise. This was very serious business as Glen did not want to be humiliated again by these private security guards from the Idaho desert.

Geno's men were in the middle of their intense practice. They were climbing walls, and they were shooting at targets from every imaginable position. They were running and doing all sorts of real-life scenarios with every man concentrating on bringing home the honors to their fearless leader. This looked like a paramilitary unit getting ready for actual combat.

As the excitement and intensity of the drill increased, there was a call from a neighboring FBI division to the south requesting assistance from the Salt Lake SWAT Team. It seemed there was some sort of an armed standoff on the Indian reservation near the four corners area, where Utah, Colorado, Arizona, and New Mexico share a common boundary. Shots had been exchanged and the situation looked dire.

The Salt Lake City SWAT Team was already assembled, had their gear with them, and could be on the road within minutes to help defuse this very dangerous situation.

But wait! What was the purpose of the practice going on at Camp Williams?

It was certainly not to help out some other FBI office with a very legitimate and potentially lifesaving stalemate involving armed desperados. Again, the priority here was to make sure the SRT Team from the INEL did not win again.

Geno messaged back to the requesting field office that his team was not available as they were "fully engaged in their own special" and unable to assist.

McWade's source on the team reported that Geno suggested they request help from other nearby field offices that could respond.

Now here was a boss who knew his real priorities.

These are the things that make regular agents roll their eyes and shake their heads. These managerial blunders seemed to always go unchallenged and again would lend credibility to the oft used statement, "Screw up, move up!"

To try to understand the driving forces behind men like Glen Geno was like trying to herd cats!

Involuntary Volunteering

Mick O'Lara, SAC of the Omaha Division, wanted to impress the United Way (UW) leadership in the city of Omaha by giving them a large donation check. He could visualize himself handing the UW folks a rather large check and making sure, of course, that the newspapers and other media were there to capture his smiling face proudly handing over the donation check. To make his dream come to pass, he sent out a memo to each and every agent in the entire division, which, again, took in the states of Iowa and Nebraska. This memo basically ordered every agent to make a generous donation and send it to his secretary by the next week.

McWade just told the secretary he had already donated to the UW in Scottsbluff and the subject ended for him. However, another agent (let's call him Shear Cannon), in one of the outstate Nebraska RAs, foolishly dared to tell the secretary that he was choosing not to donate, did not believe in some of the entities the UW funded, and certainly was not donating to the Omaha chapter of the UW. Given the short fuse and the hot temper of O'Lara, a very dictatorial superior, this was not a well-thought-out answer by Cannon.

O'Lara took this as a personal insult and vowed to cause pain to the lowly defiant mortal who had dared to challenge him.

The agent, also a bit salty and obstinate, dug in his heels and basically told the boss he was out of line for ordering him or anyone else to make voluntary contributions when it was not their desire to do so and certainly not of their free will.

The paper war of memos and phone calls that ensued was truly awesome to watch, and yet every agent in the division feared for the ultimate fate of their poor comrade. These things had a tendency not to end well for the guy on the bottom of the proverbial Bureau totem pole. McWade and the others watching from the sidelines in the various squads and RAs held their breaths and tried to get the feisty Cannon to just donate a few bucks to make this thing go away.

McWade was even tempted to send the boss twenty bucks under Cannon's name but then, knowing the explosive personality of O'Lara, thought better of it. This thing was now getting totally out of hand.

In a rage, O'Lara pulled every single case file Cannon had worked for the past six months as well as his entire caseload of pending investigations. He combed over these files with the precision of a Swiss watchmaker, looking for flaws, mistakes, or anything he could second-guess or pin on the uncooperative, mutinous troublemaker.

He settled on an unresolved kidnapping case Cannon had been working with the local authorities in a central Nebraska town. The wild-eyed and thoroughly pissed-off dictator gave Cannon a long list of criticisms about the handling of the case, along with a longer list of totally unrealistic things to be done promptly and along with the drastic consequences that would befall Cannon if he failed to do these things.

O'Lara had underestimated Agent Cannon, who called his bluff and went to a higher level. With the entire population of street agents now cheering Cannon on, he took things to a higher authority. Before the matter ended, the dreaded Inspection Staff descended on Omaha, and statements and affidavits were taken from virtually all agents under O'Lara's command.

O'Lara was now tarnished goods. He was no longer a Bureau rising star and soon was transferred from Omaha into Bureau oblivion. McWade smiled to know that, once in a while, a "loose Cannon" can hit a moving target and bring down one of the Bureau's own anointed ones.

SCUD, Father of Lies and Cockroaches

During the mid to late 1980s, Omaha was blessed with an ASAC from the depths of outer darkness. This guy had absolutely no concept of truth versus lies. Because he was so morally challenged in that area, he must have assumed others were like him. The first Gulf War had ended, but not before Saddam Hussein introduced to the world the SCUD missile, the Iraqi military's dreaded threat to the US and especially to the immediate countries around Iraq. The SCUD proved to be basically worthless. Although touted as accurate, it was not. Dependable, nope!

So it was no surprise that the reprehensible ASAC soon became known as SCUD by the street agents in Nebraska. He fit the description of the unreliable Iraqi projectile that seemed to always miss the target, but he also lacked judgment, honesty, and leadership ability.

One agent whom McWade knew about had been promised a transfer to another field office as a hardship when an opening was available. This promise had been made by the Bureau transfer section in the form of a letter. SCUD had worked hard to make sure this transfer did not happen as he was just being himself living up to his nickname.

The agent in question had lost his wife to cancer and having children to care for had wanted to locate closer to family in the west. SCUD, in all his glory, had told the agent, "The Bureau didn't issue you those kids." On another occasion, he had referred to the letter promising the hardship transfer as being worthless by saying, "You should know by now that the Bureau lies!" This guy was off the charts and getting more brazen by the day.

Finally, he made a fatal mistake and pushed the cheese too far into the wrong corner. There was a very nice, pleasant African American female secretary just across the hall from his office in Omaha. With nothing better to do, SCUD found a cockroach crawling across the floor. He killed the cockroach, then took the lifeless creature across the hall where he taped it to the mouthpiece of the secretary's telephone. He then waited, like a jackal, until she arrived at her desk. A call was promptly made, and as she went into hysterics, after putting the receiver to her mouth, he laughed like an overgrown juvenile delinquent.

As if that wasn't enough self-destructive behavior, he had gone to the evidence room and removed a $25,000 diamond necklace. The not-so-smart leader actually gave it to his wife to wear at an FBI office party. Unfortunately for him, the agent who had worked the jewelry theft case recognized the prized item hanging around Mrs. SCUD's neck and promptly filed an official complaint.

Again, the Inspection Staff made their way to Omaha. By the time they arrived, it was reported that our illustrious ASAC had again found his way to the evidence room and had helped himself to a variety of very rare books seized in a theft case in Iowa. He claimed he didn't know it was against policy to remove items of evidence for personal use.

But ignorance was not a valid excuse, and now with sexual harassment, violations of evidence rules, and general incompetence, he was busted as an ASAC and sent to the streets of some dark and dreary East Coast city as a regular brick agent. McWade and others that knew him and suffered under him thought he deserved a much-greater punishment. Even though stripped of his title, he was allowed to keep his same pay grade, which seemed unfair. His face, for obvious reasons, was never seen again in the Omaha office. This was the Bureau's way of handling a rotten apple in management who happened to have been exposed.

Right after the SCUD fiasco, one of McWade's sources wandered into his RA and gave him a drawing of a very official-looking American eagle with its head cocked to one side and its eyes crossed. Below the drawing, it merely stated, "Really, you still trust the FBI?" There seemed to be some validity to that as it pertained to management.

This Man's Army

Omaha was a somewhat unique field office located in the center of the country. It appeared to McWade that a new SAC seemed to appear on the scene about every two years. These new leaders, anointed by the Director himself, seemed to fall into two very distinct camps. The first group were those younger managers who were real blue flamers and were known as rising stars. They usually had connections (agents called them rabbis) somewhere in the hierarchy of the Bureau or, at times, in political circles on or close to Pennsylvania Avenue. Any agent in the office, with eyes on a management career, would hover around these up-and-comers like helicopters looking for a landing pad.

The second group of SACs were those who had fallen into disfavor with those in the ivory towers at HQ. Omaha was a place to put them while they were on their downward descent toward retirement. It was felt that in Omaha they couldn't do that much PR damage to the Bureau as it (Omaha) was looked at as an unsophisticated cow town anyway. These leaders were looked at by the eager agents looking for upward mobility as being very unhelpful, career-wise, and generally not worth worrying about. They were to be tolerated, avoided if possible, but not feared. They were often the types who looked like they were very deep in thought 95 percent of the time but were actually just thinking about what they were going to eat later in the day.

When Herbie Hawkeye appeared as the new SAC in Omaha, the underground information network cranked up to warp speed. Everyone wanted to know who he was, what to expect, what dirt anybody had on him, where he had been, what he liked or disliked, and, above all, was he the type to help or hurt people. McWade had not really made up his mind about him in this regard.

Then came the memo instructing every agent in the division to travel to Omaha to meet the new boss. So far, about all McWade knew about him was that he had served in the Marine Corps as an officer and supposedly had Semper Fi tattooed on his buttocks. He had earned the reputation as a no-nonsense guy who was not very large in stature and suffered from the proverbial "Little Man Napoleon Syndrome." Being a seasoned Marine, this trait, it was said, seemed to magnify greatly after a few two-fisted drinks during his happy hour.

The agents all gathered, with some apprehension, in the conference room awaiting Hawkeye's appearance. At exactly the scheduled time of his appearance, at 1400 hours (he insisted on military time), he marched in with his spit-shined shoes and freshly ironed pants. McWade wondered if he accidentally ever cut himself on that razor-sharp crease.

Herbie cleared his throat and began his obviously well-rehearsed speech meant to inspire the awaiting agents in the room on to bigger and better achievements. "Gentlemen," be began authoritatively, sounding much like George C. Scott portraying General Patton in the movie *Patton*. "In this man's army, if you will just give me one half day of good honest work, we can conquer the world!" Not much else was said before he sat down, leaving every agent with their head now spinning.

We have been busting our butts ten hours a day and now he is asking only for a half day. Good grief! thought McWade and others.

Shortly after Herbie's arrival, there was a National Academy Nebraska Chapter meeting to be held at the Legion Club in Chadron, Nebraska. Herbie showed up with a certain flare, accompanied by his FBI office entourage, at exactly 1700 hours for the beginning of happy hour. Somehow, the chef thought dinner was to be served at 1900 hours rather than the scheduled time of 1800. Needless to say, Captain Hawkeye was irritated but soon realized this just meant more happy hour drinks on his empty stomach while awaiting dinner.

He was soon feeling like he could storm the shores of Tripoli all by himself and, with each drink, was gathering even more bravado. It was then he looked across the dinner table and saw one of his agents from the Grand Island RA wearing a very casual and loud Hawaiian shirt. His face turned bright red and his nostrils widened as he considered this agent, "in this man's Army," to be out of uniform.

The casually clad resident agent did not take kindly to the loud threats and insulting innuendos flowing forth from the former Marine's mouth and stood up towering over the smaller spitfire, ex-military SAC.

The music in the hall seemed to stop, and all 150 national academy members became totally quiet and focused on the entertainment unfolding before their very eyes. The raging boss and the daring cavalier agent were now nose to nose as the Marine was threatening to kick his ass and was loudly inviting the Grand Island agent outside.

This was all happening in McWade's territory, and he could only see trouble from on high should this escalate any further. He was thinking of the reports, affidavits, Inspection Staff interviews, and press inquiries. Ted Vasman, now the Chadron Chief of Police, was looking a bit nervous himself as the drama unfolded, wondering if he was going to have to arrest the unruly ex-Marine for disorderly conduct or, perhaps, assault.

Finally, McWade was able to get both of them to calm down, unclench their fists, and sit down. Luckily, Ted announced that dinner was served, and another visit by the Inspection Staff was averted.

There is a saying that money does not buy class. As McWade and Vasman, also an ex-Marine, both breathed easier over the defused situation, they both agreed that, just like with money, rank and titles do not make a person classy either.

McWade always smiled at Captain Herbie's lecture, knowing, as he looked at his watch every day at twelve noon after a full half days work, that he was well on his way of capturing the world.

Hawkeye had his platter full while in Omaha as he was the SAC when the case involving an Omaha-based African American agent, Ron Dochon, rocked the entire country. Dochon filed a complaint against the FBI, claiming discrimination due to him being a black agent. This was just another time McWade was so happy to be in his one-man office in Scottsbluff, 452 miles away, as he was virtually the only Omaha Division agent not named in Dochon's charges as being racist. McWade had gone native but was not a racist!

Unverified stories, told by various credible Omaha agents, portrayed Dochon as being likable but not able to measure up as an agent. They told of him spraying the snow off his driveway with a garden hose in the sub-freezing Omaha temperature and not being able to stand up on the concrete for two days. They told of Dochon idling his Bureau car all night long in his driveway so it would be warm in the morning. As a result, the office mechanic, Smitty, had to replace the engine, which overheated and burned up.

No other agent McWade had heard of opened his car door without looking, only to have it torn off by another approaching vehicle from the rear in downtown Ohama. No other agent was rumored to leave his assignment on a major stakeout to go for a swim in a public pool with a chlorine malfunction. His skin was somewhat burned and bleached, and he had to check into the ER for a chemical burn treatment. No other agent took a pillow with him on a major stakeout and surveillance and crawled in the back seat to sleep, over the protests of his partner then, in the end, yelled "Racist!" against his fellow agents, who commented on his ineptness. One of the agents he called a racist was an African American like him.

Captain Herbie had to handle the Bureau inquiries as well as the press on all this and then watch in dismay from the sidelines as Dochon became a smiling millionaire after his settlement with the government.

Our fearless ex-Marine leader was eventually transferred and was heard crying loudly, "Semper Fi!" as his car left Nebraska to conquer the great state of Arizona from his penthouse office in Phoenix. McWade often wondered if he could actually do it by himself one half day at a time. Time would answer that question, but then, that was another question to be played out in exciting and tragic detail on another day and at another time.

To be forever remembered were a couple pearls of thought and philosophy given to McWade by Herbie during routine inspections of the Scottsbluff RA. "I wouldn't have to work so hard on trying to manage my anger if people around me would just learn how to manage their stupidity!" he once shared as he reflected on his days in the corps and as SAC.

He also stated in a matter-of-fact way that "if I crossed the name of everyone that was a horse's ass off my list, I would soon be just standing there looking at myself in the mirror." He was definitely a case study in McWade's "book of managers' past."

The Pulitzer Prize of Supervision

If the Pulitzer Prize for American exceptionalism could somehow be expanded from music, literature, and journalism to the category of failed leadership and supervision skills, the all-time contender would have to be none other than Fred Rupinsky, SAC of the Omaha Division. His radio call referred to earlier wanting to know his 10-20 would be akin to some very aging, memory-challenged elderly patient in a nursing home continually asking, "Nurse, where am I?"

Unlike Captain Herbie, who only asked for a half day of effort, Rupinsky loved to charm and inspire the Omaha agents at his all-agents conferences by challenging them to give 120 percent. After those less-than-inspirational pep talks, the agents would gather for their happy hour or dinner visits, where McWade would always laughingly volunteer to contribute that extra 20 percent that mathematically doesn't exist to the office effort in the pursuit of perfection. It was usually a time when each agent would share their own wacky story about their present boss and the individual interactions they had with him.

Some newly arrived agent would always have to ask, "How did this guy ever make it into the Bureau, let alone make SAC?" Then one of the old salts would answer by going into graphic detail telling how Rupinsky, although having a subpar GPA, had managed to get into college. He apparently knew how to throw a football and became quarterback on some no-name East Coast team with a losing record. But as fate would have it, he dated and won the heart of the girl he eventually married. This young lady just happened to be the daughter of one of the very most influential United States senators in the country.

With an advocate of that stature in your corner, the fight to get into the FBI as a new agent was definitely rigged, and his jet propelled rise to the office of SAC was not only predictable but almost guaranteed. Only his total propensity to draw attention to himself in an adverse way kept him from climbing higher on the Bureau's management ladder. The Peter Principle brought his managerial ascent to a screeching halt at the SAC level. He had far exceeded his level of incompetence and was shuffled off to Omaha where it was thought he could do the least amount of damage. The old adage which had been pounded into McWade's head during new agents' training was still around and in effect: "Don't embarrass the Bureau!" Therefore, Omaha was to be blessed with Fred Rupinsky until he was able to retire and fade into the Bureau sunset.

Rupinsky drove the entire 452 miles across Nebraska to visit McWade's outpost in the panhandle. Upon arriving in the midafternoon sun, he began licking his lips and mumbling about how dry the air was, wondering aloud where he could get a drink. It was known that it was not the pure sparkling water from a tap or water bottle he was asking about as the entire office knew of his drinking problem. A reach into his suitcase seemed to provide the answer to his own question, and he was then able to collect his thoughts, look around, and reflect on the long road trip he had just made.

That's when he made the famous statement. "I hope you never screw up, McWade, because I couldn't find anyone else crazy enough to take this assignment and live in this godforsaken place."

The rest of the visit with the boss went as expected, and McWade sighed a sigh of relief as the black Bucar disappeared down US 26 to the east. Now fast-forward only two short weeks when McWade had to be in Omaha for a required file review and business meeting with the AUSA. He had arrived in the Omaha office well before 7:00 AM but had forgotten to sign in with his time of arrival on the office's number one register. This sign-in sheet was located in the foyer outside the SAC's office.

At a few minutes after 8:00 AM, one of the agents in the agents' bay approached McWade and told him he had noticed that McWade had forgotten to sign in on the register. Upon hearing that, McWade went to the foyer and promptly signed directly below the agent who had last signed in at 7:10 AM. He signed the register "McWade 7:13 AM" and went back to the open agents' bay to continue working on preparing his cases for his file review.

About ten minutes later, the silver-haired Rupinsky entered the agents' bay where McWade was busy at his desk with the other twenty to twenty-five agents in the common work area. The silver-haired fox stood in silence, peering around the room as if he was looking for a chicken to pounce upon for lunch. He then cleared his throat loudly, which brought every agent in the room to full attention. "Which one of you is McWade?" he demanded in a voice obviously meant to reflect irritation and to project authoritative fear to his captive audience of mere street agents.

Since every eye in the room was on the Scottsbluff RA visitor, there was nothing he could do but answer, "Here, sir!"

"Into my office and now!" came Rupinsky's demand.

Even though McWade had heard stories about this guy, *How could he not remember that he had just spent two days with me two weeks earlier?* he wondered.

The office was cold and formal. "What time did you sign in this morning?" were the first words out of his mouth.

McWade tried to explain what had happened, but the man behind the mahogany desk was not able to grasp the matter. He was too caught up in himself to even listen. Never mind the fact that McWade worked by himself in a one-man remote office and certainly would not come into Omaha and try to bump the books for a few minutes when he could bump it for a whole day in the RA should he be that type of dishonest person.

He glared over his glasses, still not seemingly remembering his trip to Scottsbluff and telling McWade how it was such a godforsaken place and that he couldn't get anyone else crazy enough to live there. That being said, he then profoundly threatened McWade, "If that's the way you operate your damn RA, it will get you nowhere but transferred." With that parting shot over the bow, he excused the seemingly derelict McWade back to the agents' bay, where he and the other agents could add this story to the growing list of Rupinsky tales.

"Incompetence, just like ignorance, is like a disability that must take some effort to keep and maintain," laughed McWade as he drove back to his own little empire in the west.

Less than a month later, Rupinsky was at it again. He sent out an all-agents memo, instructing each and every RA in the entire two-state area to each recruit one clerical employee to send to Washington, DC, to fill their employment needs at HQ. Instead of considering the source and just ignoring the order, which he had probably already forgotten, McWade was brazen enough to send back a short memo of his own. In this, he pointed out how it was not exactly fair to give a one-man RA like Scottsbluff the same quota as a sixteen-man RA such as Des Moines.

Within hours, the big long-range gun in Omaha was pointed west and fired that the same memo back in the direction of McWade's mailbox. When it arrived, the margin was filled with large, almost unintelligible writing in blue ink (he was trying to be like Hoover): "With an attitude like this, it will get you nowhere but transferred!" McWade again chuckled at the transfer threats and at the boss's poorly functioning memory.

Upon being able to retire from the Bureau, McWade heard that Rupinsky, using his title as FBI Special Agent in Charge, secured a high-paying job as head of security at a large facility racetrack in west Omaha. He took a young office clerk, nicknamed Moose, with him as his assistant, primarily to have someone who actually knew how to do something without screwing it up. Within a year, management at his new job realized that a title does not a man make and fired him for being inadequate and unqualified. Ironically, they hired Moose, the former office stenographer and clerk, to take his job as head of their security operation. Moose was well-liked and highly successful in his new position.

Apparently, total managerial incompetence in the real business world is just like a flat tire on a car. You just can't go very far without fixing it. However, unlike in the private sector, inside the FBI, as well as in many other government agencies, it was noted they sometimes drive on flat tires even at the highest levels for years and years at a time.

Meanwhile, defying all scientific laws to the contrary, unlike back on the farm, the real cream was working hard and somehow managing to stay at the bottom of the can, thus allowing the FBI to continue to function as the premier law enforcement agency in the world despite the many Fred Rupinskys, Glen Genos, and SCUDs within their ranks.

Chapter 32

Gray Sunset: Montana's Freemen

McWade had just returned from Salt Lake City smiling. Every office has one. The agent who reeks of enthusiasm in almost everything he does to the point of being obnoxious to those in his surroundings. So mounting the treadmill in the newly finished exercise room was no exception.

At full throttle, the belt on the machine was virtually humming a fight song and his legs were a blur as they tried to keep up the impossible pace. The man on the machine was none other than the resident agent from the Vernal, Utah, RA. He was impressive as his long John Wayne—looking legs, white from the lack of sunshine, flashed like lightning bolts in the dimly lit room.

Then it happened, those legs became confused and wrapped around each other like two pretzels. The spinning belt caught his helpless six-foot frame and literally catapulted him completely through the dry wall partition into the other room.

As his body was hurled through the wall, his arms and legs outstretched in a position of panic, he left a definite image.

Witnessing the scene, McWade didn't know whether to act concerned for the agent's safety or to burst out laughing because, there on the wall, was the very clear silhouette of one of his childhood cartoon heroes. It looked as if Wile E. Coyote had just been flung through that wall after again being outsmarted by the Roadrunner.

The only injuries sustained were to the pride of the agent, who soon after retired to write his own book about the trauma of being an

FBI agent and serving as a lay church bishop at the same time. But to McWade and those who recalled this incident, he would forever be known not by his real name but as Wile E. Coyote.

The smile was short-lived on McWade's face as he received a call from the Beehive Federal Credit Union in Madison County, Idaho, that a couple of men from Thompson County were trying to cash some peculiar-looking drafts to pay off loans and tax obligations.

The local newspaper, the *Standard Journal,* carried an article about the flood of totally fraudulent lien drafts showing up in the area and warning the citizenry about not accepting them. The article referred these drafts as funny money and explained how the drafts were signed by two militants belonging to a group calling themselves the Montana Freemen.

The philosophy of the Montana Freemen seemed simple enough. The group claimed the United States Government owed them 2.5 billion dollars as a result of some completely bogus, deceptive, and spurious claim the group had conjured up. The group of anti-government zealots held their own trial, found the government guilty, and rendered themselves the 2.5 billion dollar judgment.

The imprudent group then began issuing and distributing documents they called lien drafts or comptroller warrants against their brazen self-rendered judgment. The Montana Freemen, calling themselves an anti-government, Christian Patriot Group, were, at the time, headquartered on a small parcel of land about twenty miles outside the small town of Jordan, Montana.

Shortly after the phony paper started circulating in McWade's Idaho Falls RA territory, a couple leaders of the group were lured out of their isolated compound and arrested. This infuriated the other Freemen left behind in the compound, which they now referred to as Justus Township.

The FBI had arrest warrants for eight other militant Freemen who were, with other family members, holed up in the safety of Justus Township. Shots had now been fired at the FBI by the group, and it has evidence this could be a long and drawn-out ordeal as the group seemingly possessed ample firearms and supplies.

The Bureau, still licking its public image wounds from the tragic incident at Waco, Texas, and the Randy Weaver standoff at Ruby Ridge in Northern Idaho, was being very cautious about this matter. There was not to be another Branch Davidian or Ruby Ridge incident at any cost and the orders had come down from on high to that effect. With the small cluster of buildings, located in a low depression, surrounded by the isolated grassland hills overlooking the scene, there was very little cover for the occupants of the township. Also, the checkpoints on the roads leading into the area were very open and provided no cover for agents on duty at those stations.

The takeover of the village would only take minutes if the Bureau were to unleash their gathered SWAT teams. But innocent people would be hurt and that was something the government could and would not allow to happen. So the compound was surrounded and the waiting began.

By now, McWade had been ordered to make the trip to the scene of the special, now code-named Gray Sunset for some peculiar reason.

When he arrived in the small town of Jordan, population three hundred fifty, he found there were more agents and law enforcement in town than actual residents. In addition, the place was crawling with reporters and camera crews from all over the world looking for a story and drama.

"This is Deja Moo," he mused, meaning that he had the feeling he had seen and heard this bull before.

Since the Montana Freeman considered themselves to be Christian patriots, this was setting itself up to be a long drawn-out nightmare. Whenever religion enters into the formula, it seems rational thinking goes out the window and emotional thinking becomes the rule of the day. Those who are religious zealots tend to be conditioned, not to think for themselves, but to react emotionally toward the information to which they have been exposed. These people did not feel they should have to pay taxes. Well, who does actually like to pay them? But most people rationally think their way through the process and manage to become mainstream taxpaying citizens.

But add religious emotional thinking to the mix and there is no reasoning with those particular disciples. The more reasonable facts presented to the radicals, the more they entrenched, and the backfire effect was the result.

As McWade made his way into town, he easily found the Garfield County fairground complex, which was set up as the command post for the entire Gray Sunset special. It was an unseasonably wet spring in 1996, and all the unpaved roads in the area were quagmires, requiring four-wheel drive vehicles to get to and from Justus Township.

McWade, along with several other FBI agents, took up temporary residence in a small local church, which had been rented as living quarters by the Bureau. He could now tell his wife and family he attended church daily. Food was obtained at the fairgrounds where an excellent catering service prepared meals for the law enforcement troops.

If the rain was unpleasant, the unending wind blowing across the barren landscape was pure misery. Day after day it blew. The portable toilets set up around the command post and the muddy fairgrounds had to be tied down with hurricane straps to prevent them from drifting away like fiberglass tumbleweeds. It was not a spot anyone wanted to plan a vacation around. The local streets into the countryside carried names like Hell Creek Road or Devil's Road, which seemed appropriate.

In the midst of all this confusion, a new female agent appeared on the scene from one of the big-city offices on the East Coast. Apparently, using a porta potty was a new experience for the out-of-place city woman. When the young lass received a call of nature, she entered the small shanty. With her mission accomplished, she exited the little outhouse all excited and smiling about how well equipped these things were. "Why, they even have a nice little purse holder to hold my purse!" she exclaimed. Obviously this was the first time she had seen a urinal in an outdoor privy! It was grounds for a good-natured laugh at the expense of the prissy, young, well-dressed city dweller turned real-life agent.

The local newspaper in Jordan, dated May 2, 1996, was head-lined "Freemen Issue Defiant Statement." The article then quoted Bo Gritz, a former Green Beret colonel, who had just visited Justus Township to negotiate as saying, "The Freemen believe God makes them invincible in their standoff with the FBI, and they have taken an oath never to give in."

The backfire effect toward reasonable dialogue had kicked in big-time. The Montana Freemen diehards were sounding just like the Sioux leaders at the original Battle at Wounded Knee, South Dakota, in the late 1890s. They also believed that if they partici-pated in the sacred Ghost Dance, they too would be invincible to the bullets of the soldiers, who had surrounded them with superior firepower. How did that work out?

The newspaper article went on to quote Gritz: "The Freemen have had communications with God, Yah-Wah, and vowed never to leave their ranch unless their demands are met."

"Members of the anti-government group are wanted on state and federal charges ranging from writing fake checks to threatening to kidnap and kill a federal judge. The FBI believes eighteen Freemen are still in the compound," the news article concluded.

The days dragged on endlessly on the windy, dreary landscape. Boredom became a very real concern. Jogging while off duty along Hell Creek Road could only eat up so much time, and the town of Jordan was so dead even Nurse Ratched could not have located a pulse on her very best day.

Never before had McWade seen little round marble-like balls strewn along the top of the roadside terrain in countless numbers. The local old-timers explained to him that a single grain of sand, driven by the wind, would pick up a small speck of mud and then another until, eventually, like a snowball rolling down hill, a mud ball was formed. The blazing hot sun would then dry these balls into the natural phenomenon scattered all over the barren countryside.

One bit of excitement during the Gray Sunset standoff was when five exact, identical automobiles approached his checkpoint, located on an unpaved road leading to Justus Township. These vehicles came riding in from the east at a high rate of speed for the condition of the road at the time.

The tension was high! McWade and his fellow agents manning the checkpoint were, of course, apprehensive and ready for anything. Here, in this godforsaken country, hundreds of miles from anything called real civilization, were five beautiful Ford Thunderbird cars. They came in like an invading force from the outside world, and the first thought was that they were sympathetic to the radicals at the compound and were bringing in supplies, weapons, or reinforcements.

With weapons in a ready position, the alert agents reined in the flock of T-birds, forcing them to land. As if from another planet, the spokesman for the group, in the lead car, seemed clueless about the Montana Freemen and the ongoing standoff. He claimed they were test drivers, hired by Ford Motor Company, to put those Thunderbird cars through rigorous, exhaustive, and thorough testing.

They were escorted by the Montana State Patrol back to the command post at the fairgrounds, where their stories were checked out and verified. They were last seen heading out of town on an alternate route.

The local newspaper carried a cartoon trying to make some humor out of the ongoing fiasco taking place in their county, which gave most of the agents at the Gray Sunset a chuckle.

The parody, or caricature, was a picture drawing of a redneck-looking man with an old long-barreled shotgun peering out the window of a tumbledown shack. Near the window, on the cabin siding, was a sign which read "We is Freemen. Git! We don't want no U S Gummint Here. We has SeeSeeded."

Under the cartoon was the caption, "Cover me. I'm gonna make a dash into town to pick up our welfare checks!"

Hanging proudly, high on the wall inside the Gray Sunset command post, was a sign some enterprising agent had made: "Freeman's Motto: Don't Think. Just Act!"

Finally, in the middle of June 1996, the Montana Freemen surrendered, thus ending the very long eighty-one-day standoff with the Bureau. Apparently, although their Yah-Wah had convinced them that they were invincible, they got even more bored than McWade and, thankfully, submitted to reality.

Quaking Aspen trees are known to share a common root system. Eliminate a single tree and the grove lives on without concern. The Montana Freemen, those misguided souls following their blind leaders, found the common roots of their Christian Patriotic Group were diseased and deeply flawed. When certain of their leaders went down, unlike the Quaking Aspen grove, the entire system could not sustain life without them.

LeRoy Schweitzer, their fearless leader, whose name appeared on the funny money lien drafts at the Beehive Federal Credit Union, traded his cabin at the Justus Township ranch for a twenty-two-year prison sentence in a federal penitentiary. He never saw his beloved compound again as he died in prison at the age of seventy-three. Additionally, several other Freemen, associates of Schweitzer, also lost their freedom as their cases were processed through the federal court system.

The newsmen left the small Montana town looking somewhat dejected. McWade had the distinct feeling, after his interactions with them, that several wanted there to be a shoot-out similar to Waco or Ruby Ridge. After all, dull days of standoff do not sell newspapers like action-packed confrontations.

Another cartoon from the *Chicago Tribune*, titled *Inside the Paranoid Mind*, seemed to relate to the Freemen mind-set at Justus Township. It showed a rather large, overweight, and simple-looking paramilitary figure being interviewed by a reporter.

The reporter asked, "So why are you guys so heavily armed?"

The militant answers, "Because the government is after us!"

To which the reporter asks, "And why are they after you?"

"Because we are so heavily armed!" came the reply.

But the FBI had learned their lesson well and had endured eighty-one long tedious days of total restraint. It was now time to dismantle the command post, haul away the portable toilets (with their nice purse holders), pay all the bills for the operation, and send the troops home.

The five-hundred-plus mile drive back to his RA gave McWade ample opportunity to reflect on his time in the middle of nowhere. New friends had been made though he knew most of them would never be seen or heard from again.

It was now time again to concentrate on the full-time job of going "Native", as his own time in his beloved Bureau was getting much closer to its own "Gray Sunset!"

Chapter 33

An Old Man's Wish

Don't cry because it's over, but smile because it happened!

—Dr. Seuss

By law, FBI agents face mandatory retirement at the rather young age of fifty-seven. McWade was no exception to that rule and found himself racing down that one-way street much faster than he liked.

During the first twenty years of his service, he often found himself fantasizing about retiring and living a carefree life on the beach or in the mountains. These dreams were of a life completely devoid of supervisors, SACs, ASACs, AUSAs, deadlines, quotas, unrealistic caseloads, criminal informants, ghetto informants, annual inspections, annual physicals, fitness-for-duty tests, firearms, road trips, long nights alone in motel rooms, crazy phone calls from unbalanced people, and the myriad other phenomenon that constitute being a native in a small isolated RA.

Then something very magical happened.

He turned fifty years old, and his view of his world completely and totally changed overnight. He was now eligible for retirement with full benefits. Now miraculously, it was much more enjoyable to face each day knowing that it was his choice. The fear of dictatorial management was gone as they now did not hold a death grip on his future.

There were no more concerns of being transferred at the whim of some supervisor. The option of being able to quit anytime was now there and brought a smile each day.

Now the quote from Buddha took on a completely new meaning when he said, "The trouble is, you think you have time!"

He found himself at times reflecting back on unusual cases he had worked. He recalled the fugitive he had arrested in a small Nebraska town who claimed he had an identical twin brother and that McWade had the wrong twin. The guy strangely and conveniently just happened to have copies of both his and his brother's birth certificates in his pocket. He was yelling and screaming foul and how he was going to sue McWade's ass all the way to the Cheyenne County Jail in Sidney. McWade was able to fingerprint the young felon, classify his prints using the old Henry Classification Method and determine he was the right twin. Luckily, he had stayed awake in training school the day the instructor taught that no two individuals, including identical twins, have the exact same fingerprints. The look on the guilty twin's face was priceless as he peered through the jail cell iron bars.

The lesson learned on that one was that it can sometimes come in handy to be attentive in class.

As he reminisced back to the arrest of Ernie LeRoy Sanders, who claimed to be the nephew of Colonel Sanders of Kentucky Fried Chicken fame, he again smiled. This guy was a drifter who left a trail of forged checks behind him like Hansel and Gretel had left bread crumbs—all the way from Kentucky to Nebraska.

The guy actually looked like his famous uncle, complete with the goatee and silver-white hair. At trial, he put on an Academy Award-winning performance for the two handpicked ladies in the jury that was nothing less than masterful.

He was elderly and pretended to be sick. Even though it was summer and the courtroom was hot, he wore a heavy overcoat he had purchased from the nearby Salvation Army store. He had hired a private nurse to baby him and attend to his needs every time he coughed in front of the jury. He used a cane and required the nurse to assist him whenever he tried to walk. Whenever he would cough, his nurse would jump up, administer medicine to him, and wouldn't sit back down until the fake coughing spell subsided. Meanwhile, he knew how to look as pale and sickly as a healthy person could possibly look.

Each time the jury recessed and left the courtroom, he would jump up, take off the ridiculous coat, stroll unassisted out into the hall, smoke a cigarette, and strut around like a banty rooster looking for a hen. Before the jury returned, he again assumed his sickly role and the acting resumed.

The court-appointed defense attorney passed a note to the prosecuting AUSA which McWade read and smiled. On the paper was scrawled, "What do you think the movie rights to this performance would be worth?"

The ladies he had handpicked for jury duty could only picture their own aging father and voted tearfully to acquit the poor creature.

He miraculously left the courtroom on his own power, leaving his props behind. He smiled broadly, turned and waved good-naturedly to McWade and the attorneys, and left the federal building a free man.

Three weeks later, the AUSA called from his office in Lincoln, Nebraska, to tell McWade that our Colonel Sanders look-alike, had apparently stolen a pad of checks from his court-appointed attorney and had forged and cashed them in several cities across Iowa. He was presently in custody at Harlan, Iowa, facing state charges. He had impersonated his court-appointed barrister using the man's own good name while forging his latest round of documents. So much for showing gratitude to his attorney in Nebraska for helping him get acquitted. This was worth a good laugh.

Maybe his actions were the result of his philosophy he had expressed to McWade at the end of one of their long interviews about the forged checks. "Don't piss me off. The older I get, the less life in prison is a deterrent!"

Still in the mood for pondering his past, McWade realized that, just like many managers, there were also street agents who were not capable of making rational decisions. Take, for example, a fellow agent in the Omaha Division assigned to the Davenport, Iowa, RA. Tim Spellbound, was on his way to solve his latest great case when he came upon a state of Iowa road crew pouring fresh concrete on a stretch of highway. Not wanting to be bothered with a long wait and detour, our supersleuth went around the flagman in his Bucar, drove on the road shoulder for a few hundred yards, and then aimed his car up onto the newly poured cement.

Yes, you guessed it! The FBI car became mired down in the concrete and had to be quickly retrieved by on-site heavy equipment before it set up solid. The cost to fix the road was estimated at $75,000.

The *Quad-City Times*, serving Davenport, Iowa, carried a headline explaining everything necessary on this matter: "Davenport FBI Agent Faces Charges After Driving Car in Fresh Concrete." The article continued, "Criminal trespass is a serious misdemeanor and can carry a penalty of up to one year in jail plus a $1,500 fine."

As Jeff Foxworthy would say, "Here's your sign!"

And then there was the time an NSP trooper issued a speeding ticket to the Scotts Bluff County Sheriff, Phil Warbucks, on a lonely stretch of county highway.

The irate sheriff asked the clueless trooper, "What about professional courtesy?"

His question fell on deaf ears.

An upset sheriff called an emergency meeting involving each and every one of his deputies. The meeting was unusually short and to the point as he angrily waved the newly issued citation in front of his wide-eyed staff.

Then came his order: "Get your asses out on every Scotts Bluff County road, and don't one of you even dare come back into this office unless you are holding in your sorry ass hand a ticket with the name of a Nebraska State trooper on it!"

The war was on in Scotts Bluff County. Not an NSP cruiser was seen without a county deputy bird-dogging behind like a coonhound on the trail of its prey. They were looking for any kind of reason under the sun to pull the troopers over to issue a ticket. They didn't care what the violation—whether it was failure to signal when changing lanes, rolling through a stop sign after making a California stop, or a burned-out license plate light. Citizens were scratching their heads at the show.

It finally got so pathetic and nonsensical that the NSP Captain of Troop E called a top summit meeting with the Sheriff. They apparently ironed out their differences, called a truce, and agreed upon a ceasefire.

The skirmish was short-lived but will be talked about by old-timers in local law enforcement circles for years to come.

And that, folks, is why *professional courtesy* is still practiced by most law enforcement in that area to this day!

But wait a minute! Not every NSP trooper seemed to be blessed with common sense. Trooper Andrews was stationed in Gordon, Nebraska, which is as far from the Troop E headquarters as possible, and maybe there was a reason for that.

This super trooper had just entertained his father-in-law and his mother-in-law over the Christmas holiday season. They left to go back to their home in eastern Nebraska and had not driven far on US Highway 20 before they were pulled over and issued a speeding ticket by their own son-in-law. Rumors were they had hired an attorney to make sure this guy did not get a penny of his wife's inheritance from the family farm.

The word *clueless* just took on a new meaning. Would you risk losing your wife's inheritance and those coveted season tickets to watch the Huskers at Memorial Stadium just to make your point with your in-laws?

His mind now drifted back to the present and his full attention was on a simple bank robbery of a bank on East Seventeenth Street in Idaho Falls the previous day. The robber was an older man in his late sixties. He had driven up to the drive-in window of the First Interstate Bank where he stopped his car. He looked at the teller, with no disguise whatsoever, smiled a broad happy smile, and placed a note in the sliding drawer.

The teller read the note demanding money and telling her that this was a bank robbery. The bandit then held up what appeared to be a gun and made a gesture as if telling her to give him the money.

McWade had almost laughed out loud when the story of the robbery was told to him by the folks in the bank. The teller actually gave him $3,600, and he never even had to get out of the car. The entire incident happened with the bank teller sitting safely on her chair behind bulletproof glass.

As the robber drove away at a senior citizen pace, the young teller observed that his getaway blue Buick bore Tennessee license plates.

A call was made by the teller to 911 and a police watch in the area failed to locate the Tennessee Buick.

The next day, McWade had traveled to Salt Lake City for routine training on the new computers the office had acquired. He was in deep thought, trying to understand the complex DOS operating system when he was summoned to the office of the bank robbery coordinator.

A call had been received that a senior citizen driving a blue Buick with Tennessee license plates had been arrested by the West Bountiful, Utah, Police Department. He had drawn the attention of the police when he was driving the wrong direction on a one-way street. The arresting officer observed he had a plastic toy handgun and was in possession of almost $3,600 still in bank wrappers.

A few phone calls by the police to Idaho and it was obvious he was the senior citizen robber who had hit the bank in Idaho Falls and left with the loot. The old man had been taken to the Davis County Jail in Farmington, Utah, where he was booked and was being held on the bank robbery charge.

McWade left the conference accompanied by an extremely attractive blond-haired female agent. She was newly arrived from her new agents' training and was to help interview the old man and to get his statement about the incident.

Arriving at the county jail facility, McWade and his attractive miniskirted blond partner were escorted down the long corridor leading to our awaiting felon. Even the Mormon Tabernacle Choir, with all three hundred members, singing at the top of their lungs, could not have drowned out the noise from the inmates in their cells. It was as if they had never seen a pretty woman. Their shouts, whistles, catcalls, and proposals of various kinds rang out in an earsplitting chorus. It was at that time that McWade, for the first time, noted just how mini the skirt was that this new lady agent was wearing and how much of her shapely legs were being displayed to the howling inmates.

In the stark prison interview room, the tired-looking elderly gentleman was waiting with a friendly smile. His name was Gary Lee Franklin and his story was sad. McWade could begin to sympathize with him almost immediately. His FBI rap sheet was eleven pages long and outlined the last forty-five years or so of his life story like an autobiography. The first arrest was January 30, 1948, for grand theft auto in the state of South Carolina. From that point, there were thirty-nine other entries ranging from burglary, robbery, escape, distributing marijuana, etc. It was easy to see where he had spent most of his entire adult life.

It was quite obvious to McWade, as the interview began, that he had wanted to be caught. After all, the money was still in the bank wrappers; no effort had been made to disguise himself or his vehicle, and the plastic toy gun was intentionally left out in plain sight for the police officer to observe.

When asked to give his statement, he began, "Agent McWade, since Christmas is approaching, I want you to know that since the age of seventeen, I have never seen or spent a single Christmas outside of a jail cell. I will make your case easy for you and will enter a plea of guilty if you will just promise to make sure I get prosecuted federally rather than by state authorities in Idaho."

McWade paused and promised that, although this was not his decision, he would push the AUSA in Idaho to have it handled federally.

It was quite obvious, and verified by Franklin, that his flight interstate from Idaho to Utah, where he purposely drove up a street the wrong direction, was to help ensure federal handling.

Franklin continued with a certain sadness in his voice, "All my lifelong friends are federal inmates, and I want to be back with them. I have absolutely no one on the outside to turn to, which is why I robbed a federally insured bank. I really want to be back with my friends. Besides, the federal prison system had treated me much better than the state prisons."

It turned out that Franklin had been mandatorily released from federal custody in Knoxville, Tennessee, and placed in a halfway house while on parole.

He told McWade, "At my age, I just could not adapt to all the changes in the world that had taken place over the years, and I just wanted to be back inside with my buddies. So I stole a car, drove to your state, and robbed a bank."

Franklin had further told McWade how difficult it had been to try to work as a store employee while at the halfway house. "It was as if I had suddenly be awakened, like Rip Van Winkle, from a long sleep of several years, only to find technology and civilization had left me far behind. I absolutely just could not handle it."

McWade had read a statement that he felt, at the time, applied to him but now realized it applied even more to the aging professional inmate. "As I get older, I realize it's not as important to have a lot of friends—only a few real ones!"

This man knew where his real friends were and wanted to spend his last years with them.

Little satisfaction was felt in helping Franklin get his Christmas wish, but McWade was happy to do what he could to help.

The federal judge in the District of Idaho, at Pocatello, heard the case, accepted his guilty plea, and then fulfilled his wish by sentencing him to twelve and a half years in a federal prison. He was ordered to pay $37.92 in restitution to the First Interstate Bank. The $37.92 was the amount of money he had spent on food and gasoline during his brief time as a bank robbery fugitive. The rest of the $3,600 had been recovered and returned to the bank.

As he finished the final reports on the case of Gary Lee Franklin, McWade thought to himself, *I must really be getting soft. There was a time, early in my Bureau career, that I might have wanted them to throw the book at this guy. But now, I really feel melancholy about where this poor man's life choices have left him.*

He really hoped that this man could make peace with his past so it would not unduly screw with his present and with the remaining time he had with his friends.

"I guess, just like Franklin, I always knew I'd get old. The real surprise is just how fast it all actually happened." Whether inside a jail cell or on the outside working as an agent, it goes until, one day, you look in the mirror and realize that you, too, are older.

It was hoped that both the lawman and the criminal could look at the statement from Dr. Seuss and relate: "Don't cry because it's over, but smile because it happened!"

McWade also hoped that his upcoming mandatory retirement into the outside real world would be easier for him to adapt to than the life on the outside had been for Franklin.

Only time would tell.

Epilogue

Many Shades of Sleaze

Marvin Weiner

It was a very routine fugitive lead. Weiner was a rather low-life character wanted by the Denver FBI Division as an escapee. My lead was simple: contact his elderly grandmother in Mitchell, Nebraska, to see if she knew his whereabouts.

The interview with his grandmother was informative in that Weiner had stayed with her two weeks prior and had left in the middle of the night to places unknown.

After feeding and housing the fleeing felon, she told McWade, with tears in her eyes, that she did not know he was wanted at the time and that he had taken with him her only means of transportation. Her wheelchair had disappeared with him and was found to be pawned for $25 cash in nearby Torrington, Wyoming, leaving her unable get around.

Now this guy is the gold standard for sleazy grandsons, McWade thought as he left the little old lady's home.

Or maybe, just maybe, he was just trying to live up to his family name!

Dick Freebie

Dick Freebie was in a class of his own. The thirty-two-year-old was arrested by McWade near Swan Valley, Idaho, on July 4, which turned out not to be his Independence Day at all. The young thirty-two-year-old had figured out the system and had become the king of student loan fraud on the East Coast of the United States.

He would assume several identities, enroll in college under each, obtain as big a loan as he could under each false student's name, and attend just enough of the classes to allow him time to cash the checks. He then either withdrew or disappeared with the cash which amounted to over $500,000 before he was indicted and warrants issued.

Fleeing the East Coast, he migrated back to the mountain west close to where he grew up in Pocatello, Idaho.

His new scheme now was to find rather plain-looking and perhaps overweight, lonely women with steady jobs, homes, and a good credit rating. He would always move in with them, turn on the charm, and eventually persuade them to sign with him on a rather large personal loan using their good credit and their home equity as collateral.

Once the money, usually in the range of $40,000 to $50,000, was in his wallet, the young, suave Dick would disappear like a thief in the night, leaving the defrauded and defrocked young heartbroken maidens in tears and essentially in debt to pay back the money he stole.

After his red Mazda sports car was spotted, he was chased down by officers from four different departments, including the FBI.

Dick, the pathetic self-proclaimed Romeo, had learned to keep a detailed personal journal while he was serving his two-year mission for his church. This journal, in his own handwriting, recorded each and every detail of his crimes and conquests.

He detailed by name, date, and time each of his lovemaking sessions with his lady victims. He even had gone so far as to develop a rating scale, from one to ten, to rate and evaluate their bedroom and lovemaking skills.

He had totally used and abused these women both sexually and financially and then had the brazenness to rate them as to how they measured up to his expectations in the lust department.

How ironic! McWade thought. *This guy, just like the wheel-chair-stealing grandson, had measured up to his name very well.* He really was a real Dick!

The fact that it was a hot July day when he was arrested and that he had to lie on the uncomfortably hot blacktop of the highway, behind his getaway sports car while being handcuffed, did not seem to make McWade feel all that sorry for this disgrace of a human being. "Assuming there to be an afterlife, this guy deserves a special kind of reward for the hurt caused to others."

He, too, is therefore in the running for the king of sleaze.

Normalee Warbucks

Normalee worked as a respected bank officer at the First Security Bank, St. Anna, Idaho. It was not enough for her to have embezzled over $150,000 of the bank's money, so she turned her eyes to the safe-deposit boxes maintained by the bank for additional fraud.

In addition to her bank duties, she was a bookkeeper on the side and did tax returns for select clients. One such client was a severely disabled and mostly blind elderly woman living on the Egin Bench area of Thompson County, who maintained a large number of US savings bonds in her personal safe-deposit box.

Soon Warbucks, while having the elderly lady sign tax documents, was having her sign over large numbers of the series E and EE savings bonds. Over $100,000 was quickly and quietly pilfered from the old lady into Normalee's own blossoming account. To be successful, it was anticipated that the old lady would just die and that no one would know about or ever question the vanished bonds. Since Lady Warbucks did her tax returns, it was easy to cover up the red flags that would have arisen on the federal tax interest obligation on the stolen bonds.

Given the callous nature of the crime and the total lack of compassion for the elderly victim, two short years in federal prison did not seem enough.

She told McWade, "I was just seeing the world that way until I didn't."

"Don't we all?" was the answer.

It was always strange how being caught and exposed to the whole St. Anna community tended to bring about sudden remorse and sorrowful expressions of repentance. For her, seeing her name in the local newspaper was a bummer in the small religious town. People in St. Anna tended to be somewhat judgmental and often just could not see beyond the beam in their own eye.

She promptly moved from Thompson County shortly after her release from prison, but not before being nominated for some kind of award.

Bond Napper

Bond Napper was the president of a small bank in the Sand Hills ranch country of Nebraska, where cattle were king and million-aire ranch owners were the norm. He was a rock-solid pillar in the small town of Hyannis and was respected by all. The only prior dirt on him that McWade could find was how he ran wires around his meter box to steal power from the electric company.

From the electric power theft to stealing money and bonds from an eighty-nine-year-old millionaire widow rancher's safe-deposit box in his bank only seemed natural to the smiling schmoozer. He could have given Normalee Warbucks lessons in the art of safe-deposit box theft as he started out small, gained the widow's trust, and kept on until he had stolen the grand total of $357,089.

"She was old and had more money than she knew what to do with. Besides, she would probably die before it was missed," Napper told McWade, justifying his actions.

McWade was starting to wonder if they should just call these things deposit boxes and drop the word *safe* as they did not seem always that secure to a predatory bank officer wanting access.

When interviewed, the elderly widow was charming and help-ful. She lived on a several-thousand-acre ranch a few miles south of Hyannis and was indeed extremely wealthy and a millionaire several times over. Despite this, at the end of the interview, she turned down McWade's laughing offer to be her adopted son.

She explained, with a twinkle in her eye, that her own son "would probably not go along with that."

The last comment from Napper was a saying he claimed to have heard that said essentially, "When you die, they say you may not know that you are actually dead. All the pain is felt by the people around you that you left behind. The same thing is true of my stupidity."

Was Napper trying to say that he was stupid and had caused pain? Or stupid for getting caught? It was not entirely clear to McWade.

You decide!

Since he lacked a trustworthy moral compass and seemed to be totally self-serving and greedy, he too is on the list.

Leggy Morefat

One huge problem about going native as an FBI agent in rural America, as alluded to earlier, is that most people in the area know who you are and where you live. Blending in unnoticed is impossible.

So it was when a neighbor three doors away knocked on the door that Christmas season. She was a large-framed woman about fifty years old, seemed pleasant and neighborly, and identified herself as Leggy Morefat. She wanted to give McWade's wife one of those little multicolored Russian nesting dolls. It was made of wood and had carved and painted dolls of decreasing size placed inside each other.

McWade felt uneasy about the gift, especially after Leggy mentioned her frequent travels to Russia. But McWade's wife was insistent on accepting anything free.

Morefat had always been a fan of the International Dance Festival at nearby Madison County and had, through that activity, met some Russian dancers. She now frequently traveled to Moscow, where she was engaged in charity work of some type.

Nothing more was thought of this meeting until a year or two later when she became the target of a rather large international fraud scheme. Our neighborly do-gooder had advertised nationally that she could arrange for the adoption of Russian children to worthy families and had been collecting thousands of dollars in advance fees for this service. The problem seemed to be that no one was getting the kids and that Leggy was getting lots of money.

On top of that, our own neighborly adoption queen was having huge cargo containers of donated goods, shipped from the US, free of charge, inasmuch as it was for a charity and international humanitarian purposes, to Russia. Before any of it went to charity, it was discovered that she and her live-in lover, Boris, there in Moscow, would sort through all the goods and sell any prescription drugs and things of value on the Russian black market to mobsters.

This looked like a great scheme with minimal overhead. Get things donated, free shipping, cash from the mob, near-free lodging in Moscow by shacking up with Boris, where they could have sex, smoke pot, and do drugs. Then for more cash, take $10,000 each from victims all over America who were hungry to adopt kids.

McWade listened to victims of the adoption fraud weep as their promises for a child disappeared just like their bank account balances. Some prospective parents had even gone to the expense of traveling to Russia to meet with Morefat while the stall tactics of the operation played out, costing them even thousands more.

In the end, after a year's worth of investigation, Leggy Morefat died of a drug-related disease seemingly directly related to her sleazy lifestyle.

Her premature death denied her the opportunity to finish out her five-year probation and restitution sentence handed down by the judge on a fraud by wire violation.

However, she could still be given some kind of an award, at least an honorable mention, posthumously. There are people from California to New Jersey who would love to give her their upvote.

Dr. Feel Good

The little town of Bingham, Idaho, seemed to be a pleasant place. It was off the beaten path and a place where the most excitement each day was watching the sun sink into the potato and sugar beet fields to the west while watching them grow.

Dr. Feel Good truly believed, with every fiber of his being, that he was above the law and once told McWade so in a careless undercover moment in so many words. His actual statement was, "At times I just feel that I and my special treatments are much more important than the rules."

Soon the word spread like an Idaho wind-driven wildfire. "There is a doctor in Bingham who is performing modern-day miracles. He can make arthritis patients feel pain free and could make the sleepless enjoy a peaceful night's rest."

McWade, along with ten other agents, wandered into his office at 8:00 AM, just as he was opening for business, one beautiful spring morning, without an appointment. But instead, they were armed with a federal search warrant, ordering them to look for and seize the good doctor's entire inventory of magical medicine he was giving to his patients.

His prescriptions had been proclaimed by a long list of older patients to make them feel younger, less anxious, and more able to deal with all their age-related symptoms. In fact, these patients were arriving in droves as the FBI secured his entire office and waiting room, keeping anyone from entering.

McWade had long believed in a saying that he simply called McWade's law of aging. It stated what he had observed over his life experience dealing with people. "Kind and gentle younger people generally grow into old folks who become even kinder and more gentle." On the opposite side of the coin, he found that "cranky, rude, and obnoxious younger people oftentimes grow into crankier, self-assertive, vocally unfiltered, and even more obnoxious old farts."

Those arriving for their appointments with the naturopathic doctor seemed to generally fit the latter category and were not amused at what the FBI was doing to their lifesaving caregiver. They were actually really pissed!

Dr. Feel Good usually gave virtually all his patients a month's supply of little black pills referred to as "Black Pearls."

However, the FBI lab had concluded that these black pearls contained diazepam, a tranquilizer similar to and often found in Valium, as well as other controlled substances. Of course, these little miracle pearls made his patients feel great, but the list of dangerous side effects and warnings on this drug would make every dishonest lawyer shudder.

The angry older patients soon left after growling their displeasure at the FBI and the whole process. McWade noted they seemed to have the same desperate facial expressions as drug addicts when they see their pusher taken away in handcuffs.

There is nothing better for business than a happy customer that feels a real need to return. This had been the secret to success for the thriving Bingham clinic.

After a brief interruption, a good attorney, and a slap on the wrist by the court, the clinic reopened to once again serve the well-being of its clients using other miraculous cures and placebos.

It was rumored that Feel Good's grandfather, also claiming to be a country doctor, was run out of a nearby town along the old Oregon Trail by the old county sheriff for selling a snake oil and substandard laudanum. His covered wagon was confiscated and his little black pills, containing a well-guarded secret family formula, were thrown into the nearby Snake River before the American Falls Reservoir was built. Or were they?

Family ties are deep-seated and run much thicker than the mountain-fresh water.

Our twentieth-century witch doctor should be considered for some kind of feel-good award.

Operation Disconnect

The next sleaze-capade episode takes us down I-15 to the Beehive State, America's biggest hotbed for white collared crime and telemarketing fraud. The case was code-named Operation Disconnect and had been in the investigative and planning stage for several months, if not years. The homework had been done, the search warrants obtained, and it was now time for them to be executed.

McWade was only a small tooth on a gear of the large investigative machine that had been put in motion on this operation. The SLC FBI was leading the charge on this matter and was considered the office of origin (OO). But there were several other field divisions and several hundred agents involved in what was to be the simultaneous execution of warrants all over the US.

As the clock struck 10:00 AM sharp, MST that morning, telemarketing deceivers on both coasts and several locations in between, were simultaneously greeted by smiling teams of agents, who began seizing boxes of records, cash, and computers. The most pain and trauma came when these fast-talking fraudsters were asked to turn over the keys to their fancy sports cars purchased with the fruits of their crimes. Federal law allowed the seizure of these cars which were the outward status symbols of their success. This caused more pain than the thought of jail time to some.

"Dammit, next time I'll just lease a car!" McWade heard one of the pissed-off men complain as he watched his red Porsche being impounded out of his corner office window and disappear down the street.

The seized records were a bonanza of very sad stories. Most victims were trusting elderly folks who were targeted because of their two primary qualifications. They were folks with money to be cheated out of, and secondly, they were vulnerable and not fully savvy to the tactics these high-pressured charlatans used on them.

On the team McWade was assigned to work with, there was an actual photograph of an elderly woman from eastern Utah that one of these sick and twisted purveyors of misery had schmoozed her into sending him. He had flirted with her and laughingly passed her picture around the office, joking about her age in a derogatory and lewd manner. All this happened while relieving her of the $300,000 insurance settlement she had received when her husband had died. The sobbing widow ended up losing her home because of the fraudulent investment scheme she, like so many others, fell for head over heels. This scum had sucked away her entire nest egg like Hoover's vacuum sucks up loose bread crumbs.

However, McWade nicknamed this guy Sherwin Williams; inasmuch as by keeping such accurate records of his scheme and recordings of his lewd and incriminating statements, he had successfully managed to paint himself into a corner.

He was just one of fifty-six salesmen indicted by the federal grand jury in the District of Utah. His Porsche was part of the two million dollars seized that day in the valley of the Great Salt Lake.

The number one piece of advice offered and to be shared with elderly parents or loved ones would be to "be careful who you invite into your life. By answering an unsolicited call from an unknown telephone number, you may just be doing that. In many ways, it is just like picking up a hitchhiker who is difficult for you to get out of your vehicle and can cause you untold harm."

When thinking about telemarketers, McWade recalls a quote from an unknown source that has particular meaning: "With so many things coming back in style, I can't wait until morals and honesty become trends again."

Head Start Hannah

To work with and teach little children is a very noble and honorable thing and something McWade believed in firmly. But to those professing to be saviors of the little children and then stealing money from the programs set up to do just that, well, not so much!

Hannah was a genius in the art of obtaining government grants and had obtained hundreds of thousands of dollars to run her Head Start program in Eastern Idaho. But soon this grant money was being spent on things that were for Hannah and her husband rather than for the little tykes.

An old home near a ski resort in Driggs, Idaho, was purchased with her own funds so they could ski on weekends. So what could possibly be wrong with using government funds to put on a new roof, new windows, new flooring, and new furniture? To make it look legit, all she had to do was rent the building to her Head Start umbrella group to be used as a branch classroom should the need ever arise. And what would a home near a ski lodge be without a four-wheel-drive vehicle to get up the hill with your skis?

So why not just buy an old Isuzu Trooper from a man in a high government office she had met at a seminar. This deal seemed harmless until McWade uncovered that she was having an ongoing extramarital affair with the guy behind the back of her husband. So with Head Start funds, the worn-out Trooper was purchased at above book value despite warnings from a mechanic who looked at it and called it a piece of junk.

The first item of business, after buying her lover's high-mileage Isuzu, was to use government funds to put in a new engine and transmission at a cost of over $8,000.

"After all, when going skiing, you have to have a reliable vehicle," one witness observed.

The jury winced at the extent of her brazen fraudulent financial gymnastics.

The US district court judge did not think an $18,000 expenditure on their roof and windows should be a taxpayer obligation any more than the fiasco concerning her boyfriend's old Trooper. He was not amused! However, the jury was in and out of deliberation as quick as a fiddler's elbow with a guilty verdict.

Hannah was given a two-year probation and ordered to pay restitution for the counts on which she was convicted. Never addressed by the court were the thousands upon thousands of dollars Hannah obtained in phony per diem and business expenses, which were too numerous to be addressed and too difficult to be proven.

The sentence handed down was lenient and merciful. But McWade was quite sure the little children from whom Hannah stole would be very understanding.

When it came to just how much she could steal, our good Hannah seemed to be "always striving, but never arriving at that limit."

Add Head Start Hannah to our growing list of greedy, somewhat despicable types!

Spoiled Meat for Kids

Forrest Gump's favorite saying was, "Life is like a box of chocolates. You never know what you're going to get!"

McWade was asked to assist the US Department of Agriculture, Office of the Inspector General, on a case where a company in Western

Nebraska was ultimately convicted of selling millions of pounds of hamburger to the school lunch program. That hamburger was substandard, contaminated, and made from animals that were already dead or rejected and should have been sent to rendering plants.

The owner of the company was convicted, sent to prison for six years, and fined millions. This individual could deny his fraudulent actions so fast that he needed a speed bump between his brain and his mouth.

McWade always wondered if anyone could be lower on the sleaze scale of life.

McWade's updated version of Gump's philosophy might be, "School lunch burgers are like a grab bag at a carnival. You never know what you are going to get!"

Spoiled and rotten meat for kids should be up there somewhere on the Hall of Shame. What kind of a man would do that for money?

Lightning from Heaven

Scottsbluff and Gering, Nebraska, needed another bridge across the meandering North Platte River to link the twin cities together. This river was mentioned in the journals of early pioneers traveling the Oregon and Mormon Trails as being a foot deep and a mile wide.

This area was a great place to raise a family in the 1980s. A kid could have a paper route, wander the canyons and ravines, and play all day in the badlands below the towering Scotts Bluff National Monument until his mother called him home at night for supper. But like so many other Midwest towns, drug dealers appeared on the scene, and the moral landscape gradually began to deteriorate.

One such small time drug kingpin was a guy by the name of Jose Heine. He was a typical punk who was soon arrested by McWade's friend, NSP investigator Action Jackson, and sent away for five years' hard time in the Nebraska State Penal Complex in Lincoln.

He was continually filing appeals for an early release without any success. Even though Action Jackson was not necessarily a religious person, he once told Heine, "If God closes a door on you, maybe you should quit banging on it and just do your time!"

However, Heine finally convinced the judge that his mother was sick and needed him closer to home. He soon appeared back in the Scottsbluff-Gering area on a supervised work release program after landing a construction job working on the new bridge over the North Platte River.

Jackson was a firm believer in the basic police mentality that these guys usually don't change and, therefore, expressed unhappiness that his work jailing Jose was seemingly in vain.

However, Action Jackson soon became a total believer in the supernatural. He entered the doughnut shop one morning with a tale of what he considered a modern-day miracle. An act of divine justice.

The day before had been a very hot cloudless day in the area. There were fifteen workers busy on the new bridge project, and none even noticed a small cloud appear from the west and drift across the blue Nebraska sky. Suddenly, and without any warning whatsoever, a bolt of lightning, with pinpoint accuracy, leaped from that single cloud and struck down the drug-dealing Heine. "A sniper could not have had more of a direct hit!" exclaimed Jackson, who, to this day, firmly believes that a higher judge over ruled the work release decision.

"Drug dealing is deplorable, but drug dealing to kids is despicable," added Jackson, who, it is rumored, has not missed a single Sunday at church since his faith-altering experience.

Add Jose's name posthumously to the growing list of nominees.

The Idaho Potato Pirate

In Texas, they have a history of hanging cattle rustlers. Steal a man's horse in Wyoming and risk being shot or hung. Steal an man's wife in Utah and he will just find five or six more. What would you guess they would do to a potato thief in Idaho?

A man claiming to be Nestor Balaco, doing business as NA produce, called twenty-nine different potato-processing warehouses in Southeastern Idaho wanting to buy potatoes. Being a new buyer, he usually had to do some convincing in order to get the processors to ship him the produce. But he had a good line and told them just what they wanted to hear. He had long before learned that "everybody believes what they want to believe, usually based on what they feel they need to believe."

It was a simple con. He was a buyer, and the sellers wanted to sell, so they believed him. The first train carload was usually paid for to earn the trust of his customer. Then would come a larger order to be filled and then the purposeful delays and stall tactics were set in motion.

He knew enough to order and ship only Idaho's very best famous potatoes. The Burbank Russet Potato, grown in the volcanic ash soil of Southeastern Idaho, with its cool summer nights and favorable daytime temperatures, was exactly what he wanted. Soon the train cars were arriving at his Newark Farmers Market destination in New Jersey, loaded with his prized cargo.

The potatoes were sold all over the eastern seaboard, but the suppliers in Idaho were ignored. Soon Balaco became hard to find and the victims' telephone calls went unanswered; McWade found that his warehouse in New Jersey was now vacant and that Nestor Balaco did not exist. This was just one of the many aliases of a man by the name of Artemious Koufagonnakis, who happened to be a con artist well-known in the produce markets of New Jersey. By the time McWade had visited all twenty-nine warehouses in Idaho and obtained all the documents and details, the authorities in New Jersey had already thrown him in jail on another fraud matter. It seems he had defrauded Kraft Foods out of several thousand dollars on a giant ketchup scheme.

Unlike the states of Texas, Wyoming, and Utah, Idaho proved to be very compassionate to their potato thief as the federal judge gave him only five years in prison to serve concurrent with the time he was already serving on his ketchup caper. The $166,000 in restitution ordered by the court would only be a fraction of the value of the purloined potatoes.

Koufagonnakis should be considered for your vote even if his name is hard to spell.

McWade was very aware that small-town agents work small-town cases. It was all part of going native, and it was good. Every day seemed to bring him just a little closer to the image of the agent in Hoover's nightmare.

The Snow Machine Bandit

Nicknamed the "Polaris Kid" by McWade, the daring robber parked his stolen snow machine in the parking lot of the credit union on the north edge of Idaho Falls. In full snowmobile attire, including a helmet with a dark face cover, he entered the small East Idaho Federal Credit Union. Brandishing a pistol, he ordered everyone on the floor, leaped over the counter, and quickly filled his bag with the cash from each teller's drawer.

A quick return to his waiting machine with his $21,000 and he was soon flying down county roads and through the fields to his waiting car, which he left along the side of US Highway 20 a few minutes earlier. Abandoning the stolen snowmobile in a small steel building, he disappeared into westbound traffic.

The "Polaris Kid" should have put more thinking into the disposing of his "borrowed" suit and helmet. Instead, he dumped the items into a dumpster at a truck stop on the far south edge of town and sped away with his cash.

In this information age, ignorance is a choice.

The news of the snowmobile bank robbery was on every station within the hour, and so when an alert citizen saw the helmet and suit in a dumpster, they called the FBI. Our clueless robber had stolen the outfit from a relative, who had placed his name inside the helmet and on the collar of the suit.

It didn't take Dick Tracy to solve this one as soon the relative gave the name of his shiftless nephew, who had been staying at his house. It seems the Polaris kid and the ensemble had all gone missing at the same time.

Soon the thief was tied to the theft of the Polaris sled and the robbery. The federal grand jury that indicted him was amazed but not amused.

The local *Post Register* newspaper penned a catchy headline after the jury found him guilty and the judge handed down his sentence.

It stated boldly on the front page, "Snowmobile Bank Robber Put on Ice for 8 1/2 Years."

When was the last time you heard of a bank robbery like this in Los Angeles, New York, Detroit, or Newark? In Idaho, the natives drive sleds during the winter months!

Bad Santa

Within days of the "Polaris Kid's" daring escapade and with the Christmas season baring down on the wary citizens of Idaho Falls, something else happened right out of a storybook setting.

In rapid succession, Santa Claus walked into the Bank of Commerce in Idaho Falls as well as in nearby Ririe. Instead of "Ho ho ho," it was "Hit the floor!" Brandishing a pistol that the tellers thought was as big as a cannon and using words most of the employees had only heard in R-rated movies, he leaped over the counters and filled his Santa bag with money from the teller drawers.

At both banks, Santa stopped before exiting the door, turned and waved, then with a jolly shopping mall Santa's voice, exclaimed, "Ho ho ho and Merry Christmas!"

As was often the case, the surveillance cameras were very poorly maintained and almost worthless. These cameras were no exception as the only shot that turned out was at the Idaho Falls bank, which showed a very grainy black-and-white shot of Santa's backside.

Santa had disappeared into the cold Idaho winter with $3,000 from one bank and $15,000 from the other. Other than the fact that he was a slender, athletic male with a foul mouth, there were virtually no other leads at this point other than the one worthless photo.

Trying to, at least, get a little humor into the situation, McWade made up a photo lineup using five other photos of various Santas in full Christmas uniform. Our man was easily picked out as he was the only Santa with a skinny butt facing directly into the camera lens.

With every slender Santa in town now a suspect, a few tips came in from informants, and before long, the headline in the local paper was, "Santa Claus Robber Sentenced to Prison." Another headline followed up, "St. Nick Receives 21 Years in Jail."

It was observed that two small believing kids were traumatized to see Santa, the guy in whom they had undying faith, use such bad language, threaten to kill people, and steal money right before their young and innocent eyes. One little tyke was heard asking his mother, "Mommy, what did Santa mean when he asked for the f—ing money? What kind of money is that?"

It turned out that Mrs. Santa was his getaway driver on both jobs, but her attorney managed to get her off with wearing an electronic ankle monitoring and tracking device as part of her five years' home detention. She was scheduled to get regular visits from her probation officer to make sure she was happy and doing well.

Tarnishing the image of Santa in the eyes of kids should qualify this guy for a nomination. Both he and the "Polaris Kid" should get some small-town votes for the sleaze ball award.

Damn Those Elk

Ignorance sometimes is like a disability that takes ongoing effort to maintain, thought McWade as he wondered how Mike Vonsor thought he could get away with stealing over $500,000 and then blame it all on a few Idaho elk.

He drove fancy new pickup trucks that made other farmers in the Madison County area turn their heads in wonderment. He had the newest and best farm equipment, and he took trips with his wife to exotic places. Life on the farm was good for Mike, or so it seemed.

This great lifestyle was all a charade. He had devised what he thought to be a foolproof way to live high on money he illegally obtained from his friendly local banker. This was in the form of loans obtained by furnishing false and deceptive financial statements.

Vonsor operated a grain-farming operation in the high country located in the eastern part of Madison County, which was often hard to get to during several months of the winter and early spring. On this land, he maintained a large Quonset storage facility where he stored his wheat.

The bank examiners measured and verified the existence of the grain and certified there was enough in storage to pay off his bank loan should he default.

Well, default he did! The money was purposefully spent on his lifestyle that even made his neighbor, the Joneses, a bit envious as they just could not keep up.

The bank eventually foreclosed and planned to get the wheat as soon as they could get trucks over the muddy unpaved roads to the huge isolated Quonset. When they finally arrived to take possession of their collateralized half-million dollars' worth of wheat, it had magically vanished.

In a feeble effort to explain the missing grain to McWade, he blamed it on to a herd of elk roaming the hills, which had somehow managed to get inside the Quonset and had eaten the grain.

"Those damn elk got in there and did a number on my grain. They just flat out ate it!" he said with a tone of fake anger in his voice.

Investigation soon showed that he had sold the missing grain the previous fall by mixing every other load with his current crop and then selling it to the buyers as if it was coming right out of his freshly harvested fields.

He even tried, unsuccessfully as far as McWade knew, to collect yet again for the missing grain from the Idaho Fish and Game Department. He submitted to them a bill for the grain that wasn't even there, claiming the elk broke in and ate it during the winter.

So in summary, he gets the bank loan for $500,000, then secretly sells the wheat, which actually belonged to the bank, for several hundred thousand, which he pocketed. He then blames the innocent elk for the crime and tries to collect from the state of Idaho.

To obtain approximately a million dollars in this kind of a fraud scheme is less than admirable, even for our churchgoing Vonsor. But to blame a herd of poor defenseless Idaho elk for the fraud is not only unsportsmanlike but quite contemptible.

None of the elk hunters on the federal grand jury or those sportsmen on the jury at his trial took these accusations lightly. Even the AUSA, with his photo album full of roadkill pictures thought this was outlandish bullshit.

He was sentenced to some jail and probation, ordered to pay restitution, got his name in the headlines of the local newspapers, lost face in the community, and possibly even had to come up with some story to justify himself to his local congregation, where he held a high church position.

The AUSA did a masterful job painting a true picture of Vonsor and his scheme to the jury at the trial. Mrs. Vonsor, a black-haired spitfire, did not like what was happening to her husband and verbally attacked the AUSA with a foul barrage that would make any punk gangster proud and embarrass a San Diego sailor.

"Coming from you, ma'am, I consider that a compliment," was the reply from the cool-mannered prosecutor (the same one with the roadkill photo album).

Both Mike and his less-than-charming wife should not be ruled out of any contest for "down on the farm" despicable behavior.

The Charming Con Man

"Git R Dun" was the motto of old Fuss Parker, who was liked by almost everyone he swindled. And that proved to be almost everyone that did business with him, McWade was to find out.

He had the dealership for a popular line of small orange-colored Kubota tractors in the Eastern Idaho area and was a man of true vision. Since the company manufacturing the tractors would floor their units at his dealership, he was then to pay the company when he sold one of these to a local farmer or homeowner.

Soon he was selling the tractors and pocketing the money. When the examiner from the company would come to verify the units on the floor of his business, he seemed to know of their arrival a few days in advance. He would then call the several farmers he had sold the tractors to and offer them free servicing if they would just have those units there a day or so before his expected examiner. Hence, he cleaned the units up as if new, parked them on the dealership grounds and the inspector verified the numbers, and went on his way. Then it was back to the fields for the tractors.

He also took in hundreds of items of equipment from farmers in a four-state area on consignment to sell. There were large tractors, small tractors, scrapers, augers, plows, grain drills, potato planters, and any other item of machinery imaginable.

Since farm equipment only has serial numbers but are not titled by the state, he was able to obtain loans for hundreds of thousands of dollars from five different banks at the same time and use the consigned equipment as collateral. So smooth was Parker that no one even questioned the true ownership of the listed machinery on his five financial statements.

As if that was not enough, he even sold some of the consigned equipment without paying the owners and just played dumb as to where it disappeared. One large White diesel tractor worth several thousand dollars vanished forever.

His friendly fraud schemes were so entangled that even with nice spreadsheets it was impossible to trace everything.

When McWade finally felt he had all his ducks in a row, he called Parker into his RA office in Idaho Falls. For some unknown reason, he showed up with his wife and insisted that she be there during the interview. As it progressed and the questioning became more accusatory and specific, he began to get fierce and piercing looks from his wife, who was, by now, glaring at him in disbelief. It was obvious she had no clue about his fraud and was so disgusted at him McWade feared she may kill him on the spot.

When asked by McWade what he planned to do, Fuss replied, "Well, I haven't done a very good job convincing you that I'm innocent, so I don't suppose I would be able to convince a jury either. So I guess I might as well plead guilty."

The *Post Register*, the Idaho Falls areas main news source, ran the following headline, "Rigby Man Faces Bank Fraud Charges."

McWade laughed at the scores of people, including some of his victims, who wrote letters of recommendation to the court vouching for his honesty and character. These letters came from naive church friends and neighbors, as well as family and uninformed know-it-all do-gooders.

Several letters to the editor of the newspaper scolded the FBI and the government for falsely accusing such an upstanding citizen.

Two years in prison and a $250,000 fine was the sentence.

McWade was told by a close friend of Parker that he was actually happy to go to prison where it may be safer. He was concerned and afraid that his wife, now knowledgeable about his fraud, may have her own punishment in mind that would be far worse. It was rumored she was a distant relative of Lorena Bobbitt, the famous woman who had cut off her abusive husband's penis while he was sleeping.

The two years would pass quickly, but where do you think he would come up with the $250,000 for his fine? McWade laughed as he noted that Parker went back into the farm implement business and wondered if some of the same victims would fall for one of his schemes a second time.

It has been said that "action is the only truth." And the truth of the matter was that Fuss Parker was again back in action. He would take your vote with a smile and a pat on the back. But watch your wallet!

Whores, Band Uniforms, and Cop Cars

The *Chicago Tribune* told the story of Shoshone County, Idaho under the following headlines: "Sheriff of Tough Idaho Town Now on Other Side of the Law—Wallace, Idaho." The article continued, "This tough town of hardworking rock miners, already in the history books as one of America's most colorful and raucous frontier towns, is now in the law books as well."

A federal grand jury last week indicted Frank Crnkovich, fifty-eight, Shoshone County sheriff, on charges that he used his office, his seven deputies, and his access to law enforcement computers to protect prostitution and gambling enterprises.

"Local reaction to the charges against the four-term Crnkovich were, 'So what's new?'"

The local high school band marches in uniforms provided by the town *madam* at the former Luxette brothel, and other prostitutes donated a car to the police department.

"Site of the biggest single silver strike in American history, Wallace has been a major US mining center since 1884 when legendary gunslinger Wyatt Earp was sued in the local court for claim jumping. Bar owners in Idaho's Silver Valley openly ran coin-operated gaming machines in at least fifty-eight saloons, and brothels broke the law for years, safe in the knowledge that the sheriff's office was keeping a lookout for the state and federal police," the grand jury indictment charged.

"The seven deputies testified that Crnkovich had assigned them to notify each tavern, either by telephone or in person, whenever state inspectors were to make a tour or undercover state police tried to pose as customers at the brothels.

"Whenever the prostitutes or gaming operators suspected that a stranger passing through town might be a law enforcement officer, the indictment said they contacted the sheriff's office, which ran the checks on the license plates through the national law enforcement computer networks (NCIC-National Crime Information Center).

"Fritz Hansen, a salesclerk at the Silver Capital Arts Store on Wallace's Main Street drag, agreed that I think most people will vote for Frank if he ever runs again because they like him and know he just inherited a situation that has been going on forever."

During the investigation leading up to the indictment, McWade and scores of others participated in the information-gathering process against the popular lawman. Covert undercover visits were carried out, surveillance operations were conducted, and other various forms of highly technical information gathering methodology were used.

The good sheriff's comment on June 27, 1991, to a nearby Spokane, Washington, newspaper, the *Spokesman-Review*, was perhaps one of the dumbest and most amazing denial statements ever made. "This whole thing catches me by surprise," said Sheriff Crnkovich of the raid that seized nearly two hundred video poker machines from fifty-eight bars and three residences. "I had no idea gambling was going on in my (Shoshone) county." The article concluded as follows: "The political clout of the once-proud Silver Valley has played out! Don't play dumb, Boss Hogg, the jig is up. The party's over, Frank, but it was fun while it lasted."

The "my county" mentality seemed to infect not only Shoshone but also Thompson County in the southeastern part of the state. Both counties seemed to resist being brought into the present by clinging brutally to the past. *If their consensus of thought was that education into the modern world was too costly,* McWade wondered, *just how costly being ignorant was going to be for them?*

One former resident of the Silver Valley shared with McWade how it was a very common practice and tradition for young men of the area to be introduced properly into manhood by real professionals at one of the several brothels. He admitted that he himself had been properly instructed by one of the madams on his eighteenth birthday. He added with a broad smile, "It was a day I will never forget as long as I live. All those years marching in the high school band made me feel proud to be a Wallace miner, and I wanted to do something to help compensate for those uniforms the ladies had supplied. I thought giving that nice lady my business was the least I could do to show my genuine appreciation."

Taking bribes and selling his official sheriff's office to the underworld should place Frank in contention for some kind of a special sleaze trophy.

Raiders of the Lost Signal, Porn Ltd.

During the 1980s General Instruments (GI), the company that owned the small VideoCipher boxes designed to unscramble television signals, was unhappy. It seemed there was a virtual epidemic of piracy going on where professional buccaneers would alter their unscrambling boxes for a fee of $400 each, which allowed the customer to then watch HBO, the Playboy Channel, and any other premium channel coming from the satellite operated by GI free of charge.

Each month, GI would come up with another code to confuse the pirates. However, the code was soon compromised and sent to all the thousands of customers with the altered boxes, enabling them to update the code to their unit and again continue watching all stations free of any monthly fees. The fraud was costing GI millions in lost revenue, and they were livid.

This was one of the last cases McWade immersed himself in before leaving the great state of Nebraska. GI sent their own version of Dick Tracy, with a vast technical background, to work side by side with McWade and the other agents, executing search warrants on the actual pirates. It was soon discovered that some of the pirates were also big into kinky sex practices, complete with *special* rooms and tools to help act out and stimulate their fantasies. The free pirated adult channels were only part of their game to help arouse themselves and set the mood.

McWade, accompanied by Tracy and other agents, executed a surprise search warrant on the king of kinky in a small central Nebraska rural town in the middle of the corn belt. The man had his own master bedroom-playroom complete with every imaginable and even unimaginable tool, device, and play toy known to the industry, including a large television for viewing his pirated channels as well as a large TV monitor.

It didn't take Watson, Holmes, or Tracy to discover the purpose of the monitor. Our king of kinky had built a very nice, secluded themed guest room, complete with a hot tub, large waterbed with fancy satin sheets, mirrors, and everything else that comes with a themed room in his basement. This one, however, had something else—a series of hidden closed circuit cameras to follow every move of his invited guests. These cameras were hardwired directly to the large monitors in the master bedroom to allow him to watch the live action taking place in the secluded room by his live actors—his very own invited special guests. The action, played out before his eyes, was recorded for further viewing, which allowed him to watch, with his queen of kink wife, the activity in their guest room over and over. Depending on how exciting or arousing the action captured on the VHS tapes was would determine its rating and playback appeal.

McWade, in his naive way, wondered why all the invited female guests to the special guest room seemed to be well-endowed, shapely, and well suited for his home's unrehearsed porn show movies. Most looked like porn stars themselves.

In addition to the king and queen of kink, McWade found that several other raiders of the lost signals were respectable churchgoing folks, who were otherwise outwardly trustworthy people. Somehow, they didn't seem, in their minds, to connect the dots of their deeds as being dishonest. However, he found that almost all these folks, too, were involved, at least to some degree, in their own version of porn and deceit.

One was a member of his own church congregation and held a leadership position where he held his head high on Sunday in judgment of others. This guy's particular fetish was very heavyset nude women. This assumption was based on materials found during the search of his service truck where he traveled out of town to alter customers GI descramblers.

People seem to act out in secret what they are programmed to secretly believe and desire was one of the lessons McWade learned on this matter.

The Questionable Cop

He was asked to watch his neighbor's house while the man was away on an extended vacation in the northwest. Being a trusted police officer, the guy had no qualms whatsoever about leaving his house keys in the officer's possession. But then how was he to know that he would die of a heart attack and never see home again?

When the call came in reporting the death of the trusting neighbor, our Good Samaritan police officer immediately became an experienced burglar and methodically removed everything in the house that could not be identified or tied specifically to him. He was careful to do his evil deed under cover of darkness and out of the eyes of any unsuspecting onlooking neighbors.

A television set, watches, jewelry, tools, small appliances, and items too numerous to mention all seemed to sprout legs and walk across the yard and into the home and waiting garage of our trusted friendly lawman. To serve and protect seemed to be replaced with to loot and pillage!

Meanwhile, his wife, Bonnie, was in serious trouble for stealing blank checks from a business where she worked as a bookkeeper. She had then issued these checks to bogus businesses and managed to benefit personally to the tune of over $90,000 before her scheme was uncovered. It seemed, according to the word on the street, that our pilfering policeman and his embezzling wife were into about everything unconventional they could find.

Their lingerie parties were quite novel and usually involved tossing the car keys in a bowl and taking home whoever belonged to those keys drawn out. Wife swapping, in addition to the basic underwear modeling by the women, made for an exciting evening for our duo. But by now, McWade was beginning to think this was just something some folks did to pass time during the long, cold winter nights and was not that unusual. He was learning not to be judgmental.

Our trusting officer also was rumored to have lost a pickup truck in a fire and claimed his wife's diamond ring worth $10,000 was lost in the flames. They then had a friend, another wife-swapping man-in-blue police officer, keep the ring in his personal safe until the insurance money was collected and it was safe to get the ring back out.

Bonnie eventually pleaded guilty to a federal charge of fraud by wire, went off to federal prison for two years where she enjoyed a cell right next Lynette "Squeaky" Fromme, the would-be assassin of President Gerald Ford in 1975. The two apparently became close friends, whatever that means.

A former county attorney, shortly before being convicted himself for theft, stated to McWade, "If you lose a bunch of weight without building muscle (through exercise), you'll just end up being a skinny fat man."

Conversely McWade wondered, *If you lose your integrity without changing your ways as a police officer, would you just end up a shallow empty shell of a man?* (sort of like the skinny fat man).

There should be a special place on the ballot for our dishonest wife-swapping cop and his convicted partner in crime.

Setting Fires to Fight Fires

It has been said, "The world is not full of idiots. But they are strategically placed so you seem to run across at least one every day."

Kalter Wishline prided himself as one of Chadron's best police officers. He was active in community organizations. He was a deacon in his church, a volunteer fireman, a member of several civic groups, and a likable man with a ready story to tell to anyone willing to listen. Most folks in town enjoyed him as a friend and a good neighbor.

Every time one of his friends would see him, they would always ask, "Hey, big guy, what's happening?" Sometimes it would be, "Kalter, old buddy, anything new?"

Soon he became weary and bored with his own answers. "Nothing!" "Not much!" and "It's been kinda slow lately!" were getting harder and harder for him to say.

He was starting to long for some action just so he could have a good exciting firsthand story to tell and again be the center of attention.

First there was a mysterious fire in an old abandoned building a few blocks from the downtown area. Wishline just happened to be the officer on duty to spot the fire and call it in on his portable radio while on foot patrol.

The volunteer fire department was called into action and soon, with the help of their own Kalter manning the large hose, extinguished the flames, thus saving the city from a disaster. He was the center of attention the next morning at the coffee shop as he told in graphic detail how he had discovered the fire, called it in to the PD, rushed to the fire department, and then helped put out the blaze. He relished in the spotlight.

Soon the same scenario was repeated two weeks later and then a couple weeks after that.

Ted Vasman, the same Chief of Police who had stood bravely face-to-face with the Indian threatening to shoot him with a bow and arrow, was alarmed at the rash of fires in his small town. He was more than alarmed, and being having been specially trained at the FBI National Academy, he was actually very suspicious.

He called McWade for assistance and recounted in great detail exactly how each fire had gone down. It seemed more than a coincidence that the same officer had discovered all three fires while on foot patrol. All the calls were recorded and the playbacks seemed interesting.

Maps of the fires were plotted on graph paper showing distances from the fires when the calls came in and how long before Kalter arrived at the station. It was soon determined that the portly out-of-shape officer would be eligible for the four-hundred-meter race in the upcoming Olympics given his remarkable speed.

Using his interrogation skills learned while serving with the California Highway Patrol and at the National Academy, Vasman soon had a confession rolling forth from the lips of the pathetic police officer. He was convicted in state court and, for the next two years, had a burning desire to tell his story about arson and firefighting to fellow inmates at the Nebraska Penal Complex in Lincoln, Nebraska. He was definitely a class act, and for violating his position of trust, he should be considered a worthy contender for an official sleaze certificate.

Written in Blood

The 1980s seemed be a period of change in the North Platte Valley. Since Scottsbluff-Gering was located geographically between Denver and Rapid City, it seemed a logical stopover for drug dealers and the criminal types attracted to that activity. Soon the small river valley had its own share of those adhering to that culture and the violent activity it spawned.

McWade listened with interest as his friends—the investigators from the Scotts Bluff County SO, the NSP, and the Scottsbluff PD—gathered around the table at the Holland Bakery in the 1900 block of Broadway in Scottsbluff. It was early October 1988, and the discussion was concerning the details of the bloody murders of two rural residents on the previous September 19.

The victims were Richard Paldez, a known local drug dealer, and his nineteen-year-old pregnant girlfriend, Sharon Condy.

In the weeks leading up to the double homicides, Paldez, age twenty-five, had allegedly told members of his family and some friends that he feared for his life and that someone may be planning to kill him. The individuals he told this to claimed he confided to them that if he was killed he would attempt to write the name of the killer in his own blood with his last ounce of strength, thus identifying the murderer.

When the detectives arrived at the rented farmhouse, the scene of the bloody mayhem, Paldez had apparently been able to live up to his predetermined plan, for there on the wall and on the floor next to his lifeless body was written in white grease and blood the letters *JFF BOPE* and *JEFF*.

Based on that very dramatic dying testimony, attention was quickly directed toward another local drug dealer by the name of Jeff Boppre. Shell casings from the crime scene matched casings from Boppre's gun found at his home. Additionally, at least three witnesses gave testimony, saying they had heard him talk of killing Paldez.

His .32-caliber pistol, determined to be the murder weapon, was eventually recovered in New Mexico where he had allegedly disposed of it while in that state.

He was sentenced to life in prison for the double murders but, to this day, spends his time writing petitions for a new trial. He and a following of supporters all maintain he was unjustly convicted of a murder that some other unknown person committed.

In the months immediately following the incident, there was a very public outcry from the members of the drug community that local law enforcement was actually the culprits and Boppre was simply the person on whom they placed the blame. There was a widely circulated rumor that the local Scotts Bluff County attorney, Brian Silverman, was captured on a secret tape proving that he (Silverman) was corrupt and the actual kingpin of the rapidly expanding drug trade in the area.

These accusations completely fell apart as all leads were chased down and debunked by the FBI. The origin of each baseless lead was, as you guessed, persons whom Silverman had prosecuted and sent to jail.

The talk around the doughnut shop in the months following the rural murders frequently drifted back to this unique case proving that the dying testimony from a person can actually be very compelling in a jury trial when written and sealed in his very own blood. These are the cases that dime store detective novels are made of, but this one happened all too close to home.

Having gone completely native by this time, McWade knew and trusted each and every officer whose name had been tarnished in the local newspapers by the unfounded and reckless gossip and accusations surrounding this matter. It was for that reason that an FBI agent from outside the Nebraska panhandle was called in to investigate this matter. The allegations surrounding the county attorney and the other officers were evidently put to rest, or at least to the satisfaction of the Bureau and the DOJ.

Or is it at rest? Sometimes these matters seem to just take on a life of their own as is apparently the case with this unusual occurrence.

McWade was reminded of a sign he had seen posted at the gate of one rather notorious self-proclaimed tax protester near Chadron, Nebraska. It simply read, Is There Life After Death? Trespass Here to Find Out!

In this case, there was no proof shown of life after Paldez's death, but his testimony, scratched with his finger, in his own blood, spoke loudly, clearly, and with remarkable believability from the grave.

In Summary

So-called experts in the field of human behavior spend their entire lifetime attempting to understand why people act the way they do and why they do the things they are caught doing. This study is often more of a form of art than an exact science. It is much more complicated than merely toasting a slice of bread to different shades of darkness.

During the several weeks at the Behavioral Science Unit, McWade realized the complexity of humanoid conduct, at least to some degree. He learned just enough to realize how very little he actually understood and that understanding people's behavior is very difficult at times and is not always achievable.

He was a firm believer in the fact that people actually believe what they need (or want) to believe. This can, and often does, translate into their actions and their own justifications for those actions.

Furthermore, it has frequently been said that, to a large extent, a person is the sum total of each and every decision they have made since their birth. The reasons for these beliefs and, hence, actions are as numerous as the people making those choices. They each, in their own minds, feel they have valid reasons for each act.

With all that said, how do you determine which case of sleazy behavior should be at the top of the list?

Stealing your crippled grandmother's wheelchair?

Stealing bonds from the safe deposit box of elderly and helpless women?

Defaming the name of Santa Claus by dropping the f-bomb in front of kids while robbing a bank at gunpoint?

Pretending to be a doctor with a cure for old age when the only thing you were doing was making elderly patients' wallets much lighter and drugging them with illegal drugs?

Blaming innocent elk for your theft of a million dollars' worth of grain which you stole?

Playing on people's emotional desire to adopt a child with the express goal to defraud them?

Setting fires so you can be the hero who saves the town from burning?

Inviting unsuspecting house guests to spend time in your themed room while you make a porn movie starring them?

Feeding kids at school spoiled and rotten meat in their hot lunch program meals?

Grooming susceptible women into signing for large personal loans and then, before leaving them, rating their sexual skills in your personal journal for your future gratification?

Selling your sworn services as sheriff to protect unlawful whore-houses and gambling establishments and bars from legitimate law enforcement officials?

As a good neighbor and police officer, stealing your neighbor's TV set after he dies? His own version of grave robbing.

The list of deplorables could go on and on almost endlessly. The low caliber of their moral conviction reminded McWade of a quote from an old cowboy friend in the ranch country of Nebraska when he said, "We have upped our standards, now up yours!" Clearly these folks had set their moral bar quite low to enable themselves to jump over it without so much as tripping too often.

In looking at all the cases above, comprising the Shades of Sleaze, outlined in brief summary form, they all were disgusting.

However, none of these could compare to the two low-life creatures from North Carolina, who were prostituting those two little girls, ages ten and twelve, at truck stops across the Midwest. The mental picture of those little barefooted girls, standing in the cold Nebraska rain, crying and sobbing while offering their innocence to some trucker, will not easily be forgotten.

That indeed is a shade of darkness beyond most others. The moral compass of those offending monsters is broken and probably beyond repair. Their character is like a piece of toast that is completely burnt beyond redeeming value.

When describing religious followers of high demand religions or cults, George Farquhar penned the oft quoted statement, "Those who know the least obey the best." Those two little beautiful girls knew so little about life and obeyed out of fear and obligation. Their low-life kin, who caused such abuse, deserve all that the law could throw at them and more.

Those two proved beyond a doubt that the following is a true statement: "There is a big difference between being a human being and being human!"

I have heard it said that it is never too late to have a happy childhood. I hope that statement is true for the two little victims in our Nebraska rest stop fiasco that most certainly scarred them beyond what most normal folks can comprehend.

Glossary

AIM: American Indian Movement, founded July 1968 (Aim not A I M).

APC: Armored personnel carrier, armored vehicle used to transport troops.

ASAC: Assistant Special Agent in charge of a field division (pronounced A-Sack).

AUO: Administratively uncontrolled overtime.

AUSA: Assistant United States attorney.

BNRR: Burlington Northern Railroad.

BSU: Behavioral science unit, located at Quantico, Virginia.

Bucar: Vehicle owned by the FBI and used by individual agents for official work.

buhelp: Slang term coined by McWade for anyone helping on any Bureau project or assignment.

Bureau: Term used interchangeably with FBI.

CIR: Crime on an Indian reservation. FBI investigates the most serious crimes in Indian country (reservations), such as murder, violent assaults, drug trafficking, etc., in partnership with the Bureau of Indian Affairs.

COP: Chief of police.

CNWRR: Chicago and North Western Railroad (or Railway).

CVIN: Confidential Vehicle Identification Numbers.

DOJ: Department of Justice, headed by the attorney general of the United States.

FBI: Federal Bureau of Investigation, primary investigative arm of the DOJ.

FBIHQ: FBI Headquarters, Washington, DC.

FBW: Fraud By Wire. Cases where the fraud was accomplished by use of wire, telephone, radio, television, etc. (title 18, USC, section 1343).

FD-302: The name of a report used for the written account of the testimony of an individual witness. This write-up can stand alone and be removed from a larger and more complete prosecutive report.

FOA: First office agent, the first assignment to a field office for a special agent after completing his new agent training.

ITCP: Inter-theater transporting of contraband popcorn (see chapter 24). Only a prosecutable offense in Madison County, Idaho.

ITSP: Interstate transportation of stolen property (violation of title 18, USC, section 2314).

KMA: When an agent turned fifty years old, with twenty years' service, he was eligible to retire and join the KMA Club. KMA had the usual street meaning of "kiss my ass."

MP: Military police.

NA: National academy. FBI-sponsored courses held at Quantico, Virginia, for select law enforcement officers throughout the United States and worldwide.

NAC: New agents class. Presently held at the FBI Academy, Quantico, Virginia. Prior to the academy being opened in the early 1970s, these classes were primarily held at the historic Old Post Office Building (presently refurbished into the Trump International Hotel), Washington, DC.

NSP: Nebraska State Patrol. Headquartered in Lincoln, Nebraska.

OP: Office of preference. Agents were allowed to list any of the FBI field divisions as the office to which they would like to be assigned. (In most cases, these were just wish lists until the agent had seniority in that particular office or had a rabbi in some high place within the Bureau.)

OPR: Office of Professional Responsibility. Used interchangeably with the term Inspection Staff or Goon Squad. Assistant Inspectors pulled in from other field offices to aid in an inspection were known as rent-a-goons.

PVIN: Public Vehicle Identification Number. The vehicle identification number of a vehicle posted within plain sight as opposed to the CVIN placed in a confidential location on the vehicle.

POA: Personally owned automobile by an agent to be used on his or her own personal business.

PRIR: Pine Ridge Indian Reservation, also called the Pine Ridge Agency, is located primarily in the state of South Dakota. Approximately one square mile of the reservation is located in the state of Nebraska, west of Whiteclay, Nebraska, population fourteen. Whiteclay has the lucrative but shameful reputation of supplying liquor to the PRIR. On any given day, they would sell an estimated average of thirteen thousand cans of beer.

RA: Resident Agent, referring to the Special Agent assigned to that particular Resident Agency (the actual office). A Resident Agency is supervised by a Field Division.

SAC: Special Agent In Charge of a field office. This is pronounced S-A-C and not "sack." That error would give you up immediately as an outsider.

SO: Sheriff's office.

SRA: Senior Resident Agent. Assuming the RA has more than one agent assigned, the SRA would be in charge. In a one-man office, such as the Scottsbluff RA, the agent would be referred to as the Resident Agent.

TIO: Time in the office. This term was coined during the Hoover era and was the actual time an agent spent in the office at his desk. The Director assumed that if you were not physically out on the streets, you were not solving crime. The magic TIO figure FBIHQ established was approximately two hours per day.

TURK: Time Utilization Record Keeping. A system set up by FBIHQ to keep track of various classifications of cases worked by individual agents and entire field offices. This allowed HQ to evaluate which offices were working priority cases versus non-priority routine cases, so they could assign manpower accordingly.

VIN: Vehicle Identification Number.

WFO: Washington Field Office. The field office division located in the District of Columbia, where assigned agents worked normal FBI cases as opposed to FBIHQ, which was more supervisory and administrative by nature over the Bureau at large.

About the Author

Wade Shirley was born and raised on a small farm in the Upper Snake River Valley of Idaho, literally in the shadows of the Tetons. Looking for a change from this difficult farm life, he earned a BS degree from Utah State University and went into teaching. Four years later, he accepted an appointment from J. Edgar Hoover as a Special Agent (SA) with the Federal Bureau of Investigation. Upon the conclusion of his training in Washington, DC, and Quantico, Virginia, he was assigned to the San Antonio Division on their fugitive squad.

A year later, he received his dream assignment to the small remote resident agency in Scottsbluff, Nebraska, where he spent the next twenty years in a world far removed from the big-city FBI depicted on TV. While in Nebraska, he was trained at Quantico's Behavioral Science Unit to act as the Criminal Profiling Coordinator for the State of Nebraska, along with his regular duties as an SA. His last transfer took him back near his original home to Idaho Falls, Idaho, where he served until retiring in 1999. After a period of self-employment as an investigator, he finally fully retired and presently lives with his wife, Beth, where they split their time between homes in Eastern Idaho and Yuma, Arizona.

CPSIA information can be obtained
at www.ICGtesting.com
Printed in the USA
LVHW041029171120
671900LV00003B/141